SLIVERS

OF

BONE

This special deluxe edition is limited to 1,000 signed copies.

Ray Garton

RAY GARTON

Slivers of Bone

Ray Garton

Slivers of Bone

Ray Garton

CEMETERY DANCE PUBLICATIONS
BALTIMORE
- 2008 -

SLIVERS OF BONE

All stories © 2008 Ray Garton

Cemetery Dance Publications 2008

Signed Limited Hardcover
ISBN-10: 1-58767-094-1
ISBN-13: 978-1-58767-094-7

All rights reserved. No part of this book may be reproduced or transmitted in any form or by any means, electronic or mechanical, including photocopy, recording, or any information storage and retrieval system, without permission in writing from the author, or his agent, except by a reviewer who may quote brief passages in a critical article or review to be printed in a magazine or newspaper, or electronically transmitted on radio or television.

All persons in this book are fictitious, and any resemblance that may seem to exist to actual persons living or dead is purely coincidental. This is a work of fiction.

Dust Jacket Art: © 2008 by Alan M. Clark
Dust Jacket Design: Gail Cross
Typesetting and Design: David G. Barnett
Printed in the United States of America

Cemetery Dance Publications
132-B Industry Lane
Unit #7
Forest Hill, MD 21050
http://www.cemeterydance.com

10 9 8 7 6 5 4 3 2 1

First Edition

This book is dedicated to the person most important to my career, the person who put me where I am, who has allowed me to keep writing for the last 23 years. That person is you, Dear Reader. Because you keep coming back again and again, reading the books and novellas and stories, because you've been so supportive and accepting, I dedicate this book to you.

And, as always,
For Dawn

My appreciation and gratitude go to Scott Sandin, Derek Sandin, Brian Hodges, my brother-in-law Bill Blair and my sister-in-law Michelle Blair, Jen Orosel, Bill Lindblad, Tod Clark, my wife Dawn who makes it possible for me to write, Steven Spruill, T.M. Wright, Alan and Jude and the wonderful people at Borderlands Books, my sister Roxanne De La Cruz who reads them all, my agent Richard Curtis, and Rich, Mindy, and all the great folks at Cemetery Dance.

The Guy Down the Street	11
Second Opinion	51
Website	67
The Homeless Couple	93
411	119
Monsters	205
Hair of the Dog	339
Punishments	361
Weird Gig	375
The Other Man	393
The Picture of Health	411
Screams at the Gateway to Fame	437
Myiasis	469

The Guy Down the Street

1

Look at her. Bare ass up in the air, feet apart. A big smile on her upside-down face as she looks back between her thighs. Now she reaches down and moves her fingers between her legs. I can't believe it. She's laughing, having fun. She's not being forced to do anything against her will. She's *enjoying* herself!

The man shooting the video tells her to get on the sofa. He has a friendly voice, not exactly effeminate, but hardly masculine. Soft, gentle. And familiar. I've heard it before, but cannot pin it down.

"Beautiful," he says as she spreads her legs on the sofa. "Yeah, that's hot. You wanna tell us a little about yourself, Tiffany?"

Tiffany? What a repugnant name. I bet that was his idea. She would never choose to be called something as precious and tiara-friendly as *Tiffany*. But I could be wrong—it seems there is a lot I don't know about her.

"Well, what do you want to know?" she asks.

"Tell us what kind of boys you like."

"I don't like boys. I like *men*." She laughs again, fondles herself as she talks.

"And what do you like to do with your men?"

"Well, I like to…" She pauses, giggles. She is embarrassed. Sitting there naked, masturbating on the Internet in front of anyone who wants to watch, and she's embarrassed to talk about what she likes to do with her "men." I don't know whether to pull my hair out screaming, or to laugh.

"Go on, you can say it," the man says. "They all wanna know."

"Well, I like to…y'know, give head. Some girls don't. They're all, '*Eeewww!*' and like, 'It's so *gross!*' Some won't do it at all. But I'm totally into it. As long as he, like, goes down on *me*, y'know?"

"So, you're very oral."

"Yeah."

I feel a chill, and my stomach begins to churn.

They go on talking until she becomes distracted and quiet. He says nothing for awhile and lets her masturbate.

I have to look away. Horror and rage and guilt mix badly in my stomach, like three kinds of cheap liquor. I am not supposed to see what's on the screen. I don't *want* to see it. But there she is, for all the world to watch. I clutch the small plastic armrests of the chair, squeeze and pull them so hard they creak. My fingers become numb, wrists hurt, but it keeps me from crying out. From throwing up.

They're talking again. I turn my head slowly toward the screen—not all the way, though—eyes narrowed down to razor-thin slits, hand ready to cover them. The way I used to watch scary movies as a kid.

"You look like you're really into that," he says.

She turns on her side with a shrill squeal, presses her legs together. Says something into the cushion.

"What?"

"I said, I forgot you were there."

"Well, don't stop now. Looked like you were getting close."

She sits up, tries to continue, but is overtaken by giggles.

The camera wobbles as he approaches her. "You just need something to take your mind off the camera," he says.

"Like that big bulge in your pants?" she asks with a laugh, pointing at his crotch.

He turns the camera down so we can see his erection pressing against denim.

"Well, you said you like doing it, Tiffany."

"I do." As she leans forward, she looks up at the camera with a naughty, teasing smile. It's a face I have never seen before. A face I was never meant to see.

She unfastens his jeans easily, pulls them down, and when his penis springs free, she takes it in her mouth.

My jaws burn from clenching my teeth. I turn away again and stand, walk around the desk. My voice is hoarse and unsteady as I say, "I can't watch any more of this."

"He shows himself pretty soon," Wylie says. He stands against the wall next to the window, behind the chair I was sitting in a moment earlier.

It is his office, his computer. With the exception of shopping for Christmas presents, I have managed to stay away from the Internet. I waste enough of my time as it is, I don't need a new distraction. But over the last year or so, he had become an Internet junkie.

Wylie lives with his wife Nadine and their two teenage daughters, Erica and Cherine, across the street from us. "Us" being my wife Renee, our daughter Melinda, and myself. He is an officer of the Redding Police Department. Gregarious, generous, always asking us over for drinks or a barbecue. Sometimes we go, sometimes not. Wylie can be moody, temperamental, quick to anger. This is sometimes, but not always, connected to alcohol. He's fine as long as he sticks to beer, but as soon as he switches to Jack Daniels, it's time to leave, or at least lay low. Sometimes something will set him off while he's sober as a judge. But for the most part, we enjoy his company, and Renee and Nadine are good friends. But if Wylie and I were kids, he'd be the kind of kid I would avoid, knowing that sooner or later, there would be trouble, whether we got into it or Wylie caused it. Trouble just seems to be a part of Wylie Keene, like the smell of his cologne.

Wylie called me over earlier, said he wanted to show me something. He kept smiling. An odd smile, not friendly in the least. The smile of a crocodile.

"This isn't going to be easy to watch," Wylie said as he clicked his mouse a few times. He stood and told me to take the chair.

Wylie was right.

"Can't you fast-forward it, or something?" I ask, pressing fingertips into my temples.

"Nope. Can't fast-forward the RealPlayer."

"Then just tell me who it is, Wylie. I'm assuming you know, right?"

"Yeah, I know. But it's important you *see* it."

"*Why*? See what?"

"In a minute. Okay, here it is. Come on." He beckoned me impatiently and I returned to the chair.

The camera apparently is mounted on a tripod now. Naked, the man kneels in front of her and puts his face between her thighs. She makes breathy sounds of pleasure. He is small, lean, and wiry, pale as milk. His back is covered with freckles, moles, and a patch of acne between the shoulder blades. He has rusty hair, pulled back tight in a ponytail.

I don't need to see his face. I recognize him immediately. The name of the man having sex on the Internet with my sixteen-year-old daughter Melinda is Teklenburg. Charles Teklenburg, but he likes everyone to call him Chick. For short. Maybe forty-five, a bit of a relic with his long hair, ponytail, and hippy clothes. He even drives an old Volkswagen van from the late sixties. He lives alone with his two Chows. Just down the street, at the very end. People sometimes use his driveway to turn around when they realize Gyldcrest goes nowhere. They never see the sign.

I stand so suddenly, the chair wheels away and Wylie catches it before it hits the wall. "My God, Wylie, why aren't you *doing* something about this?" Tears burn my throat and eyes, and my crippled voice is all over the scale.

"What do you mean?"

"I mean, you're a *cop*! Why is that son of a bitch still living comfortably in his house at the end of the street? Why are you coming to *me*, for Christ's sake, you're a *cop*, why haven't you—"

He puts his hands on my shoulders, squeezes them hard. "Whoa, hold it down, okay? I haven't told Deeny about this yet. Cherine's on the website, too, Clark. So are other girls from the neighborhood. Our neighbors' daughters."

"Oh, Jesus."

"Yeah, I'm a cop, and yeah, we're gonna do something about this, that's why you had to see it. But the two don't have anything to do with each other, okay?"

"What…what do you mean?"

"I mean, we're gonna kill the bastard."

2

There will be no sleep until we talk, but I get into bed anyway in my T-shirt and boxers.

I was unable to concentrate enough to hold a conversation at dinner, and Renee noticed. I snapped at her, she snapped back. A couple martinis before dinner probably didn't help, something I normally do only on weekends. On top of that, Renee tried Deeny's recipe for spinach-stuffed chicken breasts tonight and thought I hated it because I only took a couple bites. I did not eat it because I could not eat.

"I can't tell you what to do," Wylie said that afternoon in his office. "But I think telling Renee'd be a bad idea. I'm not telling Deeny. Not till we're done. Then I'll tell her and we'll deal with Cherine. I wouldn't tell Melinda, either, I was you. Keep her the hell away from Teklenburg, but wait till we're done with him before you sit her down. Like I said, it's up to you. But I wouldn't. Women just can't keep their damned mouths shut."

I know Wylie is right—about keeping it to myself, anyway—but I don't know how I can keep it from Renee. And how can I not confront Melinda? I want to shout at her and vent my rage, my confusion. I want to hold her tight in my arms and never let her out of the house again.

Doesn't she feel *any* kind of repulsion at the idea of having sex on the Internet with a man almost three times her age? In front of the whole world? That's not the girl we raised.

I punch my pillows a little too hard as I try to get comfortable in bed.

Could Melinda be taking drugs? That would help explain it. But how could I miss that? How could Renee and I not notice something like that? We know what the warning signs are, but we have not seen any of them.

Fortunately, Melinda ate dinner in her bedroom, where she spent the entire evening. Summer vacation ends in a few weeks. She will go back to school, and I will go back to work teaching English at Shasta College. But those weeks will be an eternity if I do not deal with her soon. First, I have to tell Renee.

People usually laugh when I say I tell my wife everything, but it's true. Renee does the same with me. Not as a duty, but because we want to. We married a few years out of college, each with two lovers under our belts, and have been faithful to our vows for almost twenty years (more than twenty-three if you count the years we lived in Sin before marrying). Adulterous opportunities have arisen for both of us, and we have turned them down. Not as a duty, but because we wanted to. We always tell each other about them later and laugh together. I was taking my problems to her even before we started dating. Renee is smart—a lot smarter than me—and level-headed. She approaches problems with confidence, fully intending to best them. She almost always does.

But I'm not sure how she will approach *this* problem. We already lost one child—our first, at the age of four, before Melinda was born—and I know if she sees the video I watched at Wylie's, she will fall apart as completely as if she's lost another. That cannot happen. I have to tell her, and now. It seems I've had this bottled up inside me for weeks, months, not just a matter of hours.

Renee comes to her side of the bed and stands there in her lavender robe, arms interlocked over her breasts. "Are you going to tell me what's wrong?"

I smile, pat her side of the bed. "Yes, I promise. Come to bed." My lips won't stop trembling as I smile, so I stop, bite my lower lip.

Renee does not fall apart at the news as I suspected. I thought there would be tears, sobbing. Instead, her response is one of ferocious anger. I have never seen her so enraged. Her eyes become dark and her chin juts, lower teeth visible between her lips. Rigid cords of muscle stand out in her neck and her voice becomes a low growl.

"How long have you known about this?" she asks. "Why didn't you tell me sooner?"

"I told you, I just found out this afternoon, and I—"

"And you're telling me *now*?"

This is going to be more difficult than I anticipated.

When she was a little girl, Renee was sexually molested by her father. She sometimes jokes about killing him, and sometimes I wonder how serious she might be. I did not consider this before telling her about Melinda and Teklenburg. I should have. She is seeing this not only from the viewpoint of a mother, but from that of a cruelly abused child. I wonder if now, along with her father, she wants to kill Chick Teklenburg too.

I hold her close and she shivers in my arms as I tell her the rest. About Cherine, and that other young girls in the neighborhood are on Teklenburg's website. Other daughters.

Renee bounds from the bed and paces the floor, fists clenched at her sides. "I want to kill him," she says, voice low but trembling. She stops pacing at the foot of the bed and faces me. "Give me your gun. I want to kill him now. Right now, tonight."

I get out of bed and go to her. "Wylie feels the same way. And he wants me to help."

"He's a cop. Why does he need your help? He should take care of this himself, right away, Goddammit, why hasn't he already, why hasn't—"

"He wants us to *kill* this guy, Renee."

She looks at me for several seconds, teeth clenched and eyes wide. "Then do it. No jury in the world would convict you." She is very serious.

I shake my head. "Honey, that's premeditated murder. The reason behind it won't make much difference, if any at all."

"He's a cop," she says again. "Do you think he's going to let you two get caught? Don't you think he knows what he's doing?"

Yes, I do think he knows what he's doing. That makes it all the more appealing. I *want* to kill Chick Teklenburg. I want to dismember him with my bare hands. But it would mean life in prison, maybe the death penalty, if we're caught. Who better to keep that from happening than a friendly, like-minded cop?

I stroke Renee's hair as I hold her. "We can't say anything about this to Mel yet."

"Are you out of your mind? I'd like to go to her room right now and—"

"She might warn Captain Video that we know what he's up to," I whisper.

She pulls away and frowns at me. "Do you really think she'd do that?"

"Did you think she'd do *this*?"

I pull Renee close again. She trembles rigidly in my arms, as if feverish. Her tears fall on my neck, but she is not really crying, not screwing up her face and sobbing. She's too angry for that. I can hear her anger boiling just beneath the smooth surface of her low, level voice.

"I want to help you," she says against my shoulder.

"What? Help me—"

"I'll do whatever you want. I'll cut him up into tiny pieces for you. I'll even kill him, if you want. I think it should be something slow. And painful."

The even, serious tone of her voice chills my blood. I tell myself she's just not taking this well, that's all. She'll feel differently once it sinks in. But I'm not so sure. Without comment, I lead her slowly back to the bed. I am exhausted and want to sleep, but I know I won't until Renee calms down.

She takes a Xanax and we go back to bed. Renee talks in whispers, partly to me, but mostly to herself, I think. About torturing Teklenburg, killing him. I stroke her neck and make small sounds of acknowledgement in my throat as she talks, and try not to visualize the things she is saying. Her whispers fade, words become garbled and farther apart. I am relieved to hear her quiet, purring snore. But sleep does not come as easily for me, and I spend most of the night staring into the bedroom's darkness. Watching that stringy old hippy fuck my daughter.

3

Chick Teklenburg moved into the house at the end of Gyldcrest just short of a year ago. Like the family of strict Jehovah's Witnesses who lived there before him, he keeps to himself. He's friendly enough if you meet him on the sidewalk, even calls hello from across the street. But he makes no effort to get to know anyone in the neighborhood. He put up no decorations last Christmas, which pissed a lot of people off because it probably cost Gyldcrest a special color photo spread in the Christmas Day edition of the Redding *Record Searchlight.* Gyldcrest won that honor four Christmases in a row—but then the Jehovah's Witnesses moved in. Chick was the only one on the street who did not participate in this year's Gyldcrest Spring Yard Sale, an event that grew bigger and drew more attention from around the state each year. Those who gave him a pass at Christmas were not so charitable about the big yard sale weekend.

If everyone on the street were to find out about *this*...I'm not sure what they would do. But it would not be good for Chick Teklenburg.

Minutes after Renee leaves for work this morning, Wylie calls. Says he wants me to meet a friend of his. Deeny and the girls went shopping, so I should just let myself in the front door. So I do.

His friend is a nervous little guy he introduces only as Ricky. A colleague, he says. He looks more like one of those guys who washes your windshield without asking at a red light and then expects a tip for it. He wears a dirty white T-shirt beneath an open blue chambray, torn jeans, dilapidated sneakers. He looks in his mid-thirties, but that stubble on his face might add a couple years.

"Nice to meet you," I say as I sit on the sofa.

Ricky sits hunched forward on an ottoman and Wylie wanders around the living room with a tall glass of orange juice.

"See, I own Ricky," Wylie says, then laughs. "I've owned Ricky since 1993. Ain't that right, Ricky?"

Ricky shrugs a shoulder and smirks, but it is not a pleasant smirk.

"Ricky's my snitch. When he's not in jail, of course. He's a pyro. A firebug. I got a couple things on Ricky, here, could send him away for a long time. But I look the other way as long as he keeps his eyes and ears open for me. And helps me out if I happen to need it every once in awhile. Like today. He's gonna help us out."

A few of my internal alarms go off, and with a jerk of my head, I silently ask Wylie to accompany me to the kitchen.

"Something wrong?" he asks. He gulps the rest of his orange juice, puts the glass on the counter. I can smell no alcohol on him, so I guess the juice was nothing more than juice. I hope.

"Look, Wylie, I haven't exactly said I'm going to do this."

He grins. "Well, y'gotta do it now, Clark."

"What do you mean?"

"Because you know *I'm* doin' it. If you don't do it, then I gotta kill you."

Before I can stir up enough saliva in my suddenly dry mouth to respond, Wylie slaps me on the back and roars with laughter.

"You got any plans for dinner this evening?" he asks, still chuckling.

"Just the usual. Eating."

"Don't make any. I'm throwing a little barbecue for our flower child down the street. Think Renee would mind making her potato salad? She makes the best damned potato salad."

"She's working today, I doubt she'll have time."

"Too bad. Which do you like better, chicken, or burgers and dogs?"

"I always prefer burgers and dogs," I say, patting my softening belly.

"Burgers and dogs it is. Let's go." He puts his arm around me and leads me back into the living room. Says to Ricky, "You ready?"

Ricky stands, nods.

"Where are we going?" I ask.

"We're gonna walk down to Teklenburg's house," Wylie says.

"To invite him to the barbecue?"

"Yeah. Just making a friendly visit. Give Ricky a chance to look the place over, see what he's working with. Just go along with whatever I say, Clark."

"What are you going to say?"

"I don't know."

Dread constricts my throat. "Look, Wylie, I'm no good at this kind of thing, okay? I'm a lousy liar, I can't—"

"What's to be good at? Just smile and be friendly, Clark, that's all. You can do that—I've *seen* you!" More laughter.

An unfamiliar Volkswagen Jetta is parked at the curb in front of Chick Teklenburg's house. His old van is in front of the closed garage. Loud music plays inside.

On the front porch, Wylie knocks hard on the door. Several seconds pass before he pounds harder, longer, then says, "He can't hear us. Let's stroll around to the backyard."

I quickly say, "Wait, do you think that's a good idea?"

"Sure, we're neighbors, aren't we? Why?" Wylie lowers his voice. "You don't think good ol' Chick's doing somethin' back there he'd be *ashamed* of, do you?" He laughs as he goes back down the steps and crosses the lawn.

I start to follow, but look back when Ricky doesn't move. Just stands on the porch looking the front of the house over carefully.

"You guys coming?" Wylie calls, and we jog across the lawn to catch up with him.

"He's got a couple of big Chows, remember," I say as Wylie opens the gate in the tall, weathered, old wooden fence that surrounds the backyard.

"Chick!" Wylie calls as we walk along the side of the house. "Hey, Chick!"

The music's volume drops by half. There is movement in the house, just beyond the wall to our left. The curtains in the window just ahead of us part. Teklenburg lifts the sash, smiles at us through the screen wearing jeans and no shirt.

"Hi, guys. What can I do ya for?"

"Hey, Chick, how goes it? We catch you at a bad time?"

"Kind of. I'm working."

"Working? Yeah, that's right, you said you're self-employed. What kinda work you do, anyway?"

"I'm an artist."

"An artist!" Wylie turns to me for a moment, eyebrows high. "Hey, Chick, you've met Clark, haven't you? Clark Fletcher from up the street. And this is Ricky, a buddy of mine. So, Chick, what kind of artist are you?"

His ponytail flops as he glances over his shoulder, preoccupied. "Um, the digital kind. My art is computer generated. It's, uh, kind of like—"

The high laughter of a young woman comes through the open doorway behind him, followed by the young woman herself. Through the screen she is little more than a silhouette, but a shapely one.

Teklenburg turns to her and says, "I'll be there in a sec, okay? Just go back and wait for me."

"I suppose she's a professional model posing for you? Huh?" Wylie asks with a devilish grin.

Teklenburg smiles and nods. "Yeah, she is."

I cock my head to one side and say, "You need a model for computer generated art?"

He clears his throat. "Well, uh, I've been trying some real world art lately. Sketching and painting. I'm painting a nude right now, and the model doesn't come cheap, guys, so—"

"Hear that, guys?" Wylie says over his shoulder. "How come you haven't invited your neighbors over to watch you work, Chick?" We all laugh then.

The pale, stringy hippy laughs with us, showing only the slightest hint of nervousness. The ease with which he lies makes me want to kill him right now, no waiting around. "I've gotta get back to it. Was there something—"

"Yeah, I wanted to invite you over for dinner tonight," Wylie says. "We're having a few people over for a barbecue. Just people from the neighborhood, here. Nothin' special, really, just a spur-of-the-moment thing. Burgers and hot dogs, potato salad."

"It's nice of you to ask, Wylie, but I'd probably be a bother. I'm a vegetarian."

"No bother at all! We got vegetarian hamburger patties. My wife's mother's a vegetarian, so we've gotta keep the freezer stocked."

"Really? You know, that sounds like just the thing I need. What can I bring?"

"What's your beverage of choice?"

"Usually white wine."

"Bring some. About six-thirty, okay?"

Teklenburg smiles. "See you then, guys." Starts to close the window.

"One more thing," Wylie says. "You mind if I take my buddy here in the back and show him your koi pond? He's thinking about starting one."

"Sure, man. Go ahead." He closes the window and the curtains fall back into place.

My heart is going off like a machine gun in my ears. Walking beside Wylie, I whisper, "How did you know he has a koi pond?"

"He told me. Sometimes I run into him while he's walking his dogs, and we shoot the bull a couple minutes."

As Wylie and I go to the attractive pond with a small wooden bridge arching over it, Ricky walks slowly along the back of the house.

"What's he doing?" I whisper.

"Trying to get a feel for the place. The plan was to go inside so he could look around. Didn't work out that way. You know what he's doing in there, don't you?"

"I've been trying not to think about it."

"Yeah, but that don't stop it. He's got himself another little girl in there. Got her in front of the camera. You think that car out front belongs to her parents? Or maybe it was a gift for her sixteenth birthday."

My fists are clenched so hard, my fingernails dig into the flesh of my palm. "Look, if you want to kill him now, right here, fine. Otherwise, knock it the hell off, okay?"

"Yeah. Sorry, Clark."

We watch the pretty fish in the pond until Ricky says he's ready to go, and we walk back to Wylie's house.

"Since when is Nadine's mother a vegetarian?" I ask. "She makes the best beef stroganoff in the world."

"Since a few minutes ago," Wylie says. "I made it up, figured he'd be more likely to come if we already had veggie burgers in the house. I'll have Deeny pick some up at the store." In the kitchen again, Wylie pours himself another orange juice. "Whatta you think, Ricky? Any good?"

Ricky takes an apple from a bowl of fruit on the small kitchen table, bites into it loudly. "Yeah, no problem."

"Sorry we couldn't get inside, but—"

"Nah, forget about it. That house is no big mystery. I get inside, I'll be fine."

I turn to Wylie. "Inside? When is he going inside?"

"During the barbecue." Wylie smiles. "All you gotta do is keep the vegetarian entertained, make sure he don't decide to go back to his house until Ricky's done."

"Done doing what?"

Wylie's big shoulders sag as he sighs. "You gotta pay attention, Clark, okay? Didn't I tell you Ricky's a firebug? He's a pro. Been doing it since he was a kid. Give him half an hour, he'll set up a fire to start whenever he wants it to, and once it does, nobody gets out." He smiles again. "*That's* what he's gonna do. After tonight, Clark, that fuckin' lettuce-eatin' prick's days of getting the little neighbor girls to take off their clothes are over."

Again, internal alarms are sounding. A brief wave of dizziness passes over me as I wonder what I've gotten into. "Wait, wait, how do you know there won't be someone in there with him?" I ask.

"Is Melinda gonna be over there tonight?" Wylie asks.

"Hell, no!"

"Neither is Cherine. And that's all I need to know."

I get a glass from the cupboard, fill it with icewater at the refrigerator door. Take a few long, hard gulps of it. "What do you need me for, Wylie?"

"Need you? I don't *need* you. I'm doing this no matter what. If you think I'm gonna let that son of a bitch get himself a high-priced attorney and squeak by with probation and some counseling, you're outta your fuckin' mind! I thought you'd feel the same way. I thought you'd want to know what he was doing with your daughter.

Hell, I thought you'd *want* to help me with this. Otherwise, I wouldn't have brought it up."

I don't want to say it. It sounds so weak, so cowardly. But it is real, something I cannot ignore, so I say it, anyway. "Wylie, no one wants to hurt that guy more than I do, I swear. But if I get caught…I've got Renee and Melinda to take care of. I can't do this if there's a chance—"

Wylie laughs hard, shaking his head. "Renee makes more money with her realty business than you do teaching—whatta you mean, you've got Renee and Melinda to *take care* of?"

As he laughs some more, I have an urge to punch him right in the face. It was a rotten thing to say, but my anger diminishes quickly. Too many other things eating at me, I guess.

Wylie finishes off his orange juice. "You don't have to worry about that. Won't happen."

"You don't know that. You can't."

He sets his empty glass on the counter hard and steps close to me. "I can't prove it to you, no. But I *know* it. You'll just have to trust me. If that's something you can't do…well, I thought we were friends, Clark, but maybe I was wrong."

I am surprised and touched, and feel a pang of guilt for not feeling the same way about him. I put a hand on his shoulder and say, "No, of course not, Wylie, you're not wrong about that."

"I mean, you're the only one I *told*, for cryin' out loud. I didn't tell the Hentoffs or the Griffens, and their daughters are on that website. So's the Elliott girl. I figured you and me, we could take care of it for everybody, and they wouldn't have to know. And even if we get nailed, Clark—and that's *not* gonna happen, I'm tellin' ya—but if we do, the shit's gonna land on me, not you. What the hell have you done? All you're gonna do is keep Tofu Boy occupied for awhile. I'm the one employing the services of a known criminal. I'm the one playin' with fire here, no pun intended." He puts an arm around me, leads me out of the kitchen and to the front door. "You got nothing to worry about, Clark. You have my word. Now go home and do whatever it is you do. You started preparing for classes this fall yet?"

"I started doing that six weeks ago," I mutter.

He opens the door. "Then you've probably got work to do, huh? Just go home and keep busy till I give you a call, okay?"

"Okay," I say, stepping through the door. "See you later." I cross the street in a kind of daze, wondering what happened to my life. I had it just yesterday and it was perfectly fine.

4

Every summer, I wonder why the hell I live in Redding, California. The summers are miserably hot, and each one seems worse than the last. With August just starting, the worst is yet to come. It's too hot to cook indoors, so summer evenings always smell of meat cooking on grills in the open air.

It is muggier than usual this evening. There is no breeze. The air feels clenched.

"I don't understand why *I* have to do this," Melinda whines as we start across the street together. "Can't I stay home and eat a sandwich, or something?"

My voice is tense as I say, "We're going to eat, you can visit with Cherine and Erica, and then we'll go home. I don't want to hear any complaints. And don't even *ask* if you can go anywhere, because you can't."

"I wasn't going to—okay, what'd I do?" Melinda asks as we start up Wylie's steep driveway. "How come you're so pissed at me. Am I being punished?"

"Watch your language," Renee says.

"You're not being punished. Yet. But tonight, we need to talk."

Melinda stops walking and I turn to her. She looks at me with dread.

"Talk about what?" she asks.

"We'll talk about it tonight, at home. Come on." That will give her something to chew on for awhile. She'll be so busy trying to figure out what I'm talking about, she won't have time to get into trouble.

The only guests to arrive before us are Monica and Phil Halprin. Chick Teklenburg is nowhere to be seen. Wylie greets us loudly, then beckons me over to the barbecue, where he stands in a bib apron that reads "Kiss My Skillet!" on the front.

It's a standard Weber kettle-style barbecue. None of those pansy-assed gas barbecues for Wylie. At barbecues past, he has proudly claimed the title Master of the Charcoal Brickette. But not this evening. He curses the brickettes as he replaces the lid.

"I invited the Morgans and Elliots," he says, "but the Morgan boy's having a big pool party for his birthday, and the Elliots are helping out. They're probably gonna burn down the neighborhood with those damned torches. People like that even scare the hell out of Ricky."

Wylie refers to the tiki torches the Morgans have been lighting up in their backyard two or three times a week since the luau they threw back in June.

"Why isn't he here yet?" I ask.

"Don't worry, it's early."

"Where's Ricky?"

"In the kitchen cuttin' up carrots and celery."

My heart skips a beat. "Are you serious?"

"Yeah. What, you think he can't cut up carrots and celery?"

"No, I mean, why is he *here*? Shouldn't he be out of sight, waiting for—"

"Would you just calm down? Everything's cool. Jeez, look at you, you look like Don Knotts in *Alien*." He laughs. "There's nothing to worry about, Clark, I mean it. You wanna know when you can worry? When *I* get worried. *Then* you can worry. Can I get you a beer?"

I take a couple deep breaths, trying to calm myself. My veins are already pumping with adrenaline and nothing has happened yet. "Yeah, a beer sounds good," I say, but quickly backtrack. "No, wait…are you drinking tonight, Wylie? No offense, but I'd really appreciate it if—"

He laughs. "Boy, you're coverin' all your bases, huh? No offense taken. I'm workin' tonight, Clark. I never drink when I'm workin'. But that don't mean you can't. In fact, you need to. C'mon, let's get you a beer, then you can mingle."

I don't feel like mingling. Honestly, I don't feel like being here. And for awhile, I thought we wouldn't make it over here.

I told Renee about the picnic when she got home from work, and she groaned.

"Can't we just stay home and have pizza delivered?" she said. "I had a lousy day."

"I wish we could," I said. I told her Teklenburg would be there.

Her mouth dropped open, eyes widened impossibly, and her hands began to tremble. "Clark, you can't expect me to go to a barbecue with that...that...oh, *God*, I'd put a fork in his throat, Clark, I wouldn't be able to *help* myself!"

I led her to the kitchen, poured her a glass of wine. We went out on the back porch, sat on the swing and I told her Wylie's plan in whispers. Several emotions battled for dominance on her face as she thought about it. Finally, she whispered, "We can't take Melinda if he's going to be there."

"You want to leave her here by herself? No way. She's coming. It'll be interesting to see her reaction when she sees him there. When we get home tonight, we'll sit her down and have a talk."

More seconds passed. "So, you're really going to do this?"

"What do you mean? Last night, *you* wanted to do it."

Suddenly, she threw her arms around me and held me close. "What did we do wrong, Clark? I mean, if he had forced her...if it had been against her will...that would be different. But you said she seemed to enjoy it. This is something she's been *keeping* from us. What did we do wrong?"

I could not answer her question, so I said nothing, just held her.

Wylie's stereo plays the Dixie Chicks through speakers mounted around the covered patio. In the center of the patio, a large metal tub of ice holds beer and soft drinks. Melinda huddles with Cherine and Erica in a corner, each with a soft drink in hand. Renee is helping Nadine in the kitchen and I wish she were with me now. I sip a Heineken, smile at Melinda. She turns away, looks pissed. I chat with Monica and Phil for a couple minutes, until Wylie joins us, says the burgers and dogs will be on the grill in no time, then takes me aside.

He quietly says, "Why don't you go out front, see if that little alfalfa-sprout-eating prick is out there. Maybe he's not sure which house I'm in."

"Sure. Do me a favor and keep an eye on the girls, okay? Melinda is not to leave the premises."

"I told the girls if they even think of going anywhere tonight, I'll kill 'em, have 'em stuffed, and we'll drag 'em out at the holidays to prop up at the table."

We laugh, then I cross the yard, walk along the far side of the house toward the front. Kate and Barry Murchison are on their way to the backyard and smile.

"Wylie got them burgers cookin' yet?" Barry asks.

"I think the brickettes are giving him a hard time tonight, Barry."

"Oh, shit! Brickettes givin' *Wylie* a hard time?" His laughter sounds like a bad case of hiccups. "Man, that *can't* be good. I bet Wylie's pissed!"

"Why would Wylie be pissed?" Kate asks.

Still grinning, Barry says, "Shut up," and they walk on behind me.

I spot Chick Teklenburg coming up the street on this side. Head down, four fingers stuffed into each pocket of his jeans, something tucked under his left arm. He's not very big. I could overpower him easily. Get him in the shadows beside Wylie's house and kill him. Strangle him, maybe. Or maybe I'd just stomp on his skull till it was flat. It would feel so good.

"Hey, Chick," I say with a smile.

He smiles back, coming closer. "I hope I'm not late."

"Not at all. Wylie's still battling the brickettes." I turn around and we go up Wylie's driveway together.

"I got involved in work and lost track of time," he says. "I couldn't remember what time Wylie told me to come, and I was afraid I was late."

"Must be nice to do something you enjoy so much, you can lose track of time like that," I say, wanting to wrap my hands around his scrawny neck, dig my thumbs into his larynx.

He nods. "It's the only way to live, man. I love my work. It hasn't made me rich and famous, but it's made me very happy."

I want to scoop his eyeballs out of their sockets with my fingers and shove them into his mouth. Instead, I say, "I enjoy my work, but not that much." He is about to ask, but I don't wait. "I teach out at Shasta College. English. I like working with young people." I smile at him. "Of course, the young people *I* work with all have their clothes on."

He stumbles to a stop, turns to me. "Huh? I mean…what?"

"The model at your place this morning. You said she was naked."

His head tips back and he laughs, starts walking again. "Oh, yeah. She was, man. And she was beautiful."

He must know Melinda is my daughter. Unless he's an idiot. For just a second, there, I thought I'd scared him, but now I'm not so sure. He's so relaxed, so casual.

"But when you're working on something," he says, "you really don't notice. I mean, the work takes over and you don't even think about it."

A yelp of laughter gets out before I can stop it. I ignore it and say, "That's interesting."

His head bobs a few times. I'd like to put it on the end of a stick.

We round the corner of the house to the backyard. "Would you like a beer?"

"Wylie told me to bring this," he says, taking the bottle of wine from under his arm. "I had it in the 'fridge for a while to chill."

"Let's go in the kitchen for a glass. I'll introduce you to my wife," I say, thinking, *Oh yeah, she's just* dying *to meet you, buddy.*

Nadine is laughing her loud, wailing laugh as we walk into the kitchen. Ricky is washing his hands in the sink and Renee is taking a platter of deviled eggs from the refrigerator, setting it on the counter.

"Renee?" I say. "Chick's here."

As she turns, I feel genuine suspense. I have no idea what will be on her face, what she will say.

She is grinning.

"Hey, Chick," Ricky says, drying his hands on a couple paper towels.

"Chick, this is my wife Renee. Renee, this is Chick Teklenburg, our neighbor who keeps to himself."

He glances at me and chuckles.

Still grinning, Renee rushes toward him, and for an instant, I fear she's going to pounce on him, take him down to the floor, strangle him, and I almost step forward to stop her when she reaches out for his hand.

"Well, it's so nice to meet you, Mr. Teklenburg," she says as they shake. "You know, I've wanted to drop by a few times, maybe bring you some cookies, or something, but you're so quiet down there at the end of the street, I'm afraid I'll be disturbing you, or interrupting something."

If it weren't for the fact that I know what is going through her head at that moment, if I weren't in on the whole thing, I would have no idea she wants to kill the man. She is genuinely warm. I married Meryl Streep.

"He's an artist, honey," I say, smiling.

"Really?" She turns to Nadine. "Did you know we had an artist living on the street?"

"I had no idea!" Nadine says loudly. She is even more outgoing than Wylie. I'm surprised she hasn't hugged Teklenburg yet. After all, she has no idea what he did to her daughter. "All this time we've been running into each other at Raley's a couple times a week, and you never said a *thing*." She swipes the dishtowel at him. "Self-employed, he says. You're too modest, Chick." She points at the bottle. "Can I get you a glass for that, or are you drinking it straight from the bottle tonight?"

He laughs, nods. Nadine takes the bottle to open it.

"What kind of artist are you, Mr. Teklenburg?" Renee asks. She's giving him the same look she gives her clients, the you-are-the-only-other-person-in-this-room look.

"Call me Chick," he says. "Mr. Teklenburg is my dad, and man, if *he's* here, I'm gone." Renee laughs. "I'm a digital artist."

"That's fascinating," she says.

Nadine hands Teklenburg a glass of wine and we leave the kitchen, go outside to join the others. Renee and Teklenburg chat the whole time.

"Hey, Chick!" Wylie says. "Didn't know if you were gonna make it. I hope you brought an appetite."

"I'm ready to eat."

"Won't be long now. I'm having a little trouble with the brickettes. Deeny bought a case of some off-brand at Costco and they're not worth a piss into the wind. Lessee, you got your drink. Here comes Deeny and Ricky with the appetizers."

Nadine and Ricky carry the trays to the patio and put them on a table. Wylie heads back to the barbecue and we go to the table, munch on celery, potato chips.

The sun is going down and long shadows are being dissolved. The lights in the covered patio have not been turned on yet, but in spite of the murkiness, I can see Melinda talking with Wylie's girls. They are leaning close, as if conspiring. She has not noticed Teklenburg. Not yet. Suddenly, Melinda stands up, looks around until she spots me. She hurries around the tub of ice.

"Dad, if it's only for a minute, can I go with Cherine and Erica to Target for a—"

"No."

"But we'll only be gone for a—"

"I said, *no*. And I've got news for you. Cherine and Erica can't go anywhere, either. Wylie told me. Have you met our neighbor?" I turn to Teklenburg, who is facing the table, dipping a chip. "Chick? This is our daughter Melinda."

As he turns, he lifts a chip with a glob of green dip on it to his mouth. It freezes an inch from his parted lips when he sees her.

"Melinda, this is Chick Teklenburg," I say, smiling. "He's a digital artist."

She freezes, too, jaw slack.

As if cued by God Himself, the patio lights come on and they gawk at one another for a second. Finally, he pops the chip in his mouth, wipes his hand on his jeans, and extends it to her.

"Melinda," he says. "Nice to meet you."

"Yeah. Nice…to meet you, too." After a single shake, she drops his hand and turns to me again.

"No," I say before she can speak.

With a long sigh that sounds like her whole life is one big torture, Melinda turns and goes back to the corner to rejoin Cherine and Erica.

Teklenburg turns back to the table. To compose himself, I'm sure.

"She's a very obstinate girl," I say, slowly shaking my head.

Renee says, "We're thinking of selling her into slavery. You know anybody who'd be interested, Chick?"

His head turns to her in jerks and he stares at her a moment, mouth open. When Renee laughs, I laugh with her, and Teklenberg's whole body relaxes as he smiles slowly, finally laughs with us.

Lights on the back of the house brighten the backyard. Barry Murchison and Phil Halprin have started a horseshoe game on the lawn. Wylie is hovering nervously around the barbecue. He checks his watch. Ricky joins him and they confer, heads close together.

"Clark says you have a lovely koi pond," Renee says.

"Oh, yeah," Teklenburg says, head bobbing. "The koi. They need a lot of attention, but they're so beautiful, they're worth it."

"I've been thinking about putting a koi pond in the backyard," she says.

"You have?" It's the first I've heard about it.

"Oh, I haven't told *you*, of course, because you'd just say no and complain about what a bad idea it is, and then I'd go off and do it, anyway. I figure, why bother you with it," she says with a smile, puts an arm across my shoulders.

Teklenburg laughs.

"Anyway, I *have* been thinking about it," she says. "I just haven't looked into it. I know nothing about koi, or ponds. I've tried to find information on the Internet, but I just can't figure out those damned search motors."

"Engines," I say. "Search engines."

"Whatever." She turns to him, hooks a thumb in my direction.

"He's no help, because he doesn't know any more about the Internet than I do."

I shake my head. "Not interested, thank you. I've got enough distractions in my life."

"Do you have much experience on the Internet, Chick?"

His eyebrows rise above his wire-framed glasses as he puts another potato chip into his mouth. Chews slowly a moment before saying, "The Internet?"

"Yeah. You know, I bet you could sell your work on the Internet. Or, maybe you do. Do you?"

He empties his wineglass with one gulp.

I say, "I've heard a lot of people are making money on that, um…what is it?"

"eBay," Renee says, nodding. "I have a client who makes little animals out of hot glue, puts eyes and ears on them. Makes a fortune selling them on eBay. So, do you sell any of your work on the Internet, Chick?"

His head bobs again, but he is tense. "Yeah, I've sold a few things on the Internet. At online art galleries, that sorta thing. Uh…" He looks around, eyes darting. "Could I use the—"

"Do you surf the web a lot?" Renee asks. Suddenly, there is an edge to her voice that I have heard before. It means she's getting angry and is about to blow.

"Well, not a lot," he says uncomfortably. "Could you tell me where the—"

"It's nice to know there's *art* on the Internet," she goes on. "I mean, the way people talk about it, you'd think there's nothing but naked girls and people having sex out there." She laughs, but it is a laugh that could cut flesh.

I close my hand on her elbow, squeeze. "Honey, I think you're keeping him from going to the bathroom."

He smiles and chuckles, but it's forced. "Could you point me in the right direction?"

"I'll take you, Chick," I say with a jerk of my head in the direction of the house. I lean close and whisper in Renee's ear, "Keep an eye on Snow White, over there. And calm down. Have another beer."

I take Teklenburg into the house. As I turn to close the kitchen door, I see Wylie hurrying in my direction.

"Right down that hall," I say, pointing. "Second door on the right."

As soon as he's gone, Wylie comes in, speaks in a whisper. "Goddamned brickettes wouldn't burn. I just put the first batch of patties and weenies on the grill."

"Where's Ricky?" Without meaning to, I whispered, too.

He leans close. "Down the street."

"I thought you were going with him."

"I was, but I couldn't get the fucking brickettes going. Figured I'd have a buncha burgers done by now. You wanna take over the grill for me?"

"Not if I'm supposed to keep an eye on him, too."

"Okay, maybe I'll have Deeny do it. But I don't want it to look like I'm sneakin' off somewhere."

"Get a couple veggie burgers cooked. Give him some food, and I'll try to keep him occupied for awhile. How long will it take?"

"As long as it takes."

"Come on, Wylie, I can't keep him here forever."

"Shouldn't be more than thirty minutes. Just don't let him leave till we get back."

"You don't know how long it'll take? I thought you had this *planned*."

"Give me a break, I planned this overnight. If it hadn't been for—"

Footsteps in the hall shut him up. Teklenburg comes out of the hallway frowning, a hand on his stomach. "You know, guys," he says, "I'm not feeling so well. I'm thinking maybe I should go home and lie down."

Panic hits me hard for a moment. Ricky is already in the house, but if Teklenburg decides he really wants to go home, how can we stop him?

"You just need to eat, that's all," Wylie says with booming enthusiasm. "I'll put a coupla yours on right away."

"No, really, I think—"

"You want some Alka-Seltzer?" Wylie asks. "Some Pepto-Bismol? Maalox? I got 'em all."

I put an arm around Teklenburg's shoulders and my insides recoil as I smile. "Can you try to stick around a little longer?" I ask. "This is the first time a lot of us have had a chance to meet you. Nadine would be very disappointed, I think, if you—"

"Oh, Deeny'd be beside herself," Wylie says, going to a kitchen cupboard. He opens it and removes something, hands it to Teklenburg. A packet of Maalox tablets. "Chew up a coupla these. If they don't help, then you should go home. But for Deeny's sake, stick around awhile. I'll get you a burger."

Wylie hurries out ahead of us and I follow with Teklenburg at my side.

A few more people wander in and the music changes from Dixie Chicks to Garth Brooks to Faith Hill. Not my kind of music, but it's just white noise. Nadine brings us hamburger patties and hot dogs on paper plates. We take them to the table where the condiments and buns are waiting.

"You feeling better?" I ask Teklenburg as I apply mustard and lettuce and onions to my burger.

"Yeah, I think so. A little hungry after smelling this."

"Good. You looked pretty sick for a few seconds, there."

He simply chuckles and says, "Yeah." Then bites into his burger.

Nadine is cooking at the grill. Wylie is nowhere to be seen. After we finish our hamburgers, Renee suggests a game of horseshoes.

"I know!" Renee says. Her beer is showing. "We can play in teams." She turns back to the patio and calls, "Me*lin*da! Come play horseshoes with us."

Melinda mutters something grouchy.

"This is neither a suggestion nor a request, Melinda. Come, *now*."

She comes out of the patio with her head down, shoulders slumped.

Renee says, "You and Chick against your dad and me."

"*Mom!*" Melinda says, dragging the word into two long syllables.

Teklenburg smiles and holds up a hand, palm out. "Um, maybe I'll sit this out, 'cause I'm pretty stuffed, and I—"

"Oh, don't pay any attention to *her*," Renee says. "She's just feeling persecuted this evening. Come on, let's play!"

We walk over to the two metal stakes in the lawn and take sides. Teklenburg and Melinda talk to one another quietly, but try to keep their heads down when they do it. Probably hoping we won't notice. As we play, Renee and I whisper back and forth.

"I can't believe you did this," I say.

"I can't either. You should never let me drink."

"Right now, they are two of the most uncomfortable people in the world."

"Yeah. Ain't it a riot?" Her words are cold, without humor. "What do you suppose they're saying to each other right now?"

"I don't know, but the only reason I'm allowing it is that I know that son of a bitch is gonna be dead in awhile."

I nearly burst out of my skin when someone claps me on the back.

"All systems go, Houston," Wylie says in my ear. Then he raises his arms high, waves his hands and shouts, "Deeny and I play the winners!"

5

We're smiling and holding hands, Renee and I, as we walk home. Melinda mopes a couple steps behind us.

Laughter and shouting and splashing come from behind the Morgan house, just two up from us. Obnoxious rap music, too. The glow of their torches hovers over the backyard and tendrils of smoke rise above the roof of the house. Several unfamiliar cars are parked on both sides of the street. A couple adults stand on the front lawn smoking cigarettes.

"Well, that was a pleasant evening," I say on the way up the front walk.

"Yes, it was," Renee says. "Did you have a nice evening, sweetheart?" No response. "Melinda? Did you have a nice evening?"

"No, the evening *sucked*."

I stop and turn to her. "Hey, you want to watch your language, little girl? Especially when you're talking to your mother. Maybe you talk that way around your friends, but not with your parents, do you under—" I interrupt myself by spinning around and going up the steps to the door. "Nevermind, we'll talk inside." I take my keys from my pocket, unlock the door, and go in the house.

Melinda slinks away and heads down the hall, for the sanctuary of her bedroom.

"Oh, no, you don't!" I say. "In the living room."

Sighing and harrumphing, she turns and goes into the living room. A second later, the sound of a studio audience laughing itself silly comes from the television.

We're still standing in the entryway when Renee whispers, "You sure you want to do this now? I've been drinking."

"That's right. And you're happy and cuddly and a lot less likely to kill her."

She tries to suppress a laugh, but it snorts through her nose as she nods. She smiles, hooks her arm through mine, and leans on me as we go into the living room.

Melinda sits at the end of the sofa, legs curled up beneath her, watching *Family Ties* on television.

"Turn it off," I say.

She aims the remote, turns down the volume.

"I said *off*, not down."

Jutting her jaw, she turns off the television as Renee sits at the other end of the sofa. I sit in my recliner, swivel it toward her. Lean forward with elbows on knees. "Did you enjoy meeting Mr. Teklenburg tonight?"

She fidgets, brings her legs out, hugs her knees to her, and stares at the television as if it's still on.

"Didn't you find him interesting?" I say. "I mean, Chick being an artist, and all, I thought he was *fascinating*, didn't you?"

She ducks her head lower, trying to hide behind her knees. Her eyes glisten with unfallen tears.

"I'm talking to you. *Tiffany*."

She buries her face between her knees. Her body quakes a few times, but she does not make a sound.

"I saw your video," I say. "One of them, anyway." I wait for some response. Instead, the phone chirps. Renee, who has been unusually, almost unsettlingly, quiet so far, starts to get up. "Let the machine get it," I say, and she nods. I turn to Melinda, open my mouth to continue, but I cannot. Out of habit, I am unable to ignore the answering machine. After my recorded voice, the beep sounds, then:

"Renee? You there, honey?" Renee's mother, Enid. She pauses a moment. "I been thinking about that neighbor of yours, and I think you'd better have Melinda checked for AIDS, and make sure she's not pregnant."

Melinda lifts her head, face red and streaked with tears, and shrieks, "*You told Grandma?*"

Enid's voice drones on as I say, "Dammit, Renee, I told you—*no* one."

Renee spread her arms wide. "Who's she gonna tell? She lives twenty minutes away in Cottonwood, it's not like she hangs around the neighborhood here."

Dropping her feet to the floor, Melinda grabs a throw pillow from the sofa, puts it in her lap and pounds a fist into it repeatedly. "Jesus *Christ*, I can't *believe* you told *Grandma!*" Her voice is quivery and thick with tears. "Who *else* did you tell, Mom? Did you put in the *Recycler?*"

Renee's voice gradually raises as she says, "You're in no position to complain, young lady, so I don't want to hear any—"

"Whoa, hold it," I say, "can we quiet down, please? This is not going to be a shouting match. We're going to discuss this calmly and quietly, okay? Now, Melinda. Can you tell us, calmly and quietly, why you've been having sex with Chick Teklenburg on the Internet?"

She pounds the pillow again, then tosses it aside and stands. "You weren't supposed to know, you were *never* supposed to know!" She paces between Renee and myself.

"But we *do* know," Renee says. "And even if we never found out, how could you live with yourself, Melinda? Why would you do such a thing?"

Melinda shrugged and spread her arms. "Why is it such a big deal? It's *not* a big deal! Nobody was hurt, and it's not like I was some, y'know, innocent virgin he, like, *corrupted*, or anything."

"But on the *Internet*!" Renee's anger breaks through and she stands, steps in front of Melinda. "My God, why didn't you just do it in the street? Or on television? Don't you have *any* shame?"

"Look, he pays good, and Cherine knew I was saving for a car," Melinda explains, calmly, rationally, as if her words would solve everything.

"He *pays* you?" I ask. "Don't you have a problem with that? Don't you know what that's *called*?"

Renee's voice trembles as she says, "It's called prostitution, Melinda, and it makes you a *prostitute*."

"He doesn't pay for the *sex*!" She rolls her eyes. "He just pays for the right to use my image on his website. I would've had sex with him whether he was videotaping it or not."

Covering her eyes with a hand, Renee says, "Oh, sweet Jesus."

Someone shouts out in the street. Sounds like an angry teenager. I ignore it. My attention is already overtaxed as I try to keep up with the conversation, and at the same time, I'm preoccupied with how angry I am at Renee for telling her mother. My anger seems misdirected, though, because it's unlikely that Enid would be able to—*No!* a tiny voice in the back of my mind cries. *No, it is likely, it is!* And I know the voice is right, but I'm not sure why. It's just beyond my memory's reach.

Melinda takes a deep breath, rubs her hands over her face. Speaks softly in a monotone, never meeting Renee's eyes. "Look, Mom, sex is...well, it's just not like it was when you were my age."

Outside, a couple more voices shout at one another angrily. I glance in the direction of the front window, but stay in the chair.

"Don't give me that," Renee says. "You think your generation has reinvented sex because you're doing it on computer screens? You've just found a better way to degrade it, that's all. Sex is still *sex*, Melinda. And it still spreads diseases and gets you *pregnant*! We had this talk when you were nine, Melinda, remember?"

"Yeah, but—"

"No, I don't think you do! We've had a lot of talks about boys, too, haven't we? About how some will try to take advantage of you and—"

"I don't like boys, Mom. I like men."

Renee drops back onto the sofa, leans forward and puts her face in her hands.

Something clangs in the street outside, more voices shout. Frowning, I stand and go to the front window, pull the drapes apart.

The Morgan boy is walking down the street. The Elliott boy hurries to catch up with him. There are others, too, all walking toward the end of the street. My first thought is, *It's happened already? His house has already gone up in flames?* But I know that's not right. The voices would be different if that were the case, they would sound distressed, not angry. And they wouldn't be carrying torches. The Morgan boy and the Elliott boy are carrying burning torches. Tiki torches. And a hammer, the Morgan boy has a hammer. And behind him, Garry Elliott is jogging along, beer gut bouncing, a torch held in one hand, a large gun in another.

"Oh, shit," I say as it comes to me, the thing that's been bugging me about Renee telling her mother about Teklenburg.

"What?" Renee says, and I hear her and Melinda hurry toward me, feel Renee's hand on my back as she pulls the drape back further. "What's happening? Where's everybody—"

"Your mother," I say as I back away from the window, turn to her. "When did you talk to her?"

"This morning."

"Was she on her way to a hair appointment, by any chance?"

She turns to me, eyes round. "Yes! How did you—oh, God."

Enid Plummer, Renee's mother, has her hair done at the Golden Orchid, always by the same woman, one Janet Smidden, who lives with her husband and triplet toddlers just up the street and around the corner on Madison Way.

I step forward, jerk the drapes apart and look out the window again. Some are carrying golf clubs, others tire irons. Teenage boys, grown men. And women, too—there's Rita Bartlett, whose daughter recently turned seventeen, and she's carrying what looks like a .22 rifle, and behind her, Kate Murchison, who has two adolescent girls, carries a machete.

I shake my head and say, "Dammit, Renee, you had to tell your *mother*?"

"She can't be responsible for *this*," she says. She's emphatic, but I can hear the doubt in her voice.

"Are you kidding? She told Janet Smidden all about it, then Janet came home and made a few phone calls, word got around—" I point at the people going up the street. "—and now they *all* know."

"Oh, my God, what're they gonna *do*?" Melinda asks. There is real concern in her voice, her eyes.

"They're going to kill him, that's what," I say, heading out of the living room.

Melinda moves close to the window, palms flat on the pane. "He hasn't done anything wrong!" she cries.

"You have no idea how idiotic you sound," Renee says as she follows me out of the living room. In the entryway, as I reach out to open the front door, she asks, "What exactly are you planning to do out there, Clark?"

I freeze. I have no idea what I will do out there. Try to hold them off? Shout at them, *Hey, you people can't kill this guy*—we're *killing him*! My hand drops from the doorknob and I go to the phone in the kitchen, call Wylie. Nadine answers.

"Wylie said you might call," she says. "I'm supposed to tell you not to worry, he's got everything under control."

"Oh. Okay."

"What's going *on* out there, anyway? He told me and the girls to stay inside."

"That's probably a good idea, Nadine. Thanks." I turn the phone off, return it to its base at the end of the counter.

"What did she say?" Renee asks. "Where's Wylie?"

"Both of you stay in the house." I go back to the front door, but this time step outside and close it behind me.

Most of them have passed by now, but I can still hear them, voices and footsteps fading to my left. I cross the down-sloping lawn to the sidewalk and watch them. I can't tell how many there are, but six...no, eight of them are carrying torches.

What do they intend to do, anyway? Drag Teklenburg out of the house and lynch him in the front yard? Thanks to them, maybe he will be out of the house when it goes up in flames.

Across the street, Nadine stands at the window, trying to see down the street from an impossible angle. She turns and hurries away, probably to go to another window.

Up and down the street, dogs are barking. The air is still and warm, and still carries the aromas of cut grass and outdoor cooking. It is a perfectly normal late-summer evening. Except for the angry voices and the jewels of fire bobbing through the night, all the way to the end of the street.

Wylie's voice rises above the others just before they reach Teklenburg's house. I cannot understand his words, but the neighborhood mob has come to a stop. Whatever he is saying, they are listening to it.

But they do not listen long. Another male voice shouts in protest. Then another. Some of the torches move forward, then the whole crowd. More shouting. A gun fires and my feet leave the sidewalk for an instant.

"What's *happening*?" Renee calls from the porch.

"Stay inside," I say.

"Who's shooting?"

Someone is running up the street, away from the mob.

"I don't know. Go inside!"

I recognize the shadowy shape and step off the sidewalk, hurry down the road to meet him. "What the hell is going on?"

"Cat's outta the bag," Wylie says, winded. "Who'd you tell?"

"Renee. And she told her damned mother."

"Yeah, you gotta love women. If their mouths worked as much in bed as they do the rest of the time, we'd be happy men, huh?" Glass shatters at the end of the road, followed by pounding, pounding. The shouting crescendos as more glass breaks.

"What should we do?" I ask. My voice wavers in time with my heart, which is beating in my throat.

"Well, I did all I could. I couldn't stop 'em."

"Who fired the gun?"

"Oh, that pompous ass Garry Elliott. Fired it in the air. I was hopin' it'd come back down and land right in his brain."

I can only see three...no, four torches now. Where are the other four? I turn to Wylie. "What do we *do*, dammit? They're going to kill him!"

Wylie laughs. "You're funny. Well, I'll go inside and call the station, tell 'em I did what I could. Have 'em send a couple cars down. An ambulance and a fire truck."

"A fire truck?"

"Yeah, I really oughtta make that call right away, but I'd hate to miss it. It should be any—"

A heavy *whump*—not quite an explosion—sounds from Teklenburg's house. Windowpanes blow out with a sudden clapping sound and flames belch from a few of the windows. It's impossible to tell where the fire started because suddenly it is everywhere, glowing in all the windows. But I can't hear it burning. Not above the screaming. Men and women screaming as they run from the fire, taking the flames with them, staggering, falling. Burning figures—I don't know how many—scatter and fall and scream.

Wylie chuckles, slaps me on the back. I turn to him, and he's grinning, watching the fire. "Yeah, that was something. Well, I gotta go make that call. You better run inside like you're in a hurry, too. Case somebody's watching us." He takes off at a jog, disappearing up his driveway.

I realize I'm standing in the middle of the street. Wylie was right—if somebody's watching, they're going to remember me. I turn and hurry back up the lawn, into the house.

As I go inside, the screams fade to nothing behind me. But I can still hear them in my head. I rush into the bathroom and vomit.

6

Three people were killed in the fire—Garry Elliott, his seventeen-year-old son David, and Chick Teklenburg—and nine were injured, five of them seriously. Fire trucks arrived, but by the time they were done, the house was nothing more than a black skeleton.

Although there was nothing left in the remains of the house to incriminate Teklenburg, police were told about the website. Wylie told his buddies on the force that he knew nothing about Teklenburg's activities until that evening, when people started talking. He helped question everyone on the street, including myself and Renee, which was a lot less stressful than being questioned by an unfamiliar officer in uniform.

The website remained on the Internet, and police confirmed the story. Somehow, Janet Smidden's name never came up, so police never questioned her to learn that she heard about what Chick Teklenburg was doing from Enid Plummer, which would have led them to contact Enid and learn that she'd heard about it from her daughter.

As Wylie predicted, everything went smoothly. No evidence of arson was found—Ricky was as good as Wylie said he was—and it was assumed the fire was started by the torches carried by those who had burst into the house.

But you've probably heard about it all by now. It was in the news for weeks.

Renee handled it all very well. Melinda, on the other hand, became silent and brooding for weeks afterward. We have decided to send her to a private school, and are looking around to find the one that's strictest with its students. We have been talking about taking her to a psychologist as well, maybe a psychiatrist. Her behavior has only gotten worse since the fire. We discovered she's been crawling out her bedroom window at night, going out with friends and getting drunk, stoned. She becomes more unfamiliar every day. I have little hope that counseling will help, but I've put up an optimistic front for Renee.

I don't talk about what happened, not with Renee or Wylie. As far as they know, I'm fine. But it eats at me inside. Probably always will.

Betty Elliott and her two remaining children—both girls, one eleven, one fifteen—moved out of their house on Gyldcrest almost immediately and went to live near Betty's mother in Mt. Shasta City.

Slivers of Bone

The FOR SALE sign stood in front of the house for more than three months. Just a few days ago, two men began moving in. I met them the first day, Sidney and Leo...I don't remember their last names. Nice guys, both of them in their late fifties. Sidney is an artist, and Leo is a retired florist. They moved up here from San Francisco, tired of city life, looking for a place to relax with their four cats.

The remains of Teklenburg's house were leveled, the lot put up for sale, although I don't know by whom, and do not care to find out. A new house will be built there eventually, and someone else will move in. I have no intention of getting to know the new residents. But even then, with a new house standing at the end of the street, the black and broken bones of the previous one long gone, the fire's scars will remain on the street. In the pink and twisted faces of those burned by it.

"What the hell you doin' out here in this cold, tryin' to catch pneumonia?" Wylie asks as he comes up the back steps to the porch.

I am sitting on one of the two chairs on the porch, beside a small table. The lamp on the table casts its glow on the John Irving novel I'm reading. "It's not that cold," I say. "And this is a warm sweater."

Renee and I have turned down the last few invitations to cross the street to eat or drink. Renee would have gone, but I didn't want to. It would be just like Wylie to joke about what happened. A lot. I knew I couldn't take that. I thought Wylie would get the hint, but no, I doubt it ever occurred to him I didn't want to see him.

"What you been up to, Clark? Haven't seen you in awhile."

"Busy with classes."

He's wearing a fat down jacket and removes a Heineken from each pocket, grinning. Hands me one, sits in the other chair as he twists the cap off.

"Are you sure?" He takes a sip. "Look, Clark, if I've done something to offend you, I want you to let me know, okay? I'd do the same for you. I don't believe in holding things in, y'know?"

I'm surprised, but keep it to myself. I'm not sure what to say for a moment. Then: "No, Wylie, you haven't done anything to offend me."

"Anything wrong?"

I slip my bookmark into the book, close it. "It's just…well, I don't want to talk about…about what happened."

"What happened when?"

"You know what I mean."

He leans forward in the chair. "Clark, I've already forgotten it. It's over with, a done deal. You oughtta do the same."

I am tremendously relieved to hear Wylie say that. But it's not something I could ever forget.

"You meet the new neighbors yet?" he asks.

"Yes. Have you?"

"Yeah, I met 'em. Didn't think I'd ever see it. This town's gone right down the shitter."

"What do you mean?"

"I mean I've lived in this town all my life, and it's always been a good family town, a good place to raise kids. But in the last ten or fifteen years, with all them people moving up from the Gay Bay, I just can't say that about Redding anymore."

I sip my beer and close my eyes so Wylie won't see them roll.

"It's one thing to see 'em swishin' around in the mall, or in restaurants," he goes on. "But I'll be damned if I'm gonna sit by and watch 'em move in on Gyldcrest. Hell, first our girls were being preyed on, now it's our boys who're at risk."

The beer does not sit well in my stomach because suddenly I have a sense of where Wylie is going.

"We're just gonna have to do somethin' about it, Clark. And the sooner, the better. You don't wanna let them fags get too settled."

Suddenly, I am very cold. But from the inside out.

"I'm not sure how we'll handle it yet," he says, "but I'm gonna think hard about it. I wish you'd do the same, Clark." He chuckles. "You're a college professor, you're probably a hell of a lot better at thinkin' than I am. I think it's way too soon for another fire, so Ricky's useless. Maybe we could—"

"Wylie, I-I'm hoping you're joking. You…you *are* joking, right?"

"Joking? Shit no, Clark, I'm as serious as a heart attack. Just because we don't have any boys doesn't mean we shouldn't be worried about the rest of the neighborhood."

I squint at him as if he's far away, shake my head. "What…what the hell are you talking about?"

"Boys! Little boys!" He stands, a little angry all of a sudden. Sips his beer as he walks the length of the porch, then comes back, saying, "You know how them fags are. The older they get, the younger they hunt. Those two'll be goin' after the tender meat we got here on Gyldcrest. And we're not gonna let that happen."

My mouth hangs open as if I've had a stroke. I can't remember ever being this afraid in my own home. On the back porch, anyway. He means everything he's saying, and that angry edge to his voice said he was willing to prove it.

"Wylie…Wylie…" My tongue feels thick. "I…I can't, Wylie. I can't."

Towering over me, he looks down at me the way he might look at a cockroach before he stomps on it with the heel of his boot. "Can't? You can't what?"

"I can't do it again. I just can't. Look, we're friends, right, Wylie?"

He nods slowly, still glaring. "That's what I've always thought, yeah."

"Well, if you're really my friend…I know you won't ask me to do something that I…that I just can't do."

His face relaxes when he laughs. He hunkers down in front of me, smiling. "Hell, no, I'd never ask you to do something like that, Clark. I'm not askin' you now." He lowers his voice, almost to a whisper. "I'm tellin' you. I don't think you realize how easy it'd be for me to put you behind bars for a long time, Clark. That fire? Those deaths? All them people walkin' around lookin' like dog vomit on two feet? I could pin *all* that on you and make it stick. I'm a cop, remember? I work the law from the inside. I can get you out of a jam…or put you into one." Still smiling, his voice becomes little more than a breath. "And just in case that don't work—it would, don't worry, it would—but just in case, I can always come into your house in the middle of the night, tie you up, and make you watch while I fuck your wife and daughter. Then I'll kill 'em, and make you watch me fuck their corpses. By the time I get around to killing you, you'll thank me for doin' it."

Wylie stands so suddenly that I gasp in surprise.

"But that ain't gonna happen," he says. "Because, like you said, we're friends. And we're gonna do the right thing. And the right thing is getting ridda them cocksuckers." He takes a swig of beer, then turns and goes back to the porch's doorway. "I gotta get home. Hey, tell you what. Why don't you come over tomorrow night for dinner. Deeny's gonna fix a big stir fry, and there's always way too much. Bring Melinda and the girls can run off shopping after dinner. That's all they ever wanna do, is shop."

My mouth still hangs open as I watch him go down the steps.

"I'll see you tomorrow, Clark," he says. Then he disappears into the darkness that presses close against the screened-in porch.

Second Opinion

Do you know what it's like to cut up your best friend with a hacksaw? Probably not. Most people don't. That narrow metal blade, with its fine, sharp teeth, makes a very distinctive sound while it's cutting through human bones. I know that sound very well, and I'm not bragging. Not at all.

The food is very bad today, worse than usual. Instead of eating, I've been going over and over things in my head. One of the orderlies gave me this crayon and some paper, so I decided to start writing it all down. After all, that's what I do best, isn't it?

I called him Hank, but everybody else called him Henry Carr. His work had won a lot of awards, including the Pulitzer, which he called, in characteristic humility and nonchalance, the Putzpuller. He was truly a great writer, one of the best ever in my opinion, and I don't give a damn *what* any of those bonehead critics wrote or said about his work. The man was an artist with words, a genius.

Aside from being a great writer, he was a great man. Just a great person, plain and simple. He was my best friend and my mentor. He took me under his wing after reading one of my stories—the third that was actually published—and tried his best to prepare me for the rejection that every writer has to tolerate with ease if he or she is to succeed. Hank recognized my talent and tried to make sure that I remained true to it. I very likely would have been a much different person if I had not known him, and a much different writer as well—certainly not a good one, if I'm any good at all. In fact, I might not have been a writer, period.

Yes, Henry Carr was a great writer, a great man and my best friend and mentor. And I cut his arms and legs off, then cut those into small pieces, and wrapped his severed head in aluminum foil and plastic. I hate myself for it, but I've never ever forgotten the reason I did it.

«« — »»

When I heard Michael's knock at the front door, I hurried from the kitchen to answer it, still wearing my apron, which carried splotches of tomato sauce like battle wounds.

"Come in, come in," I said jovially as I opened the door, working hard to cover my anxiety, my discomfort.

Mikey shuffled into the house nervously, still behaving as if this were our first meeting and he was still nothing more than a young beginner. That wasn't the case at all.

I'd known Mikey for seven years, and he *always* behaved that way, showing me deference that I didn't deserve. It bugged me a little, because he was every bit my equal. The fact that he didn't realize that yet was a bit annoying.

Michael Anderson's latest novel was number one on the bestseller list, and it wasn't his first trip to the top of that mountain, no, it was his third. He'd consulted me several times on the first two novels, but not at all on the third, and I saw that as a good sign. He'd found his voice, his rhythm, his niche. He'd set sail on his own, and that was good.

When I first met him, he'd written a couple of critically acclaimed novels that had been purchased by a grand total of about eight people, and I tried to encourage him to keep writing in spite of that, because his talent was very obvious. I knew that he just needed some seasoning and a little guidance...not unlike the guidance I had gotten from Hank.

"Jeez, Greg," he said, "I haven't seen you in so long."

"Yeah, I know. Been busy."

"Well, that's good, but...*nobody's* seen or heard from you in a long time. We've all been kind of worried about you, Greg. I was really surprised when you called me out of the blue. Pleasantly surprised, I mean. Are you sure everything's okay?"

"Fine, just fine, everything's fine."

It was raining hard outside, and Mikey's black overcoat was soaked. After closing the door against the storm, I peeled the coat off him, put it on a hanger and hung it in the open doorway of the hall closet to dry.

"You don't look so good, Greg," Mikey said, frowning as he looked me over. "Are you sick?"

He was right. I was pale and had lost a lot of weight, and I was pretty thin to begin with.

"Oh, no, not sick," I said. "Just tired. I've been working too hard, haven't slept well the last few nights." That was putting it mildly. I hadn't slept at *all* in the last week, and every time I ate, I threw up the food a few minutes later. I'd been a wreck for a little over a year, to be honest, but especially bad this past week. Mikey was right; I hadn't called or seen anyone in about a year and I hardly even listened to the messages on my answering machine. I *never* answered the door when the doorbell rang. I hoped he couldn't see my hands shaking.

"You cooked Italian?" Mikey asked, sniffing the air.

"Spaghetti," I said. "With my own special sauce. *Which,* by the way, if I may say so myself, is the best you'll have in *this* lifetime."

I set the table and served up the salad, spaghetti and garlic bread. Before we began to eat, I put Vivaldi's *The Four Seasons* on the stereo.

"This is *great,*" Mikey said as he ate. "I mean, this is delicious, really, Greg." He took a few more bites. "You said you wanted me to come here because something, um...well, you said something important had happened."

I shook my head as I chewed my food. "No, no, that's not exactly what I said. I said I wanted you to come here so we could discuss something important."

He began nodding rapidly, apologetically, and said, "Okay, yeah, that's what you said. I'm sorry, really, I'm—"

"Dammit, Mikey, would you stop apologizing! You didn't do anything wrong, and you don't have to treat me like I'm a member of the royal family, okay? Are we clear on that? I mean, my *God,* you've never figured that *out,* have you? I'm just another writer, just like you, no better, no worse, so stop acting like I'm a Goddamned *movie* star or something!"

Mikey nodded slowly, clearly surprised by my harsh tone.

I sighed and shook my head. "I'm sorry. I didn't mean to snap at you like that, I've just been...well, kind of tense, on edge. But Mikey, you and I have known each other for a while now, and you've got more pull than I ever had. I'm happy about that, happy as hell, but don't act like you're afraid of me anymore, because you don't have any reason to be, and you know it. Okay?"

"Hey, Greg," he said with a big grin, "I've never been *afraid* of you. It's just that I...well, you know, I don't want to offend you, or anything. I don't want to do anything wrong."

I smiled back at him and said, "I'm not a Mafia don, Mikey. Hell, I'm a fan, you know that."

He laughed appreciatively and went back to his meal.

"But I did ask you here for an important reason," I said as I began to eat too.

He gave me a questioning look as he sucked a string of pasta into his mouth.

"I wanted to talk to you about a story," I said. "A story I've been working on for a long time. But I...well, I can't seem to end the damned thing. It's been hounding me. Haunting me. I know it's a good story. A *great* story. The kind of thing that could really revive my career. Bring me back. But this ending...well, it just keeps slipping away from me. It's been eating at me so much, I can't sleep well, I can't work on anything else...but I just can't crack it. So, I want to ask for your thoughts. If, of course, that's all right with you. I mean, if you don't mind."

He gawked at me, frowning, from across the table with a bit of sauce on his lips.

"You mean, uh...you want my opinion on this story of yours?" he asked.

"That's right, Mikey. And don't act like it's a big deal, because it's not."

He seemed to freeze for a moment, then smiled and said, "Sure, Greg. Sure. You want me to read it?"

"No, not yet. I want to tell it to you. Is that okay with you?"
"Sure, sounds like fun."
"Okay, then. Eat your food and listen up."
With a light, casual tone, I began to tell him the story.

《《—》》

Hacking through human bone is not like cutting wood, not at all. For one thing, when you're cutting wood—if you know what you're doing—it's usually dry; for another, wood isn't wrapped in skin and muscle tissue. It's a messy business, wet and tedious and sickening. It's especially sickening when you're cutting up the bones of someone you care about.

I don't think I can emphasize too much just how deeply I cared about Hank, and I still do, even though he's gone. But what I did had nothing to do with my feelings for him. My decision and subsequent actions were entirely separate from our relationship, sort of like competing for a promotion with a coworker who also happens to be your friend.

Even though I'm a writer and words are my business, I can't seem to find the right ones to explain why I did what I did. I've never had this problem before. The most I can say is that I did it for selfish reasons, to breathe life back into my career, which had been wheezing along for years, barely alive. The success I'd once known, thanks to my mentor's tutelage, was gone and I was a has-been. My last three novels had barely broken even, and my current advances withered in comparison to the money I'd gotten during the height of my career.

That was it, simple as that. The height of my career was behind me, and I wanted to bring it back. I wanted it desperately. I wanted to reach another peak, and I wanted the notoriety and fat advances that I knew would come with it. This sounds quite odd, but I knew in my heart that Hank would have wanted that for me, too. That's why I killed him, because I knew that he would want me to have the success that his story could bring me.

Like I said, this sounds quite odd, but somehow I knew right away that Hank would have to be dead. *I* certainly don't want to lead anyone to believe that I heard voices—for months now, I've been trying to convince my doctor of that, but I'm not sure he believes me—but my own internal voice, the one that has spoken to me every day of my life, the same internal voice possessed by everyone, yourself included, that voice, it told me that Hank would have to be gone. My own internal voice, as familiar to me as breathing, told me that there was no other way.

Plagiarism was out of the question. Once again, I don't know how to explain this, other than to say that in order for it to work, Hank had to be dead. If he'd moved to an island in the Caribbean and become a recluse, his life, his very existence, no matter how far away, would have been a constant obstacle, and I knew immediately that he had to disappear, and that the only way to make that happen would be to kill him myself and hide his body someplace where it would never, ever be found.

I didn't own a gun—I've never possessed one—so I used a length of rope. I brought him over to my house one evening in my car, ostensibly for dinner. Early in the evening, while he was looking at a gift that I'd received from a friend—a first edition signed copy of *Naked Lunch*—I wrapped the rope around his neck from behind and strangled him.

It certainly wasn't like it is in the movies. He did not make a simple gagging sound and fall limp after a few seconds. He fought like the devil. He kicked and tried to scream and threw his fists backward over his shoulders to hit me. He knocked over a bookshelf, a table and lamp, poked me in the eye, scratched my face twice with his fingernails, and kicked my shin hard with his heel.

When he finally died, he emptied his bowels into his pants with a wet farting sound and smelled up the entire room. Dinner was still cooking, so I hurried to the kitchen and turned off the stove. But when I returned, I had the hacksaw and was prepared to do what I had to do.

I dragged him to the bathroom and stripped off his clothes, then hefted his corpse into the tub. I cut him up in there, running the faucet to wash the blood down the drain. I wrapped each piece in foil and plastic.

I did not stop until I could fit his entire body into a suitcase.

Late that night, after I'd cleaned up the mess and had dinner, I drove with the suitcase to a dense patch of woods about thirty miles away from the city or any residential neighborhoods. I hiked deep into those woods, dragging the suitcase and a shovel with me, and buried his remains at least five feet underground between two monstrous redwoods. I covered the grave well and made sure there was no sign of freshly dug earth. Then I went home.

I'm not a violent person. I've never raised a hand to anyone, and I've never been in a fight, not once in my life. But killing and dismembering my friend was pretty simple, I'm afraid. Not once, not for one moment during the entire process, did I ever doubt that I was doing the right thing. And not once after that, either. In fact, even now I have no regrets. Something deep inside myself says that I probably should, but I don't.

I can honestly say that I would do it again for the same reason I did it the first time. I so passionately wanted, once again, the success I'd known before. It didn't work out that way, of course, but I would still do it all again.

«« — »»

"Would you like more spaghetti?" I asked. Mikey's plate was empty and he was slumped in his chair staring off into space.

For the last ten or fifteen minutes, I'd been pacing as I told the story, acting out the roles, changing my voice from character to character. He'd eaten slowly the whole time, watching me, listening intently. Now his plate was empty and he looked exhausted, his face rather empty.

"More spaghetti, Mikey?" I asked again.

He blinked a few times and lifted his face to look at me. "Oh, yeah. Please. That was delicious. Yeah, I'd like some more."

"Okay," I said, taking his plate. I was on my way out of the dining room and into the kitchen when he stopped me with a question.

"Why did you tell me that, Greg?"

I stopped and turned to him. "What do you mean?"

"That story. Why did you tell me that story?"

I saw something in his face at that moment that made the skin at the back of my neck shrivel up. His eyes were different, no longer as open and eager as usual. Now they were dark, shaded, as if some sort of protective membrane had closed over them.

"Well, I just wanted to hear your take on it," I replied. "Like I said, the ending has been driving me nuts, and I just wanted an outside opinion."

"But why me? I mean, you've been at this so much longer than I have and you—"

"There you go again," I said testily, taking my seat at the table again. "Mikey, listen to me. Every writer, I don't care if it's F. Scott Fitzgerald or Judith Krantz, *every* writer, now and then, goes to another writer to talk over a story, to get an opinion, whatever. Hell, even Hank came to me for advice sometimes, God rest his soul."

I regretted saying it even before the words had come all the way out of my mouth. I didn't want the conversation to go down that road, but it was too late.

"What?" Mikey asked, frowning.

"I said, even Hank used to—"

"No, not that. You said 'God rest his soul.'"

Every muscle in my body tensed and I stood from my chair and began pacing again. "Well, yeah."

"But I thought he hadn't been found."

The words poured from me in a rush. "He hasn't, Mikey, but my God, he's been gone for nearly two years, and I know Hank well enough to know that he wouldn't just disappear like that without contacting someone if he could, especially me, because we were really close. I knew him better than anyone, and I haven't heard from him, so I'm just assuming the poor guy's dead, that's all. That's why I said that, okay?"

After a moment, he asked, "How long have you been working on this story?"

"Oh, I don't know, a year and a half, maybe more."

"So you didn't show it to Hank."

"Well no, of course not, but what's the big *deal,* Mikey? If Hank were here, I would show it to him, just like he used to come to me with stories. Just like Leonard used to ask Hank for advice on his work. That's what we *do* Mikey, *all* of us, so what's *the problem,* why are you so *surprised* by this?"

"You mean Leonard Avery?"

"Yeah. Leonard took Hank under his wing, just like Hank took me under his, and like I've tried to help you out. But age and experience don't mean that much when it comes to writing. Sooner or later, we all go to each other for advice, for an opinion. That's just the way it works. Now I'm coming to you."

He frowned thoughtfully. "They never figured out who killed Leonard Avery, did they?" he asked, his voice quiet and rather distant, as if preoccupied.

I stopped pacing and stared at him, confused. "What the hell has that got to do with anything?"

He shook his head, as if to jar his thoughts back into order, then looked at me and smiled. "I'm flattered that you've asked me to help you, Greg. I guess I'm just a little surprised. I figured you'd go to someone with more experience, but if you think I can help, then I want to. I just thought you'd show it to someone else first, that's all." He stared at me silently for a moment, still smiling, then asked, "You haven't shown it to anyone? At all?"

Once again, I saw something in his eyes that chilled my blood, something much stronger than before, something deadly.

"No," I said, my voice a mere whisper. "I haven't shown it to anyone."

He simply nodded silently, his smile never faltering. Then: "Can I read it, Greg?"

I was filled with a dread that clogged my throat for a moment, but I finally said, "Sure. If you'd like. I'll get it."

The manuscript was on my desk and I hurried to get it, all the while suspecting that I was making a horrible mistake, doing something so wrong that it would alter my life forever, even more so than my experience with Hank.

I returned to the dining room and handed him the pages as I asked, "Would you like some more spaghetti, Mikey?"

"Oh, please. It was delicious."

I took his plate to the kitchen to dish up some more for him.

I had scarcely touched my own meal, and I knew I wouldn't eat any more, not tonight. After seeing what I had seen in Mikey's eyes, I was sick with fear, and I began thinking thoughts that made me suspect the lack of sleep had finally gotten the best of me, that I'd gone around the bend, over the edge. They were the thoughts of a madman, but they were insistent, and they grew rapidly, filling my mind with a scenario that suddenly seemed so obvious, I could not understand why I hadn't thought of it before.

For the first time, I began to vaguely consider myself a victim…just as much a victim as Hank had been.

As Hank had taken me in and shared with me his experience and knowledge, he'd been taken in by Leonard Avery. I'm sure you've heard of him. His work was quite popular during the fifties, and three of his novels had been made into successful movies, one of which was directed by John Huston and starred Humphrey Bogart, and was nominated for a slew of Academy Awards. When I met him, he was old and in ill health, and he would have died soon anyway if he had not been brutally murdered.

Leonard was seventy-eight when he was killed in what the police concluded was an interrupted burglary. He was shot four times, but the fatal wound came from a large knife in the chest. It was amazing to everyone who knew him that he didn't die instantly, because he was suffering from pancreatic cancer at the time. But according to the medical examiner, he struggled and fought with his attacker, and it took that knife in the heart to do him in, even after two bullets in the chest and two more in the gut.

I remember talking to Hank the day after Leonard's murder. He wasn't as emotional as I expected him to be: rather, he was quiet and reflective, and he kept looking at me with a sad smile and saying, "He fought, Greg, can you believe that? He already had a foot in the grave, but he fought like a man half his age, maybe younger. He struggled and kicked and fought like the great man he was."

I didn't think much of it at the time. To me, it was just Hank talking with admiration about the death of his dearest friend, nothing more.

In fact, I thought of Leonard as I was tightening that rope around Hank's neck. I remembered what Hank said about Leonard fighting so hard at the very end, and it occurred to me that Hank was proving himself to be every bit the man Leonard had been, because just like Leonard, Hank had gone out with a hell of a fight. I remember thinking that if Hank were still alive to talk about his own death, he would have spoken of it just as admiringly as he'd talked of Leonard's final moments. He would have been proud of himself.

Leonard had been killed two years before I killed Hank. During those two years, Leonard's death was nearly all Hank could talk about. That, and the story.

During those two years, especially the second—the last year of Hank's life—he was consumed by that story. He mentioned it to me in conversation, just in passing, but never gave any details. All he ever said was that it was something big, a story that might very well bring him back from the dead.

In spite of his many awards and years of critical praise and commercial success, Hank's career had been swamped for a long time. By this time, the editors of magazines that once fought over his short fiction wouldn't even return his calls. Hank could not, as they say, get arrested. But he kept working, picking up what money he could while his savings from the glory days were whittled down to nothing.

By the time he finally shared the story with me and asked for my input, he was a mess. He hadn't been out of his house in months, all his groceries were delivered, and he *never* answered his phone. In fact, there were times when I'd dropped by his place and knocked on the door but got no answer, although I knew he was inside because I could hear him moving around; sometimes I could even hear the television or radio playing. But he finally opened up and admitted to me that he had a great story that could put him back on top...if only he could come up with an ending. It had been killing him, he said, trying to find a way to tie up this absolutely perfect story, the best thing he'd ever done in his life. He'd lost sleep and couldn't eat, he said, and all he needed was a little advice, a pair of objective eyes to look over the pages he had so far, the opinion of someone he really trusted. So he showed me the story. And I killed him for it.

All of that ran through my mind as I was in the kitchen, dishing up Mikey's spaghetti. He was out in the dining room reading the story and waiting for his second helping, and I was standing there over the stove, suddenly not so sure I wanted to go back out there.

I didn't think he suspected anything; it wasn't that at all. No, I was suddenly very worried about how much he would like that story. That damned story.

The thoughts shooting through my mind were insane, the stuff of nightmares and campfire stories. And those ugly thoughts made me quite afraid of the young man sitting at my dining room table...just as Hank might have been afraid of *me* if he'd had the same thoughts.

But I don't think he did. I really don't. I suspect he had no idea what was coming, which would account for his incredible struggle. It was a surprise. In fact, I don't even think he knew who was killing him. I was behind him the whole time. He didn't know who was killing him...but did he know why? In those last moments, did the reason for his death come to him in a flash?

Once I'd filled Mikey's plate, I set it on the counter and crept back through the kitchen and across the hall to look through the doorway and into the dining room. He didn't hear me, because he didn't move. He was hunched over that manuscript with all the intensity of a doctor performing brain surgery. I backed away and returned to the plate on the kitchen counter, picked it up, and walked into the dining room with a smile on my face, hoping it didn't look forced.

"Here it is," I said.

He didn't move, didn't look up, didn't even seem to know I was there.

I stood beside him, holding the plate in one hand, waiting for him to move the manuscript so I could set it down.

"Mikey?" I said. "Here's your spaghetti."

He flinched and lifted his head, looked up at me and stammered, "Oh, oh, yeah, uh, yeah, sure, um, thanks, Greg, thanks." He pulled the manuscript away and I set the plate down.

When his fist flew up holding the fork, aimed straight at my throat, I surprised myself by moving quickly, as quickly as if I'd expected it. I grabbed his wrist and stopped the fork; its tines were about an inch or so from my throat. Then, I made the mistake of looking at Mikey's face.

It was a fright mask, tense and wide-eyed and determined to kill me. I knew there was only one way I would survive this: I would have to kill Mikey.

My left hand was clutching his right wrist. With the thumb of my right hand, I pulled his little finger back, away from the fork, just kept pulling until the finger straightened out, and I kept pulling after that. The wild expression on his face began to pinch, until it was screwed up with pain. I pulled the finger back until it broke with a thick pop.

Mikey screamed like a child, dropping the fork as he fell off the chair. The manuscript fell from his other hand and the pages scattered over the floor.

I pressed a knee to his chest, holding him down, and shouted, "Why did you do that?"

He struggled, crying in pain, but did not answer.

"I said, *why* did you *do* that, Mikey?"

He looked at me, his eyes showing nothing but agony, and whimpered, "Jesus, Greg, help me, please...my finger...it hurts."

"Why did you do it?" I asked quietly.

"The story!" he screamed. "The...story. Dammit, I can...I can handle that story...the end...I can do it."

"And you were gonna kill me for it?"

"No, Greg, jeez...you just misunderstood, that's all, I was just...I guess I moved too fast, and...that's all...I moved too fast and you thought I wanted to hurt you, but...I didn't. Not at all, Greg, not at all."

As he spoke, I guess my grip on his wrist loosened and I probably relaxed my hold on him, leaning back just enough so that my weight was no longer on his chest. My fault entirely. I'm not used to holding violent people on the floor. After all, I'm not a cop. I'm just a writer.

Mikey swept his left hand up and grabbed my crotch in his fist, squeezing my testicles hard as if they were nothing more than bread dough. I cried out and fell backward to escape his grip. Before I knew it, my back had hit the floor hard and Mikey was on me. We'd traded places. But now he had the fork in his left hand.

I watched as Mikey lifted his left hand high, then brought it down with an ugly sound from deep in his chest, and I fought back my own pain to lift my hand and stop him. I grabbed his arm and pushed it back, but he was younger and stronger, and I knew I didn't stand a chance.

I grabbed his right hand and pushed his little finger with my thumb.

Mikey screamed.

I wrapped my fist around the finger and pulled, as if I were trying to remove it from his hand.

He screamed even louder and fell backward in a faint. He wasn't out for long, but long enough for me to get to my feet and grab the fork.

The moment he regained consciousness, he began to fight. But I was ready. I had the fork.

I have no idea how many times I stabbed him. I've been told, after the fact, that he was stabbed forty-three times, but I find that hard to believe. I just wanted to stop him. Sure, I wanted to kill him, because I knew then that I needed to. I knew then exactly what was happening, and if I did not kill him, he would kill me, because he had to, just as I had to kill Hank, and just as Hank had to kill Leonard. But forty-three times? No. I can't believe that. I can't imagine I would do *that*.

All I know for sure is that I killed Michael Anderson with that fork. Beyond that, I remember very little. I have a vague memory of leaving my house, covered with his blood, and screaming for help. My neighbors came out of their houses one at a time, stepping cautiously onto their porches, their porch lights coming on one after another as I cried for help, begged for help. And someone called the police.

But that wasn't what I wanted. I wasn't screaming for help from the police, I was screaming for a kind of help that I knew I could never get. I wanted help because I knew I was a victim of something that no one would ever understand. In fact, I remember what I was screaming.

"Help! Please help us! It's killing us! It's killing us all! My God, it's killing us all!"

That's what I screamed to my neighbors. They had no idea that I was talking about a story. Just a simple, exquisite, absolutely perfect, but unfinished story.

«« — »»

As I sit here in my room with its mattressed walls and locked door, I can't remember everything that happened that night. But I remember why it happened. The story. That was the only reason. All of my crazy, insane thoughts were not so crazy and insane after all. I know now why all those lives were lost. Leonard Avery, Henry Carr, and eventually Michael Anderson's. They all died because of that story. The perfect story with no ending.

I wonder how many others died before Leonard, and I wonder how far back it all goes. After all, the story, set in a village in no particular country, no particular time period, is absolutely timeless.

But it's absolutely perfect as well, and I must admit that I've still been trying to crack that unreachable ending, even here, in my room, in this place.

I have no idea what's happened to my copy of it, but it will most likely fall into the hands of another writer. In any case, I can do nothing from this room. And I know that the more I talk about it, the longer I will be in this room, in this hospital. I have to behave the way they want me to so they won't keep thinking that I'm crazy.

But that doesn't change anything. It's still out there. Waiting to be read.

«« — »»

My doctor just visited me. Dr. Culley is tall and rather round, soft-spoken and apparently kind. At least, he's been very kind to me, and I still consider him kind in spite of what I know is happening.

This was our third conversation, and he still seemed very concerned about my well-being. He asked how I was being treated, what I thought of the food, things like that. Then he started asking the questions that made me see my future.

"I've gone through your personal effects," Dr. Culley said, "and I found a story. It's very interesting."

As I watched him and listened to him, I realized that he was trying very hard to make me think that the story enabled him to understand me a little better, but posed some sort of mysterious question that he hoped I would answer. All of that was so obvious that it was difficult not to smirk. But I did not.

"I am very intrigued by this story," he went on. "It is untitled and unfinished. Do you know which story I'm talking about?"

I couldn't hold back my smile. "Yes. I know."

"Did you have an ending in mind? I'm very curious, because I think this story might provide some important information about your problems. So, did you? Have an ending in mind?"

Sitting on the edge of my bed, I looked up at him with a big grin and said, "No, I didn't. Do *you*...have...an ending? In mind?"

He flinched and took a step backward away from me, then smiled and chuckled and said, "No, no, of course not." He chuckled again. "Look, Greg, just wait right here. I'll be back in a minute."

I shrugged and said, "I'm not going anywhere."

«« — »»

Dr. Culley has just returned. He's smiling and saying something, but his words make no difference. I see the syringe in his hand.

So that's how he's going to end it.

**Dedicated to the memory of
Francis Feighan
My best friend, and the one
I always turned to for a second opinion.
I miss you.
-RG-**

Website

ONE

It was a beautiful spring day, but I didn't notice the weather any more than I noticed the blood drying on my hands and making my fingers stick to the steering wheel of my car. Under normal circumstances, I would've been sickened by the stench of the curdling blood that was splattered all over me. But circumstances weren't normal...otherwise the blood wouldn't have been there.

I was looking for my wife Heather. I'd heard from a reliable source that she was in a dirty little motel on the edge of town with someone. All I'd seen was a picture of Heather's car parked outside the motel room; I didn't know which motel it was or who she was with because my source, although reliable, had a cruel streak. That's why I'd just killed my source—and, I'd *thought*, my only friend left in the world—with a baseball bat.

My blood-gloved hands made moist smacking sounds on the steering wheel as I drove slowly through the outskirts of town, up one street and down another, looking for that familiar orange door with Heather's blue Geo Storm parked outside. She was still there, my source had told me that much. Not enough to help me...just enough to make me crazy.

Oh, well. I'd been crazy before. I guess old habits really do die hard.

«« — »»

TWO

I drove onto the information superhighway on my thirty-eighth birthday. Heather and the kids presented me with a Hewlett-Packard Pavilion computer, with 200 MHz, 32 MB RAM, and a 2.1 MB hard drive, with six months prepaid with a local Internet Service Provider, all of it set up in the sewing room, so called because that's where Heather kept her seldom-used Singer. That night, my best friend and business partner came over with his wife to show me how to use my new toy.

I knew only what I needed to know about computers. We used one down at the store to catalog inventory and handle our finances, but beyond that, they were a mystery to me. But Kurt was a computer nut. He showed me how to get on the Internet, how to make bookmarks and get and send e-mail and showed me a few of his favorite sites on the World Wide Web. Naturally, he ended up at a pornographic website.

"You're gonna be amazed, Martin," he said. "Did you know you can have a live naked woman on your computer screen and she'll do anything you want? You just tell her and she *does* it."

"I'm happily married, remember?" I said, smirking.

He chuckled coldly. "Yeah, happily married. So am I. That's the *point*! It's completely safe and anonymous."

Kurt and I had grown up together and gone through twelve years of religious schooling. In high school, we nailed a life-sized inflatable sex doll to the cross in front of the administration building. Friendships that are bound with that kind of exhilarating perverse glue tend to last.

Heather came in with Kurt's wife Joy, who wanted to have a look at the computer. I started playing a CD-ROM game while Joy watched over my shoulder. She made sounds of disgust in her throat and said, "Oh, it's so violent and bloody! What's it called again?"

"Doom," I said.

Joy muttered, "Well, I should think so."

As much as I loved Kurt, I could never warm up to Joy. She was nice, very pleasant…but that was the problem. She was always grinning, always happy, no matter what. It made me nervous. She didn't work, she *volunteered*. She didn't go to (or even *do*) lunch, she attended *luncheons*. She was a fine addition to any party she attended, and she attended all of them. I just never bought her act. But I never shared my feelings with Kurt. Best friends or not, some things are better left unsaid.

As I played *Doom* and Joy hovered over me like some kind of impatient vulture, I felt something warm and wet slap onto the back of my left hand. It was a dark red splash between two knuckles. Another landed on the keyboard, between the G and H keys, then another between B and N. I looked up and saw Joy's hand over her mouth and nose. Blood dribbled between her fingers and Kurt stepped forward and put an arm around her shoulders.

"She's been having these nosebleeds," he said. "The doctor says it's stress."

Heather rushed out and came back with a box of Kleenex as Joy looked down at my keyboard and said, "I'm so sorry!"

"It's no problem at all," Heather said. "I'll clean it up."

She did, too. I've never been the least bit mechanical, but Heather could always take things apart, fix them, and put them back together again with ease. After Kurt and Joy left, she opened my keyboard, cleaned up the mess with some Q-Tips and a little rubbing alcohol, then put it back together again. After the kids went to bed, she pulled up a chair and sat with me as I surfed the 'Net. When she announced she was going to bed, I embraced her and gave her a long kiss.

"Thank you, sweetheart," I whispered in her ear.

"I'm glad you like it," she said.

I knew exactly why Heather had given me the computer. She wanted me to have a window to the world while I was stuck at home recovering from my madness. But we didn't bring it up. We didn't need to. I didn't feel sleepy, so I stayed up with my gift and explored cyberspace.

Yes, there was a lot of pornography on the Internet, but there was a lot of *other* stuff, too. Games and news and movie clips and homepages...a *lot* of personal homepages. I was amazed to learn how many people out there were so desperate for attention. Millions of them were taking advantage of this revolutionary information powerhouse called the Internet by displaying pictures of their pets, kids, and stamp collections in personal websites, as if the whole world gave a damn. I decided Andy Warhol had been more correct than he ever imagined.

I was surprised when I received e-mail. I figured it was from Kurt. He was the only one who knew my e-mail address. I waited for it to come up.

Dear Martin,
Please visit this brand new website! Here's a link:
http://www.website.com
You won't be disappointed!

The address to the website was written in bright blue letters. Kurt had told me that was called "hyperlink," a direct link to the website. I clicked on it, and my e-mail window was replaced by a white screen. I expected to see obscene pictures...a woman and a horse, or something involving urination, the kind of thing Kurt would do.

A gray, marbled background appeared with five large, black words at the top:

THE OFFICIAL MARTIN BOYLE WEBSITE

A moment later, the rest of the page appeared, but there wasn't much:

=THIS PAGE IS UNDER CONSTRUCTION=
Please come back tomorrow, Martin.
There will be fascinating things to see and hear.
For now...go to bed and get some sleep.
You need it.

My mouth dropped open and the skin on the back of my neck shriveled. There was nothing more on the website. I read the lines several times, then bookmarked the site just as Kurt had taught me, and went to bed. I slept eventually, but not well. I kept thinking about that website, wondering if I'd just imagined it. After all, I was crazy, right?

The next morning, I kissed Heather goodbye, made breakfast for the kids and got them off to school, then went to the sewing room and sat down at my computer. I logged up, or booted on, or whatever the hell the computer geeks call it, and checked my e-mail. Nothing. I went to my bookmarks, intending to return to the website I'd visited the night before, but I had no bookmarks. None. Something wasn't right. I logged off the 'Net, then got back on and tried again. There were *still* no bookmarks. But I had e-mail.

Dear Martin,
Looking for me? Here's a link to your website:
http://www.martinswebsite.com
See you there.

Annoyed, I clicked on the link and waited for the page to come up.

HELLO, MARTIN!
This is your life!
On this page, you will find everything there is to know about *you*!
The smiley face link below will take you to the index. Enjoy!

Below that, a stick figure wearing a hardhat stood beside a black-and-yellow-striped hazard sign, and beneath him was a caption: **This site is under constant construction.** Farther down, animated balloons bounced and confetti flew around a yellow smiley face. I clicked on the link.

The website began to show me things that had no business being on the Internet, and my life has never been the same since.

THREE

I don't know how many times my psychiatrist told me not to use words like "crazy" or "insane," "loopy" or "wonky" to describe my condition. But I use them anyway, because they describe what I became. Of course, the crazy person is always the last to figure out that sort of thing. Looking back on it, I can see a lot of warning signs, but they were so small and insignificant that none of them caught my attention, or Heather's. It's a pretty sneaky thing, wonkiness.

Everyone around me figured it started with the death of my parents. Unlike most people I know, I had a great childhood and enjoyed my parents' company, so losing them both at once was quite a blow. Mom and Dad had dinner with us the night they died. Their car wouldn't start, so I drove them home. They wanted to stop by a convenience store on the way, which was fine with me because I'd promised Heather I'd pick up some Cherry Garcia. As I was searching the ice cream case in the back of the store, gunshots rang out and a woman screamed. There was a horrible clamber and the bell over the entrance went wild. By the time I got up there, my father's brains had been splashed over the floor and the front of the counter. My mother was still alive, but two holes in her chest made wet sucking sounds. She didn't live long. By the time the police arrived, I was the only living person in the store.

Everyone suggested therapy after that. I was a mess, of course, but I didn't think I needed a shrink. Heather and I talked about it at length, and she eventually agreed I was fine. But the truth was, I hadn't been fine *before* my parents were murdered. Kurt insisted I take some time away from work, and I figured he was probably right.

A couple years earlier, when I was working as the manager of a toney sports shop called The Coliseum and Kurt was trying to hold together a failing yard maintenance business, we went to work on an idea we'd been kicking around for awhile. We figured there were a lot of people with yards who didn't want to buy the expensive equipment to tend them, but who would be willing to rent that equipment if the prices were reasonable. We got a loan, put up some of our own money, and opened By the Yard.

At the time of my parents' death, we'd only been open for about nine months, and things weren't going as well as we'd hoped. Kurt had given up a business that was on its deathbed anyway, but I had abandoned a managerial position with good benefits, and months earlier, Heather had lost her job as office manager at a doctor's office. By the Yard meant a lot to me, to both of us. If it didn't work, we'd both be neck-deep in failure. Staying home didn't work for me. I was restless and troubled and needed something to take my mind off seeing Dad's brains splashed all over the place, off hearing the final gurgles of Mom's lungs. After a couple weeks, I went back to work and things were fine.

But I was washing my hands a lot. I brought a toothbrush and dental floss to work and used them often because I was sure my gums were rotting and curling back from my teeth. I became convinced the front counter was filthy because it was constantly being touched by people whose hands had been God knew where, so I kept a can of Lysol handy and used it a lot. At closing time, I checked everything three times. Kurt said he thought I was being a little obsessive, and I said I was protecting our investment.

If a light was left on in an unoccupied room at home, I became angry and shouted at Heather and the kids. I know how it sounds, but it was incredibly important to me at the time. I used the electric bill excuse a lot, but actually I was *terrified* that a neglected light would burn the house down. My mind often flickered with hideous images of myself and my family burning to a blistering crisp because a light had been left on and a glitch had occurred in the wiring.

I started keeping a diary, too. I didn't know why at the time, and I'm still not sure what got me started, but I wrote frantically in a spiral-bound notebook. My psychiatrist, Dr. Fiona Webb, told me that even as I recovered I might still hold on to some of the odd things I did during my breakdown, and she said that was okay. I guess writing things down is one of them, because I'm writing this.

Slivers of Bone

One night, I couldn't sleep and got up for a cup of hot chocolate. I turned on the clock radio on the kitchen counter and listened to a talk show host interview a man who said the world would end in two months, when an asteroid would hit the earth. He backed it up with news stories, statistics, and quotes from the Bible; the book of Revelation called the "great star" Wormwood, and prophesied that it would wipe out a third of all life on the planet. I listened for the rest of the night and became *convinced* the world was going to end.

The next morning, Heather and the kids found me at the kitchen table. Frantically, I told them the world was going to end and we had to prepare for it. Heather took me to our bedroom and told me I was scaring the children, behaving like a crazy person. I tried to explain that the world really *was* going to end, but she just told me to stay put for a minute and left the bedroom. She came back after the kids were off to school, then looked at me with an expression that melted my heart with its love and concern, but humiliated me with its certainty that I was crazy. She told me very firmly to get help or she would seriously consider leaving me. So I got help.

I saw Dr. Webb once a week, lying to her from the beginning. I tried to make her think I was fine, just stressed. I did not discuss the end of the world, although I knew it was coming, or how dirty my hands felt all the time, or that my teeth were loosening in my rotting gums. By my third appointment, I was sure she'd tell me there was no reason to continue our sessions. But she'd been reading me like an open book with large print.

"You're very scared, Martin," she said calmly. "But what's frightening you?"

My mouth opened, and a moment later I said, "Everything."

She nodded. "I'm sorry to hear that, but I'm glad you're being honest."

"Everything," I whispered tremulously. "My...my teeth are going to fall out and my family is going to die and...and the world is going to end."

She nodded again. "You're right, all those things are going to happen. But let's try to organize them in a way that makes them easier to handle. Okay?"

That's what we did. But first she suggested some time in a "specialty" hospital. That's the current politically correct term for a loony bin. There, I was given anti-psychotic drugs and Dr. Webb came to see me every evening. Somehow, it all seemed to twist the Silly Putty of my psyche into a better and healthier shape. When I left the hospital, Heather and the kids were very affectionate and made it clear they were glad to have me back home, and I was indescribably grateful. My first night home, I tried my best to let them know how happy I was to be with them again. But over dinner, I let them know I wasn't quite right yet.

"You know, this isn't over," I said quietly. "I've got a ways to go. I'll be seeing Dr. Webb four times a week, and I have to stay on the medication. And I'll be—"

"It's okay, Dad," Jeremy interrupted. "We want you to get better."

"Yeah," Deborah agreed, nodding. "Whatever you have to do is fine with us."

Heather grinned as she took my hand. "I got a job. A *great* job. You don't have to worry about money," she said. "The store's doing well, I've got this job…all you have to do is get better."

So Heather went to work as office manager at an answering service, and I stayed home and played Mr. Mom. I'm not complaining. The store and my prior job had kept me so busy I'd had little time to spend with my kids. Jeremy was fourteen and Deborah (never Debbie) was twelve. I'm surprised even now by how much I enjoyed getting to know them better, by how happy—and how awed—I was to learn they were such good and practical people. They are brighter and kinder and funnier and more fun than I ever imagined, and I'm ashamed I had to go crazy to figure that out.

At the time of my thirty-eighth birthday, I'd spent nearly eleven months at home, trying to get better. I thought I was doing a pretty good job of it…until I found that website.

«««—»»»

FOUR

A month or two later—I'm not sure exactly how long—I began to wonder if Heather or the kids were beginning to suspect anything. At first, I only went to the website when I was home alone, but that didn't keep me from thinking of it when I wasn't. I was afraid no amount of effort from me would keep them from knowing something was on my mind. Sometimes my thoughts became so loud, I was afraid Heather and the kids would actually *hear* them.

I got an e-mail from Kurt my third day on the 'Net, and I knew immediately he wasn't pulling a prank. The anonymous e-mails looked nothing like Kurt's; they had none of the information at the top, only a subject line and a **TO:** line with my address. Besides...we'd known each other all our lives, but even Kurt didn't know as much about my life as the person behind that website. It was hard to imagine such a person existed. Only Heather could know most of those things, and even she couldn't know *all* of them.

So where had this website—*my* website—come from? The countless personal websites glutting the Internet don't appear spontaneously; they're *put* there by people who *want* them there, no matter how few of the rest of us care. So who was behind *mine*? It had high-quality pictures and videos and elaborate animation, sound and music. It was an incredible job, done by a professional. But who could know such personal, intimate things about me?

Then again, maybe it wasn't there at all. No matter how many times I marked the site, the bookmark was gone the next time I got online. I could never find the website in any search engine (although I was stunned to learn how many Martin Boyles there are in the world, perhaps living other versions of my life), and the only time I could access it was when I received a link in an e-mail, which never had a return address or identifying name. I saved the e-mails, but they were always gone the next time I checked. I didn't go to the website...the website came to me. Only when it wanted to. Only when it had something new to show me.

The website knew everything about me. Things general and

things specific, things so deeply personal even *I* barely knew them. Things about my childhood and parents, about Heather and Jeremy and Deborah...things about the regularity of my bowel movements, for God's sake.

The first time, the website's homepage had a bright yellow background rippled with blue and sprinkled with dark green speckles. Animated elf-like figures pointed down at the index of links beneath them. Two strips of photographs of me at various ages, from newborn to present, flanked the index. The links flashed a cheerful blue. But the website never looked the same twice, and the things it showed me, the way it made me feel, often changed drastically. As if the website was moody. At first, it showed me wonderful memories, like it was proving that it knew me better than anyone. But other times, it showed me painful moments from my life, as if it enjoyed the ache it created in my chest.

It didn't spend much time on the past, though. It caught up to the present quickly and showed me video of Heather at work at the very instant I was sitting there at my computer. I saw the clock and the calendar in her office! It showed me the kids at school, Kurt working at the store, Joy working in some soup kitchen and trying hard not to touch the unwashed homeless folks. Nothing in particular was going on in the video clips; everyone was just going about their business. Pretty boring. I soon realized what the website was doing. It wanted me to know how much it saw and knew, that it could show me anything, everything, things I never would have known otherwise, things I might be better off not knowing. And eventually, that's exactly what it did.

FIVE

"There's something you're not telling me, Martin," Dr. Webb said.

"What do you mean?" My pulse quickened. I didn't want to tell her. I knew I would eventually, but I wanted to find out for myself if it was my craziness or some nightmarish prank being pulled by a sick heckler, or hacker, or whatever the hell they call those nerds. Then, I could discuss it with Dr. Webb and see if she had any insights.

"I mean something's upsetting you, something you haven't brought up yet. You're tense and preoccupied, not unlike you were when we first met. It concerns me. Would you like to talk about it?"

"Oh, it's n-nothing, really. I mean, later, maybe, we can talk about it. I-I think it's just a case of cabin fever, you know, from being in the house so much. That's all. I-I'm just anxious to, you know, get back to work."

"Have you thought about doing some volunteer work?" she asked. "It can be very therapeutic sometimes. And fun, too. You might want to consider it."

Like Joy? I thought. The idea of spending time with whole groups of Joys made me shudder.

"Maybe you should spend less time on that computer Heather gave you," she said with a smile, standing.

Does she know? I thought. How *could she know? No way! Unless...*

I imagined Dr. Webb hunkered over a keyboard in a dark room, face bathed in the glow of the Internet, fingers clattering over the keys as she listened to tapes of our session. I dismissed it almost immediately. That idea was so crazy it wouldn't work in a bad movie. Our session was over, but Dr. Webb saw the thought cross my face and stopped smiling.

"You're sure everything's fine? You're taking your pills and—"

"I'm fine, just fine," I said, standing. But outside in the parking lot, I realized I was perspiring on a chilly, cloudy day.

SIX

"I'm going to bed," Heather said, standing in the sewing room doorway.

"Okay," I said, glancing at her. "G'night." When she didn't leave, I looked up and smiled. "I'll be in soon."

She came into the room and I quickly changed windows on my computer so she wouldn't see the website. She put an arm around my shoulders and leaned down until her face was close to mine. "Why do you close the door?" she asked. "You never used to when you came in here. When you first got the computer, you used to let Jeremy and Deborah come in and play games with you. Now, you don't want anyone in here. Why?"

I turned to her and stared. My lips made a few moves, but nothing came out of my mouth.

"How long since you mowed the lawn?" she whispered, her eyes sparkling with worry and sadness. "And the vegetable garden in the back is filled with weeds. You've been spending all your time in here, Martin. How many times in the last week have we had take-out food for dinner? The kids don't even see you anymore. When I bought you this computer...well, that's not what I had in mind. I thought it would be a nice diversion. But it's become a...an obsession." She took a deep breath and asked, "Is anything wrong, Martin?"

I diverted my eyes, shifted in my chair, and shook my head.

"Well, I'm sorry, but seeing you closed up in this room all the time scares me a little. A *lot*, actually."

I found some kind of sick strength in myself that allowed me to turn to her and smile, take her hand and squeeze it. "I'm fine, honey. Guess I've just become a bit of a 'Net-head, that's all. You're right, I've been ignoring things. This Internet—" I forced a chuckle out of my chest. "—it's pretty addictive! But you're right. I've been neglectful. And I'll stop, I promise."

She stood up straight and looked down at me, unsmiling.

"Nothing's wrong," I said. "Really."

Finally, she smiled and put a hand to my cheek. "Good," she said. "I'm glad."

SEVEN

One bright afternoon in late spring, I clicked on four blue-flashing words: **Boys Will Be Boys**. It showed me video of Jeremy and two boys walking through the park. Jagged rap music pounded from a small boombox carried by the bigger of the two boys, and the other carried a satchel on a strap over his shoulder. A sexless, inflectionless, but not unpleasant voice narrated the video.

"Those boys are Josh and Sig," the website said. "They talked Jeremy into skipping school after lunch. Josh is Jeremy's age, but Sig is two years older, a drop-out, and often in trouble with the law. The boys are in Criminal's Corner...where your parents always told you not to go. Remember, Martin?"

That corner of the park was frequented by drug addicts and prostitutes and wasn't safe for anyone, not even in the afternoon. I tensed as I watched Jeremy and heard an echo of my mother's voice reminding me to "stay away from Criminal's Corner."

The boys settled on a huge boulder, opened the satchel and removed a bottle of whiskey, a Ziploc Baggie and a glass pipe. I watched my son take pulls on the whiskey bottle and hits off the pipe, and my heart throbbed in my throat and fingertips. I was frightened for Jeremy, and furious with him.

I waited for him in his bedroom that day. He seemed later than usual, but I hadn't been paying much attention to when the kids got home from school lately. When Jeremy entered the bedroom, he jerked to a halt and stared at me, reeking of Binaca, eyes red and a little puffy. He looked afraid, as if he'd found a total stranger doing something obscene in his room. I was too worked up to worry about that, though. I tried to keep my voice down but was shouting before long as I lectured him on the dangers of drugs. I told him to steer clear of Criminal's Corner, and if he didn't have enough sense to stay away from kids like Josh and Sig—especially Sig, who'd already been in trouble with the law—I'd turn them all in myself. Jeremy didn't move the whole time, didn't even blink. He stared at me with an expression of abject horror, mouth and eyes wide. His expression hurt me at first; I was concerned for him, trying to help him, but he was *afraid*.

Unable to say anything more, I hurried out of the room and went down the hall to the bathroom. I was startled by my reflection in the mirror. It was a face I hadn't seen in months. My crazy face, wide-eyed and perspiring, taut with fear and anger and confusion. Suddenly, the past months of recovery had never happened and I was a lunatic again. No wonder Jeremy had looked so afraid. His wonky dad was back.

What if he hadn't gone to the park with Josh and Sig and done drugs and drunk booze. What if he didn't know them, or they didn't even exist? Maybe someone was playing an elaborate high-tech hoax on me. Or maybe I really was crazy again. All that mattered to me then, though, was the fact that I'd frightened my son. And he would tell Heather. What then? Back to the specialty hospital, maybe?

How could it be my mental illness? I'd been taking my pills regularly, although reluctantly because the website had shown me what they were doing to my liver. It had shown me video of a fit, active, healthy, possible me…if I weren't on the pills. I stared at my fright-mask reflection and tried to remember taking my pill that morning…or the night before…or yesterday morning…and I couldn't. I hadn't taken it in quite awhile.

I went to my nightstand and opened the drawer where I kept my pills. They weren't there. I sat on the edge of the bed, thinking back. The website had shown me all those medical journal articles about the side effects of the pills, and I'd tossed them. All of them. How long ago? I couldn't remember. But it had been awhile.

"What did you say to Jeremy?" Heather asked, coming into the bedroom and stalking toward me. "What did you do to him? He's terrified!"

I gawked at her, wondering what I could possibly say.

"And I got a call at work today," she said, not waiting for a response. "From Fiona. She said you haven't been in for six weeks because you've got the flu!" She laughed coldly, without smiling. "Six weeks, Martin?"

My chin moved up and down and I finally asked in a weak voice, "Has it been that long?"

"Martin, what is happening? I thought you were getting better."

I smiled and said, "I am better."

"You're not! You're getting worse again." Her eyes began to

glisten. "We've tried so hard to help you get better, Martin. *I've* tried so hard. Everything I do, everything I think...it's all connected to helping you get better. But now you're getting worse again, and it's like...it's almost like living alone. We haven't made love in, what? Five or six months? Longer? I want to help you, Martin, I've *tried*, but...I don't know what I've done wrong."

Guilt flowed through my veins like adrenaline. I hugged her tightly and whispered in her ear, "You haven't done anything wrong. It's just me, that's all. Me."

She pulled away enough to look into my eyes. "You're taking your medication, aren't you?"

"Of course," I lied. That was when I decided I had to kill the thing that forced me to lie to my wife. *Kill* it.

I spent that evening with my family in the backyard, where we barbecued hamburgers. I took Jeremy aside and whispered my apology to him, hoping he wasn't still afraid of me. He hugged me, told me he wanted me to be well, then got a bat and ball and I tossed him a few. It was a wonderful evening, one of the most enjoyable I'd ever spent with my wife and children.

I managed to avoid going into the sewing room for the rest of the evening. I lay awake in bed that night, wondering what the website had to show me, wondering what I'd missed, fighting the urge to get up and go see. I wondered where all that information was coming from and who was sending it to me. Had someone wired the house? Were we all being watched through hidden cameras, listened to through tiny hidden microphones? I didn't sleep much that night, but was awake and a little jumpy the next morning, still preoccupied with the website and its secrets, trying not to let on as I fixed breakfast.

Before leaving for work, Heather reminded me to call Dr. Webb and make an appointment. I assured her I would and kissed her goodbye. Once the kids were out of the house, I headed for the sewing room. I stopped outside the door in the hallway and thought about the decision I'd made the night before. To kill it. I went into Jeremy's room first, then approached my computer armed with his baseball bat.

I stared at the HP Pavilion for a long time, thinking about the fear I'd seen in Jeremy's face, the pain I'd seen in Heather's eyes, what I was putting them through by...

By doing what? What had I done? Okay, so I hadn't been taking my medication for awhile, and I'd skipped a few visits with Dr. Webb. And I'd gotten a little wrapped up in my birthday present. So what? I hadn't hurt anyone, had I? At the most, I'd slowed down my recovery a little, that's all.

But I had terrified Jeremy yesterday by shouting at him about some nonsense I'd seen on my computer screen. And I'd upset Heather, who had been so patient with me throughout my craziness.

I hefted the bat and set my jaw as I glared at the sleeping computer. Lifted it over my head and clenched my teeth.

What would Heather say? She'd complained because I'd been spending too much time with the computer, but it had been a birthday gift from her and the kids, an expensive one. What would she say when she came home to find it bludgeoned to death?

I lowered the bat slowly and stood there for a long time, thinking things over. Finally, I decided I just wouldn't turn it on. I'd neglected the yard, so I'd spend the day working out there. I hadn't gotten much exercise lately; it would do me good. I started to leave the room, but decided to check my mail.

Come to the website right away, Martin.
There are things going on behind your back
you need to know about. Follow the link:
http://www.martinsmarriage.com

I had put down the bat, but the website had decided to play hardball.

EIGHT

As usual, a list of new links awaited me at the website. But this time, there was no colorful background, no animated decorations.

Just blackness behind links that glowed a shiny gold. I started at the top and worked my way down.

It showed me video of Heather's desk at work. She was not there. The clock read 11:27.

It replayed a few moments from my birthday: Kurt and me at my computer, Kurt saying, "Did you know you can have a live naked woman on your computer screen and she'll do anything you want? You just tell her and she *does* it."

"I'm happily married, remember?" I said, smirking.

He chuckled coldly. "Yeah, happily married. So am I. That's the *point*!" It rewound. "Yeah, happily married. So am I. That's the *point*!" Again and again, and each replay included that snide chuckle. I hit my browser's BACK button.

The next link replayed part of my conversation with Heather the day before. "Everything I do, everything I think...it's all connected to helping you get better. But now you're getting worse again, and it's like...it's almost like living alone. We haven't made love in what? Five or six months? Longer? I want to help you, Martin, I've *tried*, but...I don't know what I've done wrong." It rewound. "...it's almost like living alone. We haven't made love in, what? Five or six months? Longer?" Over and over, until I went back to the links on the main page.

The next link showed me Heather's unoccupied desk at work again. By then, the clock read 12:14. And the next showed me her Geo parked in front of a dingy motel room with an ugly orange door. I could hear traffic nearby, a mechanical rattle, like maybe an old soft drink machine.

My hands felt dirty, sticky, so I went to the bathroom and washed them. While I was there, I brushed my teeth. I went through all the links again, then logged off the Internet, got the cordless phone and called Heather's work number. An unfamiliar female voice answered. "Is Heather there?" I asked.

"She's at lunch. Can I take a message?"

"Lunch," I said flatly.

"Yes, and I think she had an appointment."

"When do you expect her back?"

"I'm not really sure. Is this her husband?"

I hung up. Paced awhile. Washed my hands. Paced some more. I didn't need to go back to the website to hear her saying, over and over, *We haven't made love in, what? Five or six months? Longer?* Kurt kept interrupting her in my head with that cold, sarcastic chuckle, and: *Yeah, happily married. So am I. That's the point!*

I hadn't seen much of Kurt since my birthday. We usually spent a lot of time together, but he'd been very scarce. I picked up the phone and dialed By the Yard.

One of our delivery boys answered and I said, "Hi, Matt, is Kurt there?"

"No, he's out."

"Out? To lunch?" I asked with a catch in my voice. Kurt never went to lunch. He always had somebody bring him something from one of the nearby fast food joints.

"Uh, I'm not sure. Want me to have him call you, Martin?"

"No. That's okay." I hung up. Paced some more. Washed my hands. Gave my teeth a quick brush. Then got back on the Internet. Another e-mail, with another link to the website. This time the background was blood red and the links were black, all different.

It showed me soundless video of a huge lumpy shape hurtling through black space. It looked authentic, like NASA footage, because the real thing never looked quite as real as the special effects in the movies. The next link led to video of a pudgy middle-aged man speaking at a lectern. He didn't look familiar, but I'd heard the voice before. On the radio. The man was talking about Wormwood, the great star that would fall from the sky and wipe out a third of all life on earth, as prophesied in Revelation. The man said he'd miscalculated last year, when I'd heard him on the radio. He now claimed Wormwood was to strike the earth in August. I went back to the footage of that huge thing shooting through space.

My mind frantically shot from Heather and Kurt to the end of the world and back again. My best friend was screwing my wife and there were only months left on earth. I didn't know what to do, couldn't think, washed my hands, brushed my teeth, and kept going back to the website, clicking the new links, waiting for it to tell me what to do.

When I heard the kids get home from school, I locked the sewing room door. When Heather got home and knocked, I didn't respond. Not even when she began shouting. She threatened to call nine-one-one. Without taking my eyes from the screen, I said in a trembling voice, "Don't worry, I'm fine. Just leave me alone."

She went outside and talked to me through the window. I lowered the blinds. "All right," she said outside, sounding hurt. "Just as long as you're…okay. Let me know when you want to talk, Martin. But if you don't come out of there soon, I'm calling Fiona."

I didn't come out, so she kept her promise and made the call. I didn't find out until later that Dr. Webb was out of town. It wouldn't have mattered, though. I was already too far gone.

NINE

I lost track of time. Especially after Heather took the kids to her mother's for awhile. I was too busy to look at a clock, hardly ate, but I washed my hands and brushed my teeth. A lot. And all the while, the website kept feeding me information. It made me realize the medication Dr. Webb had given me was only to sedate me, numb me to the truth, keep me calm while my wife fucked my best friend; I never saw them together, but they were always gone from work at the same time, and I saw Heather's car parked in front of that motel room, and a couple times in front of Kurt's house. It dulled my perceptions while my son sneaked around the park doing drugs and jacking off with a couple of juvenile delinquents, and my daughter let boys feel her up in a neighbor's garage. It showed me everything. Made me realize everyone around me was just trying to keep me sleeping so they could go on with their dirty little secrets. Fiona Webb wasn't a psychiatrist, she was part of the Mind Patrol that medicated people when they started to see the truth. Otherwise there would be panic in the streets because people like me would warn everyone about the dirty things going on behind their backs, tell them that Wormwood was coming and there was no escape.

That was why Heather had left with the kids. She and Jeremy and Deborah knew I was becoming more and more aware of their filthy deceptions and they were afraid of me, afraid of exposure.

I no longer wondered who—or what—was behind the website. It was on my side, so what did it matter? It was the only thing on my side. Just the website and me against the world.

Sometimes it took me awhile to understand what it was trying to tell me. Like when it started showing me pictures of all the chainsaws we had in stock down at the store. It took awhile, but I finally got the picture, figured out what it was saying. That was the day Dr. Webb came by.

"Martin," she called from outside the sewing room window. "I want you to let me in so we can talk." When I didn't respond, she said, "I know you're in there. Your family is very worried about you. I'm sorry I was out of town when you needed me. I had family business to tend to. But I'm here now and I want to talk. So please let me in." I didn't move from the desk. "If you don't, Martin, I'm afraid I'll have to have you committed. It'll just take one phone call. My cell phone's in my bag."

That scared me. I couldn't afford to be locked up. Then they'd *force* medication on me with their needles. I went to the window and peeked through the blinds. She seemed to be alone, but it was hard to tell. She could have a bunch of white-coated thugs out there waiting for me to open a door. Just to be safe, I didn't leave the sewing room alone; I took a friend.

"You're alone?" I asked with the front door open a crack.

"Of course," she said.

I let her in. Behind my right leg, I clutched Jeremy's baseball bat, which had been leaning against the wall of the sewing room. She came inside and I closed and locked the door.

"Let's sit down and talk, Martin."

When I turned and faced her, I knew we weren't going to talk. After everything the website had revealed to me, what was the point? It would just waste time, and with Wormwood on the way, there was precious little left. She was starting to turn away when I lifted the bat and brought it down on the very top of her skull. She hit the ceramic tiles hard and her legs began to kick. I put her out of her misery with three more swings, stepped over the spreading pool of blood and went back to the sewing room, still holding the messy bat. I paced. Washed my hands. Brushed my teeth for a long time. There was blood on my toothbrush. Just as I'd suspected, my gums were rotting fast.

I wasted no time changing out of the sweatpants and T-shirt I'd been wearing for days. I got in the car and drove to By the Yard. The store had been closed for about forty-five minutes, and everyone had gone home but Kurt. I knew he'd be in back, checking and cleaning the equipment returned that day, so I parked behind the building and went in the back door. He was bent over, funneling gas into the tank of a rototiller. When he stood and turned, he gasped and nearly dropped the can.

"Jeez, Martin, you scared the hell outta me."

I didn't speak as he looked me over, his eyes widening.

"Hey, Martin, are...are you okay? I mean...well, you look awful." He put the gas can down and stepped toward me. "Heather told me she's been really worried about you, that you'd locked yourself up in the—"

"You can actually say her name to me?" My voice was a rasp.

"What?"

I looked around until I spotted what I wanted, then went toward it slowly.

"I called you several times," he went on, walking with me, paying no attention to where I was going. "I left messages on the machine. I even came by twice, but nobody was home. We've been friends too long to—"

"Friends?"

He looked hurt. Such a good performance. "Yes, Martin, friends. Hell, we've known each other all our lives."

I looked him in the eye and said, "A friend wouldn't fuck my wife."

He craned his head forward as he squinted, then his eyes slowly widened. "Whuh...what?"

I lifted the eighteen-inch Stihl chainsaw and pulled the cord once, roaring it to life, all in one quick movement. Before Kurt could react, I swung around. The chain chewed into his left side, just below his ribcage, all the way to the middle of his abdomen. He did a little dance, sang an ugly little song, and fell to the concrete floor before I was finished with him.

When I left, I took the saw with me and put it in the passenger seat. I went back home, stepped over Dr. Webb, slipped a little in her blood, and settled down at the computer. My bloody fingers turned the keys and mouse red. I opened the e-mail I knew would be there, clicked on the link and watched as the website appeared. There was only one link:

Meanwhile...
On The Wrong Side Of The Tracks

I clicked my mouse and saw the same video I'd seen so many times before: Heather's Geo parked in front of that ugly, dirty, orange door.

"B-buh-but..." My voice was a dry croak. My head shook back and forth, slowly at first, but faster, faster, all by itself, without any help from me. "What is this, a *rerun*?"

The website didn't respond. I'd talked to it before, but it only spoke in its own way, its own time.

"She...she *can't* be there now. He's *dead!*" I clicked my browser's BACK button...but nothing happened. Just that same static shot with sounds of traffic in the background. I clicked and clicked, stood up so fast I knocked my chair over, still clicking.

I froze when I realized I'd been tricked. The website was not on my side, never had been. I didn't know why or how, but it had been a trap all along.

I leaned down and swept up the bat from the floor. It was dark and lumpy with Dr. Webb's blood and hair and brain matter. I began pounding the computer, fast and hard, going back and forth between the CPU and the monitor, pounding and pounding, shattering, breaking. Blood spattered the air. I couldn't tell if it was coming off the bat or from the spilled guts of the wounded computer, and I didn't care. The scuffed old desk collapsed beneath my blows. I didn't even pause to breathe, just kept pounding until I lost my balance and fell back against the wall and slid to the floor. There was an ugly sound in the room; I soon realized it was a low, wet, panting growl in my chest.

I stood slowly. It was dead. Dismembered and mutilated.

I hurried out of the sewing room, slipped and fell in Dr. Webb's blood, crawled, stood, rushed out to the car, sped away from the house, and drove around...

...until I found that clown-hair-orange door at the Starlite Motor Inn a block away from the bus station. I parked behind Heather's Geo, grabbed the chainsaw and got out. I tried the knob; it was locked. Pounding on the door, I shouted, "Heather? Heather!"

I heard clumsy movement inside and Heather's panicked hiss: "Ohmygod, Martin!" More movement, but no response.

I was in no mood to wait. I fired up the saw and started chewing through the door. Peeling orange paint flew through the air like shreds of torn flesh. The flimsy old door came apart easily and I kicked my way in as Heather screamed. There was another scream, too, another woman's scream. I stood just inside the door, chainsaw roaring, and stared at Heather and Joy, both half-dressed, their backs against the wall, arms wrapped around each other, wide eyes staring at me in horror.

Joy. She'd been sleeping with Joy, not Kurt. So I'd killed poor Kurt for nothing. My oldest friend. But I didn't dwell on that. I decided I'd kill them both. Of course, if I killed Heather, I'd have to kill Jeremy and Deborah, too. I didn't want them to go through life knowing their father had chainsawed their Mom. They were a part of this whole elaborate scheme, anyway, so they had it coming.

I started moving toward them when somebody grabbed my arms from behind. I was struck on the head once with something hard, and the room tilted severely...then again, and I lost consciousness.

TEN

The rest is pretty boring. You could probably write it yourself, even if you *haven't* read about it in the papers or seen me on one of those damn tabloid TV shows.

I was arrested, of course. Locked up and tried. I had no one on my side but a public defender at first. Then, when my face started showing up at grocery store checkout stands and Letterman and Leno started making cracks about me in their monologues, some grandstanding showman of a defense attorney—one of those guys who makes more money off one client than I'd make in my whole life—came forward and took on my case. He knew I couldn't afford him; he was after the publicity, and that was fine with me. I didn't care about anything by then. I had a pretty good idea what was coming and resigned myself to it.

Heather was not exactly supportive; I guess she'd run out of compassion and patience, and love. She attended the trial every day with Joy at her side, both of them puffy-eyed and holding hands. Their eyes never met mine.

My attorney decided to keep me quiet through the trial, but I was surprised to learn Jeremy would be taking the stand. While my attorney was questioning him, I sat numb and shackled in my seat, barely hearing my son's voice above the constant drone that had been in my head ever since…well, I couldn't remember when it had started. But something Jeremy said snapped me out of my medicated state. I'd missed the questions—something about "odd behavior"—but I caught Jeremy's response.

"One day, I got home from school and Dad was waiting for me in my bedroom," he said. "He…he was upset with me."

"Why was he upset, Jeremy?" my attorney asked.

"He said I'd cut school that day and gone to Criminal's Corner—that's a pretty dangerous part of the park—with a couple guys named Josh and Sig. And that we'd been, um…drinking and doing drugs." He bowed his head a moment and took a deep breath before continuing. "I'd just *met* Josh and Sig," he said, shaking his head slowly. "I didn't know anything about them. I didn't find out till later that Sig had been in trouble with the police. But Dad knew, he told me that day in my bedroom, he knew where we'd gone, what we'd done...and I don't know how. There was no way he could know."

My attorney seemed uncomfortable with the direction Jeremy was taking, so he asked another question, but I'd already tuned them out again. I'd heard everything I needed to know, and a great crushing weight lifted off my shoulders, off my brain. Jeremy *had* gone to Criminal's Corner with Josh and Sig that day...and probably all the *other* days the website had shown me. What I'd been shown on my computer screen had been real.

I knew it wouldn't change things, but it gave me something to cling to no matter what happened: I hadn't been wonky. I hadn't been loopy. Insane. Crazy. It had been *real*.

I was found guilty but insane and sentenced to spend the rest of my life in a state facility for lunatic criminals.

It's not that bad here, really...even if I'm *not* a lunatic. I get three so-so meals a day, and the medication keeps me pretty happy most of the time. I go to group therapy four times a week and see my new psychiatrist almost every day. There's a TV room, lots of board games and books to read, plenty of crafts to kill time and occupy the mind. They even have computers available to most patients, with limited access to the Internet.

But I don't use those. I decided to take up painting instead.

The Homeless Couple

For Oscar: we'll miss you.

Roland Pearce walked to and from work every day, all year long, in rain, snow, or heat of summer. Ever since he'd lost his wife, the walk had been as much a part of his daily ritual as waking up in the morning and going to bed at night. Roland's job at the accounting firm of Schallert and Timmons allowed him no physical exercise, and he spent most of his time there—he nearly always arrived early and left late—so the brisk walk helped keep him healthy and trim. It was fourteen long city blocks from Roland's apartment to the building where he worked. That meant he had to leave earlier than he would if he took the bus or subway in order to get to work on time, but he didn't mind. By the time he'd spent the night alone in his apartment, he was ready to get out of there. He usually didn't sleep much, anyway, and was wide awake by five every morning, leaving him more than enough time to have some coffee and watch the morning news.

On this particular morning, it was raining hard. The charcoal sky seemed to hang just above the tops of the city's towering buildings. Roland held a large, deep, black umbrella in his right hand, and a matching briefcase in his left. The rain made such a loud roar as it fell on the umbrella that the sounds of the city seemed far away.

As he did every morning, Roland stopped at Mellenger's diner on the way for a breakfast of half a grapefruit and toast or a bagel with cream cheese and another cup of coffee. There was always a newspaper on the counter and he usually gave the headlines and the business section a cursory glance and exchanged empty pleasantries with the proprietor, an enormously fat man with a walrus mustache. Roland had been eating breakfast there for years, but he did not know the man's name, and it had never occurred to him to ask. The diner was just another part of his route, and he paid no more attention to it every day than he did the rest of his surroundings. The entire walk to and from work had become so routine, he hardly needed to look where he was going.

Occasionally, something extraordinary would occur during Roland's walk, and he would stop and take notice. The previous summer, he'd been on his way home when a woman had screamed across the street. He'd turned toward the scream, like everyone else around him, to see a woman clutching her purse as a small, filthy-looking man pulled on it repeatedly, trying to snatch it away from her. The man slammed a fist into her chest and she fell backward. He ran away with the purse, and the woman continued to scream for help as she struggled back to her feet. Roland had walked on then, along with the other pedestrians who had stopped on the sidewalk. He wasn't about to chase after a drug addict for a purse, and he'd thought that if she was smart, that woman wouldn't either. There was nothing she could keep in there that would be worth his life, hers, or anyone else's.

The year before that, a battered old pickup truck had jumped the curb half a block ahead of Roland and driven through the window of an American Cancer Society thrift store. The wreckage quickly drew a crowd, but as Roland approached, he stepped off the sidewalk and walked around it.

Such things seldom happened, of course, and that was fine with Roland. Since his life had changed so drastically seven years ago, he had come to appreciate routine, to crave it. He had no interest in change or surprises. So when he walked to and from work, he remained within himself, noticing as little as possible on his route, thus giving each walk a bland sameness.

Roland enjoyed letting his mind roam as he walked, letting it spiral up toward the sky like a helium balloon trailing a string that had been released by a child. He tried not to let anything get hold of that string and pull the balloon back down to earth.

There was one distraction that wouldn't go away: the Homeless

Couple. He didn't know their names, so he thought of them only as the Homeless Couple. He'd first seen them midway on his route about eight months ago, beneath an aluminum awning that stretched about twenty feet from the entrance of a tiny convenience store to a phone booth. They wore what had once been clothes but were now little more than layers of filthy rags, and they never seemed to move from their spot, where the man asked passersby for change and always said, "God bless you," no matter what kind of response he received. He had done that the first time Roland had seen the two of them.

That first time, Roland had seen the woman first. She'd stood in the telephone booth against the wall of the building. Normally, Roland wouldn't have turned his head to look at her, but peripherally, there seemed to be something wrong with the way she was standing—slumped and leaning against the inside wall of the booth—as though she'd been injured. It was an old-fashioned phone booth, the kind with a circular fluorescent light overhead that came on once you'd stepped inside and closed the accordion door. Roland hadn't seen one like it in years—the booths had been replaced by banks of open payphones that took up much less space—and he'd *never* noticed that particular phone booth before. It had been there for a long time, though. It was marred by graffiti and a couple of the Plexiglas windows were broken out. A strip of plastic over the doorway used to read TELEPHONE, but someone had used a marking pen to cross out TELEP and crudely change the N into an M, so it looked like this:

HOME

The other reason he'd turned to look at her was that the door of the phone booth was open and, in spite of the sounds of traffic, Roland had heard the woman crying as she talked into the telephone receiver, sobbing between garbled words. He hadn't stopped, or even slowed his pace, just glanced to his left at the woman in the phone booth…and the man appeared in front of him, making it necessary for him to stop.

"Excuse me, sir," the man had said, running a hand over his hair, which was long and slicked back in an almost stylish way, except that instead of styling gel, it glistened with grease from not bathing. His voice was hoarse and his eyes were bleary and bloodshot, red around the edges and had pockets of puffy flesh beneath them. "Could you please spare some change? See, my wife and I—" He jerked his head toward the woman in the phone booth. "—we haven't eaten in a couple days, and we could sure use a little—"

"No, I'm sorry," Roland said as he stepped around the man and continued walking.

"You don't have to apologize," the man called after him. "God bless you."

As Roland walked away, the woman's deep, racking sobs had faded behind him.

He'd seen them every day since. A few months after they'd first appeared, the man approached him and started to ask for change again, then he'd recognized Roland and backed away with a weary smile.

Nearly every time he saw them, one or the other was in the phone booth, talking on the phone, and whether it was the man or the woman, they were always upset about something. Sometimes even the man was crying. Now and then, Roland would catch a few words as he passed.

"No, baby, it's gonna be all right. I promise, I promise…"

"…listen to me, sweetie, don't cry…"

"I'm so glad we can talk…so glad…"

"I miss you so much."

It occurred to Roland that, for two people who couldn't afford to eat—and it was obvious from their appearance that they were seriously malnourished—they certainly had a lot of change to spend on emotional phone calls in that booth.

Roland didn't understand the "homeless problem." He was forty-two years old and his grandparents had raised his parents through the depression. Back then, work had been almost nonexistent. The entire country, with the exception of the very rich, had been made poor overnight, and suddenly, everything from food to clothes were too expensive. They had to get by on wits and potato soup.

Apparently, it had been a different time that had produced a different breed. There was certainly no depression now. The economy was in great shape, Wall Street was singing...and yet there were homeless people begging on the streets. The only conclusion Roland could come to was that they had simply given up on the responsibilities that most people lived with every day. They had decided to go out and ask others for their money. Oh, sure, *they* didn't see it that way. *They* honestly believed they were at the end of their ropes. But that was only because they had decided not to reach out and grab all the other ropes dangling around them. A low-paying job was better than no job. Sometimes McDonald's was all that was available, whether for food or work. But they didn't want that. In being above such menial work, they had put themselves below everyone else...begging on the streets.

Roland refused to believe that he was not compassionate. He realized there were many people in the country who had the rug pulled out from under them and needed some help getting back on their feet. But in such a thriving economy, it was hard to believe so many people were "homeless" because of financial misfortune, and unable to recover from the situation. Most of them were simply people who had given up their lives in favor of drugs or alcohol, or both. They all reeked of booze as they staggered the sidewalks, asking for change. That was why Roland refused to give them handouts. They would only use it to buy more of whatever substance had them at the end of their ropes anyway, and he did not want to contribute.

Although Roland realized, as he turned the corner and headed into the business district, that the man who had stepped in front of him eight months ago had smelled of nothing but body odor.

But the most annoying thing of all about the Homeless Couple was that they never left their spot next to the phone booth, against the wall of the insurance building. The city was filled with shelters and programs to help the homeless get back into the mainstream...but they never took advantage of them. Just a few yards from where they stayed was a small convenience store. Every once in awhile, Roland saw them eating, but it was always food from that store: Twinkies, Hostess Fruit Pies, packaged sandwiches. He wondered if they had other people get the food for them when they could afford it, because they never seemed to get more than a few feet from the phone booth.

Something odd had happened twice in the eight months that they'd taken up residence there. Roland had been passing them when the telephone in the booth had rung. They'd been sitting on the sidewalk, their backs against the wall of the building, but the second they heard that ring, they'd shot to their feet and scrambled to the booth, nearly tripping over one another. He'd only been passing, so he'd heard none of the conversation...but he was sure it had been the same emotional wailing he'd heard and seen before. It didn't make sense. Who would be calling the likes of them? On a payphone?

Roland rounded a corner and passed through a storm of rap music coming from a group of teenage boys huddled beneath an awning outside a newsstand. On his right, a car horn honked repeatedly and someone shouted an obscenity into the rain. But Roland was remembering a vacation he and his wife had taken once, before they'd had the baby, to California's wine country. It had been a beautiful week, over much too soon. They'd sipped more wine that week than in both of their lives combined, before or since. It had been a honeymoon more than a vacation, actually, because when they *should* have taken their honeymoon, Roland had been roped into working because of a plague-like flu that had swept through Schallert and Timmons and had left a dangerous number of positions empty.

He was starting to feel a nibbling of guilt deep in his chest and immediately pulled his head out of the Napa Valley. He had to be careful with memories; even now, he sometimes found it very easy to upset himself.

He'd been lectured by well-meaning friends and his sister—*especially* his sister—about his failure to grieve. Not so much lately, but relentlessly in the year following her death. They'd been worried because he'd remained so calm, even stoic, before, during, and after the funeral. It was unhealthy to hold back, they'd told him; it was natural, even necessary, to mourn, and if he didn't allow himself to do it, it would come out later, perhaps in some other way, some way that *wasn't* so natural. He'd listened to them all and thanked them for their concern, and he'd tried to tell them he was mourning, in his own way. When they didn't believe him, Roland had understood. None of them had ever really known him, not even his sister. The only person who would've understood *his* way of mourning—which, like everything about him, was very private and quiet and solitary—was his wife. Of course, by then, she'd passed the point of being understanding.

Roland took a deep breath, filling his lungs with the cold, damp air, then exhaled slowly, cheeks puffed, lips curled up in a small pucker. He would be at work soon. He needed a clear head, a place where numbers could dance.

"Mister! Hey, *Mister!*"

Roland barely heard the call, as if it were coming from the farthest end of the block.

"Mister! *Please!*"

The skin at the base of Roland's skull tingled and his brow wrinkled slightly.

"*Briefcase man!*" The voice was loud, but brittle and cracked.

Roland's step faltered and his shoes made scritching sounds on the wet sidewalk. He looked around quickly, his head moving in bird-like jerks, eyes squinting through rain-misted glasses. Roland spotted the homeless man behind him and to his left.

Although the aluminum awning kept the rain from falling directly on him, the man was still soaked. His cheeks and temples had fallen away, making his face and head look too long and impossibly narrow. What there was of his dark beard stood out sharply against his pale skin; some of that skin glared through the wiry beard in spots were no whiskers had grown. He was sitting against the wall, legs stretched out, with what looked like a large bundle of rags in his lap.

"Help me," the man said, holding out a dirty hand. "Please, you gotta help me."

Looking around, Roland saw everyone else on the sidewalk moving around him from both directions, as if he were a tree growing in the middle of a stream. He looked at the man again.

"I-I-I...I told you once before," Roland began, shrugging, but the man didn't let him finish.

"No, not *that,* not...not *me.*" He shook his head slowly, wearily. "My wife. Please, you gotta help my *wife.*"

Roland frowned, took a couple short steps toward the man and leaned his head forward slightly, staring at the bundle of rags. After a few seconds, the image changed, clarified. It was the homeless woman, lying in a fetal position across her husband's lap, covered with something that might have served as a blanket at one time. With that realization, Roland's frown deepened.

"What, uh...what's wrong?" Roland asked as he took a few more slow steps, moving closer to the Homeless Couple.

"My wife," the man said. "She's sick. Duh-dying, I think." On the last three words, his voice broke, became throatier, as if he were about to sob. "I don't know what to do...what we *can* do. We...weeee...we have nothing." There was pain in his voice, not whininess, but a great, raw pain. He was either near tears or had been crying before Roland got there and was about to start again.

The surprisingly small bundle on his lap suddenly quaked with a series of deep, ripping coughs. She rolled away from her husband and her face became visible as she continued coughing. Bright red blood sprayed from her mouth with each cough and rained down on her skull-like face, spattering her ghostly-pale skin. There were already dried streaks of blood on her face where she'd tried to wipe it off with her fingers. When the coughing stopped, her hand appeared from beneath the rags and wiped the fresh blood, smearing it with the old.

Roland gasped at the sight. "My God," he said. "She's got to see a doctor."

"Well," the man said with a cold, hollow and unsmiling chuckle, "in case you haven't guessed it already, we don't have a doctor."

She coughed some more, sprayed more blood. Some of it speckled her husband's pale, sunken cheek.

"Well, she needs medical attention," Roland said. "Right away. If she stays out here in the rain like this, she'll—"

"Please help us," the man said, his quivering voice nearly a whisper.

"But I-I-I'm not a doctor. I don't even know why you...why *did* you call me over here, anyway?"

"I see you walk by every day. You're...familiar. I thought you'd...do something, I guess."

Roland looked at the woman's blood-stained face again and muttered, "Well, I-yuh, I could, uh..." He walked quickly to the phone booth, fishing some change out of his pocket. He closed his umbrella and stepped inside, hanging the umbrella on his forearm by its hooked handle. As he closed the accordion door, he heard the man calling to him again.

"Wait, wait, no, don't—"

Roland ignored him, lifted the receiver, dropped two quarters into the slot and put the receiver to his ear. His forefinger froze an inch from the 9 button when he heard a strange sound in his ear. He'd expected a dial-tone, but instead heard an open connection, echoing and whispery, crackling with static. Over the line came the nonsensical sing-song burbling of a small child, a toddler.

"Hello?" he snapped. The child continued. "Could you please hang up the phone? I have an emergen—oh, why bother." He pressed the lever down with two fingers, waited a couple seconds, then let it up again. The child was still there, distant and hollow-sounding. And then, from out of the nonsense words and baby sounds:

"Daa-*deeee!*"

Roland's jaw became slack and his eyes widened suddenly beneath his frowning brow. Gooseflesh crawled beneath his clothes as an image flashed in his mind, vivid as if he were walking in on it for the first time all over again. His wife Deborah on the kitchen floor, rocking their dead baby in her arms as she hummed a lullaby.

The receiver rattled when Roland slammed it back into its cradle.

He fumbled with the door until it opened, then tripped out of the booth and opened his umbrella. He looked up and down the sidewalk, then across the street, for another phone.

"That telephone doesn't work," the homeless man said as Roland walked toward him. "Please, could you just—"

"If the phone doesn't work," Roland interrupted, shaken and suddenly angry for no reason he could readily identify, "why is it that every time I walk by here, one of you is *talking* on it?"

Before the man could reply, his wife heaved with more coughs. It sounded as if chunks of her lung were tearing away and were about to shoot from her mouth with the spray of blood.

"The county hospital is just a few blocks from here," Roland said. "They can't turn you away. I could call a cab and—"

"I won't take her there. She wouldn't want me to. They killed our little girl."

Roland slowly hunkered down beside the man and leaned forward slightly, his throat suddenly dry and scratchy. A wave of nausea passed through him and he swallowed hard a couple times. "They killed your...you...you lost a daughter?"

"She was just eighteen months old when she got sick. Just a year and a half old. She wasn't important enough, though. People like us...we're not important enough. They let her die. They killed her." He bowed his head and looked down at his wife's bloodied face, his upper body rocking slightly.

"Well, I-I...I don't have a car," Roland said. "I don't know what I can—"

"I don't know what I expected you to do," he muttered without looking up. "Sorry for bothering you."

Roland stood there for a long moment, just watching the Homeless Couple. The man never looked up again. The woman kept coughing. He walked on finally, still frowning, his pace a little slower than before, as unsettling thoughts flitted through his mind. But it wasn't the Homeless Couple he was thinking about. It was the voice on the phone, the child who had said, "Daddy?" And no matter how hard he tried, he could not shake the crystal clear image of his wife, in shock on the kitchen floor, rocking their dead baby in her arms. Nor could he shake the sickening certainty that the voice on the phone had been his daughter's.

"Years ago," he muttered to himself under his breath. "That was years ago."

He was distracted all day. He made errors in his work, forgot about a meeting, and even forgot what he was doing at one point. It wasn't like him. Others noticed, and a couple people asked if he was feeling all right. He took advantage of the opening and said he thought he was coming down with the flu. Someone suggested he go home early and get plenty of liquids and rest. He paused to think about it, and it confused him a little. Go home early? Why? What would he do? If he really were coming down with the flu...well, that would be different. But to just go home early?

He told his coworkers he would make it to the end of the day, then went about his work, trying hard to focus, to ignore his dark, disturbing thoughts. That proved to be difficult, though. They would not go away.

Roland and Deborah had Melanie at the beginning of their fourth year of marriage. When they first married, they'd agreed they weren't ready—emotionally, and especially financially—to have a child and had decided to wait. As Roland got to know his new wife better, he was glad of that.

She was...fragile. During the year and a half they had known one another before marrying, he'd learned early on that she was very sensitive, that she was easily hurt, that she'd been abused as a child and again as an adult in two relationships before they'd met. But later, he realized that she was just fragile, a person with vulnerable feelings and a delicate personality. She wasn't just sensitive about certain things; she had a difficult time handling crises, drastic or unexpected changes in routine, or even the anticipation of those things.

That didn't bother Roland. If anything, it made him more protective of her. She had a job for awhile, working in an antiques store. But when she couldn't take that anymore, she just stayed home. He brought her something every evening: flowers, candy, a balloon, a sentimental card. They kept to themselves after she quit work, stayed home in the evening watching videos, or regular television, reading aloud to one another, or making love.

Slivers of Bone

He came home one night to find Deborah crying. It wasn't the first time; he'd come home to find her crying quite a lot. But this time, it was about something. She was pregnant. "And we're not ready," she said. "We're just not ready yet." But Roland thought they were. He had already made advancements at work and was making more money than when they'd married, and there were more advancements to come. He told her they could afford it, and of course they were ready, because they loved one another so much and were so happy, and that was all anyone needed to have a baby, right?

Once baby Melanie was home, Roland saw a change in Deborah, a change he'd expected. She was happier than he'd ever seen her, ecstatic. Her entire life embraced the child, and Roland never came home to find her crying again.

Until fourteen months after Melanie's birth, when he found Deborah on the kitchen floor, back against the cupboard doors beneath the sink, legs splayed before her, holding Melanie in her arms. Deborah's eyes were wide, but in an empty way, and she seemed to stare at something a great distance away. She stroked Melanie's hair and half-sang, half-moaned some off-key lullaby as she rocked the baby in her arms.

Roland spoke to Deborah repeatedly, but she did not reply, or even acknowledge his presence. He took his daughter's right hand between his thumb and fingers; the ends of her tiny fingers were black and she felt unnaturally cold. Heart beating faster, he knelt beside them and pressed two fingers to Melanie's neck to find a pulse. There was none. He gasped and fell away from them onto his back, crawled backward a few feet, then grabbed one of the chairs by the kitchen table and climbed up, until he was standing again. "My God, my God," he muttered, staring at his dead daughter and absent wife.

An ambulance came, and with it, two police cars. A metal hairclip was found on the floor in the dining room beneath an electrical outlet. Apparently, Melanie had found one of her mother's hairclips and had stuck it into the outlet. And apparently, it was more than her mother could take.

Melanie was taken to the morgue, and Deborah was taken to the psychiatric ward of the Sisters of Mercy Hospital. Roland handled all the burial arrangements. Deborah's doctor told Roland that the funeral would only worsen Deborah's condition, so she did not attend. Roland visited her twice a day—once before work and once after—until she came home two months later.

Those two months were the longest and loneliest of Roland's life. Their small apartment seemed cavernous when he was there alone, and yet the walls always seemed about to close on him and smash him flat. He tried to keep himself occupied by eating dinners at a reasonably priced cafeteria and seeing a double feature a couple nights a week, no matter what was showing, at the Phoenix. His sister visited a few times, and he was always glad to see her because he thought it would kill time, fill some emptiness. But he always found himself wishing she would go a few minutes after she arrived; her tears and condolences were needles driven into his skin, and when she said they could always have another baby, he wanted to scream, to break something. He didn't, of course. He held it all in.

When he was in the apartment, he kept the television or radio on to bury the silence, to cover up the absence of Melanie's crying or sweet babbling. He did everything he could to keep away the knowledge that he would never hear those sounds again, never change her diaper or make her laugh by playing tug-of-war with his tie. When he did let such thoughts in, they made him feel helpless, impossibly small, tiny as an insect, and they fell on him with breathless finality, blocking out all light, crushing him.

When Deborah finally came home, Roland was so happy to have her back that he didn't notice how drained she was. Drained of personality, of interest in anything, of life. She was to see her doctor twice a week and attend group therapy twice a week. Roland made *arrangements* at work so he could drive Deborah to her appointments. He'd expected her to be different, to need time to heal, and he was prepared to do whatever necessary to bring her back to the person she'd been before.

After a few months had passed and there had been no improvement, Roland became concerned. If anything, it seemed Deborah had gotten worse. She seldom spoke, and shook her head whenever Roland suggested they go out to eat or see a movie. He often found her crying, and sometimes awoke in the middle of the night to find her sitting up beside him, sniffling and muttering to herself. He finally decided to be very frank with her, sat down beside her and told her she was not to blame for Melanie's death, it was an accident, the kind of thing that could, and does, happen to millions of people, but it happened to *them* this time. Her only response was to shake her head and sob.

Shortly after three o'clock on an early, moonless spring morning, Roland was awakened by a sound. He assumed it was Deborah, crying again. But as he rolled over, he found she wasn't there. The room was cold and Roland was surprised to see the window open. When he heard someone shouting urgently down below, he gasped and threw the covers off, bounded to the window and leaned out. From fourteen stories up, it was impossible to identify the body on the sidewalk below with any certainty, but he knew it was Deborah.

More burial arrangements, another funeral. He'd gone home once again to an empty apartment, but with the knowledge that it would remain that way, empty except for him. He'd decided to move almost immediately.

At Deborah's funeral, her doctor had approached Roland. He'd said Roland appeared a little too calm, too composed, and suggested Roland make an appointment with him. When Roland did not, the doctor called him at home twice to make the suggestion again, with a little more urgency. "Grief is a natural and necessary process," he said. "Not grieving in the aftermath of a great loss is unhealthy and can lead to serious problems. It's entirely possible for one to experience a complete breakdown as a result of not properly grieving the loss of a loved one. I strongly suggest that you make an appointment with me, Mr. Pearce."

But he had not seen the doctor. Instead, Roland had moved to a new apartment. That was when he'd started walking to and from work, leaving the apartment early and coming back late.

By the time he left work that evening, everyone else was gone and the sun—hidden behind charcoal clouds all day—had set. It was still raining, but harder now than it had been that morning. And

Roland was still unable to clear his head of the upsetting thoughts that had been with him all day.

He considered taking a different route to avoid passing the phone booth, where he knew the Homeless Couple would be. He wondered how the woman was, and the thought made him wince, made him angry at himself. It was a useless, stupid thought, she was going to die without medical attention. The next thought came without warning:

And with his daughter and wife dead, he'll be all alone. Just like me.

Roland sucked in a sharp breath, as if he'd experienced a sudden pain.

Midway through his walk, he saw several red and blue lights spinning atop vehicles directly ahead, and he slowed his pace. An ambulance was parked at the curb along with two police cars, one beside it and one about a car-length behind it. As he got closer, Roland heard someone shouting desperately up ahead. There seemed to be a struggle going on, and Roland was about to cross the street and go around it when he recognized the voice.

"No, please don't, *please* don't take her. *PLEASE! DON'T TAKE HER!*"

Roland moved slowly closer to the group of people moving erratically on the sidewalk.

"*Goddammit,* you son of a *bitch,* get your hands *off* her!"

Feet shuffled and scuffed on the pavement. There were grunts and muffled curses.

Traffic sped by, tires making *shush…shush* sounds on the wet road, as if to say the whole thing were a secret, to be kept under wraps.

Roland stopped in front of the convenience store and watched as two police officers fought with the Homeless Couple, tried to remove the woman from her husband's arms. Two paramedics stood nearby next to a waiting stretcher, talking to one another quietly. The police officers finally separated the Homeless Couple, knocking the man to the sidewalk, and the paramedics stepped forward.

As the paramedics lifted the woman onto the stretcher,

Roland's mouth dropped open for a moment, then he snapped it shut. She was stiff. Her arms and legs did not move, her bent body did not straighten.

The telephone rang in the open booth. It wasn't the chirp of a cordless phone or cell phone. It was a genuine, old-fashioned ring, the sound of a rattled bell, and it cut through the night like a scream.

The paramedics loaded the corpse into the ambulance and the two police officers approached the homeless man again, one of them removing his handcuffs from his belt. The homeless man scrambled to his feet and shot around them, got into the phone booth and slammed the door behind him. The overhead light was dim and flickered erratically as the man grabbed the receiver and said, "Hello?" He said it so loudly—shouted it, really, in a raw, torn voice—Roland could hear it even through the pouring rain outside the closed phone booth. The man began to speak rapidly into the phone, clutching the receiver with both hands as he tossed nervous glances at the two police officers approaching the phone booth.

The doors on the back of the ambulance slammed and the paramedics headed for the front of the van.

The man in the phone booth pressed himself against the accordion door, still talking frantically, preventing the police officers from getting in.

Roland hurried over to the paramedic who was about to get into the passenger side of the ambulance.

"Excuse me," he said, "but...are they going to arrest that man?"

The paramedic turned and faced him. He was about twenty-five, already balding. A toothpick worked back and forth beneath his blond mustache.

"Sure," the paramedic said with a smirk. "He hit one of the cops. Punched him right in the face."

"Who called you?"

He shrugged. "Someone called and said there was a woman bleeding on the sidewalk here. She had blood on her, but she hadn't been bleeding in awhile. He wouldn't let go of her, so we had to call the cops." He climbed into the van.

Roland put his hand on the door before the paramedic could close it and asked, "What will happen now? To his wife, I mean?"

"His wife? You know this guy?"

"No, I just...I see them here when I walk back and forth to work, that's all."

"Well, if you know him, the cops might wanna talk to you. In case he doesn't have any ID, or something, y'know?"

There was an explosion of sound and Roland turned to see the two police officers reaching into the opened phone booth, trying to pull the man out. He was still clutching the receiver, in one hand now, its metal cord taut as he tried to hold it to his ear.

"I'm coming, honey!" he shouted. "Don't worry! I'm coming! I'll be right there, just—"

The receiver slipped from his hand and he and the two police officers tumbled backward out of the phone booth. All three of them fell onto the wet sidewalk.

The paramedic chuckled, shook his head, then said to Roland, "See ya." He slammed the door shut as the ambulance's engine came to life.

The two police officers got to their feet quickly and lifted the man up between them by his arms. The officer with the handcuffs began to speak to the man in a low voice with a sort of sing-song rhythm.

Even though he couldn't hear the words, Roland knew what the police officer was saying from a lifetime of television programs. He was telling the homeless man his rights.

The ambulance pulled away from the curb slowly, careful not to hit the patrol car parked beside it, and drove away, disappearing in the evening traffic.

Roland sighed as he stepped toward the curb, planning to get off the sidewalk long enough to walk around the two police officers and the homeless man. Before he took a full step, he heard two pained grunts and another quick scuffle of feet on wet concrete, then an outburst of voices all speaking at once.

"He's got my gun!"

"You just back off!"

"Drop the gun *now!*"

Roland turned to the three men and froze. One of the police officers was getting to his feet while the other stood beside him, fumbling his gun from his holster. The homeless man stood about eight feet away, facing them, holding a gun between both hands. The man's arms were stiff, elbows locked, but his hands shook severely.

"You wanna take me to jail, you're gonna have to *kill* me first!" The homeless man smiled as he shouted at them.

Before he even knew he was going to speak, Roland said, "No, don't do that! Please!"

The man looked at him for a moment, surprised, as if he'd just noticed him there. "Stay outta this," he said. "This is none of your business."

But it is, Roland thought. *I shouldn't have walked away.* He knew that once he found the payphone didn't work, he could have gone into the convenience store and used the phone to call an ambulance.

But the payphone had *worked,* he told himself.

Daa-*deeee!*

Roland shuddered.

Both police officers were standing now, and the one who still had his gun was aiming it at the homeless man.

"Drop the gun, buddy! I'll shoot!"

"You duh-don't want to do this," Roland said, taking a step toward the man.

"Back away, Mister," the police officer with the gun said.

"Look, you tried to help today, and that was nice, but this is none of—"

"No, I didn't do enough! And I'm sorry. Doing this…it won't help anything. I…I-I know how you feel right now, I know what you're—"

"You don't know *shit!*" the homeless man barked, keeping an eye on the police officers.

Another step toward him. "Yes, I do! I…I had…" His throat was suddenly very dry and seemed ready to close on his words as he spoke them. But even though it would make him feel as if he were standing naked there by the street, he wanted to say it, felt a *need* to say it. "I had a...a wife and daughter, too. And I...lost them. Both of them."

The man's eyes stayed on him for a long moment. "They're both...both dead?"

"Yes."

"Goddammit, Mister, back *away!"* the police officer shouted.

The telephone in the booth rang. It startled the homeless man and he turned the back of his head to Roland to stare at the phone booth for several seconds. When he turned to the police officers, he was grinning. He raised the gun, as if aiming at something over their heads, and fired.

The police officer shot him twice.

The homeless man dropped to the sidewalk like a rag doll.

The telephone stopped abruptly, mid-ring.

Roland made a small, helpless sound in his throat.

The police officer who had fired grumbled into his radio as he approached the homeless man. The other officer hurried to Roland's side.

"You know this man?" he asked. He was winded from fighting with the homeless man; his lower lip was cut and his left eye swollen and bruised.

Roland shook his head slowly, never taking his eyes from the homeless man's limp form. "No, only...only in passing."

"You know his name?"

"No."

"What's your name?"

"Roland. Pearce."

"Well, stick around, Roland. We're gonna have to ask you some questions." He joined the other officer at the homeless man's side.

Roland took a couple steps toward them. "Is he...um, is he going to be okay?"

"No," one of them replied. "He's dead."

A headache began to form behind Roland's eyes. Everything

was blurred and fractured by the water on the lenses of his glasses, and the rainfall on his umbrella had become an irritating drone that gnawed at his joints with a rat's needle-like teeth.

Another ambulance arrived, siren wailing. Another police car pulled up at almost exactly the same time.

The telephone rang again.

Roland started, as if someone had poked him in the back.

It rang again. And again.

No one else seemed to notice.

Stepping around the paramedics and their stretcher, Roland went to the phone booth and stopped just outside the door, staring at the phone as it continued to ring. He collapsed his umbrella, stepped into the booth and closed the door. He did not say hello when he put the receiver to his ear, just waited.

It was a crackly connection. Static hissed and popped, while another sound went on continuously beneath it, much quieter...a whispery sound, fluttering...like voices...many whispering voices blending into a low, echoey hum.

"Thank you," a familiar voice said.

"What? I-I...I'm sorry?"

"Thank you, Briefcase Man," the homeless man said. His voice faded in and out as he spoke. "I know you were trying to help, and I appreciate it. But I'm okay now."

Roland turned his head to the right and looked through the Plexiglas. The paramedics were putting the homeless man's body on the stretcher.

"You're dead," he said flatly.

The homeless man did not reply. Instead a small, smiling voice—a painfully familiar voice—said, "Daa-*deeee!*" The word collapsed into a fit of giggles. The line fell silent. No dial tone, no sound at all, not even the resonance of an open line. It was dead.

"No," Roland breathed. "No-no-no, hello?" He put two fingers on the chrome tongue that protruded in the middle of the receiver's cradle and hit it several times, rapidly. *"Hello?"* The only thing he could hear was his own heart, throbbing rapidly in his ear.

He replaced the receiver, turned around slowly, and gasped

when he saw someone standing just outside the phone booth, staring in at him.

"Mr. Pearce?" the female officer asked. "Could you step outside? I need to ask you some questions."

Outside the booth in the rain, the officer took down Roland's name, address, telephone number at home and work, and asked him for a statement. Roland told her everything he'd seen, trying not to leave out any details...but it was difficult to focus on what he was saying. The officer told him he would have to come down to the station tomorrow to finish answering questions, thanked him for his time, then walked away.

By then, the homeless man's body was gone, along with the other two police officers. The ambulance's engine started up and its headlights came on as it pulled away from the curb.

Roland wiped a finger over each lens of his glasses, and started to walk away. After only a few steps, he stopped and turned back, looked at the phone booth with the crudely altered word written above the door: **HOME.** He walked over to the booth and leaned inside just enough to remove the receiver from its hook and put it to his ear.

There was only the flat, silent nothingness of a dead line. Just a grimy, cold piece of plastic against his ear.

But it hadn't been dead a little while ago...and Roland knew what he'd heard. The homeless man...and Melanie.

They're dead, he thought as he started walking. He picked up his pace, quickly putting as much distance between himself and the phone booth as possible. He heard Deborah's doctor warning him the last time they spoke on the phone:

It's entirely possible for one to experience a complete breakdown as a result of not properly grieving the loss of a loved one. It's entirely possible for one to experience a complete breakdown as a result of not properly grieving the loss of a loved one.

As he hurried home, Roland wondered if that was what was happening to him.

«« — »»

He started to fix a quick dinner, but realized he wasn't hungry. He sat down to watch television, but he couldn't sit still.

Roland had two bottles of wine in a cupboard in the kitchen. He'd bought them when he first moved into the apartment. There had once been three bottles, but he'd used one for cooking. He seldom drank alcohol, but found himself craving some that evening, so he opened a bottle and, tossing manners aside, poured some wine into a tall water glass over ice.

Strong feelings were stirring in him, shooting through him like bullets going in one side and out the other. He finished one glass of wine and started on another. The wine was loosening his muscles, but not clouding his head. The sweet, giggling voice on the telephone kept sounding again and again in his mind: Daa-*deeee!*

A studio audience laughed inordinately on a television sitcom, but although he stared at the screen, Roland saw none of it. He was thinking about the Homeless Couple. Ever since they'd first appeared on his route, it seemed one or the other of them had been talking on that payphone every time he passed. Sometimes emotionally, loudly. He closed his eyes and thought back over all those walks to and from work, passing them there between the payphone and the convenience store in their filthy rags, eating junk food, doing nothing with their lives, just standing there, sitting there…or talking on that phone.

That telephone doesn't work, the homeless man had said.

To whom had they been talking on a phone that didn't work? And what had they said? What had he heard them say?

No, baby, it's gonna be all right. I promise… I promise…

…sweetie, don't cry…

I miss you so much.

He remembered walking by twice when the payphone rang, and seeing the Homeless Couple scramble to get to it, as if their lives depended on it.

They had lost a baby girl, too.

And what had the homeless man said on the phone earlier when the police officers were pulling him out of the booth?

I'm coming, honey! Don't worry! I'm coming! I'll be right there, just…

Honey? He was talking to his wife...telling her he'd be there soon. And when he'd fired the gun he'd taken from the police officer, he'd raised it first, raised it high so the bullet would go over their heads and they wouldn't be hurt. He'd done that knowing full well he would be shot immediately.

After resisting the urge for nearly an hour, Roland went to a rolltop desk next to the kitchen doorway and opened the top drawer. From the drawer, he took a framed eight-by-ten studio photograph of Deborah and Melanie. It had been a Christmas gift from them both. In front of a colorful wooded backdrop, Deborah was seated on a short stone wall with Melanie on her lap. They were both smiling, but Melanie looked as if she were laughing heartily. The picture had been on the living room wall for awhile, but Roland had never looked at it, couldn't *bear* to look at it, and had finally taken it down and put it away. He looked at it now, though, for a long time. His throat burned and the picture blurred as tears filled his eyes.

Daa-*deeee!*

His tears landed on the lenses of his glasses and he put the picture back in the drawer.

"I'm not having a breakdown," Roland whispered.

He knew what he'd heard. His baby girl had spoken to him over that payphone. That was why the Homeless Couple stayed by the phone booth and never seemed to get out of earshot of the phone's ring...because they'd heard *their* baby girl's voice over that payphone, too. And just before he was killed, the homeless man had been talking to his wife.

"I'm not having a breakdown," he said again as he closed the desk drawer.

He knew what he'd heard, and it had been Melanie's voice. And if Melanie could speak to him over that payphone, so could Deborah.

Roland moved quickly: slipped on his overcoat, took his wallet from the desktop and stuffed it in his coat pocket, grabbed his umbrella and left the apartment.

It was still raining, but it had gotten much colder. Traffic was thinner, there were fewer pedestrians and the loudest sound in the night was the rain on his umbrella. Roland walked fast, his breath puffing clouds from his mouth and nostrils, heels clicking on the shiny wet concrete.

The payphone was ringing before he even got there. He could hear it a good distance away, growing louder as he neared. He broke into a jog for the last several yards, bounded into the phone booth and nearly tore up his umbrella. He held it outside the booth as he grabbed the receiver.

"Hello?"

No one spoke at first, but he recognized the odd sound of the connection: crackling static and the hollow, echoing murmur of countless voices all whispering over one another.

"Hel...hello?" he said again.

"Daa-*deeee!*"

Tears came suddenly and tumbled down his cheeks. "Melanie? Mel, sweetie? Is that you?"

The beautiful sound of her giggles faded in and out. "Daa wook? Daa go wook?"

He started to laugh, but it became a sob. Melanie used to ask that over breakfast, before he left for work.

"Not now, baby. Daddy's going to stay right here and talk to you now, okay?"

"'Kay, Daa-deeee."

Holding the receiver with his shoulder, Roland turned, collapsed the umbrella, pulled it into the booth and closed the accordion door. "Is...is Mommy there, Melanie?"

"Mommy."

"Yes, Mommy...is she there?"

"Rollie?"

He fell against the wall of the booth, weakened by the sound of her voice.

"Duh-Deb-Deborah?"

"We miss you, Rollie. We miss you so much. Melanie's always asking for her daddy, and I...I'm so lonely without you."

"Deborah...oh, God, Deborah, I...sweetheart, I..." He could

not find words. He was blinded by his tears and his heartbeat thundered in his ears as his lips worked, mouth opened and closed, trying to speak.

The static suddenly grew louder.

The connection was severed abruptly.

"*No!*" Roland shouted, rattling the chrome lever. He pressed his forearm to the phone and leaned his forehead on it, groaning. After a moment, he stood upright again and replaced the receiver. Stood there, running a hand through his hair again and again, clenching his teeth.

He stepped out of the booth, opened his umbrella, and paced on the sidewalk.

She'd been there, on the phone with him, and he'd been unable to speak, tongue-tied like some nervous boy. There had to be some way to call back, to reach her...wherever she was. But if there was, he was unaware of it.

Melanie had called once. Maybe she would call again. Maybe Deborah would call because their conversation had been interrupted.

Roland stopped pacing and stood beneath the awning awhile, his eyes on the phone booth.

How often does it happen? he wondered. *Is there any regularity? Any pattern to the calls?*

He paced some more. He would wait as long as he had to. All night, if necessary. If he got hungry, he could always grab a bite to eat at the convenience store. It was open twenty-four hours.

Roland went back into the phone booth, closed the door and leaned against the wall, staring at the phone.

He would wait as long as he had to. He would wait forever, if necessary. He wanted to talk to his family again. He'd lost them once and had been alone—all alone in the world for seven years—and he didn't want to lose them again.

Roland Pearce waited. He waited in the phone booth, beneath the marked-up word over the door, the word that had been crudely altered to spell **HOME**.

411

As always, for Dawn

1

An ice-cold hand clutched Kaitlin's soul and ripped her from sleep with the sound of crushing metal and shattering glass and cracking bones.

Kaitlin sucked in a breath that went down her throat like gravel as her upper body shot forward in her wheelchair, both arms outstretched, hands reaching for…something. She froze that way for a moment, catching her breath, then let her arms drop in her lap. Perspiration trickled over her temples and down her back beneath the baggy sweatshirt she wore, even though the fireplace held only embers and the house had gotten cold. Her hands trembled and her heart pounded the timpani in Strauss's "Thus Spake Zarathustra." Her mouth was dry and tasted foul.

She rubbed her bleary eyes until she could see the images on the television screen clearly. When she'd fallen asleep, Humphrey Bogart had been searching for *The Treasure of the Sierra Madre*. Now, a badly colorized version of Shirley Temple was tap-dancing and singing, looking like a ghoulishly painted child-whore.

Kaitlin reached for the diet soda on the end table beside her. Her fingers, still trembling from the nightmare, lost their hold and the can hit the hardwood floor with a thunk. She let her arm fall limp over the chair's wheel as she watched the open can roll onto the area rug. Cola bled from the can with a snake's hiss and formed a small puddle that spread over the edge of the rug and onto the wood floor.

Slivers of Bone

It was just a small mess and would have been so easy to clean up twenty-five months ago. Two years and one month...but it felt like a lifetime.

Thunder cracked from a distance, and several seconds later, the windows in the living room flickered with a flash of lightning.

Kaitlin despised Shirley Temple movies. She picked up the remote and clicked until she found an old *Twilight Zone* rerun. Agnes Moorehead was being menaced by tiny, toy-like aliens.

The clock on her DVD player read 12:14. On the floor, the cola hissed poisonously as it spread.

The nightmare always stayed with her for an hour or more after waking, and there was never a chance of getting back to sleep right away. She had an early split shift at work the next day, but even if she went to bed now, Kaitlin knew she would just stare at the ceiling. She saw no point in ignoring a mess when she had nothing better to do.

Kaitlin wheeled into the kitchen, got a roll of paper towels and returned to the spill. Leaning forward in her chair, she wiped the cola from the hardwood floor and soaked it up from the rug.

Oscar, her gray tabby manx, wandered over to see what she was doing and gave a hoarse, questioning meow. She'd adopted him seven months ago from the Humane Society, where he'd stood alone inside a cage, staring at her with pleading eyes. His coarse, inordinately loud meow had bellowed from his scrawny body, from his huge yawning mouth with extra-long whiskers, from his tiny head with over-sized ears, and he'd won her heart immediately. He was far from scrawny now, with a belly that swayed pendulously when he walked and gave him a pear shape when he sat on his haunches. From the day she'd brought him home, Oscar had breathed with a loud wheezing sound. It had worried her at first, but the veterinarian had examined him extensively—he'd even taken X-rays—and had been unable to find anything wrong. He'd told Kaitlin not to be concerned, that Oscar was a perfectly happy and healthy, if noisy, cat. He was an odd cat, too, and the wheezing, which didn't seem to bother Oscar in the least, simply added to his eccentricity.

As Kaitlin wiped up the mess, Oscar sat on her hand.

"Hey, hey, c'mon," she said, pushing him away gently. "Don't you have work to do? Isn't there something in the house you haven't chewed up yet?"

Oscar's long whiskers twitched as he made a garbled sound in his throat, then turned and sauntered away.

Kaitlin wadded up the soaked paper towels, dropped them in her lap, then reached down and picked up the aluminum can. As she sat up straight, she absently crushed the empty can in her hand.

The can's metallic crunching sound traveled down her spine and through every tooth in her head, through her gums and down her arms to her fingertips, searing her mind with a sudden, brilliantly vivid flash of her nightmare. She flopped back in her chair, wincing as if with pain, as she dropped the can into her lap. Her teeth clenched and she silently cursed herself. As she wheeled back into the kitchen, she realized her hands were trembling again. She hated herself for hanging on to it for this long, for not letting it go after two years.

Kaitlin remembered nothing of the accident, and it had taken a few days for her to recall the events immediately preceding it. The party...the argument...the quick, schoolkid-like reconciliation on the way to the car. Those things had emerged slowly from dark, moist, crimson shadows. But the accident itself only came to her in nightmares, and she wasn't sure if it was an actual memory or a cruel amalgam of details heard after the fact.

She felt no pain in the dream, although she often wished she would. The absence of pain gave the nightmare a cold, documentary-like feeling, allowing her to notice other details so upsetting that during the first year, she'd sometimes vomited upon awakening.

Richard's car began to slide over the ice, black as night, and went into a skid. He corrected once, but then lost control again, and they slid into the other lane. The headlights of the oncoming car grew rapidly brighter, filling Kaitlin's vision.

No sound at all, no voices, no engine, nothing...until the two cars connected. The metal clashed with an exquisitely shrill scream and a gut-squeezing rumble. Breathing stopped at that moment. She tried to inhale, fought to draw breath into her lungs, but could not. Kaitlin felt the bones in her legs and back breaking, and the sensation of her kneecaps shattering was so vivid it was almost as visual as it was sensual. She was not wearing a seatbelt and felt herself propelled forward toward the windshield. An instant before she hit the glass, she saw the face shooting toward her from the other car…a round, pale, sexless face with bulging eyes and blood breaking out like sweat on its surface, bits of broken, snowflake-like windshield dancing backward over the shattered nose and cheeks and chin, pieces lodging in soft flesh and eyes.

All the while…not breathing, no air.

Kaitlin's face hit the windshield of Richard's car and she felt and heard the cartilage in her nose crunch, the bones in her cheek and jaw crack and grind together, her teeth break and spew from her mouth, all without a hint of pain.

And that face bulleted toward her as she headed toward it, both with mouths open wide, as if about to lock in a bloody, tattered, broken kiss.

No breathing…no air.

Kaitlin flew through that other person from the oncoming car. Their bones grated together as they passed through one another, and she continued on, through metal, more glass, on and on…until she awoke in a sweat, a scream clawing to get out of her but ultimately drowning in her inability to make a sound as she fought for breath, for life.

She wheeled back into the living room to find Oscar rolling on the floor, playing with a paper towel that apparently had slipped from her lap on the way out of the room earlier.

Kaitlin watched television for about an hour, then turned it off, turned off the lamp, and wheeled down the hall with Oscar clumping after her in a hurry. She went into the bathroom and brushed her teeth, washed her face, and brushed her shoulder-length red hair. Then she went to her bedroom.

Once she'd swung herself out of the wheelchair and onto the bed, she removed her sweatshirt and leggings. It didn't get any easier. After two years, she was still clumsy at dressing and undressing, at working around her dead legs.

Oscar hopped onto the bed and began to look for a comfortable spot in which to curl up against her.

When Kaitlin rolled over to turn off the bedside lamp, her eyes fell on the small picture of Richard on her bed stand. It was in a simple black and silver frame. The picture had been taken at Shasta Lake on a day when the sky was blue and the sun was bright and nothing could go wrong. Richard was striking a silly pose in his swimming trunks, a heroic, superhero pose, as if he were rippling with muscles, when in fact, he was just a slender, nice-looking guy with a devastating lopsided grin and the eyes of a shy boy.

He not only left her, he'd left town for, he claimed, a better job in Sacramento. She knew he'd felt responsible for what had happened to her, guilty about the car accident. She didn't blame him for leaving her, but she'd tried to tell him she didn't hold him responsible. And she really *didn't*. It wasn't his fault. It was an accident. Her friends had been next, falling out of her life, like teeth from the mouth of an old dog. She still saw them around town, and maybe they would smile or wave, but they were no longer a part of her, and once again, she was helpless to do anything about it. It had been a knife in her heart at first, but she'd come to understand and even accept it. They were afraid of her. They couldn't bear to look at her. They all knew the accident that had put her in a wheelchair could just as easily happen to them. At any time. On any day. Kaitlin's dead legs could not be more horrifying to them if the paralysis had been contagious.

To Kaitlin, her legs were the result of more than just an accident. At night, in the minutes just before she fell asleep to have the nightmare that still haunted her almost every night, she saw her paralysis as an entity…a living being…a shadowy figure that had come from nowhere and stepped into her life…and had stripped her of her life. And there was nothing she could do to lash out, to fight back.

Richard, her friends, and her legs…she'd lost them all in a short period of time. And that shadowy figure remained, standing just out of sight at all times, untouchable, unhurtable…permanent.

Once Kaitlin turned out the light and was still, Oscar curled up beside her, meowed once, and began to purr as he wheezed.

2

"*Hi, I'm Roz…what city?*" Kaitlin's recorded voice asked when her Personal Response System was activated.

"Uh, hello, I'm, uh…I'm looking for a doctor," the elderly female voice said.

"What's the name and city?" Kaitlin asked.

"I don't know a name yet. I'm looking for a foot surgeon." The old woman spoke softly, kindly, with a slight tremble in her thin voice.

"I'm sorry, ma'am, but I can't search by category," Kaitlin said. "I need a name and a city."

"But I don't know of any foot surgeons. See, I *need* a foot surgeon. I have such terrible spurs in my feet, dear, you have no *idea*. So could you just look under foot surgeons and find one for me to—"

"I'm sorry, ma'am, but I don't have the Yellow Pages. I can only give the numbers of specific names in specific cities."

There was a long silence on the other end, without even the sound of breathing.

"Ma'am? Can you give me a name and—"

"Well, then, you're just a useless twat, aren't you?"

Kaitlin's eyes blinked, then widened, then blinked again. It was her job to find the numbers the customers needed, but not to take verbal abuse. During training, she'd been told to disconnect anyone who used such language. It was her *nature*, however, to convince the old woman at the other end of the line that she was simply not able to pick out a foot surgeon for her. It was her nature to patch things up before the connection was severed. But her job performance was judged according to the amount of time spent with each customer. The ideal time was somewhere between eighteen and twenty seconds. In her twelfth week on the job, Kaitlin was still hovering between twenty-three and twenty-five seconds per call. There was no time for small talk or chitchat, and certainly no time to soothe those customers in an ugly mood.

"Ma'am, I need a name and a—"

"I thought you were *information!*" the once kindly old woman snapped. "But you're *just* a useless *twat!*"

Kaitlin hit the release button and ended the call. But she knew it would stay with her awhile…that call, and any others like it she might get in the course of the day. It would gnaw at her like an unresolved argument with her mother.

"Get a good one?" Sue asked. She was seated at the station to Kaitlin's left.

Kaitlin nodded as she turned to Sue.

"You look like you just heard about a death in the family," Sue said with a smirk. "You've really got to stop taking those things so hard. They're just pissy people who think it's safe to treat you like dirt because you're on the phone and not face-to-face."

"It was an old woman," Kaitlin said. "A sweet-sounding old lady."

"Really? That's odd. The old ladies usually *are* pretty sweet. Probably because PMS is a thing of the past for them and most of their husbands are dead."

"She called me a useless twat."

"Eh," Sue said dismissively with a cock of her head. "Sounds like a nutjob. Probably belongs in a home, if she isn't in one already. Those places really need to keep their patients away from the telephones," she said as she turned away to take a call.

Sue had been the first person to talk to her when Kaitlin had started the job, and they had hit it off. They usually sat close together, and when their schedules permitted, they chatted over lunch.

Sue had separated all the customers into groups: The "nutjobs," who were just plain crazy; the "whackjobs," who wanted someone to listen while they masturbated and talked dirty; the "dingbats," who took the word "information" literally and called to ask how to spell words, how long to cook a turkey, and who played what role in which movie; the "cranks," who were usually kids who thought it was funny to ask for the number of a Hunt, first name Mike, or spew profanities at an operator; the "coronaries," who were impatient, rude, shouted at the operators and would most likely end up having a heart attack; and the "cattle," whom Sue said were "just regular people like us."

Kaitlin took a few dozen more calls before a lull set in.

"I was going to run to that new sandwich place for lunch," Sue said. "Want anything?"

"No, thanks," Kaitlin said, smiling. "I've got a split shift today. My mother's coming to pick me up at noon. We're going to have lunch, shop for my dad's birthday present, then she'll bring me back here at six to go back to work."

"Lucky you!" Sue said sincerely.

"Well...we'll see," Kaitlin replied with a low chuckle.

"You don't get along with your mother?"

"I try. Very hard."

Sue shrugged one shoulder. "Maybe you shouldn't try so hard. Maybe then she wouldn't be a problem. I know that worked for me."

"What do you mean? You stopped trying to get along with your mother?"

"No, I stopped talking to her. About sixteen years ago."

Kaitlin heard a click on her headset and turned to take the call.

"I'd like the number of a pizza parlor," a man said pleasantly.

Not again, Kaitlin thought. Why did so many people confuse directory assistance with the Yellow Pages?

"I'm sorry, sir, but I'll need the name of a specific pizza parlor."

"Oh, okay, sure. That makes sense. Uh, let's see...how about Round Table Pizza?"

"In what city?"

"Well, in *this* city."

"Sir...I don't know what city you're calling from."

He laughed. "Oh, yeah...of course you don't. Okay, uh, I'm in...*Redding*, that's it."

Her fingers clattered softly on the keyboard.

"I have five Round Table Pizza restaurants listed in Redding, sir. Which one do you want?"

"Oh, jeez," he said with a sigh. "Five? Well, I...I don't know. Just give me one and I'll get directions."

Kaitlin rolled her eyes behind briefly closed lids. At least he was being nice about it. "I have Round Tables listed on five different streets, sir. Do you have *any* idea which one you want?"

"Oh, well, see...I'm just visiting here. I don't know the area at all. So, uh, you see my problem?" He was pleasant, and sounded young—in his early twenties at the most—and more than a little helpless.

"Do you know where you are?" Kaitlin asked. "What street you're on, I mean?"

"Oh, yeah, sure. I'm at my mom's on, uh...let's see, what *is* this street? *Orchid*, that's it, I'm on Orchid Street. No, no...*Way*. Orchid Way."

Kaitlin recognized the street. It was in a very pricey neighborhood on the western edge of Redding, nestled atop a great hill overlooking the rest of the city.

"If you're on Orchid, then you're not far from Eureka Way," Kaitlin said. "That would be the Round Table closest to you."

Before the man could reply, there was an odd *thump* in the background on the other end of the line, like someone hitting a large pillow with a baseball bat. Glass shattered once, then again. A woman screamed.

It wasn't a scream of anger or fear, or even pain. It rose from the center of the woman's soul and tore chunks out with it as it came.

"*Nooooooo!*" the woman cried.

There were more sounds of struggle.

Kaitlin heard the receiver on the other end being joggled around, as if the young man were holding it while running.

"Mom?" he called. "*Mom?*"

There was another scream. More glass shattered.

Kaitlin stiffened in her chair as the skin on the back of her neck shriveled.

The sounds of movement from the young man carrying the phone stopped and there was a brief moment of dead silence. Kaitlin stared wide-eyed at her monitor, muscles tensed, and thought he'd hung up. Then:

"Oh, Jesus! Oh, *Jeeezus*, what—"

There was another *thump*. Then two more in rapid succession.

The phone clattered loudly in Kaitlin's ear as it was dropped, obviously, to the floor. Something thunked heavily nearby...a body falling to the floor.

Kaitlin had not moved so much as a fraction of an inch. As the connection fell silent again, she realized she'd been holding her breath. Her eyes welled up and the monitor blurred. She was not crying; the tears were a natural reaction to the icy chill that embraced her. She gulped in a breath suddenly as she moved a trembling finger toward the release button.

"Hello." It was a firm male voice, deep and without inflection, suddenly speaking on the other end of the line. "Who is this?"

Startled, Kaitlin said, "This is Kaitlin. I-I mean, uh...this is directory assistance. Is...is everything all right?"

There was no reply.

"My God," Kaitlin whispered. "What...*happened?*"

After a few more endless seconds of silence, the connection was severed.

Kaitlin remained frozen in place, her finger hovering over the release button, wide, glistening eyes locked on the monitor. On her headset she heard the silence of disconnected nothingness; deep in her ears, the throbbing of her own heart. Then the nagging click of another call coming in.

She took that call, then another, and another. They were all easy, straightforward calls, but her fingers fumbled on the keyboard and she stammered when she spoke. By the sixth call, tears were trickling down her cheeks and she could hardly talk. She shut down her station and backed away in her wheelchair.

"Are you all right?" Sue asked.

"I have to talk to Margaret," Kaitlin said as she spun her chair around and headed for the in-charge desk. The desk was elevated, giving the service assistants, or SAs, a clear view of all the operators. Kaitlin wheeled up the ramp that led behind the desk and approached Margaret, a plump, tall-haired woman in her fifties.

When she saw Kaitlin, Margaret's eyes widened and she frowned, turning toward Kaitlin as she approached. "What's *wrong*, honey?" she asked as she handed Kaitlin a box of tissues.

Kaitlin told her SA about the call, told her every detail. She dabbed at her eyes as she spoke and managed to stop crying. When she was finished, she said, "I didn't know if I should tell you or not. I just...I just can't get that woman's scream out of my head. And I can't stop wondering what *happened* to her...and to that young man I was talking to."

Margaret's round, pink face tightened with concern as she reached over and patted Kaitlin's hand. "I don't know of a single person working here who hasn't had at *least* one call like that," she said. "It happens to all of us."

"But what can we *do*?"

"Well, the fact is, it's usually a prank."

"A *prank*? But...who would—"

"Kids. They do it all the time. They think it's funny. Sometimes they call up with little jokes, sometimes they talk dirty...and sometimes they plan these elaborate pranks to scare the operators."

"Maybe so, Margaret, but...I'm serious...this didn't sound like *kids*."

"It never does the first time. But you'll be ready for it next time," she said with a smile. "Why don't you take a special. Go have some coffee, or something. Okay?"

Kaitlin did not move. "What if...what if it wasn't a prank? What if it was real?"

Margaret's penciled eyebrows rose high and she shrugged. "There's nothing we can do about it. We have no way to trace calls or identify callers. That's not our job. Sounds cold, I know, honey, but...that's the way it is. If it makes you feel any better, though, I can *promise* you it *wasn't* real. Really."

Kaitlin went to the restroom, washed her face, then had a cup of coffee. When she returned to her station, she felt better. But there was still a small, hard lump of tension in her stomach that would not go away.

"What happened?" Sue asked.

"I got a bad call," Kaitlin said, putting on her headset.

"You looked pretty upset."

"I was."

"I keep telling you, Kaitlin," Sue said, smiling, "you've gotta toughen up. Let those bad ones go."

"I know, I know. My mother would say what she always says to me...that I'm too sensitive." Kaitlin put her fingers on the keyboard and took another call.

3

"You're just too sensitive, Kaitlin," Paula Callahan said as she drove her Ford Taurus into the parking lot of the Mt. Shasta Mall. "With a job like that, you're just going to have to learn to ignore the pranksters."

"It didn't sound like a prank, mother. The young man sounded like he was in his early twenties, maybe, and the woman in the background—"

"I'm surprised at you, Kaitlin. Of *course* it was a prank. Just some kids trying to frighten someone. I'm sure they had a big laugh afterward. They'll probably talk about it for days. I would think you'd remember that sort of thing. You used to do it enough."

"I never made prank phone calls, Mother," Kaitlin said, managing to keep her frustration out of her voice. "Mitch made the calls. I just got blamed for it...until one of his teachers recognized his voice and called you to complain."

"Mitch made those calls?" She frowned and glanced at Kaitlin. "Then why didn't you say so at the time?"

"I tried at first, but nobody seemed interested in what I had to say, so..." She shrugged with one shoulder. In her mind, though, the sentence finished itself: *I just went along with it so the whole thing would blow over.*

"Well, even so," Paula continued, "you know how kids are. Scaring someone, frustrating someone…getting under a grown-up's skin is the pinnacle of humor to them. You're just too sensitive. You let things get to you. You shouldn't do that, Kaitlin, you really shouldn't. The stress will make you gray before your time."

Pouring rain fell in a steady roar against the car and the windshield wipers barely kept up with it. The sky reminded Kaitlin of an old silent movie: black and gray, flickering with silver flashes of lightning, scratched with streaks of rainfall. It was nearly June, but the El Niño winter held on with an iron grip, burying spring and holding summer at bay with the worst electrical storms in decades.

Kaitlin had forgotten to bring the handicapped plate that went on the dashboard and would allow her mother to park in a handicapped parking slot. Rather than risk getting a ticket, Paula drove around the large but full parking lot until she found an empty spot at the farthest end of the parking lot from the mall.

While Paula put a plastic bonnet over her perfectly coiffed silver hair, Kaitlin opened her door and reached into the backseat for her wheelchair.

"You stay right where you are," Paula said, opening her door. "I'll come around and help you."

"Mother, I do this a dozen times a day. You don't have to—"

"Not in *my* car you don't." Paula got out, leaned in and took her umbrella from the backseat. "What do you suppose people would say if they saw me just *standing* there while my crippled daughter dragged herself and her wheelchair out of the car?" She closed her door and walked around to Kaitlin's side of the car.

Kaitlin rolled her eyes as her mother grunted and struggled with the wheelchair. Once it was unfolded beside the car, she leaned over and clumsily tried to help Kaitlin into the chair with one hand, holding her umbrella with the other. Kaitlin knew she could have been most of the way to the mall's entrance by the time her mother had her in the wheelchair.

Once inside, they decided to have lunch before shopping. They went to a little Chinese fast food restaurant called The Power Wok, got their food, and settled at a tiny moulded plastic table.

"I'd like to get Dad something he'll really love," Kaitlin said, "and I know how much he loves tools. Do you know of anything he doesn't have? Something he's been wanting but hasn't gotten for himself?"

"He's a sixty-nine-year-old retired carpenter," Paula said. "He doesn't need tools, he *has* them all. He needs pants. Some shirts, maybe. He'll never let me shop for clothes for him. Won't even let me go *with* him. So what happens? He ends up *dressing* like a retired carpenter. Outside of flea markets and hardware stores, I can't take him *any*where. He hasn't bought a suit since Reagan was in the White House, so I'm going to get him a couple. You can get him some nice pants and shirts. I'll show you the kind he needs."

Kaitlin sighed. She did not *want* to buy her father pants and shirts for his birthday, especially pants and shirts her mother claimed he needed. Kaitlin wanted to buy him something that would make his eyes light up. But she knew if she said as much, it would only start a fight with her mother, so she said nothing. If necessary, she'd buy a shirt and a pair of pants today, to satisfy her mother. Then, before Saturday, she would buy something she knew her father would appreciate, even if she had to dip into her savings. A brand new tool belt, maybe. He spent most of his time out in his shop, so Kaitlin knew he would use it. That way, everyone would be happy.

Kaitlin had become very good at avoiding fights with her mother, at keeping peace in general. From the time she was a little girl, she had been the peacemaker in the house, always trying to patch things up between her older brother Mitch and her father, between herself and her mother, and between her battling parents. Even back then, as a child, she'd often wondered how two people as vastly different as her mother and father had ended up married to one another.

Kaitlin and Paula ate their lunch quietly for awhile, then Paula put down a half-eaten egg roll and asked, "What if it was real?"

"What if what was real?" Kaitlin asked.

"The call. What you heard. What if it *was* real, and not a prank?"

"Mother, you've been telling me all the way over here that I was overreacting to a prank." Kaitlin's tone was gentle and she wore a soft smile, but she felt the muscles of her neck tensing.

"I know, I know," Paula said with a bitter frown, shaking her head sharply back and forth as she always did when impatient. She stopped and leaned forward, looking closely at her daughter. "But what if it *wasn't* a prank? I mean, let's just *say* it was real."

"Like I said, Mother, we can't trace calls. Even if it was a real call and something bad *really* happened to someone, there was nothing I could do."

"I know, I know, that's not what I'm talking about."

"What do you mean, then?" Kaitlin took a couple swallows of her Diet Mountain Dew.

"What I'm saying is, what if you really *did* hear someone being hurt?" She raised an egg roll halfway to her mouth, then looked Kaitlin in the eyes. Holding the egg roll between thumb and fingertips, she poked it in Kaitlin's direction to accent her words as she lowered her voice to a secretive whisper. "What if you heard a *murder*?" She took a bite and chewed slowly as she dabbed her lips with a paper napkin.

A shimmer of tension moved across Kaitlin's upper back, drawing her shoulder blades toward one another slightly. Her mother continued to stare at her, chewing, slowly raising her eyebrows.

It was as certain as the rotation of the earth. Kaitlin's mother would harp on her and harp on her about something, like the fact that she was so sensitive that she got upset about a simple crank call. Then, when it looked like the subject might change, taking the conversation in a safer, more comfortable direction, she would double back and start all over, this time arguing from Kaitlin's initial point of view.

Kaitlin took a bite of her chicken chow mein and stared back at her mother as she chewed.

After a moment, Paula asked, "Why are you looking at me like that? As if I just burst into song, or something? I mean, if it *was* a murder, then the last voice you heard on the line *could* have been the *murderer*."

Kaitlin massaged the bridge of her nose with thumb and forefinger. There was growing tightness behind her eyes: a headache calling ahead to let her know it would be arriving soon. "I really don't want to think about it anymore, Mother. Whatever happened, there was nothing I could do about it then, and there's nothing I can do about it now. Besides, you've been *telling* me to forget about it. So, do you think we could talk about something else? I mean, Dad's birthday party, or something? Anything?"

Paula sipped her tea and sat back in her chair. "Yes, you're right. And anyway, if it *was* the killer, he wouldn't have heard your name at the beginning of the call because he didn't make the call, right?"

"What do you mean?" Kaitlin asked.

"Well, all of you directory assistance operators have those prerecorded greetings where you give your name and ask the caller, 'What city, please?' Right? For a minute, there, I was a little worried about that, because if it *was* a real murder and the killer *was* the one who hung up on you, I thought he might have heard your name. But that wouldn't have happened because he didn't make the call." She sat up and took another bite of her egg roll. "They *were* two different voices, weren't they?"

Kaitlin closed her eyes for a moment so her mother wouldn't see them roll. "I've told you before, Mother, we don't use our real names."

"You don't? I don't remember you telling me that."

"Well, I did. A few times."

Paula sniffed. "No need to rub it in. I was just concerned for your safety, that's all. I mean, if it *had* been a murder you heard and the killer *had* heard your name, how hard could it be for him to track you down? But just forget I said anything." Her voice had suddenly changed, sounding slightly wounded.

Kaitlin opened her mouth to apologize…but she wasn't quite sure what it was she was about to apologize for, so instead of speaking, she took another bite of chow mein. They both ate in silence for a little while, with the busy sounds of the mall filtering into the little restaurant like the buzzing of a hive of bees. Although she tried, Kaitlin could not stop running the last few minutes of conversation with her mother over and over in her head.

What if you really did hear someone being hurt?...What if you heard a murder?

Kaitlin suddenly realized her mother had spoken to her. She lifted her head and said, "I'm sorry, what?"

"I said, I'm going to the restroom, and then we should get some shopping done." Paula frowned. "What's wrong?"

"Nothing, I'm fine. Yes, we should go."

Paula stood, went to the back of the restaurant and disappeared down a narrow corridor.

Kaitlin sighed as she poked at her chow mein with her plastic fork, annoyed at herself. Most people Kaitlin knew were unable to have a normal, pleasant conversation with at least one of their parents, usually both, so she knew there was nothing unusual in that. But it seemed most of those people could either ignore whatever buttons their parents pushed, or give back as good as they got. Kaitlin was unable to do either.

This time, though, something about her mother's words chewed at her with sharper-than-usual fangs...

...if it was the killer, he wouldn't have heard your name at the beginning of the call because he didn't make the call, right?

Right, Kaitlin thought. But something about the question was tying her insides into a knot.

She remembered the man's voice. After the shrill, horrified screaming Kaitlin had heard at the other end of the line, the man had spoken in a voice that was deep and steady and utterly calm.

Hello? Who is this?

Gooseflesh crawled across the back of Kaitlin's neck and made its way up over her scalp. She felt cold suddenly, as if she were sitting in a chilly draft, and the palms of her hands became clammy. The plastic fork dropped from her fingers and landed on what remained of the chow mein.

Kaitlin pressed her lips together tightly, closed her eyes and told herself to stop it...that she was being ridiculous...that she was letting her mother get under her skin yet again. But it didn't work, because she couldn't stop hearing her own voice in her head...she kept hearing what she'd said to that man when he asked, *Who is this*?

Frightened, nervous and off-guard, she had said, *This is Kaitlin.*

4

Kaitlin's initial fear, stirred up by her mother, passed as she and Paula shopped. They chatted amiably, with Kaitlin steering the conversation to safe, neutral subjects. She bought pants and shirts for her father, not because that was what she wanted to give him, but to satisfy her mother.

At work, Kaitlin returned to her station and fell back into the routine of taking calls, tapping at the keyboard, and giving numbers. During the rest of her shift, she thought only fleetingly of the disturbing call she'd taken earlier that day, and of that deep male voice she'd heard just before the connection was severed.

She had managed to leave her mother's unsettling speculations at the mall. When her mother nagged her about something personal, Kaitlin was usually unable to shake her words for days, sometimes weeks. But this time, like a rare few in the past, was different. She knew Paula was just trying to get a rise out of her, maybe even trying to frighten her, although Paula might not be consciously aware of it. Kaitlin knew that was simply the kind of person her mother was, and although she didn't like it and couldn't change it, she could, at times, refuse to let the woman's behavior under her skin. This was one of those times.

Kaitlin was on her way out at the end of her shift when she heard Margaret call her name. She turned to see the SA holding a blue ribbon with a pink helium-filled balloon attached to the top end, and a small bag of jelly beans tied to the bottom. She smilingly offered the ribbon to Kaitlin.

"You got a commendation today," Margaret said.

"Really?" Kaitlin asked with a grin. The balloon and candy meant a caller had been so satisfied with Kaitlin's work that he or she had asked to speak to an SA so he or she could compliment Kaitlin's efficiency and politeness. "My first commendation," she said as she took the ribbon and smiled up at the gently swaying balloon.

Margaret nodded. "He said you were the most polite operator he'd ever talked to."

Kaitlin's smile faltered as she thought back over the day, trying to remember a caller who had asked to talk to her SA. She looked at Margaret. "No one asked for an SA today."

"No, he called a little while after you left for your break. I got so busy, I almost forgot about it."

"You mean, he called back after he talked to me and asked *another* operator for an SA so he could give me a commendation?"

"Uh-huh. He said he'd talked to you this morning."

Kaitlin looked at the balloon again for a moment, frowning slightly, then tied the ribbon to the armrest of her chair, still frowning.

"It was odd," Margaret said. "He wasn't quite sure of the name of the operator who'd taken his call, but he thought it was Kaitlin, or something *like* Kaitlin. That threw me at first, because I know just about everybody's PRS name here, and I knew no one was using the name Kaitlin. Then I thought of you...but your PRS name is Roz. I was surprised he knew your real name." Margaret's voice became slightly more firm and SA-like. "You know, if you want to go by Kaitlin, that's fine, but you should pick one or the other. If your PRS says Roz, but you identify yourself as Kaitlin to the callers, things could get confusing. You might even miss a commendation." She smiled again. "Besides, you shouldn't be talking to them long enough to *tell* them your real name."

"He said 'Kaitlin?'" she asked, her eyes suddenly widening beneath her furrowed brow. "Not...'Roz?'"

"Mm-hm."

"Well...maybe he was referring to someone else."

"You're the only Kaitlin we have here."

"What...did he say, exactly?"

"That you were polite and friendly and patient with him when he wasn't sure which town his number was in."

"Did...did he say anything else?"

Margaret shook her head. "No. Should he have?"

"Oh, no. No, of…course not."

"Well, I've gotta run," Margaret said with a little wave as she walked away. "You have a good evening."

Kaitlin stayed where she was for a moment, staring up at the balloon.

Each operator was allowed to choose a name for his or her PRS when beginning the job. The PRS identity was partly to avoid having more than one operator with any particular name and partly to maintain the privacy of the operators. Kaitlin had mentioned her name only once since she'd started the job…and that had been earlier that day when the low male voice had asked, "Who is this?"

At least…she couldn't *remember* mentioning her real name any other time.

"You okay?"

Startled, Kaitlin looked up to see one of the other operators, a thin blond man looking down at her with concern. She realized she'd been sitting there, still as a statue, staring at the balloon. Smiling, she said, "Yes, I'm fine. Just a little distracted." As she wheeled herself out of the room, she realized her smile had been forced and her voice hollow.

In the employee locker room, Kaitlin frowned as she mechanically went through the routine of putting on her coat and removing her retractable umbrella from her locker. She wheeled to the back of the building and out the door that led to the gated employees' parking lot.

The thick rain clouds made the late afternoon dark enough for the parking lot's tall automatic lights to have already come on, although the night was still thirty or forty minutes away. In all the unseasonably gloomy weather lately, there had been no dusk; the days went from afternoon to night in no time at all.

In the covered entryway just outside the door, Kaitlin opened the umbrella and tucked it between her right shoulder and the back of her chair. Her car was just a couple yards from the door in the closest of the two handicapped spots, but it was raining so hard, she knew she'd be drenched in seconds with nothing over her head.

Kaitlin barely heard the explosive pounding of the rain on her umbrella. She was too busy thinking about the commendation she'd received, and the man who had spoken to her earlier that day.

Hello? Who is this?

Why would he call back to praise Kaitlin's performance? If he'd asked questions about her, if he'd wanted to know her working hours, or perhaps her last name, Kaitlin would understand, because if, as her mother had suggested, Kaitlin had actually heard someone being hurt or killed, the killer might consider her a kind of witness and want to silence her. He would not have learned anything about her from Margaret, of course, or any other SA, for that matter. The operators' anonymity was carefully guarded and such questions were never answered. But it would have made *sense* to Kaitlin. The fact that he'd called simply to give her a commendation was...*bizarre*.

Unless there was something Margaret hadn't told her. Maybe he'd asked something in passing, something that seemed so casual she hadn't noticed. No, Margaret would have mentioned it. The SAs were very protective of the operators and if someone called and asked anything about any of them, it was reported to the person in question.

Maybe he'd called just to make sure someone named Kaitlin really worked there.

Or maybe it wasn't the same man at all. Kaitlin smiled with relief so sudden that it punched a single little laugh out of her as she wheeled off the sidewalk down the small concrete ramp.

Of *course* it wasn't the same man! It was just someone considerate enough to call back and compliment Kaitlin's work. That didn't explain why he'd known her real name, but...just because she couldn't *remember* mentioning it to any other callers didn't mean she hadn't, especially considering how upset she'd been after that frightening call. Those last calls before her mid-shift break had gone by in a blur. She could have recited obscene limericks to callers and she wouldn't remember it.

"Thanks a lot, Mother," Kaitlin said as she unlocked the car door and swung it open. Her words were swallowed up by the sound of the rain. She collapsed the umbrella and tossed it into the car. In a smooth, fluid movement, with her left hand on the steering wheel and her right clutching the edge of the car's roof, she swung out of the chair and behind the car's steering wheel, leaned over, folded the wheelchair up and slid it into the backseat.

Back when she was newly handicapped, getting in and out of a car had been one of the hardest things to learn. She'd fallen often and scraped and bruised herself. Fortunately, it had only hurt from the waist up. She had gotten the hang of the maneuver eventually, however, and in time, she'd mastered it.

Kaitlin slammed the door and let her head fall back as she released an explosive breath through puffed cheeks. In the seconds she'd been without her umbrella, her long red hair had been soaked, and she pulled the wet strands from her face as she adjusted herself in the seat. She started the car and turned on the heater.

The radio came on with the engine, tuned to a news/talk station.

"—not only no let-up in the rain, but in the next two days, Shasta County residents can look forward to winds up to seventy miles per hour, as well as electrical storms that will no doubt top those that have hit the surrounding areas in recent days. Power outages have already been reported in—"

Kaitlin hit the FM button and Fleetwood Mac began to sing "Tusk" in stereo. Once the windshield wipers were beating rapidly to keep up with the rainfall, she backed out of the parking slot using the hand controls and drove around to the long metal gate with its simple vertical bars in their rectangular frame. When employees drove in, it was necessary to punch a code into the keypad just outside the gate to get it to open; on the way out, though, it was triggered by a motion sensor. It slid aside slowly, opening on the visitors' parking lot in front, which opened onto Stover Road. Across the street stood the JVZ Cosmetics factory, a large ugly building that looked like an airplane hangar.

Tapping the steering wheel to the beat of the music as the gate slid aside slowly, Kaitlin noticed a black sports utility vehicle parked at the curb across the street, right in front of the cosmetics factory. The only reason she noticed was that there was no parking along Stover—signs were posted up and down the street—and she'd never seen a car at the curb before.

When the gate was open far enough, Kaitlin drove forward slowly. Growing up with her brother and father around, she'd picked up an eye for cars, and she recognized the SUV across the street as a Lincoln Navigator. The windows were tinted, but the driver's window was rolled down halfway and she saw a man sitting at the wheel. He wore a dark blue New York Yankees baseball cap with the bill pulled down over sunglasses. No...as she drove closer to the parking lot's entrance/exit, she realized they were just regular wire-rimmed glasses with a tint to the lenses.

Kaitlin stopped at the edge of the parking lot and checked both ways for traffic. There was none, but she didn't pull out. Her eyes fell again on the man in the Navigator across the street.

He was looking at her.

No...not at her...at her car. The front of her car.

"Kaaaayyy one-oh-one, where the music of the seventies and eighties lives *on*! Coming up, a solid hour of non-stop music, with Elton John, the Bee Gees, Styx—"

Kaitlin turned off the radio as her car idled...as the man in the Navigator stared. She felt a sudden chill in spite of the toasty air shooting from the vents in the panel.

The man's head turned away and dipped suddenly, as if he were looking at his lap. Reading something. Or writing. After a few seconds, he lifted his head and turned to her again as the tinted window rolled up. Glistening raindrops dribbled down the dark glass like liquid diamonds.

Kaitlin waited, expecting the Navigator to start up and drive away, but it didn't. The window remained rolled up and the Navigator sat there, black and shiny-wet, as if its occupant were waiting for something as well.

Kaitlin screamed when a car horn honked behind her. She slapped a hand to her chest and took a few deep breaths, surprised by how tense she'd become. In the rearview mirror, she saw Pamela, one of the other operators, in her blue Sundance. Pamela smiled and waved half-heartedly, but the movements were forced;

she was obviously impatient. Kaitlin wondered how long she'd been holding Pamela up while sitting there staring at the Navigator across the street.

After checking for traffic, Kaitlin pulled out of the parking lot and turned left. She glanced in her rearview mirror and saw Pamela pull forward, waving again, smiling, looking a little more relaxed than before.

As Kaitlin drove away, slowly at first, she looked in the rearview mirror to see if the Navigator was following her. The black SUV didn't move as she looked repeatedly into the mirror. It remained at the curb, melting in the dreamy blur of rainwater on the rear window as Kaitlin drove on, relieved…for the time being, at least.

5

"Wait a second," Wanda said in her gravelly, cigarette-damaged voice. "You want me to go outside and look across the street for a van?"

"Not a van," Kaitlin said into the phone, "a black Lincoln Navigator."

"A van, a Navigator, whatever." She sounded annoyed.

Kaitlin had worked with Wanda only once, and she didn't like her. In her forties, she looked in her fifties and behaved like a cranky senior citizen.

"Look, Wanda, I know this sounds weird, but I'd really appreciate it. Just step out front and look across the street. Or maybe you could have someone else do it. Please?"

There was a long, phlegmy sigh at the other end of the line, then Wanda said, "Hang on a second." She put Kaitlin on hold with a muted click, plugging her into the middle of The Police singing "Roxanne."

Kaitlin was calling from the phone at the front desk of the Achievement Center. At first glance, it appeared to be a social center for handicapped people, but it was actually much more than that. It was run by volunteers who utilized the services of several non-profit organizations and government programs to provide handicapped people with wheelchairs, prosthetics and other equipment they might not otherwise be able to afford. Newly handicapped people could go to the center for training programs that helped them adjust to their new way of life, and social events were held for groups of all ages—from children to the elderly—so they could meet others who faced the same physical challenges.

At first, Kaitlin had resented the very fact that she *needed* a place like the Achievement Center, but it had ultimately been her salvation. It was there that she'd learned everything she needed to know about how to live life from the waist up. She'd made some fast friends there, as well. It took awhile for her to realize just how much she needed them.

Outside, a white flash of lightning preceded a long, cracking round of thunder.

Down the main corridor, the *clock-clock, clock-clock* of a ping-pong game rattled on steadily, rhythmically. Kaitlin assumed it was Nicole and Larry because she'd seen their cars out front. They seemed to be the only other people in the building.

On the phone, The Police gave way to Blue Oyster Cult singing "Don't Fear the Reaper." It made Kaitlin feel old to know the rock and roll of her youth had become respectable enough to be on-hold music.

Kaitlin sat alone at the front desk, staring through the plate glass window that looked out on the strip mall next to the Achievement Center. A new ice cream and espresso parlor called *Confetti!* had opened there only a few days before and a banner above the entrance read GRAND OPENING! Just above the banner, a floodlight glared, illuminating most of the parking lot.

A clown stood before the ice cream parlor holding an umbrella and wearing a sandwich board. The board read, FREE ICE CREAM CONE WITH ANY PURCHASE! Helium-filled balloons were attached by strings to his umbrella and they dipped and danced in the heavy rainfall. He waved to passing cars as he walked back and forth in his puffy white suit with huge red polka dots. But there were no cars parked in front of *Confetti!*. It seemed no one was in the mood to stop for ice cream or espresso in such unpleasant weather.

Kaitlin held the receiver in her left hand and rested her chin on the knuckles of her right as she stared out the window and listened to Blue Oyster Cult.

The clown suddenly stopped pacing back and forth. He was facing the window through which Kaitlin was staring. He didn't move for a long moment.

Kaitlin's back stiffened slightly. She couldn't see the clown's face because it was shaded from the floodlight by the umbrella. But the clown tilted his umbrella back jauntily, revealing his white face. A flash of lightning blended with the floodlight. The clown's face appeared to be in black-and-white, like an old movie…pale white skin with a huge black grin and eyes lost in dark, empty sockets. He lifted a white-gloved hand and waved, bobbing his head as if to say, *Yes, yes, I'm waving at* you, *dear*!

In the next room, the ping pong ball continued to clock against the table with a steady beat.

Kaitlin's lips parted as she pressed her back against the back of her wheelchair. Without even realizing she was doing it, she lifted her right hand and waved half-heartedly at the clown as "Don't Fear the Reaper" played on in her ear. The clown's waving hand dropped, but he continued to watch her for a moment.

What if he's watching me? Kaitlin thought suddenly. *What if he followed me and is somewhere nearby watching me right now? I was so busy* thinking *about him that I never thought to* look *for him in the rearview mirror on the way over here!*

The clown turned away and continued pacing with his sandwich board and balloon-festooned umbrella.

That's ridiculous, Kaitlin thought as she closed her eyes and shook her head firmly. *How could he know who I was? He couldn't possibly know who to follow out of that parking lot, even if he did know my first name. It would be—*

"Are you still there?"

Kaitlin jerked and gasped, so startled by Wanda's voice she nearly dropped the phone. "Yes? What?"

"I looked for that Explorer, or whatever you said it was, and it's not there, okay?"

"There was nobody parked in front of the JVZ factory?"

"That's a no parking zone," Wanda pointed out, annoyed. "There's nobody parked on the street anywhere around here. Okay?"

"You're...sure?"

Wanda lowered her voice a bit. "Look, honey...have you been maybe having a few drinks?"

Kaitlin was watching the pacing clown again. The strings that tied the balloons to his umbrella sagged as the balloons were beaten down hard by the falling rain.

"Kaitlin?" Wanda said loudly.

"Yes. I mean, *no*! No, I haven't been drinking." She sighed and licked her lips, realizing her mouth was dry. "Um, thanks for looking, Wanda, I really appreciate it. *Really*."

"All right, well...I've gotta get back to work, here, okay?"

"Sure, sure. Thanks, Wanda."

Kaitlin returned the receiver to its cradle. She was craving a cigarette, but there was no smoking in the building. She had only stopped by the center because it was on her way and she'd wanted to use the phone. She'd thought about nothing but the black Navigator on her way home from work, until her knuckles were white as she clutched the steering wheel. She'd decided to find out if the SUV was still there and hadn't wanted to wait until she got home.

She wasn't in a very sociable mood and hadn't planned to stay, but she hadn't been to the center in a few days, and its familiarity—the sound of the ping pong game, the smell of coffee from the kitchen—began to ease the tension in her shoulders and back, and slow the beat of her heart. She wheeled out from behind the front desk and rounded the corner to go to the game room when the muffled clocking of the ping pong ball came to an abrupt stop.

"*Piss* on my shoes!" Larry exclaimed. It was a phrase he used a lot in the game room.

Nicole laughed, and the hum of her electric wheelchair began to draw closer. Kaitlin met her at the game room doorway.

"Hey, what're you doing here?" Nicole asked with a grin.

"I just stopped to use the phone."

"Well, I hope you can stick around for awhile. This place has been dead all day."

Larry pulled up behind Nicole in his electric wheelchair. "Dead? What am I, chopped liver? I even let you win at ping pong."

He looked angry, but Kaitlin knew he wasn't. He always looked that way. His black and silver hair fell, thick and wiry, to his shoulder blades, but was disappearing on top. It framed a long, narrow face with permanent creases on the forehead and on each side of the mouth. A bushy mustache covered Larry's straight, thin upper lip, and gray stubble speckled his firm jaw. He had a stern face and seldom smiled—on those rare occasions, he smiled more with his eyes than his mouth—so to people who did not know him, he looked angry. But he wasn't. He had plenty of reason to be, though. Larry had left both his legs and his left arm in Vietnam. He wore a prosthetic arm with three chrome hooks that opened and closed at the end, but his body simply stopped at the waist, as if he were growing out of the seat of the wheelchair.

"*Hah*! You wish, old man," Nicole said. "You never let anybody win at ping pong in your life. You probably couldn't even let *Stevie* win at ping pong."

Stevie was a young man who frequented the center; he suffered from multiple sclerosis and had very little motor control.

"Maybe not," Larry said, winking at Kaitlin. "But I could whip him at Scrabble. That kid can't spell worth shit."

"Stay awhile and have some coffee, Kaitlin," Nicole said.

Kaitlin smiled. "Yeah, I could use a cup."

Kaitlin followed them down the corridor, the hum of their wheelchairs louder than they would have been had they not been the only three people in the center.

After the accident, Kaitlin's mother had tried to talk her into getting an electric wheelchair. "If you're going to be crippled," she'd said, "I see no point in making your life more difficult by having to wheel yourself around by hand. And *think* of how dirty your hands will be all the time."

Kaitlin had decided that if she'd lost her legs, she was going to make the best of her arms, and went with a manual wheelchair. As a result, her arms and shoulders were much stronger than they'd ever been before her accident. But her mother still worried that people would think they'd been unable to afford an electric wheelchair for their crippled daughter.

They went down the broad corridor to the kitchen, where Nicole filled a mug and set it on the table in front of Kaitlin. She complained about the weather as she poured a cup for Larry and one for herself, and Larry complained about people who complained about the weather.

Nicole was the first person Kaitlin had met at the center a little over a year and a half ago, the one who'd shown her around and introduced her to others. She was plump, with rosy, dimpled cheeks, blue eyes that were large and round, and blond hair in a short, almost boyish cut. At twenty-five, she was eight years Kaitlin's junior, but the age difference was unnoticeable. Nicole had a cheerful disposition—genuine, not forced or cloying—and she'd been exactly the kind of company Kaitlin had needed when she'd first come to the center, new to her wheelchair and unaccustomed to life without legs. They'd become almost inseparable for awhile. Kaitlin had feared she was going to scare Nicole off with her desperation to be with someone who knew exactly what her life was like, someone who was like her. But Nicole hadn't seemed to notice the desperation at all, and if she had, she'd never let on.

Nicole had been born with a severely malformed spine and had required a great deal of corrective surgery over time. When she was five years old, a mishap during one of those operations had paralyzed her from the waist down. In a lawsuit against the doctor and the hospital, Nicole's parents were awarded a sizeable amount of money. They'd put most of it away for their daughter's future, but some of it was used to start the Achievement Center. Now, Nicole practically ran the place.

Nicole and Larry were now Kaitlin's best friends in the world and she loved them dearly. Sometimes, though, she missed the friends she used to have. But she wasn't in their class anymore.

They still had legs and walked, and they didn't want to be reminded of how easily and quickly they could lose them.

"You look awful, Kaity," Nicole said as she poured some non-dairy creamer into her Beavis and Butthead coffee mug.

Larry chuckled, a low, quiet sound. "And you think nobody showed up today because of the weather. It's probably the way you're always flattering people like that, scares 'em away."

Nicole stuck her tongue out at him, then turned to Kaitlin again. "You feel okay?"

"I'm just tired. It was a long day. And I took this—" She screwed up her face and shook her head. "—I don't know, this *weird* call."

"Let's hear about it," Nicole said. "But first—" Her chair hummed as she wheeled away from the table, took a rectangular Tupperware container from the counter and put it on the table. "I made oatmeal cookies last night," she said, peeling off the blue lid. "Help yourself."

"Music," Larry muttered, steering his chair over to the boombox at the other end of the counter. "This joint needs a little music."

"Kaitlin's gonna tell us about her weird call," Nicole said. "We don't need music."

"Well, maybe you don't need music, but I need music."

Nicole and Larry were constantly snapping at each other, like a couple of people between whom little love was lost. But they had known each other for nearly a decade; Larry had been coming to the center longer than anyone besides Nicole, who had been an adolescent when they met. Sometimes they behaved and sounded like an old married couple, cozy and content in their bickering in spite of their considerable age difference. Kaitlin often suspected they were quietly in love with one another, but she'd never mentioned it to either of them.

Larry turned on the radio as Nicole turned to Kaitlin and said, "Okay, what about this call?"

Kaitlin lifted the mug to her lips and sipped her coffee, taking a moment to decide how to tell the story without sounding like a paranoid lunatic.

"—the house on Orchid Way in Redding, where she was found murdered with her twenty-one-year-old son," a male voice said on the radio.

Upon hearing those words, Kaitlin gasped and her arm jerked reflexively. The mug slipped from her fingers, hit the tabletop with a loud *clunk*, and hot black coffee splashed in all directions.

Nicole and Larry backed up in their chairs quickly, talking over each other— "Careful, careful, that's hot!" Nicole cried as Larry muttered, "Heads up, coffee on deck." —as the coffee spread over the tabletop and dribbled off the side in front of Nicole.

Kaitlin held up both hands and snapped, "Shhh, *quiet!*"

They fell silent and turned to Kaitlin, but she didn't notice because she was staring at the boombox on the counter.

"—as the murder investigation continues," the man on the radio said with finality. He paused, then: "Police in Tehama and Glenn Counties are still baffled by a serial rapist who is believed to be responsible for three murders. According to—"

"Damn." Kaitlin closed her eyes and sighed. She'd missed the story. She could feel her heart pounding in her throat. "Larry, can you find another station with local news?" she asked.

Without replying, he wheeled over to the counter.

"What's *wrong?*" Nicole asked in a whisper. "My God, you're so pale, you…you look like you're going to pass out."

Kaitlin shook her head as she watched Larry adjust the dial on the boombox. "No, I'm fine, Nicole, really." Her mouth was dry again and her voice hoarse. "I'm sorry about the mess. I'll clean it up in just a minute."

But Nicole had already retrieved a sponge and began soaking up the coffee that had pooled over the tabletop.

Larry found a station and turned up the volume. This time, the news was being read by a woman.

"—and with no witnesses or suspects, police have little to go on. We'll continue to report on this story as it develops."

As the news broke for a commercial, Kaitlin's shoulders sagged. "I missed it."

"Missed what?" Nicole asked. She finished cleaning up the

mess with some paper towels, then poured another cup of coffee for Kaitlin.

"Hey," Larry said. He sounded serious, so Kaitlin turned to him. "Are you in some kind of trouble?" His eyes were not smiling.

"I...I don't know," Kaitlin said wearily. "One minute, I think maybe I am. The next, I think maybe I'm just being paranoid."

Nicole took a cookie from the plastic container and handed it to Kaitlin. "Here. Have a cookie, and talk."

Kaitlin took a small bite of the cookie, but did not taste it. Before she'd heard the first incomplete news report on the radio—before the words "Orchid Way" and "murdered" had shot across the room and slapped her in the face—she had been about to tell Nicole and Larry of the upsetting call she'd taken at work, and of the conversation she'd had with her mother about it. But she hadn't decided whether or not to tell them about the Navigator parked across the street at work, or of the gnawing fear she was unable to shake. She was afraid even her friends would find it difficult to take her seriously about something so vague...so outrageous. Even worse, she was afraid they might find it funny.

But everything had changed within seconds. Someone had been murdered on Orchid Way...a woman and her twenty-one-year-old son. The son's age suited the voice of the young man Kaitlin had talked to...and he'd said he was visiting his mother.

Thinking about it made her feel ice cold and she leaned back in her chair and hugged herself. She had to tell someone. Even if she *was* crazy and the whole thing *was* a paranoid fantasy, she could not keep it to herself. So she told Nicole and Larry everything.

6

No one came into the center, so Kaitlin was able to tell her story uninterrupted. An occasional rumble of thunder punctuated her words; it was slowly growing closer, louder. Low chatter came from the talk show on the radio and lightning made the AM station crackle with static now and then.

"It sounds crazy, I know," Kaitlin said with a sigh when she was finished. "*I* sound crazy."

"I believe you," Larry said without hesitation.

Kaitlin wasn't surprised. Larry was quite the conspiracy theorist and had a reputation around the center for being a bit paranoid. Larry claimed that, along with his cigarettes, medication, paperback books and a couple handheld video games, he kept a loaded handgun in the leather pouch attached to the right side of his wheelchair. It was the subject of a lot of jokes around the center—many of which were made by Larry himself—but no one had ever actually seen the gun, and Kaitlin suspected it didn't exist. When Nicole was sixteen, her older brother, addicted to drugs and severely depressed, had shot himself in the head with their father's handgun. Nicole had found him. After that, the family refused to own guns any longer, and Nicole despised them. Kaitlin knew that if Larry *really* had a gun in his leather pouch, Nicole would have nothing to do with him.

Kaitlin cared for Larry very much…but armed or not, with his propensity to put stock in outlandish conspiracy theories—for example, Larry suspected El Niño was government created and controlled and part of a plan to cause just enough catastrophe and chaos to give the president reason to declare martial law—these kind of beliefs gave his acceptance of Kaitlin's story questionable value, and made Kaitlin question her own senses…something she'd already done a few times that day.

"I believe you, too," Nicole said, nodding. "I mean, that's really *scary*, hearing something like that on the telephone. But, um…maybe you're, uh…I don't know, maybe you're jumping just a little bit ahead of yourself…don't you think?" Nicole tucked her lower lip between her teeth and winced slightly, as if she expected Kaitlin to respond angrily.

"I know," Kaitlin said, nodding. "You're probably right. After that talk with my mother today…I guess I took what she said and ran with it. But *still*—" She pointed to the boombox. "—I heard him say a woman and her son had been murdered in a house on Orchid Way."

Larry nodded. "I heard it, too. Sounds to me like the guy you were talking to."

"But even so," Nicole said with more confidence, "I mean, even if you really heard that murder over the phone, there's just no *way* the killer could track you down. At least, not *that* fast. And why would he *want* to? I mean, you were just an operator on the phone, not an eyewitness. You didn't see his face, you don't know his name."

"He wouldn't know what the guy on the phone had *told* the person on the other end of the line," Larry said quietly.

Nicole turned to him slowly and spoke with warning in her voice: "Larry…"

"I'm serious," Larry said with little inflection. "The killer comes in…the young guy's on the phone. From what Kaitlin heard, it sounds like the mother was killed first, then the son. The killer knows the son was on the phone…he doesn't know who he was talking to, what he said. The killer thinks maybe the son called nine-one-one…that maybe he described the killer to the person on the other end of the line." He shrugged his right shoulder. "Who knows?"

Folding her arms on the tabletop, Nicole leaned forward and glared at him. She set her jaw and said firmly, "Even *so*, that doesn't *mean* anything. He wouldn't be able to *find* Kaitlin."

Kaitlin smirked. She could tell Nicole was trying to signal Larry to stop before he made Kaitlin feel even worse.

"Sure he could find her," Larry said.

Kaitlin's smirk crumbled and she turned to Larry. "Really? How?"

"You said you gave him your real name. Kaitlin. He knows you're a directory assistance operator. It wouldn't take much to find out if the directory assistance operators are local, or where the place is located. He drives down there, parks across the street, where you saw that black Lincoln Navigator. He sits there and writes down the license plate number of every car that drives out of that gated employee parking lot. Then maybe he—"

"Would you *stop* it, Larry!" Nicole snapped. She was serious, not joking around with him as usual.

Kaitlin held up a hand, palm toward Nicole, while she continued to look at Larry. "No, no, wait. I want to hear this. How would the license plate numbers help?"

"I don't know...maybe he's got a friend at the Motor Vehicle Department. Or maybe he wasn't writing them down. Maybe he wasn't writing anything down. Maybe he had a laptop computer. Maybe he was already *in* the Motor Vehicle Department's database and was just typing the license plate numbers in one after another, looking for one that belonged to a Kaitlin. A Kaitlin *anything*."

Kaitlin's lungs seemed to thicken, harden. Her chest felt as if a large hand were pressing on it hard and she took in a couple deep breaths, letting them out slowly, silently.

"But my first name, it's...unusual," she said. "Not common. Nobody ever knows how to spell it. How would he know from just hearing my name over the phone?"

"He wouldn't know," Larry said. "But if he had that laptop, all he'd need would be the numbers off your car's license plate. He'd keep typing them in, just waiting for a Kaitlin to pop up, and when it did...well, he'd um, you know...he'd have you."

"God*dammit*, Larry," Nicole said, slapping a palm onto the table, "why are you *doing* this?"

"I'm just going over possibilities," he said calmly.

"They're *not* possibilities," Nicole insisted. "Some guy goes into a house and kills a couple people while he's robbing the place...he's not gonna *do* all that shit! We're probably talking about some punk who didn't even graduate from high school!"

"How do you know it was a robbery?" he asked Nicole quietly. Larry asked the question casually, but with the hint of unspoken knowledge that lay beneath almost everything Larry said, as if he already had everything figured out, but was withholding information he considered too sensitive to reveal. His manner of speaking annoyed, even infuriated, a lot of people, who interpreted it as arrogance. But Kaitlin knew better. Larry would tell a dirty joke in the same tone of voice he'd use to explain how the government was going to use the Internet to eradicate the privacy of every American citizen online. It was just the way he talked, nothing more.

"Well, I...I *don't* know that," Nicole said.

"Maybe it wasn't just some punk," Larry said. "Maybe somebody *wanted* them dead for some reason. Maybe it was somebody who knew what he was doing, somebody with the ability and the resources to—"

"Okay, Agent Mulder, *okay*," Nicole interrupted. "I was just *assuming*."

Larry nodded. "Right. Speculating. That's all I'm doing. You said it'd be impossible for the killer to track Kaitlin down so quickly, and that he wouldn't have a reason to, anyway. I was just coming up with some ways he could do it, reasons he might have. Just speculating." He turned to Kaitlin. "I didn't mean to upset you. You know me. I love a mystery. Nicole's probably right. It was probably some addict robbing a house in a ritzy neighborhood to pay for his next high." His eyes smiled at her, and even his bushy mustache moved a bit.

Kaitlin took a couple more sips of coffee. "You didn't upset me, Larry. I've been doing that all by myself."

Larry went over to the boombox again. "There might be some news at the bottom of the hour," he said, turning the dial.

The sound of voices came from the front of the building and someone called, "Hey, anybody here?"

"Amazing," Nicole muttered. "Somebody actually showed up." She backed away from the table and wheeled out of the room, saying over her shoulder, "Have another cookie and I'll be back in a minute."

Loud, sharp static sputtered from the boombox as Larry tried to find a news broadcast. "If that lightning gets any closer, I'm not gonna be able to pick up anything."

"That's okay, Larry." Kaitlin leaned forward and took another cookie from the Tupperware container and took a big bite. "I'll catch the news on television tonight, or maybe in the car on the way home."

Larry came back to the table. "Look, I didn't mean to scare you, like I said before. But I don't blame you for being worried. These days, you should always be a little worried, even about something like that call you got. Because these days—" He shrugged his right shoulder. "—hell, these days, anything's possible. When I was your age, that little scenario I outlined a few minutes ago...that kinda thing was science fiction. It was *Mission: Impossible*. It was a good show, sure, but we all knew it was phony. But not anymore."

"So, you were serious? About that guy using license plate numbers and a laptop to find me?"

"I didn't say that's what he was *doing*. I just said it's *possible*. These days, there's no such thing as privacy or anonymity. Anybody who knows what he's doing and has a computer can find out everything there is to know about you with just your car's license number, or your driver's license number, your social security number, your name...and he can do it without asking you a single question, without ever meeting you."

Another sip of coffee did nothing to warm Kaitlin. As much as she fought it, an icy fear coiled around her and squeezed like a boa constrictor. "That's comforting," she said in a thin voice.

Larry shook his head slightly. "Oh, I doubt he's coming after you. That's the kind of stuff the big guys do. You know...government goons, corporate thugs, professional assassins. Nobody like that's gonna come to a redneck colony like Redding and kill some woman and her son. You're probably as safe as ever."

But all Kaitlin heard were the words "doubt" and "probably." They told her Larry was saying nothing *definite*...that he wasn't *sure* of anything he was saying. That was quite typical of Larry, and under normal circumstances, she would not have given it a second thought. But she was scared, and circumstances were not normal.

She finished her coffee and stared into the empty mug in front of her. She did not look forward to going home to her dark house. If she hadn't stopped at the center, she would have gotten home before sunset. Now it was dark, except for the lightning.

"I should go home," Kaitlin said. "Oscar's probably pacing by the door, waiting for me to feed him."

"I haven't been over there in awhile. Is that cat any fatter?"

"No, but he's still fat." She wheeled toward the kitchen door.

"Hey, Kaitlin, if you'd like, I can follow you home. Make sure everything's okay at your place, lock it up good and tight for you."

"Oh, you don't have to do that," she said with an embarrassed smile.

Nicole returned with a round, frost-crusted carton in her lap. "That was Marjie Leifer and her mother," she said. Marjie Leifer was a regular at the center, but didn't come by as often as she used to. She had fibromyalgia and her condition was worsening, making her unable to go out on her own anymore. "They were driving by and Marjie remembered I was here until closing tonight, so they went to that new ice cream place next door and brought me this. Anybody in the mood for some Oreo Cookie Crunch?"

"That sounds delicious," Kaitlin said, wheeling around her friend, "but I've got to go feed my cat."

Larry followed a few feet behind Kaitlin. "I'm gonna follow her home, Nicole, just to ease her mind, make sure nobody's dropped by her house."

"Really, Larry, you don't have to do that," Kaitlin said, turning to him. "I'll be fine."

"I've got an idea," Nicole said. She put the ice cream in the freezer, then turned to them. "I'm here for another…what?" She glanced at her watch. "Another hour and a half. And I might even close up early. I mean, nobody's gonna come out in this weather. Why don't Larry and I invite ourselves over to your place, Kaitlin? We can bring dinner. Pizza, Chinese, whatever you want. Watch a couple movies."

"Well, I *do* have the day off tomorrow."

"Great! I'll rent *The English Patient*. We can make fun of it till morning."

Kaitlin felt the muscles in her shoulders and neck relax with relief.

"I'll see you in awhile, then," she said, wheeling out of the kitchen and down the corridor.

Outside, with her umbrella up, she saw the clown again as she wheeled to her car. He was still pacing with the sandwich board. It was raining so hard now that the balloons drooped over the edge of the clown's umbrella. He stopped pacing when he saw Kaitlin and turned toward her.

Kaitlin backed out of the parking space and stopped at the lot's exit. The clown waved to her as lightning gave flickering glimpses of his grinning, eyeless, black-and-white face.

7

According to Kaitlin's street address and the prefix of her telephone number, she lived in Anderson, a small town ten miles south of Redding. She lived, in fact, between the city limits of both Redding and Anderson in an unincorporated area of Shasta County. Although her address was on Rivershore Road, her house was nearly half a mile south of her mailbox at the end of a gravel drive.

The house had been built by Kaitlin's grandfather right after he married her grandmother. It had a large fenced yard and was surrounded by fifteen acres of land, all of which had been left to Kaitlin by her grandmother.

Just short of reaching Kaitlin's house, the long drive forked at an enormous old oak tree. Beyond that tree was a triangle of thick green grass bordered by oleander bushes, and towering from within them, a cedar tree. To the left, the gravel road sloped downward sharply into a gully flanked by thick blackberry bushes, then worked gently upward and stretched across a flood plain to the bank of the Sacramento River. To the right, it wound into a circular drive in front of the house, with a detached two-car garage in the center. Kaitlin never parked her car in the garage, and her grandparents hadn't before her; it was so full of her grandparents' old belongings, and now boxes of her own stuff, there was no room for one car, let alone the two for which it had been built.

When Kaitlin was a little girl, her father had built a carport attached to the western side of the house so his parents could avoid rain and snow getting in and out of their car in the winter. It was just a few steps from the car to the door on the side of the house that led into the kitchen.

Behind the house, just beyond the back fence, the land dropped off into a pit of blackberry bushes and leveled out to become the flat green flood plain beside the Sacramento River. Every winter, the river rose enough to cover the plain, and where normally it was common to see deer grazing, ducks swam over the water on the plain and occasionally plunged beneath the surface for food.

The river had never come close to reaching the house before, but this year it had risen higher than Kaitlin had ever seen it in her life. The river had risen all the way to the top of the steep hill in the driveway's left fork. Blackberry bushes, ferns, and wild grapevines had disappeared beneath rapidly flowing water the color of mud that splashed against the trunks of tall oaks. The previous morning, Kaitlin had watched from the rear windows in her living room as one of the smaller trees on the plain below slowly succumbed to the river's angry current. It had tilted to the east very slowly as Kaitlin sipped her morning coffee and watched, and after an hour or so, fell over with a splash and floated away, its mud-crusted clot of roots bobbing in and out of sight in the roiling water.

Above the rising water and directly across the river from Kaitlin's house was *Osaka*, a Japanese restaurant. She'd eaten there once, years ago, and the food was terrible, but it remained popular because of the covered patio that overlooked the river. Sometimes, during the quiet summer months, the restaurant's music and laughter drifted across the river and could be heard through Kaitlin's open windows.

Like Kaitlin's, few of the houses on Rivershore could be seen from the road. Her nearest neighbor, a sixty-nine-year-old widow named Edith Costa, lived about three-quarters of a mile west of Kaitlin. Before the accident, Kaitlin used to walk through the woods that separated their houses and visit Mrs. Costa; now she rarely saw the woman.

The house itself was bigger on the inside than it looked from the outside. It was the house in which Kaitlin's father and his three brothers had grown up. It had a sunken living room with a beautiful view of the river, which was connected to a large dining room with a laundry room attached. There was a spacious kitchen with an island in the middle beneath two rows of hanging pots and pans. A hallway ran between the dining room and kitchen, leading to five bedrooms and three bathrooms. Only two of the rooms were still used as bedrooms, one for Kaitlin, and a guest room. In another was a desk and chair and a couple filing cabinets, where Kaitlin handled all her bills and taxes; the next was the smallest and she'd given it to Oscar, keeping his litterbox, food and water there; the third was a catch-all, a garage sale of this and that, where she put all the things that didn't belong anywhere else. The kitchen doorway and dining room doorway were equipped with sliding accordion-like partitions, each of which was equipped with a hook-and-eye latch that kept Oscar out whenever he needed keeping out.

But the house and everything in it had been built for and, until two years ago, occupied by people with functioning legs.

Upon learning of her paralysis, Kaitlin's father and brother immediately began working on the old house. All raised surfaces—tables, desks, counters, the island in the center of the kitchen—were lowered a few inches to make them accessible to Kaitlin in her wheelchair. All the steps outside the house, and the three steps leading down to the sunken living room inside, were converted to ramps. When Kaitlin returned from the hospital, everything seemed so *normal* to her that she almost hadn't noticed what her father and Mitch had done.

When she got home, Kaitlin decided she needed to clean up a bit before her friends arrived. Being confined to her wheelchair made it easy for her to forget that *other* people needed a place to sit now and then. She had a bad habit of using her sofa and chairs as tables, and mail and newspapers tended to stack up on them rather quickly. Nicole and Larry wouldn't be using the furniture, but it looked very messy and Kaitlin didn't like it.

She grabbed the remote, turned on the television, and clicked to a local channel. The evening news was just beginning. She chuckled as she picked up old newspapers and sales flyers and envelopes with Ed McMahon's splotchy picture on the front. Kaitlin didn't usually watch local news because it was impossible to take seriously. There was only one television station in Redding—KRCR, channel 7—and then there were four from Chico, a college town about seventy miles southeast. Each was a network affiliate, but all were laughably pathetic when it came to delivering the news, and channel 7, which trained pimply-skinned, voice-cracking beginners in the business, was the absolute worst. News readers stumbled over their words and read copy that was so often grammatically incorrect, it seemed to be written by school children.

But Kaitlin wasn't interested in the delivery. She was interested in learning more about the story she was pretending to ignore. She wanted to hear about the murder on Orchid Way. But she still feigned disinterest, even though she knew better, even though she was alone. She began to pick up the mess on the sofa and recliner without even looking at the news broadcast on the television. But when she heard the story she was waiting for, the story that had been eating at her, she stopped what she was doing and turned to the screen.

"Police are describing a double murder in an affluent Redding neighborhood as a robbery gone awry." In his early twenties, skinny, with a ghost of a mustache and a voice that sounded as if he were undergoing the onset of puberty, the newscaster's pronunciation of the word "awry" rhymed with "bowery." "Fifty-two-year-old Emily Nevitt and her twenty-one-year-old son Myron were shot to death in Nevitt's home on Orchid Way."

"*Shot* to death?" Kaitlin asked the television. "There were no gunshots!"

"Police say the killer ransacked the house, but have not yet determined what was stolen. No witnesses have come forward, but police believe the killer acted alone. There are still no suspects, and police are investigating their con…uh…investi—no, wait…police are *continuing* their *investigation*."

Kaitlin relaxed in her chair as relief moved through her slowly, as if it had been injected intravenously. So it *was* only a robbery, as Nicole had speculated. But why hadn't she heard any gunshots? She thought the story was over, but—

"Emily and Myron Nevitt are survived by well-known union figure Benjamin Nevitt, Emily's ex-husband and Myron's father. Benjamin Nevitt has served as a communications special for…er, *specialist* for the AFL-CIO since 1976, and Chief of Communications since 1988. Anyone who may have information about the double murder is urged to call the Redding Police Department."

"Communications specialist?" Kaitlin muttered as the newscaster moved on to the next story. "What's a communications specialist?"

"North Valley law enforcement officials believe that the serial rapist, who has been linked to three murders in Tehama County, has struck for the second time in Glenn County. Glenn County Sheriff—"

She turned down the volume. The knot that had been in her stomach most of the day unraveled a bit. But Kaitlin remained puzzled by the fact that Emily and Myron Nevitt had been shot to death. She knew what gunshots sounded like; she went target shooting with her father fairly regularly. She'd heard no gunshots during that call. Aside from the voices and the breaking glass and what she thought had been the sound of the young man falling to the floor, the only thing she'd heard had been thumping…that odd thumping.

As she cleaned up the living room, Kaitlin heard Oscar wheezing somewhere nearby, probably asleep. While most cats are easily stirred from sleep, Oscar slept as if dead, usually sprawled on his back with legs pointing in four directions, wheezing almost to the point of snoring. The vacuum cleaner, loud music pounding from the stereo speakers…nothing disturbed him. When Oscar *did* wake up, it was slowly and unwillingly; he squinted and scowled and walked unsteadily for the first few minutes, refusing to let anyone pet him or pick him up.

She followed the sound of Oscar's wheezing until she determined he was under the small coffee table before the sofa. Even as great cracks of thunder rattled the window panes—enough to make most cats scramble in a panic—Oscar slept. He *might* wake up when Nicole and Larry arrived, because he loved chewing on the hands and feet of visitors, but Kaitlin doubted it.

Finished in the living room, she went to the kitchen and opened the refrigerator. She groaned when she saw that she was out of soft drinks. She didn't even have any beer. If Nicole and Larry were going to bring the food and the movies, the least Kaitlin could do was provide the drinks.

Bridge Market wasn't far. It was more expensive than Safeway but much closer, so she wouldn't have to drive across the river and into Anderson.

In the car, the windshield wipers had a difficult time keeping up with the rain. Kaitlin drove slowly through large puddles that were growing larger, threatening to flood her long driveway and make it impassable.

A barn owl flew from a tree beside the driveway and swooped low out of the darkness as it flew over the car. It made a shrill, screeching chirp as it passed through the glow of the headlights, flapping its enormous wings once.

Kaitlin stopped as a fat possum waddled across the driveway in front of her, glancing at her once with blood-red eyes. Soaked from the rain and dragging a long, pink, fleshy tail, it looked more like a giant rat slinking through the night than a possum.

For years, Kaitlin had been telling herself to invest in a good camera and learn to take photographs at night. After the sun went down, the land around her house came alive with nocturnal wildlife.

She turned right on Rivershore, then left on Bridge Road, which took her up a steep hill. In the small market four miles from her house, she got a twelve-pack of Diet Dr. Pepper, a six-pack of Bud, and a couple packs of Benson and Hedges Lights for herself.

Kaitlin had stopped smoking about six years ago, and had nearly pulled her own hair out in the process. During her initial depression after the accident, she'd taken the habit up again. Now she regretted it. Lately, she'd been thinking about stopping again. She didn't look forward to the withdrawals, but she was getting tired of the coughing fits in the morning, and the instant panic she felt when she realized, in the middle of the night, that she had only one cigarette left in the house. But there was something else. For as long as she could remember, Kaitlin had felt she had little control over her life. Everyone felt that way as children and teenagers, of course, but she'd still felt that way as an adult. She couldn't even steer a conversation with her mother in the direction she wanted it to go. After the accident, though, she'd learned what true helplessness was really like. Then, unable to walk, confined to a wheelchair, she'd handed over one of the few slivers of control she had left to a habit that determined how she spent a good deal of her money, often made her irritable between breaks at work, occasionally burned holes in her clothes and furniture, and ultimately would most likely give her cancer.

On the way home from the market, Kaitlin thought about kicking the habit. She had two days off in a row next week; maybe she'd start then. Last time, she'd used nicotine patches and gum, and to work off the tension brought on by withdrawals, she'd jogged herself silly. This time would be different. She wouldn't use patches or gum, and...jogging was definitely out. Last time, quitting had been a miserable experience with no payoff, because even after the worst of it was behind her, she still missed smoking. But Kaitlin didn't think it would be so bad this time, because instead of giving something up, she saw it as taking something back. This time, the payoff would be regaining that little bit of lost control.

When she turned back onto Rivershore, Kaitlin saw taillights up ahead. She slowed down as she neared the vehicle because, although its brake lights weren't on, it was moving very slowly. It was large and dark, a van or...perhaps a sports utility vehicle. The flickering glow of lightning fell on its black surface and Kaitlin's breath caught in her throat like a fishbone when she saw the shiny chrome letters on the rear of the vehicle ahead of her:

NAVIGATOR.

8

"Oh, my God," Kaitlin murmured.
What was it doing *here*? So close to her *house*?
Maybe it's not the same one, she thought.

"Of *course* it's the same one," she whispered tremulously. Kaitlin was familiar with the vehicles owned by the residents on Rivershore, and no one had a Lincoln Navigator.

It's going so slow...maybe it's a visitor...someone from out of town, looking for a friend's address.

But even as she thought it, Kaitlin knew it wasn't true. At least, it wasn't someone looking for a *friend's* address...it was someone looking for *her* address...the man in the baseball cap...with a laptop, just like Larry had said earlier that evening at the center.

The Navigator almost came to a complete stop at Kaitlin's driveway, across from her barn-shaped mailbox.

Kaitlin *did* stop, about fifty feet behind the Navigator, because she didn't trust her driving. Her palms were sweaty and sticky, her chest constricted, and her heart frantic. She held her breath a moment, certain he would turn left into her driveway and head for her house, looking for her, intending to silence her just in case she had something to say about him, about what he'd done that morning on Orchid Way.

The Navigator passed Kaitlin's driveway and picked up speed. It went up the hill beyond her mailbox and disappeared over the crest.

Kaitlin held the brake, even after the Navigator was gone, wondering if he was making a U-turn up there, or pulling into someone's driveway to turn around. She expected the glow of the Navigator's headlights to ooze over the top of the hill at any moment.

Instead, headlights appeared in the rearview mirror, tearing her from her thoughts and prompting her to drive ahead.

Call the police, she told herself silently.

She didn't wait to get to the house. As Kaitlin turned into her driveway with one hand on the wheel, she leaned over, opened the glove compartment, and removed her cell phone with the other.

"Nine-one-one," a female voice said. "What is your emergency?"

Kaitlin had to raise her voice to be heard above the car's engine and the drumming of the rain on the roof. "I'm, uh...I-I have an...um, I have..."

She had what? What did she have? She'd been about to say "an intruder," but that wasn't the case. A word danced around just out of her reach, a sensational word, something from tabloids and TV movies. She groped for it, trying to remember...

"A *stalker*," she said. "I-I think I have a stalker."

"Are you in trouble right now?" the woman asked.

A hollow *beep* sounded intermittently, indicating that the call was being recorded.

"I just saw him. Near my house. He, uh...he was looking at my mailbox. Looking for my address."

Kaitlin looked in her rearview mirror. No lights.

"Are...are you in your house now?" The operator sounded mildly confused.

"No, I'm in my car."

Thunder cracked and roared overhead, and a moment later, lightning flashed, creating a wave of hissing static on the cell phone. The nine-one-one operator said something, but her words were swallowed up.

"I'm sorry, what did you say?"

"I said, you're on a cell phone." It wasn't a question.

"Yes. I went to the store, and when I came back, I saw him just outside my driveway."

"What was he driving?"

"A black Lincoln Navigator. New."

"You've seen him before?"

"Yes."

Kaitlin pulled around the garage and parked beneath the carport. She turned in the seat to look out the rear window, up the driveway. Still no lights. But her pounding heart was not getting the message.

"Can you see him now?"

"Well...no, but—" She stopped and waited as lightning created more crackling static on the cell phone. "But he's not far away. He could be at the other end of my driveway, for all I know."

"Your name, ma'am?"

Kaitlin gave her name and address and told the operator exactly where her driveway was on Rivershore.

"I'll send a deputy out there right away," the operator said. "Are you back in your house?"

"No, but I'm going."

"Do you want me to stay on the line with you?"

"No, that's all right. Just get somebody out here."

As she pulled her chair out of the backseat and got into it, Kaitlin kept looking over her shoulder up the driveway, expecting to see lights…or the black hulking shape of the Navigator moving through the rainy darkness *without* lights.

In the kitchen, she didn't bother putting the soda or beer in the refrigerator, just put them on the counter. Without coming to a full stop, she hung her purse on its brass hook at the end of the kitchen counter, then turned right out of the kitchen, going down the hall. She clicked on the overhead light as she went into her bedroom and opened the drawer of the nightstand beside her bed. Kaitlin removed from the drawer a Smith & Wesson .40 caliber semiautomatic handgun.

Her father had given her the gun seven years ago when she'd first moved into her grandmother's house. He hadn't liked the idea of her living alone in a remote area where the neighbors were so far apart. He'd done some hunting when Kaitlin was a little girl and had several rifles as well as handguns, but for the past dozen years, he'd been doing all his shooting at his gun club's shooting range. When he gave Kaitlin the Smith & Wesson, he'd shown her how to clean it and had taken her to the range to teach her how to shoot it. She'd enjoyed it so much that she still went to the range with him every few weeks to shoot some of his guns as well as her own.

When she wasn't target shooting, the handgun was kept in her nightstand drawer. She had never used it for its intended purpose—self-defense—and had never thought she'd need to. When her father had given her the gun, Kaitlin thought he was being overprotective, but had accepted it graciously to keep him from worrying. She was sure the chances of ever needing a gun to defend herself were extremely slim, and found the idea of it rather silly.

Now, she whispered a heartfelt, "Thank you, Daddy," as she looked the gun over. There was a round in the chamber and a full magazine. She closed the drawer, put the gun in her lap, then made sure the bedroom's two windows were closed and locked. Her hands trembled and she felt unnaturally cold as she went through the entire house, checking every window as thunder cracked and lightning flashed through the panes. The lights fluttered, and for a moment, Kaitlin froze, thinking they were going to blink out, but they remained on. To keep her mind off her fear, Kaitlin thought about what she was going to tell the deputy Sheriff when he arrived.

It wasn't hard to guess what kind of reaction she would get if she told him about everything…the disturbing call that morning, the appearance of the Navigator on Rivershore that evening, and everything in between. He would decide she was crazy before she got halfway through the story. She would have to keep it simple, tell him just enough to make him nod knowingly, as if he's seen it all before. All she wanted was for him to show up, hang around for a bit, maybe take a look around outside. She hoped that the presence of a police officer would make the driver of the Navigator decide to go away.

When she finished checking the windows, Kaitlin went into the kitchen and started putting the cans of beer and soda into the refrigerator. Her hands were still trembling, but not as badly as before. Knowing a deputy was on his way was reassuring.

A wind had begun to blow outside, slapping rain against windowpanes and driving Kaitlin's collection of wind chimes hanging all around the front porch wild. The small ones tinkled and rang madly, while the large ones gonged repeatedly like broken grandfather clocks. They were loud enough to make her miss the doorbell the first time it chimed, but she heard the second ring. Before going to the living room to answer the door, she took the gun from her lap and tucked it out of sight between her right hip and the side of the wheelchair. She wasn't in the mood for a lecture on gun safety.

The Sheriff's deputy wore a large dark green Gore-Tex raincoat over his khaki uniform, and a khaki baseball cap with the logo of the Shasta County Sheriff Department on the front. It was hard to tell beneath the raincoat, but he seemed to be a bulky man, with a broad, ruddy face and wire-rimmed glasses. He introduced himself as Deputy Morgan and apologized for dripping on her living room carpet.

"Now, you have a...stalker?" he asked. "Is that right, Miss Callahan?"

"Yes. Well, I...I guess that's the right word." She chuckled nervously. "Someone is following me. Watching me. Some guy."

"Do you know him?"

"No."

"What makes you think he's following you?"

"Today, he was parked across the street from where I work. In a Lincoln Navigator."

Deputy Morgan reached beneath his raincoat and produced a pad and pen. "What color was the Navigator?" he asked, writing.

"Black. And it was parked in a no parking zone. He was watching our parking lot from there. Watching *me*. As I left."

"Where do you work?"

She told him.

"He followed you?"

"Well, I didn't think so at first. But then I went to the store this evening—just to Bridge Market up the hill—and when I came back, there he was again on Rivershore. He slowed way down at my driveway, like he was...checking the address on the mailbox, looking for my name, I don't know."

"You saw him?"

"Yes, I was just a little ways behind him."

"You saw the driver?"

"Well, I...didn't actually see the driver. I was behind him."

"So all you saw was the back of a Lincoln Navigator. This was after dark?"

"Yes, just a half hour ago."

"Are you sure it was black?"

She nodded. "Yes, I'm sure of that."

"Did you get the license number?"

Kaitlin opened her mouth to reply, but instead, she closed her eyes tightly, pressed her right hand to her forehead, and let a hissing breath out through clenched teeth.

"No, I didn't," she said quietly. "Damn, I wasn't *thinking*." She dropped her hand and looked up at him again, sighing. "It's been, um...a bad day."

"I'm sorry to hear that. Have you been getting phone calls from this guy? Any letters or gifts?"

"No."

"What's he look like?"

"Well, I didn't get a very *close* look at him, but...he wore a baseball cap. New York Yankees, dark blue. And he had a mustache, dark. And glasses. Wire-rimmed, not too different from yours."

"That's all you remember?"

"No, that's all I *saw*."

"Has he approached any of your friends or coworkers and asked questions about you?"

"Um, no, not that I know of."

"How long has this guy been following you around?"

"Oh, it just started today."

His eyebrows popped up. "You mean, this afternoon at work...that was the first time you saw him?"

Kaitlin nodded.

"And this evening...about half an hour ago...that was the only *other* time you saw—uh, *think* you saw him?"

Kaitlin didn't like his tone. He suddenly seemed doubtful.

"Well, yes," she said, "but I'm sure it was the same guy. He practically came to a stop at my driveway. I thought he was going to turn in for a second."

Deputy Morgan sighed as he flipped his notebook closed and tucked it and his pen beneath his raincoat.

"You don't believe me," Kaitlin said flatly.

"It's not that I don't *believe* you, Miss Callahan. It's just that...I thought you said you had a *stalker*."

She shrugged. "Only because I didn't know what *else* to call him."

"Well, if it's anything, it's not a stalker. Not yet, anyway. Not if it just started this afternoon."

"What do you mean?"

"Look, I don't doubt you saw some guy parked across the street in a Lincoln Navigator at work this afternoon. But he didn't follow you, correct?"

"He didn't *seem* to—"

"When you left the parking lot, did you see him pull away from the curb and follow you?"

After a moment, she shook her head slowly, averting her eyes. "No...I didn't *see* him follow me."

"Okay. He was there, and maybe it was a no parking zone, but he didn't *follow* you. Then, this evening, you say you think you saw a Lincoln Navigator when you—"

"I *did* see it!" Kaitlin insisted.

Deputy Morgan held up a hand and nodded slowly, looking down at her sympathetically. "I'm sure you did, Miss Callahan, I don't doubt that. But you didn't see *him*. You don't know if it was the same guy, and unless there was some distinguishing characteristic about that Navigator that you haven't told me about, you really can't be sure it was the same one. Let's face it, Miss Callahan, there's more than one Lincoln Navigator out there."

Kaitlin reached up and rubbed her right temple hard with her fingertips. There was a headache lurking somewhere in the distance; it was taking its time, but it would arrive sooner or later. "So I *don't* have a stalker."

"I didn't say that. Not *exactly*. If this guy in the baseball cap *does* follow you around, if you *see* him following you around...if he calls you repeatedly, sends you letters or gifts, harasses you, threatens you in any way...*then* you have a stalker."

"But until that happens, I take it there's nothing you can do for me."

Deputy Morgan's voice lowered slightly and took on a kind, warm tone. "Hey, look, Miss Callahan, I don't blame you for being scared. You did the right thing by calling nine-one-one. I'm just telling you how *I* have to look at this. I have to do things in a certain way, and right now...no, there's really nothing I can do. But you know what? I wouldn't be a bit surprised if it *was* the same guy you saw this afternoon. And if you see him again, I want you to *call* again, okay? Right away, don't hesitate. Will you do that?"

She smiled slightly and nodded.

"For now, I'll drive along Rivershore, then up Cedar Road and back down Bridge, see if I can find somebody hanging around in a Navigator. I'm afraid that's the most I can do for now."

"Thank you," Kaitlin said sincerely. "I really appreciate it."

He pulled the door open, then pushed through the screen door, saying, "Now you remember what I said. If he shows up again, if he starts bothering you, don't hesitate to call. I mean it. It's always better to be safe, even if you're mistaken."

"I will. Thank you."

The wind chimes continued to tinkle and gong outside as Kaitlin locked the screen, then closed and locked the door. Her insides were shriveled with embarrassment as she went to her bedroom. She kept shaking her head and repeating, "Idiot…idiot…you idiot…" as she changed into a teal sweatshirt and dark blue sweatpants. In the kitchen, she took a Diet Dr. Pepper from the refrigerator and her cigarettes from her purse.

With the can of soda held between her thighs, Kaitlin wheeled back to the living room. She turned off the overhead light, flipped on the porch light for Nicole and Larry, and turned on the four lamps in the room, ending with the Tiffany-style lamp on the sofa's end table, her usual sitting spot. She placed her cigarettes on the end table next to the lighter and television remote, popped the can of soda and took a swallow, then picked up the remote and began clicking through the channels.

Kaitlin was confused. Maybe it *hadn't* been the same Navigator. According to the news, the woman and her son had been shot to death, but Kaitlin had not heard gunshots over the phone, so…maybe those weren't even the same *people*.

"You're such a wimp," she muttered to herself as she hit the button on the remote hard with her thumb. For the moment, she hated herself for being such a coward, for being so paranoid, for calling nine-one-one, for having a gun tucked down beside her in the chair.

She was glad her mother hadn't been around to see it. If she had, Kaitlin would never hear the end of it.

She lit a cigarette and decided to make a fire in the fireplace.

9

Beneath the sounds of the windblown chimes on the front porch, Kaitlin heard the discordant hums of two electronic wheelchairs coming up the concrete path outside, approaching the front door. She started to wheel to the front door with the television remote in her lap, but backed up when she remembered the gun in the chair beside her. Nicole didn't know she owned a gun, and Kaitlin knew how her friend would react if she found out. She opened the drawer in the end table. It was full of magazines, so she took a few out and tossed them onto the sofa, then set the gun in their place and closed the drawer. The doorbell rang while she was on her way to answer it.

Kaitlin opened the front door to a cacophony of rain, wind, thunder, and chimes. Nicole and Larry were on the covered porch, closing their umbrellas.

"I have good news!" Nicole declared as Kaitlin unlocked the screen door.

"What's that?" Kaitlin asked.

"I didn't bring *The English Patient*."

"Thank God." Kaitlin pushed the screen door open until Larry caught it, then she backed up and let them come in. Larry was the last to come in and closed and locked the door.

A fire was crackling and popping in the fireplace and the living room was just beginning to feel a bit toasty.

"You didn't say anything about *gunshots*," Larry said to Kaitlin as he rolled past her.

"What?" she asked.

"Turn on CNN," Larry said as he wheeled into the room. He sounded serious.

Nicole tilted her head back and rolled her eyes. "Oh, come *on*, Larry, *please*, can't we just relax and have some fun this evening?" In her lap, she held two large pizza boxes and a blue plastic bag with a local video store's logo on the side. "I just wanna pig out and watch some funny movies, okay?"

"Turn on CNN," he said again, looking around frantically for the remote.

"I've got it," Kaitlin said. She tossed the remote and he caught it. She turned to Nicole and said, "Let me take those." She put the pizza boxes on the coffee table and set the bag of videos beside them. "I'll get some plates and napkins. What do you want to drink? I've got Budweiser and Diet Dr. Pepper."

Nicole asked for a Budweiser and Larry, though very distracted, asked for a Dr. Pepper.

As Kaitlin went to the kitchen, she heard them arguing quietly. She realized she was feeling tense again, and tried to push it away, bury it with a few deep, relaxing breaths. Nicole and Larry were still at it when she came back with three plates, a stack of napkins, and their drinks.

"Hey, what's the problem, you guys?" she asked jovially as she handed out the drinks. She went to the coffee table and set down the plates and napkins. "You sound like a Democrat and a Republican the day before an election, for God's sake." She opened the pizza boxes—one Hawaiian and one combo with anchovies, which she and Nicole loved—and started placing slices onto the plates. The pizzas smelled delicious and made Kaitlin suddenly realize how hungry she was.

"We heard the story on the radio," Larry said in his usual quiet monotone. "Nicole doesn't want me to talk about it because she thinks it'll upset you, but I think, um—" He stopped to clear his throat. "—I think we *should* talk about it."

Her stomach filled with ice as she turned to him. His tone was far more serious than usual, more than his regular monotone. "What? Why do you say that?"

"It's on CNN," Larry said, gesturing toward the television with his prosthetic arm.

She turned to the television and saw a man she'd never seen before walking from the left side of the screen to the right in an expensive suit, smiling and nodding casually, aloofly at reporters who were barking questions. He was in his late fifties, a fit man with a full head of gray hair shot with black strands, a square jaw, and a nose that had been broken once long ago and ended in a bulbous knob. At the bottom of the screen:

BENJAMIN NEVITT CNN
Communications Specialist AFL-CIO August 16, 1995

The windows lit up with lightning. The lights flickered and the television blinked for a moment.

"That man's ex-wife was the woman you heard being murdered," Larry said.

"Emily Nevitt and her son Myron," Kaitlin said quietly, nodding. "I saw it on the news tonight." When Larry started to speak again she held up a hand to quiet him so she could listen to the television.

"—Nevitt, who divides his time between New York and Washington, D.C., has refused to speak to reporters," a female voice was saying over the file footage. "A spokesman for Nevitt says a statement will be released soon." The screen switched to two photographs against a blue background, one of a tired-looking middle-aged blond woman and a young man with a splotchy mustache and goatee. "Police in Redding, California say the murders are the result of a robbery gone wrong. So far, there are no witnesses and no suspects." The female newscaster appeared on the screen and went on to the next story.

Kaitlin frowned. "Why is this on CNN?"

"Because Nevitt's a national figure," Larry replied. "You don't know who he is?"

Kaitlin turned to him. "Yeah. He's a communications specialist for the AFL-CIO. I know what the AFL-CIO is, but…what the hell is a communications specialist?" In her stomach, the knot began to retie itself. She wasn't sure she wanted to hear anything Larry had to say. She turned back to the pizzas and continued putting slices on the plates.

"'Communications specialist' is a euphemism," Larry said. "Kind of like 'sanitation engineer' or 'ethnic cleansing.' Nevitt worked in the union business all his adult life, and he's been in this position since seventy-six. Nobody says it out loud, but he's their J. Edgar Hoover. The keeper of their secrets. His job is to use his department to spy on everybody. I mean everybody. People in power, people they might be able to use. Politicians, corporate heads, you name it. But he also digs up dirt on union leaders, just in case they get out of line. He knows about skeletons in people's closets *they* didn't even know were there. In other words, he's, uh, not exactly the most popular guy at the union Christmas party, if you know what I mean. But everybody's nice to him, for the obvious reason. He's never the focus of a story, but always around, in the background. If the unions are in the news, so is Nevitt, in one way or another."

"He's the focus of a story *now*," Nicole said, cracking her beer.

Larry nodded. "Yeah, and he doesn't seem too comfortable with it, either." He turned to Kaitlin, who was still frowning. "You didn't say anything about hearing gunshots...did you?"

"No, because I *didn't* hear gunshots." She rubbed her eyes with thumb and forefinger. "This whole thing is giving me a headache," she muttered. She told them she'd seen the Navigator—or *a* Navigator—on Rivershore that evening, and about her chat with Deputy Morgan. "Now I can't decide whether to be afraid or just *confused*. A young guy and his mother turn up dead on Orchid Way, and they sound a *lot* like the young guy I talked to, who was visiting his mother on Orchid Way. But they were *shot* to death, and I didn't *hear* gunshots. And if it was just a botched robbery, why would the guy be coming after me? How could he *find* me like that? So *fast*?" She looked at Larry. "You said only the *big* guys could do that."

He nudged at his mustache with the knuckle of his forefinger. "That, uh...that's what I'm trying to tell you, Kaitlin. Benjamin Nevitt *is* one of the big guys. And he only deals with *other* big guys."

The pizzas no longer smelled appetizing, and the grumbling of hunger in Kaitlin's stomach quickly became a nervous churning. She wheeled over to the end table, shook a cigarette from her pack and lit up. Holding the cigarette between the first two fingers of her right hand, she realized she was trembling again. After blowing the smoke from her lungs explosively, she said, "You mean...are you saying that...that this guy *had* his ex-wife and son murdered?"

"No, I'm not saying that," Larry said, shaking his head. "Well, I...I don't know, really. Maybe he *did*. Or maybe it's somebody's way of sending him a strong message. What I *am* saying is that anything's possible with people like this."

"What about the gunshots I didn't hear?" Kaitlin asked.

Larry pulled at his mustache for a moment, then scratched his head with the three hooks on the end of his prosthetic arm. "Tell me *exactly* what you heard again."

Kaitlin took another drag on her cigarette and let the smoke out with a sigh.

Nicole's wheelchair whirred as she went over to the coffee table. "I hope nobody minds, but I'm starving and I'm gonna eat." She picked up a napkin and a plate with three slices on it.

"Okay," Kaitlin said, closing her eyes, thinking. "We were talking, then all of a sudden, there was this noise. And then a scream. A really awful scream. No. Uh...no, wait, just before the scream, I heard glass shattering somewhere, like...like maybe in the next room, or something. Then, after the scream—"

"Hold it," Larry said. "That first sound...what was it?"

Kaitlin opened her eyes. "I don't know."

"What did it sound like?"

"It was a...a thump. Like somebody hitting a pillow with...I don't know, with a heavy stick, or something. After the woman screamed, she cried out, 'No!' but it was long and drawn out. Horrible, like she was...well, like someone was killing her. Then the guy on the phone, it sounded like he was running with the receiver, calling out to his mom. There was more screaming, more glass breaking, and then the guy said, 'Jesus!' a couple times. Then I heard that thump again. Twice, or maybe...no, it was three times. Once, and then two more times, right together, one right after the other. He dropped the receiver then. At least, it sounded like he—"

"Gunshots," Larry mumbled.

"What?" Kaitlin asked.

"Those were gunshots you heard."

She shook her head. "Oh, no. I'd recognize gunshots, even over the phone. They didn't sound at all like—" She stopped and blinked her eyes a few times as she stared at Larry, knowing what he was going to say as his lips parted.

"He used a silencer. Those thumps you heard were gunshots...from a gun equipped with a silencer."

Kaitlin closed her mouth and swallowed hard. Her mouth felt dry so she picked up her soda and finished it off with a few gulps.

Nicole rolled her eyes. "Larry, for crying out loud, this is *Redding*. People who rob houses in this town don't go around using *silencers*."

He nodded very slowly. "My point exactly."

Kaitlin stared at Larry for a long moment as Nicole turned slowly to look at her.

"It was made to *look* like a robbery," Kaitlin said quietly, nearly whispering.

Larry nodded. "For the police. The press. But I bet Benjamin Nevitt knows better. Either way...if he had it done or somebody did it to tell him something...he knows better." His voice became even more quiet, even more serious. "Listen to me, Kaitlin. If this guy thinks you know something, he won't stop until he finds you."

Nicole's head turned back and forth between them, her mouth open. "You mean...you mean this is *real*? All this stuff you've been talking about?"

"No," Larry replied abruptly, sarcastically, "we're writing a novel together."

"Oh, screw you," Nicole snapped. "How am I supposed to know when you're serious? You're so full of shit, I *never* take you seriously." She turned back to the coffee table and put her plate down, then went to Kaitlin's side. "Look, Kaity, maybe, um...I don't know, maybe you should go stay with your parents for awhile. You think?"

"No," Larry said. "No, I think you should call the police again. Tell them everything this time."

"She already talked to a cop," Nicole snapped. "If she goes back with a different story, they'll think—"

SLIVERS OF BONE

"They'll understand if she just—"

"They'll think she's *nuts*," Nicole continued. "They'd never believe her after—"

"Goddammit, will you shut *up!*" Larry shouted.

Nicole stared at him with a slack jaw.

Kaitlin flinched and her eyes widened. There was nothing playful about the bickering between her friends now, and she'd never heard Larry shout before, never heard him raise his voice above his usual monotone. It was startling and ugly, and it made Kaitlin realize, quite suddenly, that things were very serious.

The three of them fell into an awkward silence that seemed to go on forever. The television screen turned a silent blue when the cable feed was cut off, and the lights flickered again.

Larry slipped a hand into his leather pouch, removed a cigarette pack, and found it empty. He crushed it in his fist, reached back into the pouch, and fished around.

"Want one of mine?" Kaitlin asked.

"No. I've got a pack in the car. I'll get it in a minute." He turned to Nicole and said, "I'm sorry. Really. I'm just a little tense right now, that's all." He turned to Kaitlin. "Because I think you might be in some serious trouble. And I really think you should—"

The lights went out.

The three of them spoke at once, Kaitlin saying, "Oh, *great*," and Nicole saying, "Goddammit," and Larry saying, "Fuck me in the neck."

The only light in the room—in the entire house—came from the fireplace, a dance of orange that flowed liquidly over the hardwood floor and the rug, reaching Kaitlin and her friends as a soft, pulsing glow.

"You got any flashlights?" Larry asked.

Kaitlin was already wheeling across the room. "Right here," she said, picking up the long black Maglite that had been leaning in the corner by the front door. She clicked it on and turned to Nicole and Larry. "And I've got candles in the kitchen."

"I've got a great battery-operated lantern in the car," Larry said, humming toward the door. "I was gonna get my cigarettes, anyway."

"You're *not* going out *there*," Nicole said. "Not *now*, not after all that shit you just said!"

Larry turned his chair toward her and smiled. "Hey, we're safe right now. The cop left just before we arrived. He told Kaitlin he was gonna drive around awhile, see what he could see. That guy's not gonna move in right *now*, trust me. He made the one today look like a robbery, so he's gonna want to make this look like something else, too. Something it isn't. So he's sure not gonna come storming in right after a cop's been here looking around." He headed for the door again, saying, "I'll be right back."

"I'll go get the candles," Kaitlin said, putting the flashlight in her lap, pointing ahead of her, as she started out of the living room.

"You're not going to leave me here in the dark!" Nicole said. "I won't stay here alone!"

Larry left the house, leaving the front door open behind him. "You can close that!" he called back.

Kaitlin backed up and closed the front door, then turned to Nicole. "It's not that dark," she said.

"There are no *lights*!" Nicole replied, spreading her arms wide.

"Okay," Kaitlin said, wheeling toward her friend. She handed the flashlight over to Nicole. "Take this. I know my way around, and there's another flashlight in the kitchen."

Nicole made a noise that was somewhere between a groan and a sigh. "Thank you, Kaity, *so* much."

Kaitlin turned and left the living room, wheeling up the small ramp that led to the dining room…which was as black as the night outside. Slowly but smoothly, she made her way through the dining room, past the large window to her right which, under normal circumstances, would be filled with the glow of the porch light, and across the hall, into the kitchen. The flashlight was just inside the kitchen door, standing upright on the floor, another long Maglite. She clicked on the flashlight, put it in her lap facing forward, and went to the hutch that held her grandmother's best dishes. She opened one of the drawers and removed six long, white candles. She closed the drawer, put the candles in her lap, and opened another drawer. Shuffling around in the drawer, she found the small pewter candleholders she'd never used before. Each had a round, ring-like handle on the side and a flat, round base on the bottom. She put six of them in her lap, closed the drawer, then left the kitchen.

In the dining room, she heard the hum of Larry's wheelchair just outside the window.

"Okay," she said, crossing the dining room toward the living room doorway, "I've got six candles and we've got matches by the fireplace." The glow of the fire bled through the living room doorway and into the dining room, providing sufficient light for her, so she turned off the flashlight in her lap.

As Kaitlin neared the doorway, she heard the screen door open, heard the front door open. Larry wheeled into the house and closed the door behind him. Kaitlin waited for him to move forward and out of her way, so she could go down the small ramp into the living room. But he did not move forward.

He stood up.

"Kaitlin Marie Callahan?" he asked in another man's voice.

"Oh, *Jesus*!" Nicole cried, pointing the flashlight at him.

The light illuminated a man of average height, wearing a dark baseball cap and wire-rimmed glasses. He was dressed in black; even his hands wore black gloves.

Nicole screamed, "Kaitlin! *Kaitlin!*"

The man stepped forward immediately and clamped his left hand on Nicole's throat. She made a gagging sound as she began to pound his forearm with her fists. With some effort, and a slight grunting sound, the man lifted her from the wheelchair and pulled his right arm away from his body. The light from the fire glinted on a silver blade that extended nine or ten inches from his gloved fist. He swung the blade forward and buried it in Nicole's abdomen. He pulled it out immediately and repeated the gesture, this time driving the blade into her chest. Nicole fell limp, dangling from the grip of his hand like a rag doll. But he continued to stab her. Again and again and again. The blade made a horrible thin, wet sound going into her body and coming out.

Kaitlin opened her mouth and was about to scream...but she

realized he hadn't seen her yet. He was standing at an angle that put most of his back to her, and she was sitting in the dark of the dining room. Sick enough to vomit, she closed her mouth, backed away from the living room doorway, and headed for the kitchen again.

She had to get out of the house.

10

In the hallway between the dining room and kitchen, Kaitlin spun around and pulled the accordion door closed. She turned on the flashlight in her lap, fastened the hook-and-eye latch, spun around and wheeled into the kitchen, then did the same thing again, quickly latching the door.

She instinctively snatched the cordless receiver from the wall-phone base next to the doorway to call nine-one-one. The buttons on the receiver did not light up and Kaitlin clenched her teeth against a curse. The cordless phone was electric, and the power was out. She put the receiver on the kitchen table, then scooped the candles and candleholders from her lap and dropped them beside it, leaving the flashlight on one thigh, pointing ahead of her.

Wheeling over to the end of the counter, she reached into her purse and grabbed her keys. She had them only for a moment, then they slipped from her fingers. Kaitlin made a soft, high mewling sound in her throat as she leaned forward and pushed her hand in deeper, feeling for them, groping around change purse, checkbook, cigarette lighters, envelopes, tampons, breath mints...

Heavy footsteps thumped on the hardwood floor of the dining room, getting louder, coming closer.

Kaitlin released an explosive breath when she closed her fist on the keys. She put the keys in her lap, turned her chair, and wheeled quickly to the kitchen door.

There was a rattling from the dining room. The accordion door. It stopped for a moment, then the man pounded on it, or kicked it, hard, several times. The loud, crunching clamor told Kaitlin he was getting through the first one.

She went out the kitchen door, closed it, spun the chair around, and locked the deadbolt. He would be able to open it easily enough, but it might slow him down for a moment, perhaps long enough for her to get the car started and leave.

Through the closed kitchen door, she heard more noise. First the rattling and clattering, then the explosive sounds she'd heard inside when the man had broken through the first accordion door.

At the bottom of the concrete ramp, Kaitlin wheeled to her right and stopped at the car. She opened the door and tossed the flashlight in. It landed with a clunk on the passenger seat, but continued to shine. Leaning forward, she gripped the steering wheel with her right hand, the edge of the car's roof with her left, and swung her body into the driver's seat. Her plan was to shove the wheelchair out of the way—she couldn't afford the time it would take to fold up the chair and slide it behind her seat—so she could close the door, back out of the carport, and leave.

Something in the rearview mirror caught her eye before she could lean out and move the chair. Not a thing in particular...but the fact that the rearview mirror was unusually black, completely dark. It was a black night, with the moon hidden behind thick rainclouds, and the light that usually shined over the garage door was off because of the power outage...but the darkness in the rearview mirror was *unnaturally* black.

Kaitlin turned on the car's headlights. The taillights were reflected on a shiny black surface.

The Navigator. It was parked across the opening of the carport, blocking her exit.

"Oh, Jesus God," Kaitlin groaned.

She could still hear the sounds in the kitchen. But they wouldn't last much longer. They would stop soon, and he would come out the door.

Kaitlin reached up to take hold of the edge of the roof again and swing herself into the chair, but stopped suddenly, shaking her head.

"No, no, no," she muttered to herself chidingly as she leaned over to the glove compartment, where she'd returned the cell phone before going into the house earlier.

The clamor in the kitchen stopped abruptly. Footsteps moved over the kitchen floor.

Once the cell phone was in her hand, she put it under her chin and held it against her chest as she swung herself back into the chair, then dropped the phone in her lap.

The muffled thump of heavy footsteps marching through the kitchen sounded through the wall.

She grabbed the wheels of her chair and spun to her right, toward the driveway. There was no time to get the flashlight or close the car door, only enough to wheel forward, weave around the blocking Navigator, and put as much space between herself and the kitchen door as she could.

The knob of the kitchen door rattled and the door was jerked violently a few times.

In the driveway, Kaitlin was exposed to the rain. The wind was blowing so hard, it threw the rain into her face with enough force to sting and make her squint against it. She ducked her head, trying to avoid the rain and at the same time see where she was going.

She stopped for just a moment to pick up the cell phone with her left hand and quickly hit the POWER button. The keypad glowed a pale green as she used her thumb to punch nine-one-one, then hit SEND. She wedged the phone between her left ear and shoulder and moved on, pumping at the wheels of her chair.

There was a loud bang behind her, a sound she recognized. It was the kitchen door slamming against the wall as it was swung open.

He was out of the house.

Kaitlin was breathing rapidly as she moved forward. There was no sound from the cell phone, nothing at all in her ear, just dead silence. She'd hit the wrong buttons.

Overhead, the great crunching rumble and crash of a skyscraper being demolished moved through the black sky. Kaitlin felt it in the bones of her arms, chest, and shoulders as she pumped the wheels of her chair. The night turned a harsh, bleached white and flickered like a bad fluorescent light.

Just ahead of her, Kaitlin saw Larry's car, an old Volkswagen

Bug, and veered to the right, away from it. She didn't want to, but she stopped for just a moment, only because she *had* to in order to make the call. She held the cell phone in front of her and hit the POWER button once, then again. She punched nine-one-one again, careful to hit the correct buttons, and with the cell phone back between her head and shoulder, she continued to wheel her chair forward as fast as she could.

Beneath the constant rainfall, there was another sound behind her. Gravel crunching beneath feet. Slowly at first, uncertainly... then at a faster pace.

"Nine-one-one, what is your emergency?" a female voice asked at the other end of the line.

Kaitlin recognized the operator immediately; it was the same one she'd spoken with earlier.

"My name is Kaitlin Callahan!" she shouted into the phone, wanting to be heard above the constant drone of the downpour. "I talked to you earlier! I'm on Rivershore Drive and there's a man—"

Her words were swallowed by an explosion of thunder.

"Um, a man," she continued haltingly, still shouting. "He's here now and he's already killed—"

Lightning sent a harsh, piercing wave of static over the line.

Kaitlin kept pumping the wheels as hard as she could. The muscles in her arms burned as she fought the loose, bumpy gravel beneath her wheels.

"You're on the cell phone again," the operator said casually.

"Yes, and in my wheelchair outside my house in the rain!"

"Is the man there with you now?"

There was a rush of crunching gravel behind her, hurried footsteps...but she could not tell in what direction they were headed.

"Right *behind* me!" Kaitlin cried into the phone. "He killed my *friend*, I saw him *stab* her!"

"I can send a deputy out there," the operator said, still sounding aloof, slightly distracted.

"I need someone *now*, he's right behind—"

The left wheel of the chair hit something hard and the chair wound sharply to the left. Kaitlin cried out as she was thrown forward. Her face and palms slammed hard into sharp edges of gravel as the cell phone flew into the darkness away from her. The cell phone skittered over the gravel in a couple directions; something had broken off of it…probably the cover on the battery casing. She listened for the sound of her chair's wheels, but couldn't hear them. Apparently, it had come to a stop close by.

While her hands had landed on the gravel, her upper body had landed on something else. Something pliable…and warm.

"Oh God, oh my God," Kaitlin muttered as she moved her hands over the shape.

Thunder roared overhead, even louder than before, and lightning turned the night a ghostly white.

Kaitlin saw Larry's face a few inches from her own. His mouth and eyes were open. So was his throat.

"No!" she screamed. "No, Christ no, please God no!" But she wasn't screaming out loud…only in her mind. With everything around her soaked by rain, her hair plastered to her face and neck, her clothes clinging to her, her mouth was dry as desert sand and her tongue felt swollen, her throat constricted, and she couldn't have screamed at that moment if she'd tried. As she tried to crawl off her friend's dead body, her left hand fell on his prosthetic arm, hard as stone.

"Kaitlin," the man said from the darkness.

She closed her mouth and stopped breathing. Her sweatshirt clung to her like a second skin and she'd clamped a rope of her wet hair between her teeth. She heard his footsteps in the gravel. Coming closer.

Kaitlin ran her left hand down Larry's prosthetic arm until she found the three hooks. They were spread wide, frozen in place. She wrapped her fingers around them and began to pull. Hard.

"Kaitlin," the voice said again. "Looks like you want to be a problem, huh?" There was a slight southern accent to the low, even voice.

She jerked on the hooks, twisting the arm as she pulled, harder…harder…

The footsteps slowed as they drew closer and finally stopped next to her.

"You really want to throw a wrench into things, don't you, Kaitlin?"

She jerked on the prosthetic limb with all her strength.

A hand closed on her left elbow.

Larry's arm came loose and slid out of his sleeve.

Kaitlin jerked her elbow from the man's grasp and rolled away from him.

"Hey, hey, come on, now," he said. "Let's get you inside out of the rain before you—"

She swung the arm up at the dark shape in the darkness with all her strength, holding it with both hands just above the wrist, and it connected with something, hard but with a hollow sound. A clacking sound, too…the sound of the arm hitting his wire-rimmed glasses.

The man made an abrupt, spontaneous raspberry-like sound between his lips and gravel crunched beneath two clumsy backward steps as something small hit the gravel nearby with a tinkering sound. Kaitlin used her elbows to quickly crawl backward off Larry's body, still clutching his arm. Cold wet gravel cut into the flesh of her arms as she dragged her lifeless legs over the ground.

The man's footsteps moved quickly toward her.

She swung her body over to the left with a grunt, onto her stomach. The prosthetic arm slipped from her grasp in the process and clacked against something solid before it fell onto the gravel nearby. The wheelchair.

Kaitlin made a frustrated sound in her throat as she rose up on both arms and began to drag herself forward more rapidly. She moved in the direction of the sound the arm made, reaching each hand out as far as she could as she crawled, until her right hand fell on the upper end of the prosthetic arm, the end with the straps.

With the arm in hand, she crawled forward, and slammed her head into the spokes of her chair's left wheel.

Breathing rapidly, Kaitlin leaned on her right fist, which held Larry's arm, and reached up with her left hand to clutch the chair's armrest. She started to turn the front of the chair toward her clumsily, so she could pull herself into it.

The wheelchair disappeared suddenly, kicked by a foot that Kaitlin's head nearly hit as she fell forward with nothing to lean on. The chair rattled over the gravel as it shot away, and stopped with a clanking sound, as if it had fallen over suddenly.

"Okay, that's enough," the man said firmly.

A fist closed on her wet hair and jerked her head back.

Thunder ripped through the sky, swallowing Kaitlin's scream. She swung her right arm up hard, and with it, the prosthetic arm. It hit him in the face, and it stopped there. It did not continue its arc; it did not bounce off his skull. It stopped.

The man cried out in pain as he pulled away and took the prosthetic arm with him, jerking it from Kaitlin's hand. She turned her head to see him stumbling backward. Lightning revealed his yawning mouth, his left arm stretched out at his side and waving in circles to maintain his balance, and his right hand holding the wrist of the arm just a few inches from the right side of his face. And it revealed what appeared to be black tears dribbling down his right cheek. His glasses were gone. Darkness returned, and the man made no more noise after that single abrupt cry, but Kaitlin heard him fall. That was enough.

She lifted herself up on her arms and pulled herself forward again. The gravel was like broken chunks of thick glass beneath her hands, cutting into the soft flesh of her palms and fingers.

After the last flash of lightning, Kaitlin knew where she was in her driveway, and knew where she was going. If she continued to move forward, she would cross the triangular strip of grassy earth that separated the forked driveway. Beyond that stretched a vast, soggy field dotted with Manzanita trees, and then...Bridge Road. If she could reach the road, she might be able to get someone's attention, get some help.

Kaitlin listened for sounds behind her, for feet kicking up gravel. There was nothing.

Her heart drummed in her ears and her lungs burned in spite of the night's cold, damp air. The wind hissed through branches and high overhead, an owl released a long, piercing screech. It was nothing more than distant background noise to Kaitlin as she focused all her concentration on dragging the lower half of her body as quickly as possible to the side of the busy road ahead, where she would either get some help or be hit by a car.

Her hands splashed through a puddle and kept reaching out, pulling her forward, until she'd dragged the dead half of her body through the puddle as well. A moment later, the gravel gave way to soft mud that oozed between her fingers. She felt thick grass beneath her hands and knew she'd reached the division between the driveway's fork. Her face pushed into a thick oleander bush, and she ducked her head to protect her face from the thin branches. The oleanders hadn't been trimmed in a long time, and they'd grown thick.

Kaitlin tried to visualize where she was in the darkness, wondering on which side of her the big cedar stood. She didn't want to slam into it. Not now while she seemed to have a lead on her assailant. Once she was through the bushes, she slowed just a bit; if she was headed straight for the tree, it would be just beyond the oleanders. She stopped for just a second to reach out with her right hand and sweep her arm back and forth. Nothing. She moved forward. When she reached the next row of oleander bushes, she knew she was most likely just to the right of the tree, just south of it.

For the moment, there was only silence behind her. She was still safe.

Beyond the next strip of bushes, she reached more gravel. Kaitlin smiled. It was involuntary. She was making good time, covering a lot of ground. The muscles in her arms ached, burned, and she felt the vague beginnings of a cramp in her right bicep, but ignored it. She focused her attention on what was ahead of her in the dark.

Above the Manzanita trees in the field ahead, she saw the rushing glow of cars moving back and forth. Through the tall weeds, she could see the headlights moving north and south with a kind of sparkly strobe effect.

One hand in front of the other...left, right, left—

Her right hand landed on nothing and she dropped forward, rolling to her right as her hand scraped over gravelly mud that sloped downward sharply. She slid first, then rolled to her right, tumbling helplessly as if the earth had opened up and swallowed her. She screamed a surprised, broken scream as she realized she was rolling down the hill toward the flood plain...but she knew the flood plain was—

Kaitlin took in a mouthful of gritty, mossy water as she went under. She flailed her arms and fought to find the surface. But the cramp in her arm stopped teasing and twisted her muscle painfully, and the weight of her dead, useless legs pulled her under.

11

The thunder sounded thickly muffled and distant underwater, but Kaitlin felt it all around her, through her clothes, in her hair. Pain cut like a hot blade through her right bicep as she flailed her arms in the water, but she clenched her teeth against it, ignored it, and fought the water.

When her head broke the surface, she spat the foul water from her mouth and drew in a gasping breath. She opened her eyes to a silent, bluish-white explosion of lightning that cast a web of tree branch shadows on her and the water around her. In that brief moment of light, squinting against the rain that stung her face, she saw part of a blackberry bush above the water's surface; its vines were climbing the fat trunk of an old oak about four, maybe five feet in front of her.

Kaitlin realized she was turning away from it gradually because her left arm was moving through the water with more strength than her right. Although she was trying to ignore the cramp, it was still causing her to favor her right arm. If she kept it up, she'd never get to that blackberry bush, and might even go under again. The pain made her groan—it was more a gargling sound in her throat—as she stretched her right arm out and swept it through the water with as much force as her left. The distance between Kaitlin and the oak tree began to close, but slowly.

Before she reached the part of the bush she could see, vines pulled at her sweatshirt under the water. Needle-like thorns pierced the flesh of her breasts and abdomen and cut her as she moved in the water. Panic closed on her throat like a cold hand when she realized her legs were caught in the thorny vines. She couldn't feel the thorns biting into her legs through the sweatpants—all feeling stopped at her waist—but instead of moving forward, she was lolling in the water. Just out of reach of the tree, and her struggling arms were getting her nowhere.

A frightened, animal-like growl rose from her chest as she swept her arms through the water harder, faster. She closed the gap a little before her head went under.

Kaitlin surfaced with a garbled cry and took a deep breath. She forced herself to calm down. Struggling in the vines would only make her situation worse. She would have to use them to her advantage. She took another deep breath and went under again, intentionally this time, in control. Reaching forward with her right arm she closed her hand on a clump of the vines. Tiny razors sliced into the soft flesh of her palms. She pulled on the vines as she propelled herself forward with her left arm, then switched and grabbed some vines with her left hand, swept her right backward. She felt herself pulling free from some of the thorny bushes while hanging up on more, but at least she was moving.

Two more pulls on the vines and her right shoulder nudged the trunk of the tree. Clutching the vines that were crawling up the oak, Kaitlin pulled herself above the surface and drank in the air. She hugged the fat tree trunk, mindless of the thorns that pierced her hands and face and cut her arms and breasts and stomach beneath her sweatshirt.

With her legs before the accident, she would have been out of the water by now. Where the left fork of the driveway sloped sharply down to the flood plain, the water was at its deepest—six feet, maybe a little more—and then the road inclined gradually. It would have taken a couple strokes through the water, then she could have walked up the steep hill down which she'd rolled. But with her legs paralyzed, four feet of water could be dangerous to her. She was only a few feet from high ground...but with the water filling that gap, it might as well be miles away.

Kaitlin wondered where her pursuer was. He could be standing nearby, watching her, for all she knew.

The muscles in her arms and back and shoulders burned, and the cramp in her arm came and went repeatedly, an indecisive tormentor. She felt as if every inch of her skin had been pierced and torn, and she knew that not all of the wet rivulets dribbling down her face were rainwater.

When she thought of Nicole and Larry, she felt a different pain...not physical, but no less excruciating. She was certain Larry was dead, and she suspected Nicole was, too. But why had he killed *them*? Because of what she might have told them? Because they were *there*? Because...he simply enjoyed it?

"The more, the merrier," Kaitlin whispered to herself as she closed her eyes. She saw the long blade plunging into Nicole again and again...and Larry's throat, open in a black, leering grin. A dry, sickening sob wracked her body and she pressed her head against the tree.

It had happened again. Just like Richard and the friends she'd had before the accident, two more people had been taken from Kaitlin's life. But it had nothing to do with her paralysis this time...and she would not be seeing these friends now and then at the mall or at the occasional concert. They were gone. As permanently as her legs.

But this time, Kaitlin was not helpless. She had a chance to make sure the killer paid for what he'd done to her friends...and for what he'd done to Emily and Myron Nevitt as well. If she could just get out of the water.

Tree branches whipped in the wind overhead and rain sliced through the cold air. When thunder exploded again, Kaitlin could feel it in the tree trunk she was holding. She looked around quickly in that moment, got her bearings. She was on the eastern side of the gravel road, and the top of the hill was about five feet away.

She pushed away from the tree and the blackberry bush and the vines clung tenaciously to her sweatshirt. She could pull those vines away with her hands, clumsily and while bobbing under the water, but the vines holding her legs were a different problem.

Kaitlin grabbed the blackberry bush and pulled herself to the tree again. She reached down with her right hand to find that her sweatpants had already been pulled halfway down by the snagging vines. The sweatpants would continue to hold her back as long as they were on her legs, so she pushed them down as far as she could. With the sweatpants bunched around her ankles, the thorny vines would easily pull them over her stockinged feet as she swam away. She clawed at the vines clinging to her sweatshirt, pulling off as many as she could, then heaved herself away from the oak tree, pushing with both arms.

She moved her arms in long, powerful strokes. There was a brief moment of resistance as the blackberry vines clung to her sweatpants, but when she felt them break away, she moved her arms even harder, faster.

Kaitlin's hands scraped the sharp gravel on the hill, and seconds later, she was dragging herself over the muddy ground, out of the water, gasping for breath. She didn't want to hold still for too long, though; she was so exhausted, she was afraid of being unable to move if she stayed in place for more than a few seconds. As thunder roared overhead like the wrath of God, she put her palms to the ground, rose up on her arms, and reached out with her right hand to begin crawling forward.

Her hand fell on a shoe.

A hand hooked under her left armpit and lifted her from the ground.

In the bluish flash of lightning, Kaitlin saw the man's face just a few inches from hers. His left eye was swollen shut and black, tear-like streaks were running from it. He smiled as the lightning stopped.

"You got me," he said, and he sounded almost playful. He pulled back his left arm and slammed his black-gloved fist into her face.

Kaitlin lost consciousness.

12

I'm not dead.

It was Kaitlin's first thought when she opened her eyes. She had no idea how much time had passed or where she was...but she knew she was hanging upside down. It was still dark, she was still in the rain, and she was hanging upside down and being jarred and jostled. And footsteps...she heard footsteps in the gravel...heavy and quick and determined.

The man had slung her over his shoulder and was carrying her through the rain.

Where? Kaitlin thought. *Where is he taking me? Why hasn't he killed me? That's why he came here...isn't it? To kill me?*

Her head throbbed and her ears rang, and she tasted blood in her mouth. Her skin was on fire and her muscles felt shredded.

Thunder startled, and lightning showed her Larry's dead body on the ground. He couldn't have looked more brutally exposed if he'd been naked...one arm stretched out at his side, the other missing, no legs.

I got him, Kaitlin thought, remembering the man's eye, his words. The hooks on the end of Larry's arm must have caught him right in the eye. *Good.*

But it wasn't good enough. As bloody and swollen as his eye had looked, it didn't seem to bother him at all.

I'm not dead, she thought again. *Yet.*

The man's feet stopped crunching on the gravel drive and slapped on the wet concrete path that led to the living room door. He didn't say a word. Kaitlin could not even hear him breathing. Only the steady slap of his feet on the puddled walkway.

The screen door was whipped open so hard it slapped against the outside wall. It swung back slowly and bumped Kaitlin as the man opened the front door and carried her inside.

Not until she was in the toasty warmth of the living room did Kaitlin realize how cold she was. The man carried her to the middle of the room, leaned forward, and dropped her on her back like a sack of potatoes. She cried out in pain when she hit the floor and immediately gasped for the breath that was knocked from her lungs by the impact. She propped herself up on her elbows and saw that her sweatpants were gone. She wore only a sock on her right foot, and her panties. Her legs were torn and bloody from the blackberry bushes.

To Kaitlin's left, the fire still popped and crackled, bathing the room in its soft, dancing orange glow. Larry's chair lay on its side not far from the front door, near the wall, apparently having been kicked out of the way. Behind her and to the right, the television was still on; angry voices were arguing about the latest details of the ongoing presidential scandal. She tilted her head back and saw Nicole in the far corner of the room, sprawled in her wheelchair, arms hanging over the armrests, head tipped backward over the back of the chair, her blue and white sweater soaked with blood. The flashlight Kaitlin had given Nicole earlier lay on the floor at Nicole's feet, still shining.

The man stood up straight and smiled down at her. His eye was still bleeding. He took off his Yankees cap with his left hand and ran the fingers of his right through his dark, short, curly hair, then tossed the cap onto the coffee table. It landed on one of the pizzas, but he didn't notice. He unzipped his jacket and slipped it off.

"Let's get down to it, shall we?" he said. His voice was different now, breathier, ever so slightly tremulous, and moist with a quiet excitement.

He tossed the jacket over the pizzas on the coffee table and it dropped neatly onto the armrest of the sofa. Beneath the jacket, he wore a black long-sleeve jersey and a gun in a shoulder holster. A knife—presumably the knife he'd used to kill Nicole and Larry—was attached to his belt in a black leather sheath.

The man removed the knife from its sheath—the silver blade was stained with dark streaks—and lowered himself to one knee between Kaitlin's legs. She panicked and began to crawl backward on her elbows, her breath coming like machine-gun fire.

"Hey, hey," he said, grabbing her right ankle and pulling her toward him effortlessly. "*Knock it off!*" He slapped her in the face hard, then leaned toward her, holding out the knife.

Kaitlin cried, "Pluh-please, ple-hease, pluh—"

He slid the blade beneath her panties and sliced through the material, pulled them away from her and tossed them aside.

Kaitlin knew that instant what was going to happen next.

When he killed Emily and Myron Nevitt, he'd made it look like a robbery that had gone bad, stealing a few things, maybe tearing the place up a little. He wouldn't want to do the same thing twice in the same day. This time there would be nothing missing, and if there was any damage done, it would be due to a struggle. This time, he wanted it to look like the work of a psycho, Kaitlin was certain. Three friends sitting around having pizza...an anonymous lunatic invades their evening...kills two of them...

...and rapes the third before killing her as well.

He stood and returned the knife to its sheath, then unbuttoned his pants, opened them, and pulled them down along with his underwear. He was already fully erect.

Tears stung Kaitlin's eyes and her insides writhed.

"They'll find you," she said, her voice dry and cracked.

"Why do you say that, Kaitlin?"

"Your semen...your DNA..."

His smile became a grin as he knelt between her legs. "That won't be a problem," he said, hooking a hand under each of her knees. "I don't exist."

He released a trembling sigh as he pulled her limp legs apart while at the same time pushing them back toward her shoulders. He moved in between them, making a low, guttural sound through a smile.

Kaitlin lay flat on her back and waited till he was close enough, still smiling, the blood caking around his swollen eye. She clenched her teeth so hard they ground loudly in her head as she swung her left fist into his bloody eye. She was afraid she didn't have enough strength left to do any damage, but she was wrong.

The man bellowed like a wounded animal and fell off Kaitlin. He landed on his left side, his right hand over his eye, lips pulled back over wet teeth.

Kaitlin didn't give him time to recover from the first blow. She rolled onto her right side and brought her fist down again, hitting the back of his hand as it covered his eye. Again, hitting his right temple. Again—

His hand moved quickly and closed on her fist. He squeezed her knuckles together until she cried out in pain and dropped onto her back. He was back on his knees in a moment, between her legs, hovering over her.

"That hurt," he said, a quiet chuckle interrupting his words. He pulled his arm back and punched her in the face.

Kaitlin lost track of how many times he hit her in rapid succession. She heard and felt something in her face crunch, a horribly familiar sensation that took her back to her nightmare...to the windshield of Richard's car as her face crashed through it...as the cartilage in her nose and the bones in her face were broken, as teeth shattered and others loosened as they closed on her tongue.

A heartbeat later, she was back in her living room. The floor seemed to tilt, the room to spin and wobble. Her nose began to bleed, from her nostrils as well as down her throat.

She was only vaguely aware of the fact that he had pushed her legs up again and had her calves resting on his shoulders. Eyes closed, she turned her head to the side and coughed and spat blood, trying to keep from choking on it. Her coughing stopped abruptly. She tried to take a breath, but her throat was closed. Opening her eyes, she looked up at the man.

He was smiling again, in spite of his bloody eye. His pelvis pounded against her hard and his gloved hands were closed on her throat.

He was killing her as he raped her.

Dizziness washed over her as she flailed her arms. Her fists landed on his arms weakly, uselessly, but she did not stop. Her vision blurred as tears welled up in her eyes, making the man waver liquidly like a grinning fever dream. Kaitlin's eyes felt as if they were about to pop from their sockets and her tongue seemed to fill her mouth like a bulbous, wet piece of meat. Her heartbeat pounded in her head and the rush of blood flowing through her veins made a fluid-throbbing sound in her ears. The crackle of the fire sounded more and more distant, until she couldn't hear it at all. The fire's orange glow faded to a faint sparkle in blackness.

The hands suddenly let go.

Kaitlin sucked air into her lungs loudly, then broke into a fit of violent coughs as pain exploded in her throat. Her eyes closed tightly as she hacked and tried to gulp air at the same time. When she opened her eyes, she was startled to see the man's face an inch from hers.

"Who else is in here?" he whispered.

His face seemed to melt in the tears that still filled her eyes. Her chest heaved as she gasped to fill her lungs. She moved her mouth to speak, but had no voice; even if she had, she was too busy trying to breathe to use it.

"Who else is in the house?" he asked again.

Kaitlin shook her head, coughing again.

The man moved away from her, stood upright on his knees, and drew his gun from its holster as he looked around slowly.

Kaitlin was confused. There was no one else in the house…he'd *killed* the only other people in the house!

The man leaned forward and held his left hand in front of her face, index finger extended upward. It was a subtly threatening gesture, a silent command for her to stay where she was. He got to his feet and turned slowly in a circle, looking carefully into the room's shadows with his remaining eye. He stepped over to Nicole, leaned over, and picked up the flashlight on the floor in front of her.

She heard it then…the sound that made the man think someone else was in the house.

Breathing…thick, wheezy breathing.

Oscar.

With effort, Kaitlin lifted her head and watched him walk away from her slowly, shining the flashlight around the room. She wiped her teary eyes with the back of her right hand as she propped herself up on her left elbow. Pain moved over her and through her in a rush, from her head to her waist, and for a moment, she teetered on the very edge of consciousness. She fought to stay alert, widened her eyes, bit her lower lip. The moment passed and, still dizzy, she tilted her head forward to look under the coffee table. Beyond it, she saw Oscar, still curled up and sound asleep under the sofa.

Kaitlin lifted her head again and her bleary eyes fell on the end table. She looked at the man again. He was on the small ramp that sloped down into the living room, leaning through the doorway and peering into the dining room, moving the flashlight beam through the darkness.

She knew she could crawl to the end table, but she didn't think she could get there before the man stopped her. He had to be distracted.

He looked back over his shoulder, head cocked, listening.

It had to be now, before he figured out where the breathing was coming from.

Kaitlin rolled over on her stomach and lifted herself up on her arms. She cried out in pain—a hoarse, ragged sound—as she dragged herself in a half-circle, turning herself around.

"Look out!" she cried, as if someone were in the dining room. "He's coming in there!"

The man turned toward her, froze for a moment, then looked into the dining room again. For an instant, he was torn.

"He's got a gun!" Kaitlin screamed. The words felt like razors as they tore out of her damaged throat.

He looked angry as he bounded into the dining room.

Kaitlin dragged herself toward the end table. The room tilted to the left, then the right, and a wave of nausea swept through her stomach. Blood dribbled from her nose, which throbbed painfully. The room dimmed again, and she was afraid she was going to pass out. She kept putting one arm in front of the other, pulling herself forward.

The man's footsteps clumped around in the dining room.

Through more tears, Kaitlin saw the end table. Closer…closer…

"Goddammit," the man muttered. His footsteps started toward the living room again.

Kaitlin blinked her eyes several times, trying to clear them. She reached up with her right hand for the handle of the drawer of the end table. Her hand missed it…she wasn't close enough. She dropped her hand to the floor and moved a little closer.

"God*dammit*," the man said again, coming into the living room. "It's in *here!*"

Her hand closed on the antique brass handle and pulled. The drawer slid all the way out and dropped to the floor in front of her. The gun lay on top of an old copy of *Entertainment Weekly*. Clint Eastwood glared up at her.

"A fucking *cat!*" the man snapped.

Kaitlin put her hand on the gun, then noticed movement in front of her. She lifted her head to see the end table falling toward her. The Tiffany-style lamp landed heavily on her already battered head. Her arms collapsed beneath her as the table fell on top of her.

She opened her eyes and the table was gone. Had she blacked out? For how long?

"What the hell do you think *you're* doing?" the man asked calmly.

Not long, she thought.

He kicked her hard in the side, hard enough to roll her onto her back.

Kaitlin felt herself slipping into nothingness again as pain exploded in her head, her abdomen, her back and shoulders and arms and—

She still had the gun.

Eyes wide, breath coming rapidly, she fought unconsciousness as she raised the gun and aimed it at the man who towered over her.

The trigger wouldn't move.

The man grinned down at her.

She hit the safety and fired. Once, twice, three times.

The man's grin disappeared as his body jerked with each gunshot.

Kaitlin continued to squeeze the trigger even after the tenth shot, when the gun clicked harmlessly.

The man fell on top of her like a tree.

Everything slipped away…

13

Kaitlin awoke slowly, moving through the familiar fog of prescription painkillers. At first, she thought she had just been in the car accident with Richard, and she wondered if she'd dreamed everything and she wasn't paralyzed and she hadn't lost Richard and all her friends and she wasn't confined to a wheelchair.

That didn't last long. As she came out of the fog, a vague memory of Deputy Morgan returned to her...he'd found her in the living room with the dead man on top of her. She remembered being put into the ambulance...and going through the CT scan that had been performed not long after she'd arrived at the hospital. They were cloudy memories and seemed much more distant than they were, but Kaitlin wasn't fooled. She'd been through it only a couple years earlier, and the similarities were frightening.

At least the worst is over, she thought. *I don't have to wonder if I can still walk.*

"Hey, baby."

Kaitlin opened her eyes and saw her father smiling down at her. Sixty-nine years old and he still had a full head of hair, and most of it was still red. He leaned on the chrome rail of the bed and lightly rested his hand on her shoulder.

"Hi, Daddy," she said. Her voice sounded like two rocks being rubbed together and her lips felt impossibly swollen. Her words were slightly garbled, as if she were speaking through a mouth full of ice cubes. She became aware of bandages on her face, head, hands, and arms.

"You're gonna be okay," he said. "You're in a lot of pain now, 'cause you've been banged up like a pinball. But it's nothing serious. You're gonna be fine."

She smacked her dry, broken lips a few times and they felt as if bees were stinging them. "Daddy, tell me...Nicole and Larry, they're, uh...they're, uh...gone?"

"I'm sorry, honey," he whispered, nodding.

"She's *awake*?" Paula asked from somewhere else in the room. "Why didn't you *tell* me?"

"Hi, Mother," Kaitlin said as the woman appeared next to her father.

"Oh, Kaitlin, sweetheart," Paula said. She reached down to take Kaitlin's bandaged hand, but stopped short. "Kaitlin, I told you. I told you. Didn't I tell you?"

Kaitlin closed her eyes.

"That man," Paula went on. "He was able to find you. You heard a murder and that man came after you, just like I *said*. I've been trying to tell the police, but they won't listen to me. You need to tell them. You need to—"

"Mother," Kaitlin said hoarsely, opening her eyes halfway. "Shut up."

Paula stiffened beside the bed and clicked her tongue a couple times, the sign that she'd been hurt. "Did you hear her?" she asked her husband. "Did you *hear* her?"

Kaitlin watched her father roll his eyes. "Yes, Paula, I heard her," he said. "Did *you*?"

Kaitlin fell back to sleep in no time, and remained that way for hours.

The next time she awoke, her parents were gone and dinner had arrived. Soup, Jell-O, and a milkshake. She'd lost a couple of teeth, others were broken, and her tongue was badly cut and swollen, so she was in no shape to eat solid foods. She wasn't hungry, but the thought of a cold milkshake oozing down her throat was appealing.

Dinner wasn't all that waited for her. Deputy Morgan stood by her bed. He was in uniform, without a raincoat or cap this time.

"Hello, Miss Callahan," he said.

"Hi," she croaked.

"I'm really sorry this happened, Miss Callahan. I want you to know, after I left your house I drove around the loop twice and didn't see that Navigator anywhere. But, this guy..." He shrugged and shook his head. "He's like that."

Kaitlin frowned. Even *that* hurt. "Who's like that?" she asked.

"The man who...came to your house. I'm sure you've heard about him on the news. The serial rapist. He was getting bolder, more violent. He'd killed a couple people just to get to his target.

He started in Tehema County and stayed there for awhile, for almost a year. Then, just recently, he moved to Glenn County. He'd never hit Shasta County before, and nobody expected him to. Everybody thought he was moving south, but—" He shrugged elaborately.

"Wait," Kaitlin said. "What…what *man* are you talking about?" Her voice was thick, her words slurred, but she spoke slowly, wanting to be understood. "What about the Nevitts? Emily and Myron Nevitt."

Deputy Morgan's head tipped to one side and he leaned forward slowly, folding his arms on the bed's rail. "You know, somebody's gonna have to ask you a lot of questions, and I know now's not the time, but…what's all this about the Nevitts? Your mother was telling me about them earlier. Something about you getting a call at work. So, what's the deal?"

Kaitlin used her elbows to push herself up further on her pillows. It hurt, and she groaned, but she managed.

"You found the Navigator?" she asked.

"Yes," he nodded.

"And the laptop computer?"

"What?"

"The man's laptop computer in the Navigator."

He shook his head slowly. "There was no laptop. We found a notebook, though. Spiral-bound. He'd written down the name of each victim in that notebook, and with each victim's name…well, he did a lot of research on each one. A *lot* of research. He knew their schedules, their habits. He knew *yours*. He'd been getting around a lot. It looks like he was already researching you about the time he raped his previous victim. But, no, there was no laptop. Why do you ask?"

"He…he wasn't…" Kaitlin cleared her throat and licked her swollen lips with her swollen tongue. "He wasn't a hit man?"

"A *hit* man? No. He was an unemployed mechanic. What's all this about the Nevitts and…and a *hit* man?"

Kaitlin closed her eyes as she took a deep breath. Had it really been someone *else*? A different *man*?

There was a bustling sound of movement in the room, but Kaitlin didn't open her eyes. It was her parents, she was sure.

"Mr. and Mrs. Callahan," Deputy Morgan said pleasantly.

"Do you think you could leave her *alone*?" Paula said. *"Until she feels better."*

"I'm sorry," Deputy Morgan said. "I didn't come to question her. Just say hello and to see how she was doing."

"Thank you very much," Kaitlin's father said. "We appreciate that."

"Maybe tomorrow," Deputy Morgan said, "she'll be feeling a little better and I can ask her a few questions."

Kaitlin listened as her father saw the deputy to the door. She sensed her mother leaning over her.

"Your dinner's here," Paula said when Kaitlin opened her eyes. "Do you feel like eating?"

"No," Kaitlin whispered, closing her eyes again.

If this guy thinks you know something, Larry had said, *he won't stop until he finds you.*

She heard a deep, level voice in her ear as clearly as if she were wearing her headset at work:

Hello. Who is this?

This is Kaitlin.

"Are you sure?" Paula asked. "How about some soup? You should eat *something*. At least drink the milkshake."

"No," Kaitlin said. She wasn't hungry. There was a knot in her stomach…a knot that was tied very tightly.

…he won't stop until he finds you.

"Well, all right, then," Paula said quietly. "Maybe it is best if you just get some sleep."

Kaitlin's eyes remained closed.

Hello. Who is this?

She was not sure if she would ever sleep again.

Monsters

1

Until that cold early morning in the Munch Room, Roger never realized that blood had such an overpowering smell. But then, he'd never been near so much of it.

Blood was splashed in deadly Rorschach designs all over the wall above the dying man—

Jesus Christ, Roger thought, hugging himself in the corner, *he's still alive, dear God his chest is open, how can he STILL BE ALIVE?*

—and dribbled to the floor in long, thin black-red streaks. Dark strands of it shot from the man's chest and tattered throat in rhythmic spurts. His blood-gloved hands slapped the cement floor, leaving smeared hand prints and the heels of his boots thunked together spastically.

The alcohol in Roger's stomach burned as it tried to come back up and his own babbling voice sounded unfamiliar to his ears. He was babbling not only because of the bloodshed before him, but because of the cause of it all.

The creature that hunkered over the convulsing body was only vaguely human in shape. Its patches of mangy hair were clotted with blood; bits of flesh clung to its jagged teeth like chives; tremors of pleasure passed over its leathery skin as it plunged a clawed hand into the man's chest and tore something out with a moist ripping sound.

When it began to eat, Roger lost consciousness...

2

The drive from L.A. was like sliding naked along the edge of a razor blade. He hadn't stopped once in nine hours. A rusty nail was imbedded deep in the small of his back, he was sitting on crushed glass, and somewhere along the way he'd swallowed a rock. The rock had gotten stuck between his throat and stomach, and remained a lump of dull pain in his chest. He didn't always feel the pain—mostly just when he heard the wrong song on the radio or began to worry about returning to Napa Valley.

Which was most of the time.

3

The valley was getting ready to change color when Roger arrived that late Thursday afternoon. Fall was a footstep away and with it would come the crush, when the entire Valley would smell like a freshly opened bottle of chilled wine. But now the green of the trees had darkened on the verge of brown and the grapevines, full with leaves ready to be pruned, clung to their trellises as if shocked by the changing of their color.

St. Helena remained cradled among the vineyards, a small town that still seemed uncomfortable with blacktop rather than cobblestone streets.

Why shouldn't it, asshole? Roger asked himself. *You were only gone six years, and they didn't exactly log your departure in the fucking town records.*

The town had changed slightly in places.

Jim's Country Kitchen, a coffee shop on the south end of town, was now Molly's and looked like a giant enclosed gazebo instead of the noisy, smelly, greasy spoon it had been.

Taylor's Hardware was now a video store.

And so, he was sad to see, was Hollywood North. It used to be a store that sold only Hollywood memorabilia—posters, stills, lobby cards, decorations, greeting cards, and toys—and had been run by Josh Draper. Roger had spent many an afternoon sitting behind the counter in Hollywood North with Josh, drinking coffee, and talking about movie trivia. Josh's specialty was horror films; one whole wall of the store had been covered with posters and stills of old Frankenstein and Wolfman movies and nearly all of the Hammer vampire films, some of which were valuable originals that were not for sale. Roger was sorry to see the store closed and wondered what had become of Josh.

The sidewalks were busy with fashionably dressed shoppers who crossed the narrow Main Street indiscriminately, slowing traffic to an uncertain stutter.

Roger was glad to see that the most welcomed sight in town had not changed at all: the barber's pole in front of DiMarco's Deli.

He parked his gray Accord behind the deli and went in the back way past the stacked cases of beer and soft drinks and—

—suddenly he felt as if he'd just driven over from his house on Sulphur Springs Avenue after spending a few hours at the typewriter.

Suddenly, he hadn't decided—after finding his mutilated dog hanging over his back porch—to pack up late one night six years ago and drive to Los Angeles without telling anyone. He hadn't attended a single meeting with a preoccupied director or producer and hadn't once been told, "It's just not what we're looking for." He'd never had a gun in his mouth and he'd never *heard* of the Sylmar Neuropsychiatric Hospital, let alone seen its sterile white interior.

It was as if he'd never left St. Helena.

The place still looked more like a garage sale than a delicatessen. In the front was the candy counter and register, then the meat counter, shelves of groceries, coolers of drinks, and the sandwich counter. Above it all were shelves and shelves of souvenirs, knickknacks, mementos, photographs, drawings, and other objects unidentifiable from any distance. The walls were covered with posters, postcards, letters, photographs, and notes. Nothing was arranged in any particular order but it did not look sloppy. It looked somehow...right. As if the place couldn't possibly be any other way.

Roger was halfway to the meat counter when he heard a hoarse shriek.

"Roger Bernard Carlton!"

Betty DiMarco was already rushing toward him when he turned, her arms open wide. She laughed as she embraced him, the cigarette between the first two fingers of her right hand trailing a thread of smoke.

"Holy God!" she cried, her voice muffled against his shoulder. "How long has it been?"

"A long time, Betty. How are you?"

"Well, I'm—oh, you know how I—Jesus, but it's good to—let me *look* at you!" She stepped back, a hand on his shoulder.

Betty, a small, spare woman, wore a red plaid shirt and a pair of bluejeans that still looked good on her in spite of the graying of her curly blond hair and the deepening of the lines around her eyes and mouth.

"Come on in the back," she said, tugging his arm. "Come *on*."

She led him through a door over which a sign read THE MUNCH ROOM and seated him at a rustic picnic table. It was the very same table where he used to sit each morning drinking coffee, reading the paper, and writing.

"A sandwich?" Betty asked.

"Yeah, I was just gonna—"

"Let me. What kind?"

"Roast beef and dill cheese on dark—"

"Dark rye, no onions, no sprouts. Right?" She grinned before hurrying out of the room.

The same pictures hung in the Munch Room: Nixon and Agnew dressed as Batman and Robin, posters for a local rock group, an art show, a wine tasting, all several years old, a few old beer logos, and a painting of Betty and Leo. Mickey Mouse ticked away the time on a wall-sized wristwatch.

The far end of the room was partitioned off and held a large metal sink, a cutting board, and shelves of cutlery and containers.

A few hours ago, at lunch time, there wouldn't have been an empty seat in the room. Patrons would have been shouting to be heard above the din of voices and the single restroom would have been free for only seconds at a time.

Roger remembered sitting at the same table one day during just such a busy lunch hour. A young couple walked in, college age, both neatly but plainly dressed. He didn't recognize them, but knew immediately that they were Seventh-Day Adventists—probably students from the college up the hill—and looked away from them, went back to his writing.

A moment later, he realized they were standing by his table facing him. He looked up to see them staring, lips parted, eyes wide below frowning brows, sandwiches held before them on paper plates. He started to ask them what was wrong when the girl spit on him.

The voices in the Munch Room silenced and all eyes turned to Roger and the couple.

"You're the writer," the girl said quietly with a mixture of fear and awe, as if she were standing before a movie star who also happened to be a serial killer. "I caught my brother reading your book once. I burned it." Her voice lowered to a whisper. "You're sick." She turned and walked out, followed by her boyfriend. They threw their sandwiches into the garbage can by the door as they left, as if unwilling to eat the food of an establishment that would serve Roger.

The eyes of the other patrons remained on Roger for several silent seconds, then he said, somewhat nervously, "Probably kept the book and underlined the dirty parts."

A brief chorus of laughter broke the uncomfortable silence and the chatter continued. A man asked if Roger was really a writer; when Roger introduced himself, the man said he'd read his novel and eagerly awaited his next. They talked for a while, had a laugh over religious nuts, and the man even bought Roger lunch.

But, pleasant as the conversation had been, the lunch had not gone down well. In fact, on his way home, Roger was struck by a pain in the lower right side of his abdomen, a pain so severe that he had to pull over to the side of the road and sit a while. It was a dreadful scraping pain, as if a claw were scooping out his insides. At home that day, he'd vomited his lunch and kept retching until blood splashed red in the toilet.

It was the first sign of an ailment that would elude countless doctors. He spent the next three years undergoing test after test, none of which showed the slightest sign of an ulcer or intestinal problem, and all of which inspired the doctors to suggest he see a therapist. Although he would do so later, he wasn't quite ready to go that route when it was initially recommended.

Instead, he would sometimes spend entire days in bed curled into a ball, either waiting for the pain to go away or fearing it would return, all the while imagining it to be an ugly gnarled claw that scraped through his insides, trying to gut him like a fish...

Betty hurried back into the room and seated herself across from him, taking his hand.

"The sandwich is coming, now how *are* you? Where have you *been*, what's the—*oh!*" She held up his left hand and examined his fingers. "You're not married?"

"Uh, no." He gently pulled back his hand and drummed his fingers on the tabletop. "That...um, didn't work out."

"Oh. Well. I must admit, I'm glad to hear that."

Roger chuckled. "Should've said something *then*."

"Oh, I did. But when you're in love, honey, you'll hear a gnat fart before you'll hear your friends' warnings. You were deaf to 'em. And understandably so. She was a very appealing, very pretty girl."

"She was selfish," Roger said, shaking his head gently. "She was...deceitful...unfaithful..."

"She was a Seventh-Day Adventist."

After a pause, Roger said, "That, too."

"That in *particular*."

"Oh well. That was...Jesus, that was over five years ago." He shook his head again; he hadn't thought of Denise in a long time.

Betty asked how long he'd be in town and if he needed a place to stay, and Roger explained that he'd already rented a house on Beakman.

"Have you even seen it yet?" she asked.

"Not lately, but my friend Bill Neibord—remember Bill? The musician who believed in better living through litigation?"

"Sued Springsteen?"

"Tried to. Over a song. But it got thrown out of court. Anyway, he's lived in this house for the last two years or so and now he's moving to L.A. I needed to come *here*, so I grabbed it up."

"Why are you here?"

"I got a teaching job through Napa Community College. Creative writing and a short story class. Night classes here at St. Helena High."

"Well, that's good." She took an uncertain drag on her cigarette, cocking a brow. "Isn't it?"

"Yeah, sure. Sure it's good." He tried to give her a genuine smile as he thought, *Better than bouncing around in a rubber room or using a gun to repaint my bedroom a deep shade of brain matter.* "I've always wanted to try my hand at teaching."

"But you're still writing, aren't you?"

Roger half-shrugged.

"Well, you *are*, aren't you?" Betty was beginning to sound stern and motherly.

Someone came into the Munch Room and placed a sandwich and a Michelob in front of Roger, saving him from having to reply. He looked up to say thank you but could only stare silently for a moment at the most beautiful, loving, and frightened eyes he'd ever seen.

"Thank...um...thank you," he stuttered after a moment.

The girl quickly turned to leave, but Betty waved her back.

"Sondra, Sondra, c'mere."

The girl stopped suddenly, as if disappointed she hadn't escaped, slowly turned and came back to the table.

"Sondra, I want you to meet Roger Carlton, the writer you've heard so much about?" She turned to Roger. "I talk about you all the time and I came in here screaming my head off the morning after you were on Letterman." To Sondra: "Remember that?"

Roger was touched that she still seemed interested in him after he'd made no attempt to stay in touch for so long. But he gave that little thought; he couldn't take his eyes from the girl.

Her hair was the color of creamed coffee and her eyes—he couldn't stop watching them—were a deep dark brown, a solid brown that seemed to darken naturally into the black of her pupils.

She leaned over Betty's shoulder, holding out her hand cautiously, as if he might bite her.

"I knew who you were soon as you came in," the girl said, her eyes turned downward to the table. "I didn't see—" Her mouth was dry, so she stopped to swallow. "I didn't see you on TV but, but I saw your picture in the paper."

Betty said, "*The Chronicle* ran your picture when they reviewed *Ledges*. It was a terrible picture, Roger. You should have another taken."

Roger figured Sondra was about seventeen; she wore no make-up and her skin was unblemished and fair. There was a darkness about her eyes that made eyeshadow unnecessary and somehow made her look worried.

As Roger shook her hand, her eyes met his for just a moment and he saw something in them: flecks of gold, like miniscule slashes, tiny slits in the brown that opened up to something else.

She pulled her hand away and—Roger wasn't sure, but he *thought* he saw her wipe it on her apron.

"Nice to meet you," she said quickly, then spun around and hurried out.

Roger noticed as she left that she was quite tall, maybe taller than he.

"I just love watching the brains drip out of men's ears when she walks through the room," Betty laughed, putting out her cigarette. "Isn't she a stunner?"

"Yeah," Roger breathed. "Is she new?"

"No. She's been here about six months. That's a long time for the girls who work here. But then, everybody here's new to you. You've been gone too long." She reached over, took his face between her hands, and gave him a big kiss. "Glad you're back, kiddo." Standing, she pointed a finger at him and said, "Tonight. Our place. Seven. We've got a lot to talk about. I'll tell Leo you're here."

After Betty went back out front, Roger took a back issue of *American Film* from the basket of magazines on the floor and absently thumbed through it as he ate, just scanning the pictures and reading captions. He couldn't start an article because each time Sondra whisked in to wash some lettuce in the sink or slice some tomatoes, he had to look up and watch her go by.

She smelled only faintly of a sweet perfume—the kind of perfume a teenager would wear—and quickly rushed by him as if he weren't there, afraid that he might speak to her.

The sandwich was delicious, but Roger couldn't finish it.

The rock in his chest was hurting him again.

4

Ten years before, when Roger was going to the Seventh-Day Adventist college on the hill and living in the dormitory, DiMarco's Deli was a refuge, a place that served real meat, played rock and roll over the P.A. system, and where no one damned you for drinking a beer. Of course, if you weren't careful, you might be spotted by one of the school's many narcs who occasionally came into DiMarco's for a vegetarian sandwich and a can of fruit juice, and who would immediately report your transgression to the Dean.

When Roger quit college to write full time and moved down the hill to St. Helena, he frequented DiMarco's even more. It became a second home, the DiMarcos a second family; his own small house was too enclosed and too empty.

He'd moved to St. Helena for two reasons; he loved the town and he wanted to be close to his friends at the college. He'd grown up with most of the people he knew there because he'd gone to Seventh-Day Adventist schools since first grade. The Adventists are a very close-knit, self-contained group; they have their own schools, their own hospitals, even their own towns. One of those towns was just eight miles north of St. Helena.

Manning is populated solely by Seventh-Day Adventists and closes up from sundown Friday till sundown Saturday—the

Sabbath. Most of the students who moved off the hill settled in Manning.

By the time Roger left school, though, he considered himself an Adventist by association only, and decided it would be a lie to continue associating with them. He went to movies and bars, smoked and drank, ate meat—and worse, pork and seafood—and he didn't want to live in a community that would expect him to hold to *their* lifestyle, which included none of those things.

When he moved to St. Helena, he got a job in a Napa bookstore and drove there four days a week. The rest of the time he spent writing his book, trying to finish it as quickly as possible, hoping to sell it and raise enough money to quit his job.

He'd told only his two closest friends at the college of the *real* reason he quit school—his writing—telling everyone else that he was just taking a break.

There was a reason for this secrecy and it had nothing to do with shame. Rather than flaunt his choice to write fiction—let alone his chosen genre—Roger wanted to keep peace. As far as Seventh-Day Adventists are concerned, fiction of any kind is *not* a peacemaker. In fact, according to the writings of Ellen G. White, a self-proclaimed prophet and the voice and conscience of the Seventh-Day Adventist Church since the mid-1800's, the writers of fiction of any kind (and she includes fairy tales, comic strips, and even history books in the lot) are directly inspired by Satan to teach their unsuspecting readers to properly serve the Prince of Darkness. She even goes so far as to say in her writings that some people have been stricken with physical paralysis simply from reading too much fiction; the victims were kept in such a state of excitement by their reading material, claims Mrs. White, that their brains simply shut down and their bodies ceased to function.

Needless to say, reading fiction is not approved in Adventist circles; *writing* it is openly condemned.

So Roger decided to keep his intentions to himself.

But somehow, word got out; then everyone wanted to know *what* he was writing.

The book was called *Restraints* and Roger knew it would not be well received by Adventist friends and acquaintances. There were a few close friends who would probably appreciate it, but not many.

His novel was an erotic murder mystery that centered around a secret dominant-submissive relationship between a man and woman. When the woman is murdered, her sister—a straight-laced church organist—is determined to see justice done and find the killer herself. In the process, she discovers a dark, sexual side of herself that she never knew existed.

Roger had hoped to at least keep the book's plot under wraps, but knew that would be impossible, having had firsthand experience with the Adventist grapevine. So he prepared himself for the criticism.

It started as a quiet murmur on the hill.

What a disappointment Roger had turned out to be...

To think he'd been president of his senior high school class and used to sing in the church choir...

What a shame he was using his God-given talent to titillate and disturb rather than uplift and encourage...

He got stares when he went on campus to visit friends—stares from people he didn't even *know*. Roger thought he was imagining it at first until one day, while waiting for a girl in the dorm lobby, he was approached by a young man in a suit who asked hesitantly, "You're the writer, aren't you?"

Startled, Roger nodded; the boy stared at him for a moment, then walked away.

He tried to ignore it at first, but when he noticed that his friends were becoming increasingly unavailable—always too tired or too busy to see him—he could ignore it no longer.

Lying in bed one night, he realized he should have known this would happen, that his work, if he chose to continue it, would require him to cut himself off from the church and its people entirely—just as he should have known how difficult that would be.

As a child, Roger was taught—as was every other child he knew—that the Adventist church was the only true church, the "remnant church", and that he was fortunate to have been born into an Adventist home. He was taught to cling to his faith as if for his life—because some day it *would* be. Some day, he was told by his parents and his friends' parents, his ministers and Sabbath school teachers and school teachers—even his *gym* teachers—the government would band together with America's churches and decide that *everyone* should worship on Sunday. Because Adventists worship on Saturday, they would be considered criminals. They would have to flee their homes and hide out in forests and caves, living off the land while their enemies—all the other churches of the world—hunted them down like animals to be shot and killed on sight. This "time of trouble," as it was called, had been foreseen by Ellen White and written about at length in her many books. It was to take place just before the Second Coming of Christ; He would descend from the clouds to save His people—the Adventists—and punish everyone else by throwing them into the Lake of Fire (Adventists don't swear, so they can't call it Hell).

Ellen White's writing, with its purple prose and lofty words, conjured powerful and frightening images in young minds, images not soon forgotten and difficult to stop believing in. Every other child Roger knew was affected by these teachings; on the school playground, it wasn't uncommon to hear one child say to another, "I'll be the Adventist, you be the Catholic, and you try to kill me, okay?"

Throughout his childhood, Roger was hounded by nightmares of cowering in reeking garbage bins and dark, filthy abandoned buildings while the footsteps and gunshots of his hunters sounded all around. The nightmare always ended the moment he was discovered and about to be killed.

He had another recurring nightmare as a boy. It involved a picture his parents hung on his bedroom wall.

It was a picture of the U.N. Building; beside it stood a giant ghost-like Christ as tall as the building and wearing a white robe and sandals, his knuckle crooked, preparing to gently knock on the building, the hole in His palm clearly visible.

It wasn't a very good picture—it looked like a paint-by-number—but was very popular with Adventists and showed up in nearly every Adventist home. Posters were issued to Sabbath school rooms and school offices; there was even a wallet-sized picture available in Adventist bookstores.

Roger knew the artist had intended the giant Jesus to look gentle and benevolent, but in bad light, it did not.

In shadows, the beatific bearded face seemed to take on a sneer, a sinister grin held in check. The crooked finger seemed about to crash through a window and drag out whoever was unfortunate enough to be too close.

Christ seemed to be about to say, "I'm back, folks...and guess what I'm going to do to you for killing me the *last* time?"

Roger used to dream of waking to a tremendous rumbling and the agonized screams of people outside; a loud, angry voice that seemed to come from everywhere shouted, "Where's Carlton? Where *is* that little shit? I'm here for Roger Carlton because he reads *comic books* that he buys with his Sabbath school offering, and he watches TV on the *Sabbath* when his parents aren't around, and sometimes at night he *plays with himself*—DON'T YOU, ROGER? Where *is* the little *shit*?"

In the dream, Roger always went to his bedroom window and, with fear-weakened hands, pulled aside the curtain—

—to see two gigantic, ghostly, sandaled feet crushing cars and houses and people. There would always be a bloody hole through each foot.

The feet were always headed straight for Roger's house as the voice roared on...

"Where's Carlton? Where *is* the little *shit*?"

It was not easy to get out from under such dark clouds...the threat that the Time of Trouble might come and Roger might not be ready...the image of a gigantic, enraged messiah tearing up a whole town just to find Roger...

Even now, at the age of twenty-eight, he sometimes tensed when a television program was interrupted by a special news report, certain that Dan Rather was about to announce that a national Sunday law had been decreed and that those who break it—"Like you Seventh-Day *Ad*-ventists," he might add with a hateful sneer—would be executed. Even though Roger considered himself the farthest thing from an Adventist—he even held a burning *hatred* for them—the thought of such a broadcast chilled something in him, as if, although he'd shed the beliefs the church had instilled in him, he could not rid himself of the fears it had created.

When it came time for him to sever his ties to the church, he couldn't do it at first. It was like trying to stop smoking, something he'd failed to do; just as he needed a cigarette after a meal, he needed the approval of his Adventist friends. They were his whole life, the only friends he'd ever had. In order to disconnect himself from the church, he would have to disconnect himself from the first twenty years of his life.

Completely.

Roger needed to know that his friends didn't think there was something wrong with him—because there wasn't. He was just doing something he enjoyed, something he did well: telling stories.

As he continued writing the book, he tried to reassure his friends.

One of his closest and oldest friends was Marjie Shore. She'd been his first kiss in grammar school, his first girlfriend in high school, and his first lover in college. (In spite of stern doctrines prohibiting sex outside of marriage, Adventists—particularly of that age—are no less active, just less obvious.) They'd never gotten too serious, always dated other people, but they remained the closest of friends.

She knew he'd always planned to be a writer, she knew he wrote mysteries and thrillers; it had never seemed to bother her before and he asked her why she was suddenly uncomfortable with it *now*.

"I always thought you'd outgrow it," she said. "I never liked the stuff you wrote. I've always loved your *writing*—you're very good, God has blessed you with a wonderful talent. But I never liked the stories. All the violence and...and sex."

"But it's real. I mean, look around you, there's violence everywhere, we live in a violent world. Read a paper lately? And sex—well, Marjie, what was it we did, the two of us, remember? When—"

"I know, but it's...different. The things you write are wrong. You dwell on them, wallow in them, and they're...they're *sick*. They're wrong."

"But all those things you read, that was...*me*," he said. "My writing was a part of *me*. Yeah, they were thrillers and stuff, but they were *important* to me. I thought you knew that."

"I never understood it. I thought it would go away."

"You *read* them. You seemed to *enjoy* them."

"But I always prayed it would go away."

Roger felt like putting his face in his hands and bawling then. It was as if his entire relationship with Marjie had been a charade; she'd been waiting for him to turn into another person, and when she realized he wasn't going to—when he got serious about his writing and tried to do something with it—she just quit waiting.

She wasn't the only one.

That was the night he began to see the bridges burning all around him.

All of his friends—friends he'd known since he was a toddler—were no longer waiting for Roger to change; in their eyes, he was hopelessly lost.

Fortunately, his family gave him their support, although they remained active in the church. They told him to forget about those people, that they were never friends in the first place.

But that was what hurt the most. In spite of the histories they'd had, in spite of all they'd shared, they'd never really been his friends; they'd been waiting for Roger to shed his scaley, soiled skin, when all along, that skin had been Roger.

That was the night they began to hurt him.

Then he sold *Restraints*.

That was when they began to terrify him...

5

Roger spent the evening with Betty and Leo, sitting at the bar in their kitchen and talking over wine.

He'd spent a few hours settling into his new house; most of his things were in storage, so it didn't take long.

Leo, an enormous, solid man with a shiny bald head and a fringe of silvering black hair over his ears, pounded a hammer-like fist on the bar after finishing his fourth glass of wine, and rumbled, "Read your last book. You know, the one with the, uh—" He snapped his fingers twice in Betty's direction. "—what was it?"

"*Ledges*," Betty replied.

"Yeah, yeah. God*damn*, son, that was a horny book. Had me jumpin' on this broad every night that week," he laughed, leaning over to kiss Betty's hand. "But the movie—"

"Oh, please," Roger groaned, "let's not talk about that. It never should have been made." He sipped his wine and said, "Speaking of movies, I noticed Hollywood North is gone."

Betty and Leo exchanged a dark glance and Betty said, "You haven't heard."

"Heard what? Is Josh all right?"

Shaking her head slowly, Betty said, "He's got AIDS."

Something in Roger's chest seemed to deflate, collapse. "How bad is he?"

"Pretty bad. I saw him Sunday. He likes visitors but doesn't get many. Everybody's too scared they're gonna *catch* it," she added with quiet bitterness.

"S'a scary thing," Leo mumbled.

"Is he still living in St. Helena, Betty?"

"When he's not in the hospital. It won't be long before he'll need constant care. It won't be long, *period*, according to his doctor."

Roger finished his wine with a gulp. He hadn't been in contact with Josh in six years, but their long visits together were fond memories and he'd always meant to give Josh a call someday.

"*Meant* to," he murmured angrily to himself as he poured another glass.

"What?" Leo said.

"I'm just pissed at myself. I kept meaning to write him or call, but..."

"Go see him," Betty said enthusiastically. "He'd love that. He sits in that little house and watches old movies day and night. Pretty soon he won't even be able to do *that*. He'd love to see you."

"Yeah, I'll do that."

They talked for another hour about other people in town—

who'd moved, who'd married, who'd died—then Leo lifted his bulk from the barstool and slurred, "I'm through for the night, kids. See ya tomorrow."

After they heard the bedroom door close, Betty said, "So what's eating you? Why aren't you writing?"

"I didn't say I'm not writing."

"You didn't say you *are*."

"I am, I'm working on a new book, but it's…slow. The teaching job will do me good. I need a break."

"You've *had* a break. It's been—how long since your last book?"

"Almost two years."

"And the next one?"

"Whenever it's finished."

"Which will be—when?"

"I…don't know. Look, Betty, I need the break, okay? For however long it lasts, I *need* it." He blinked in surprise at his own words; he hadn't meant to sound so harsh. He picked up his crumpled pack of cigarettes, found it empty, and took one of Betty's and lit up. "The last couple years have been pretty…rough."

"Wanna talk about it?"

He thought about that for a few moments. Betty was just about the most understanding person he knew; she'd given him her support in everything he'd done, and always made him feel like she was on his side. But she knew nothing of Sylmar Neuropsychiatric or of his reasons for going there.

Sometimes even the most understanding people cocked a brow when they learned a friend—however close—had spent some time in a mental hospital…

"No," he said. "Someday, but not yet."

"Whatever you say."

"So. Who's that girl in the deli? What's her name—Sondra?"

"For God's sake, Roger," she laughed. "She's only seventeen."

"No, that's not why I'm asking. She's just…interesting, that's all. She seems so afraid, as if she's used to being hit every time she walks into a room. You know much about her?"

"Not much. She's awfully quiet. She's from Berrien Springs, Michigan."

"An Adventist?" Roger asked. Berrien Springs was another predominantly Adventist community.

"I think so, but I'm not sure. She always wears dresses, never pants, no jeans, no jewelry. She probably is."

"I'm surprised she's allowed to work there."

"I don't think they have much choice."

"Her parents?"

Betty shook her head. "Her parents were killed over a year ago. Maybe two. Some kind of accident, I think. She moved here to live with her cousin."

"Who's her cousin?"

"Her name's Annie. She comes in to get Sondra at the end of the day. Another quiet one, never says anything. I get the impression money's tight. I suspect Sondra never sees much of her paycheck, if any."

"Is her cousin married?"

"Yeah, but the way Sondra talks about him, he's been hurt, or he's crippled, or something. Whatever's wrong, he can't work."

Roger thought about Sondra's eyes, how they never met his for more than a second at a time, of the golden flecks in them that looked like tiny puncture wounds.

Punctures from the inside, he thought.

Sipping his wine, he muttered, "Poor kid."

6

When Roger walked through the back door of DiMarco's the next day, someone was screaming. The deli was dead silent except for the radio and wailing sobs of a girl who was leaning on Leo at the register, her fingers clutching his big shoulders and her face pressing to his chest.

Two girls behind the sandwich counter stared at her; customers stood in the middle of the store gawking at the crying girl.

Someone had died, Roger was certain.

Betty hurried by him from behind, patting his shoulder and saying, "In a minute, hon." She went to the girl's side and gently pulled her away from Leo, whispering something in her ear.

Roger stepped out of the way as Betty led the girl back to the Munch Room, whispering, "Just come in the back and sit down till we can reach your parents, okay, honey? Okay?"

The girl had long red hair and a face sprinkled with freckles and wet with tears.

Roger went to the meat counter where Leo stood beside the slicer shaking his head as he watched Betty lead the girl into the Munch Room.

"What happened?" Roger whispered.

"Shelly's fiancé was killed. The boy's parents are out of town, Shelly's parents are at work, so they called here. I went down and...and identified the body." He pulled his palm across his lips, closing his eyes a moment. "Hope I never again have to..." He didn't finish.

"What happened?"

"They're not sure yet and they don't want me to talk about it."

A line had formed at the counter; voices mixed with the radio's music; the deli was back in order.

"Roast beef and dill?" Leo asked.

"Uh, no. Just coffee for now."

A few tables were occupied; a cup of coffee sat beside the morning paper at Roger's usual place. As he seated himself, Betty came out of the restroom and joined him.

"Christ, what a horrible thing," she sighed.

"Is she okay?"

"Oh, it'll be a while before she's okay, I think." She lit a cigarette and blew smoke hard from her lungs. "They were gonna be married here. In the deli. Right up front between the potato chip racks and the cash register, can you imagine that? They met here, so they wanted to get married here." She laughed humorlessly.

"How long were they together?"

"Not long, about three months. She's—" Betty lowered her voice.

SLIVERS OF BONE

"She's pregnant. But they say they would've gotten married anyway. That they loved each other and..." She waved her cigarette before her face as if to say, *You know the rest.* "I never liked the boy. Benny Kent was his name. He was nice enough, but didn't seem the marrying kind, didn't seem...faithful. He'd come in here wearing his jogging clothes—he always wore jogging clothes, but I don't think he ever really jogged—and start flirting with the girls. When Shelly was around, he'd flirt with her, but when she *wasn't*—well, he got along very well with the others when Shelly was gone. He especially liked Sondra. Can you imagine someone trying to pick up Sondra? He asked for her phone number once and I thought she was gonna have a stroke; scared her silly. I tried to talk to Shelly about him, but..."

"She wouldn't listen."

"Sound familiar? Well, I better go back and be with her till someone comes. Later."

Betty returned to the restroom and Roger opened the paper before him, but he couldn't concentrate on the words. Instead of giving any thought to the girl whose fiancé had been killed, Roger found himself thinking about Sondra.

He wondered what she was so frightened of...

«« — »»

Roger was still in the deli two hours later. He'd chatted with a man in the wine business; he watched Shelly's mother arrive wearing a red grocery store apron and nametag, complaining about being pulled away from work and telling Betty, a bit too loudly, "I never could stand that boy, anyway." He finally read the paper and decided to have a sandwich.

When he went out front to order, he spotted Sondra coming in the front entrance.

"You're early," Leo bellowed.

She seemed to whither a bit at the attention Leo's voice drew to her.

"They...they closed school early," she said softly. "When they heard about B-Buh...the boy."

Roger thought it odd that she referred to him as "the boy" instead of by name.

As she hurried by him, hugging her school books to her breasts, he noticed there was something different about her. Something...

"Hello, Sondra," he greeted her, smiling.

She turned her head away from him and breathed, "Hi," then went into the Munch Room.

Roger got his sandwich, a beer, and went back to his table.

An old man sat at the back table noisily chewing his sandwich.

Sondra was the only other person in the room; her books were spread out on a table across from Roger. She sat hunched over her books, her long hair hiding her face, her index finger tracing sentences as she read.

What had he seen about her that was different from yesterday? Was it something about the way she walked? Something about her hair?

Her hair seemed stringier than yesterday, perhaps greasy, unwashed.

"Are you a senior this year?" he asked.

Without looking up, she nodded.

"Are you going to college next year?"

"No."

"Do you plan to go at all?"

Sondra slowly lifted her head a bit and looked at him through strands of her hair. There were blotches of darkness beneath her eyes; her face looked drawn and weary. Her voice was fragile as a spider's web: "I don't think we'll ever be able to afford it. I...I might take a few classes..."

"What would you like to study?" he asked, spreading a napkin over his lap.

She straightened a bit and pulled some of the hair from her eyes. Sondra seemed to puzzle over that question, as if she'd never given it a thought.

"I...I don't really know," she whispered, looking at the floor.

"What are your best subjects?" he asked.

"Well..." She frowned a moment. "All of them, I guess."

"You get straight A's?" he asked, somewhat surprised; she seemed too afraid of everything to be as aggressive as most straight-A students.

She nodded, looking at her book again.

"Then you'll have a lot of choices," he said. "In choosing a major, I mean."

She said nothing and didn't look up.

"Have you ever considered teaching?"

Sondra shook her head with a jerk, as if startled.

"Neither have I," Roger chuckled. "I *tell* people I have. I mean, that I'm looking forward to it. But you know what?"

Roger waited a long moment until she finally said, "What?" in a voice thin as silk.

"I'm scared to death," he said, leaning toward her a bit.

Nothing for a long time. Then she slowly lifted her head and turned her eyes to him, met his own.

"Really?" she whispered. "You're really scared?"

"Sure."

"Why?"

"Well, who am I to tell these people whether or not they can write? Just between you and me, most of them probably *can't*—but I had teachers tell *me* I was bad, that I'd never sell a word, so…" He shrugged and realized she was still looking at him, looking him right in the eye; but it was the way a deer looks into the eye of its hunter when the hunter snaps a twig or disturbs the earth. "Do you know what I mean?"

"Your teachers told you that?"

"Mm-hm."

She shook her head slightly and whispered, "But you went to school up—," then stopped suddenly and looked away.

Roger chuckled. "Up on the hill?"

A faint nod.

"Yeah, and most of my teachers didn't like *what* I wrote anymore than *how* I wrote it. Did Betty tell you that?"

No reply.

"Hm?"

He thought he saw her shake her head once.

"How did you know?"

Her book closed with a *crack* and she stood suddenly, scraping her chair over the concrete floor.

"I've gotta get to work," she said as she hurried out.

He noticed her clothes—a simple brown skirt, maroon sweater and white top—were mussed and in need of a wash, as if they'd been slept in.

She was an Adventist, all right. If Betty hadn't told her he'd gone to school up there, then one of *them* probably had. They'd probably been expecting him—probably already knew he'd arrived. Why had he, for one moment, thought otherwise?

They always knew where he was, where he was going.

They watched him.

In fact, they'd followed him all the way into a breakdown. Now they were apparently waiting for him, smiling, on the other side.

7

News of the sale of *Restraints* spread quickly on the hill, then through Manning.

The first sign of it was a phone call. It was a little after one a.m.; Roger was up working.

"Hello?"

"'Whatever is true, whatever is honorable, whatever is right, whatever is pure...let your mind dwell on these things.' Does *that* sound familiar?"

It was a woman, but he didn't recognize the voice.

"Who is this?"

"It's the Word of *God*! 'Whatever is true...whatever is pure.' What you're doing is a perversion, it's dangerous, mind damaging—"

Roger wanted to hang up but was too shocked and fascinated.

"—and God will *damn* you for it. And you were *given* the truth, *raised* in it, and—and—" She sounded almost too frustrated to go on. "God*damn* you for it!"

SLIVERS OF BONE

The loud slam that came over the line made Roger jerk the receiver from his ear; when he heard the dial tone, he replaced it in the cradle.

He called Marjie then, mostly out of habit. He hadn't seen her in three months but couldn't get out of the comfortable habit of calling her now and then. He knew her schedule enough to know she'd still be up studying; she had no morning classes the next day.

A second after Roger said hello to her, Marjie hung up the phone.

Roger stared at the receiver a while, reached down to call her back again, but decided against it. Instead, he called Bill Dunning.

He'd known Bill since first grade when they got in trouble for fighting over a crayon; they'd been best friends ever since. They'd roomed together in boarding academy, where they'd raised no end of mischievous hell without getting caught once; they'd always been a couple of teacher's pets and no one ever suspected them of the pranks that befell the school during their two years as students.

Bill was now an engineering major. They were still close but conflicts in their schedules and interests had put a wedge between them. Bill was a motorcycle enthusiast, Roger couldn't stand them; Bill was a sports fan, Roger wasn't; and rather than growing away from the church as Roger had, Bill had become more devoted to it.

That night, Bill was working the desk in one of the men's dorms; Roger called him there.

Bill immediately hung up on him.

He didn't sleep that night; he sat in front of the television staring blankly at the screen.

Two days later, he found the two front tires of his Accord slashed and flattened.

The following week, someone smeared dog shit all over the front seat of his car. He cleaned it off with trembling hands—it took days to get rid of the smell—and drove to DiMarco's.

Betty told him to call the police.

An officer came to the deli and talked with him; he took notes as Roger spoke.

"I don't know what to tell you," he said afterward, tapping his pencil on the table. "You really have no proof of—"

"I have two slashed tires and three rags covered with dog shit."

"They won't do us any good. And even if they would, our hands are tied because nothing was actually *done* to you *personally*."

"But they slashed my tires and—"

"That's vandalism, not necessarily a personal threat. We don't know why these people—"

"But I *told* you—"

"You can't prove that."

"So...what has to happen before you *can* do something?"

"They have to be caught hurting you, or trying to. And if they're from that church, like you say, you have to be able to prove it."

He never could prove it, even though it continued to get worse.

A rumor spread on the hill that Roger had broken into the biology lab late one night and stolen a dead cat to use in some kind of satanic sex ritual.

Several nights after he heard about the rumor, he got a phone call around nine in the evening.

"So what're you gonna steal next, devil worshipper?" a breathy male voice asked. "Babies out of the hospital? Or would you rather—"

Roger hung up, got in his car, and drove up the hill to Bill's dorm. He looked at no one as he hurried upstairs to Bill's room, not wanting to see the staring eyes, the sneering glances of those around him.

Bill's door was open wide and Bill lay on his bed studying. On the wall above him was a poster of the picture Roger had always hated so much; the giant spectral Jesus about to knock on the U.N. Building.

"Will you tell me what the hell is going on, Bill?" he asked, standing in the doorway on trembling legs. For a moment, he couldn't move; he was paralyzed by the alien look in Bill's eyes.

When he lifted his gaze from his book to Roger, his eyes flashed, in rapid succession, three reactions: surprise, sudden fear, then the dawn of the solid assurance—the cold steel *conviction*—that he had nothing to fear after all.

"I'd appreciate it if you didn't come in here, Roger," he said, reaching out to swing the door shut.

Roger caught it with his foot, stepped inside, and closed it behind him.

"Bill, why are you *doing* this?" Roger asked in a firm but quiet voice.

Sitting up on the bed, Bill said, "I'd really rather you go, Roger."

"We used to be so close, you and me. And Marjie? The three of us were—" Roger felt his voice weaken and start to crack; he took a breath. "—we were inseparable. Ever since we were *six*, for Christ's sake."

"Don't talk like that in *my* room," Bill snapped, standing.

"*What?*" Roger was genuinely surprised. "My swearing's never bothered you before."

Bill seemed to carefully choose his words as he shuffled his weight from foot to foot.

"I've lost patience with you," he said finally.

"Lost patience?"

"You were always interested in such...bad things. Fiction, movies...all things that you knew were wrong—and you *knew* that as well as *we* did, Roger, you *still* know it," he added quickly, as if he thought Roger might interrupt. "You were raised and taught the same way we were. But you kept rejecting the truth. No matter how much we prayed. You..." He shook his head sadly. "You're our failure."

"Fai...failure?" A moment before, Roger had feared he might cry; now he felt an anger stronger than anything he'd felt before.

"Maybe not as a writer. But you know, Roger...you *know* what you write is wrong."

Roger turned around and pressed his clenched fists to Bill's desk.

"It's not of God, Roger. And there's only one other source."

On the desk, Roger saw a paperweight he'd given Bill in high school. It was a scorpion encased in a clear half-sphere of plastic about the size of a large man's fist.

Roger touched it with his fingertips; it was hard and cool.

"Your work is evil, Roger," Bill said. "Evil."

Without a thought, Roger swept up the paperweight, spun around, and threw it blindly.

He regretted it even as his arm was slicing the air.

Bill threw himself on the bed.

The paperweight hit the poster and stuck in the gypsum wall behind it with a loud *thwack*, tearing a gash in the side of Christ's ghostly head.

Roger stared at Bill silently; he'd shocked himself.

Bill slowly rose from the bed, gawking open-mouthed at the paperweight sticking out of Jesus's head. Then he turned to Roger, looking at him as if Roger had just committed cold-blooded murder, and breathed, "I'm calling campus security."

"I-I'm sorry, Bill, really, I'm...I'm j-just so *frustrated*!"

Bill went to the phone on his dresser and began dialing as if Roger weren't there.

Roger moved toward him, saying, "Wait, Bill, just listen for—"

Looking over his shoulder, Bill said, "Don't come *near* me." His voice was unsteady and his hands trembled as he dialed; Bill was terrified.

"Just tell me who's calling me at night, Bill, just tell me—"

"Jesus Lord, protect me now from this evil," he whispered, hunching over the phone. "Shield me from whatever demon has—hello, security?"

Roger heard no more; he hurried out of the room and down the hall.

"Stay away from him!" Bill shouted from his doorway.

Doors opened and heads began to peer out.

A young man wearing a bathrobe stopped on the way to his room and stared as Roger passed.

"He's evil! Stay away from him! He tried to kill me!"

Roger resisted the urge to turn around and shout back; *what* he would shout he did not know. In the stairwell, he could still hear Bill, no matter how hard he tried not to.

"He's evil! Stay away from him! He's evil!"

He sometimes heard him still...

8

Josh looked as if he'd died some time ago but refused to admit it. He stood in the doorway, pale as fishmeat, his skin hanging from his bones like clothes he hadn't changed in a year. His brown hair was wirey and unkempt now and there seemed to be less of it.

His smile came slowly as his drawn, skull-like face craned forward on his wrist-thin neck.

"Roger?"

"Hey, Josh." Roger tried to smile and almost held out his hand to shake, but a sickening image flashed in his mind that held his hand back: Josh's arm breaking off in his hand, snapping at the elbow with a crisp, hollow crack.

Josh held out his hand anyway, and Roger could not ignore it; the hand was featherlight and too cold.

Pulling his bathrobe together in front, Josh led Roger into the house where Humphrey Bogart was shouting at Edward G. Robinson on television.

Josh walked slowly and carefully, as if his body might, at any moment, crumble into a heap of splintered, broken parts.

The temperature in the small house was cloyingly warm and Roger could smell pungent, stinging medicines.

Josh fell into a chair and turned off the television and VCR with the remote control.

Roger seated himself on the sofa and looked at Josh, wondering if he should have come. This was not the same man he'd known six years ago; he was a withered stalk of flesh and bone. Roger didn't have the foggiest idea what to say; *so how've you been?* was out of the question.

A tune from the seventies ran through Roger's head, but with slightly altered lyrics:

What do you say to a dying man?

But Josh managed to make him comfortable. Eventually.

"Did you call?" he asked.

"No, I'm sorry. I should have—"

"Oh, no, I was just wondering. I haven't checked the answering machine lately. I sleep a lot these days. Practicing, I guess."

Roger winced.

"You should hear my tape," he said with a paper-thin laugh. "'I'm sorry, I can't come to the phone right now. I'm in the bedroom rehearsing my Greta Garbo death cough.'" He laughed again, but it turned into a fit of coughs.

The joke made Roger fidget; it was funny, but he couldn't bring himself to laugh.

"You would've laughed at that a few years ago, Roger."

"But you weren't sick then."

"I am *now*, and if *I* can laugh at it, so can *you*." Then, after a moment: "Please."

Their conversation was peppered with Josh's razor-sharp jokes about his illness; it wasn't long before Roger was laughing with him.

They talked about movies, about Roger's work, then the topic of Josh's impending death moved in like a storm cloud.

"This isn't going to take me," Josh said quietly. "The doctor doesn't give me long, but I know I've got longer than he thinks. I can feel it." He placed a skeletal hand on his chest. "Inside. It'll be a while before I run out of life. But when I do...it won't be because of this."

"What do you mean?"

"I have a gun. I've never used it before, but I know how. When I feel I don't have much longer—when I *know* I'm going to die soon but while I'm still able to get around—I'm going to disappear."

"Where?"

"I'm the only one who needs to know that."

"But...why?"

"I don't want to be found here, in my home. I don't want to leave a...a mess someone else will have to clean up." He cocked his head, looking at Roger thoughtfully. "You're the first person I've told. About my plan. Keep it to yourself, okay?"

"Sure, Josh, but...well, the thought of you—"

"Don't think about it. I probably shouldn't have told you. But believe me, Roger, the thought of this thing, this sickness, taking me when *it* wants to…" He shook his head. "It has to be *my* decision."

"I understand," Roger said quietly, remembering the sensation of cold gunmetal against the roof of his mouth. "Believe me, Josh, I understand."

9

Although the police would confirm nothing, word spread that Benny Kent had been shredded like a life-size paper doll, and that parts of him had been eaten.

The police did make a brief statement, however, saying only that Benny had been attacked by a wild animal while jogging and had bled to death before he was found.

Roger knew the press would stay with the story for weeks to come, ferreting out every rumor and speculation, getting as much from it as they could. As he read about it in Saturday's paper, Roger kept remembering what Betty had said about Benny Kent:

He always wore jogging clothes, but I don't think he ever really jogged…

…don't think he ever really jogged…

…ever really jogged…

The funeral was going to be Tuesday; the high school would be closed for half a day so students could attend.

…I don't think he ever really jogged…

Roger tried to shake it from his mind; he had a habit of turning unanswered questions into mysteries with which he became obsessed, pursuing them at the expense of his work, and sometimes his sleep.

He didn't need that now.

More than anything, he needed his sleep.

10

Roger's last two years in St. Helena were like riding a roller-coaster that only went down—*straight* down.

The story of his visit to Bill's room was blown out of proportion and spread like a plague. It went like this:

Roger burst into Bill's room and began spouting some sort of evil spell in an ancient tongue; a paperweight flew across the room, untouched and of its own volition, destroying a picture of Christ. The evil force that had, for years, been so subtly inspiring Roger's unholy stories of lust and murder, was clearly making itself known. The monster inside him was finally awakening. Roger Carlton was—*obviously*—possessed by Satan.

The late night phone calls doubled.

"Are you keeping the *Sabbath*, Roger?"

"Do you know you're going to *burn*, Roger?"

"Take your demons somewhere *else*, Roger, your evil isn't welcome here."

"The Bible says—"

"Sister White says—"

"God says—"

The voices were male and female, sometimes familiar, sometimes not. He had his number changed twice, always unlisted, but the calls continued.

After the girl spit on him in DiMarco's, Roger began to spend more time at home with his dog Larry, a mutt he'd found outside the deli one evening.

Stories of Roger's "possession" began to spread among non-Adventists; while they were not familiar with the church's beliefs and taboos and did not accept the stories as gospel, they still looked askance at Roger, apparently deciding that there must be *something* strange about him to generate so much talk.

By the beginning of the last year, he saw Betty and Leo only at their home or his; DiMarco's Deli was no longer the refuge it had once been.

He began to drink more than he should and write less.

The phone calls did not stop—he kept his phone off the hook most of the time—and the police said there was nothing they could do unless the calls were specifically life-threatening.

His tires were slashed again and one morning he awoke to find a red cross painted on his front door; beneath it, written crudely, was a Bible verse: Exodus 22:18. He went to the library to look it up because he no longer owned a Bible.

It read, "Thou shalt not suffer a witch to live."

He filed yet another report with the police, but they did not see it as a threat.

That was when he finally began to think it was time to leave in spite of his love for Napa Valley.

Two nights later, feeling restless, he drove to a coffee shop in Calistoga. On his way back, as he drove through Manning, headlights appeared bright in his rearview mirror; a car parked behind a large tree sped onto the road and followed him. The headlights drew nearer, filling the mirror, and, a few hundred yards farther down the road, two gunshots rang out behind him.

The next few minutes became a blur as Roger slammed his foot on the accelerator and doubled the speed limit the rest of the way through Manning, hoping he would attract a patrolman. Rivulets of sweat cut chilly trails down his neck and back as he hunched over the steering wheel as if hugging it for protection, breathing, "Oh God, oh God, oh God," over and over. He tensed in anticipation of another gunshot, of the sensation of a chunk of lead tearing through his flesh, nicking his bone—

—but the headlights were growing smaller in the mirror and the sound of the car's roaring engine was fading away.

Roger did not slow down; he went from Manning to St. Helena, where he parked in front of the police station and ran inside, nearly sick with fear. After a glass of water and a cigarette, he calmed down enough to tell the on-duty officer—a man named Miller with a barrel chest, thick glasses and thin brown hair—what happened.

Afterward, Miller began asking questions, shaking his head slightly after each reply.

No, Roger could not identify the car or its driver or passengers.

No, he did not see the license plate.

No, he didn't actually *see* a gun, but it sure didn't sound like an engine backfiring.

"Look," Roger said, "this has been going on for more than two years now. Not as bad as this, but—well, I've reported everything."

After checking a file and shuffling some papers, Miller returned to his desk and said, "You sure have." He kept glancing from the papers to Roger and back again, noisily chewing some gum. "You've reported a lot of stuff, haven't you?"

"Everything that's happened."

"But you had no proof *then* that these things were being done by Seventh-Day Adventists."

"But the things they say on the phone, the cross and—"

"Those don't mean a thing. Listen, I've lived here most of my life, and you can't do that without getting to know a little about the Adventists. They're kinda strange—no movies, no coffee, no jewelry or dancing—but maybe it works, because they're good people. They do a lot for the community. They—"

"Yeah, I know, they collect clothes for the poor and food for the hungry, they help people stop smoking—they've got *great* PR." Roger stood. "But they're like *spiders*, Officer Miller. They eat their own."

Miller leaned back in his chair and shrugged. "Well, even if the people who shot at you *were* Adventists, you've got no ID on the car or driver, no witnesses. You've got nothing."

Frustrated, Roger started to leave.

"Wait, Mr. Carlton, I'd like to make a suggestion."

Roger stopped and turned wearily.

"Don't take this wrong, now. I'm on your side. I believe that *somebody's* got it in for you and your work. And God knows I've dealt with enough religious nuts in my time—of *all* religions—but you need solid proof. And it might be a good idea if you didn't report any more of these things till you *have* that proof. Think about it. Some kid on the hill gets a wild hair up his ass and burns down one of the school buildings. We've got no leads, don't know who did it, but we *do* have a stack of reports filed by some guy who thinks the Adventists are out to get him but can't *prove* it. Turns out *you* were home alone the night of the fire. No witnesses. No alibi. And we *know* you don't like them. Wouldn't be too good for you. That's why I'm telling you—for your own good. Think about it."

The short drive home was terrifying; each time he saw headlights in his rearview mirror, Roger's body buzzed with adrenaline.

When he got home, his front door was open a crack. With his heart pumping its way up his throat, he cautiously entered, turned on the lights, and looked around.

The lock had been broken; no one was inside and nothing seemed to be missing.

But he couldn't find Larry.

Not at first, anyway.

Larry was hanging by a rope over the back porch. All four of his legs had been twisted and broken; his abdomen had been cut open down the middle and his insides lay splashed on the concrete.

Roger moved to Los Angeles that night.

11

Sunday was covered by a shroud of gray clouds.

Around one, Roger bought a paper and went to DiMarco's. Sunday was always slow; there were a few people in front but the Munch Room was empty except for Sondra, who was seated at a corner table studying and drinking apple juice. She sat straighter than she had the day before; she looked a little healthier, more rested. Roger got a bowl of minestrone and took a seat at the table closest to hers.

"On a break?" he asked.

She nodded without looking up.

"What are you studying?"

"American History," she whispered.

She didn't seem interested in talking, but Roger didn't want to give up while she was on a break. He wanted her to talk, have a whole conversation with him; he wanted to put her at ease.

"Where do you go to school?" he asked.

"St. Helena High."

"Really? Why not the prep school on the hill?"

She slowly lifted her eyes to him.

"You are a Seventh-Day Adventist, aren't you?"

The light from the small lamp on her table glistened among the golden gashes in her brown eyes.

"How did you know?"

"Just a guess. I'm familiar with them and...well, a pretty girl like you should be wearing a little makeup, maybe a nice necklace—"

You're making an idiot of yourself, he thought.

"—but you aren't. So, I thought maybe..."

"You used to be one," she whispered, turning away from him.

"That's right. How did you know?"

"I...heard."

"Like you heard that I went to school on the hill?"

She suddenly seemed out of breath as she gathered up her things from the table.

"Where did you hear that?"

"Around."

"Is your break over?"

"Uh, no, I just have to...I have to, uh..." She pushed away from the table, stuttering, then stopped; she couldn't lie. "No, it's not over."

Roger turned his chair toward her. "Are you afraid of me, Sondra?"

She bowed her head again and blushed. "Well...not...not really. But...they say I should be."

"Who?"

"People at church."

He nodded. "Do you believe them?"

"I...don't know." She whispered this secretively as she took her seat again, as if afraid of being overheard. "You don't *seem*...um..."

"Evil?"

She nodded.

He waited because she seemed about to ask him something. Finally she looked at him and, like a fearful schoolgirl asking the principal if he *really* kept a spiked paddle in his bottom drawer, Sondra asked, "Are your books inspired by Satan?"

"No," he smiled. "If anything, they're inspired by newspapers. I write about the things people do to each other—mostly *bad* things—and about what happens to them afterward."

Here I go again, he thought, *defending myself against their lies.*

"But...if they're bad things...why write about them?"

Roger chose his words carefully. "Because if we don't write about them and read and *think* about them, they'll only get worse. We'll never figure out a way to make them stop because we won't look at them long enough to figure out why they happen. Unfortunately, everyone in the world doesn't do the things Adventists *think* they should do."

Including some Adventists, he thought.

"Don't you ever write about...*good* things?"

"Sure. About good people and bad people. Good things happen in my books, but bad things happen, too—and sometimes to good people. Because that's just the way it is. Think about it, Sondra, have you ever had a single day when only *good* things happened to you?"

As she thought about that a while, her face slowly changed, softened, and Roger thought he saw a glimpse of something that made him want to smile; she understood. It seemed to make sense to her; something he'd said had cut through probably seventeen years of Adventist teaching and thinking—Adventist *living*—and had *reached* her.

This is how a teacher feels, he thought, still wanting to smile—to *grin*—but not sure how she would interpret it.

She stood with one hand on the table and said, "Well, I guess I'd...better go." She started to walk away but quickly turned and whispered to him, "Do...do you really think I'm...pretty?"

"Very," he said, meaning it. Before she could go, he put his hand on hers, stopping her, and said, "Would you like to read one of my books? I've got some copies at home."

Her eyes moved downward to his hand and lingered there for a long time. So long, in fact, that Roger thought she was getting angry, thinking that he was making a pass, and he pulled his hand away.

Her hand followed his, gently brushing it with her fingertips, then jerked away as if burned. Sondra's entire body jolted once and she stepped back, bumping her chair and pressing her hand to her stomach.

"*Sondra?*" Roger said, concerned. "Are you—"

"I'm fine," she whispered, backing away, still holding her stomach. "Fine, just...I just...have to..." She bolted for the bathroom and slammed the door behind her.

Something fell to the bathroom floor with a *smack—*

Her books, he thought.

—and muffled retching sounds came from behind the door.

Roger lost his appetite, thinking perhaps he'd said something that had upset her, made her sick, and he pushed his soup aside.

A moment later, Betty called him from out front. As he left the Munch Room, Leo passed him coming in, grumbling.

"Where the hell are those *boxes*, Goddammit?" he snapped as he passed, heading for the restroom. "*Sondra?* Where the hell is Sondra?"

As Roger walked through the door, Betty took his arm and led him past the grocery shelves.

"Somebody I want you to meet," she said.

"Betty, Sondra's pretty sick, I think. She just—"

"Oh, it's just—" She leaned toward his ear and whispered. "—just her period. It always hits her hard, poor kid."

Betty introduced Roger to a customer who was a fan of his books. They chatted at the register for a moment, Roger answering all the usual writer questions, then froze when they heard Sondra's scream.

They stood in place for a moment, as if paralyzed, until she screamed again:

"*Leooo!*"

Roger dashed back through the Munch Room and spotted Leo's legs sticking out of the bathroom door, jerking.

He was curled on the floor, clutching his chest, pain shattering his red sweating face with countless lines and wrinkles. He was groaning, writhing miserably, wheezing for air, and as Roger knelt beside him, Leo vomited onto the concrete floor.

Sondra pressed herself into the corner, hugging her books, her face ashen.

"Call an ambulance!" Roger said in a thick voice.

She didn't move.

"Go *now*!"

Betty passed her on the way in, crying, "Leo! God, oh, Leo, oh—"

"Betty, see if there's a doctor out front—somebody who knows what to do! I think it's his heart."

Her hoarse crying voice faded as she hurried out.

Leo's face was darkening as he struggled for air; he vomited again with a long, agonized groan.

Roger had never felt so helpless, so useless; tears burned his eyes as he watched Leo's body perform its violent mutiny. "Leo, oh Leo, just…if you could just…" He didn't know what to say.

Suddenly, Leo gripped Roger's shirt with a meaty hand and pulled him closer, sucking air to speak. His words were wet and garbled:

"What…*is*…she?"

"I don't…who?"

"Son…*dra*."

Roger saw more than pain in Leo's face, in the way his mouth stayed open and his tongue darted around, in the way his eyebrows rose high above his bulging eyes; he saw fear.

"What…what about Son—" Leo wouldn't let him finish.

"I *saw*…her. I-I came in and…and she…she was—"

Leo's big body stiffened and he cried out in pain, tearing Roger's shirt with his fingers.

"What…*is* she?" he gasped.

Leo released a long sigh that seemed to come from every inch of his body; his hand relaxed against Roger's chest.

The room filled with the smell of bodily wastes as Leo's hand slapped to the floor.

12

Roger got no sleep for the next twenty-four hours.

Betty crumbled when she returned to the restroom and found Leo dead; she was taken to the hospital at the request of her family doctor, who came to the deli as soon as he heard.

Roger stayed behind to take care of things at the deli; fortunately, the girls knew what they were doing and didn't need much help because he was not up to supervising. He knew Leo kept a bottle of scotch in a box under the back room sink; after things had calmed down a bit, he had a couple of drinks to warm the cold trembling in his limbs.

When he went out front, he found Sondra sitting at the table by the front window, staring out at Main Street. Roger quietly seated himself at the table.

"Would you like to go home, Sondra?"

"My cousin is coming to get me during her next break." She was silently crying.

"Are you okay? Can I get you something?"

"No, I'm okay."

He chewed his lip a moment, debating his next question.

"Tell me, Sondra...what happened in there?"

She took a deep breath and said, "He...he came in and...he grabbed his chest and...fell over and...and..."

"Did something startle him? Were you talking when it happened?"

She stared out the window a long time, then shook her head, wiping away a tear.

What...is she?

Leo was in a lot of pain, he thought. *He was probably hallucinating.*

Another tear tumbled down her cheek as she whispered, "I didn't do anything."

"There was nothing *any* of us could do, Sondra. It was a bad one. It took him—"

Roger stopped when he noticed she was wringing her hands on the table, squeezing until the knuckles paled. Pearls of sweat clung to her forehead and her lips were a tense, straight line.

She didn't mean she was sorry that she didn't do anything to save Leo from his heart attack; she was denying that she'd done anything to cause it, and making the denial for no good reason Roger could see.

What...is she?

"Well," he said, looking at her differently now, curious about the guilt she was failing to hide, "remember what I said about bad things happening to good people? This is one of them. But Leo wouldn't want us to spend too much time crying over him." Roger stood. "He'd want us to keep the boxes stacked and the slicer clean."

The bell over the door clattered and a small, weary-looking woman came in wearing a white rectangular nametag on her pink-and-white striped smock. She smelled slightly of medicine and disinfectant, like a doctor's office. Her brown hair was pulled back snugly into a ponytail. Large brown eyes were set deep beneath a worried brow. Her cheekbones were like blades beneath her pale skin. She clutched her purse before her in both hands.

"Ready to go, Sondra?" she asked in a small voice, ignoring Roger.

He saw in Annie the same fear he saw in Sondra and found it fascinating.

Sondra left the table and went to the door. Roger wasn't sure he'd heard her whisper "Goodbye" or if it was just a soft exhalation.

"Sorry about your loss," Annie muttered, leaving with Sondra.

Roger watched them through the window for a moment. Sondra's shoulders were stiff and a bit hunched, as if she wanted to close in on herself.

Roger thought, *What could she have done in that bathroom?*

«« — »»

In the following days, Roger helped Betty arrange for Leo's cremation. She refused to hold any kind of ceremony, claiming that Leo would hate to be the reason for any man to have to put on a suit and tie. Instead, she held a gathering at her house the following Tuesday.

DiMarco's Deli had been opened in St. Helena by Leo's grandfather seventy-five years ago; the DiMarcos were a prominent family in the area and Betty received visitors from all over the valley.

Roger spent that day at the deli. Debi, the cashier, showed him how to clean the slicer and change the coffee filter.

Sondra came in late that day and said little. Whenever Roger spoke to her, she acted as if she didn't hear and hurried away.

Betty had given him the key to lock up at the end of the day, but after everyone had gone, Roger sat in the Munch Room, listening to the radio, sipping scotch, and smoking while he stared at his blank-paged notebook.

An hour later, Betty came in the back door and walked unsteadily to his table, smiling.

"Jesus, I've never had so many people in that house," she said, slurring her words.

"Did it go well?"

She lit a cigarette and nodded. "Everybody seemed...comfortable, you know? Leo would have liked it. Everybody was...well, *drunk* is what everybody was. Me, too, I guess." Her smile turned downward and tears began to fall. "Roger, I don't know what I'm gonna do. I think I...want to stay this way for a while. Drunk. You know? I was wondering if you'd mind...taking care of things here for a few days? Or weeks. I don't know how long. I'd *pay* you, of course. Just for a while, Roger, I promise."

"Sure, Betty. I don't know if I'll do you any *good*..."

"Oh, you'll be fine. I don't know about *me*." She laughed as she cried, putting out her cigarette and standing.

"Can I drive you home?"

"No, I'd like to walk."

Roger imagined Benny Kent's torn and bloody body lying in a cold, muddy ditch—

I don't think he ever really jogged.

—and became uncomfortable with the idea of Betty walking alone after dark.

He drove her home.

13

Roger met Denise in Los Angeles.

He moved in with Tony Gavin, an ex-Adventist he'd known for years. Tony constructed sets for movies and television shows and, like Roger, had bitter feelings toward the church.

The week Roger moved in, Denise Long moved in two doors down. She was a speech therapist from Colorado.

And a Seventh-Day Adventist.

Roger didn't discover that until their third date. By then, it was too late. They got serious fast and on that night, when Denise made a joke about her Adventist upbringing while they were tangled on the sofa in a half-prone position, it didn't seem very important. She knew about his writing; he decided if it disturbed her, she would have mentioned it already. She was probably a lax, back-slidden Adventist.

He was right; she went to church sporadically, was very liberal in her observation of the Sabbath, and she danced and went to movies.

And she had nothing against living together before marriage, a topic that came up sooner than Roger expected.

Three months after they moved in together, Roger announced their engagement to his parents and sister, as well as to Betty and Leo. Shortly after that, Denise read his book in progress in bed one night. She didn't talk about it until two weeks later.

During those two weeks, something changed between them.

Denise seemed preoccupied and frowned a lot. Sometimes Roger would find her staring at him as if he were a total stranger.

He thought little of it. He was happy for the first time in a long while; he was in love and his writing was going beautifully. The pain that had made him so miserable for a while had not reared its ugly head in months. He decided Denise was just buried in her work, maybe not getting enough sleep. The possibility of it all going sour seemed remote.

Until he came into the bedroom one night to find Denise reading a volume of *Testimonies* by Ellen White.

"Roger, why do you write what you write?" Denise asked suddenly.

He took his time replying, trying to give her a clear explanation for his interests in crime and the macabre.

"Why?" he asked after trying to answer her question.

She hesitantly told him that his novel had disturbed her, that she'd confided in a friend about her feelings.

"A...pastor," she said. "From Glendale. He's heard of you. *Lots* of people have, it seems. And none of what they've heard is good."

As Roger tried to decide where to begin his explanation of his reputation, she asked, "Are you *always* going to write this kind of stuff?"

"Probably. I don't know."

"Because if you are...I can't stay with you."

They did not go to bed that night; they stayed up talking. Their conversation, which seemed to go in circles, moved from the bedroom to the kitchen to the living room and back to the bedroom, Denise saying that, even in her disinterested, back-slidden spiritual state, she could not justify his work, could not understand how a person with his upbringing could use a God-given gift toward such unpleasant ends.

It was the same thing he'd heard from Marjie and Bill, and when he realized that, he couldn't fight anymore. He stopped arguing and started packing; his things were back in Tony's apartment the next day.

But it wasn't that easy. She only lived two doors down. He

knew when she walked by the door because he recognized her footsteps in the tile corridor; he saw her car in the parking lot; sometimes he thought he could smell a faint whiff of her perfume.

Roger began to look for another apartment. He couldn't really afford it, but he had a royalty check due any day. It was already four months late.

He found a studio apartment in North Hollywood. On the evening he was moving his last few boxes of things out of Tony's apartment, he got a phone call.

"We wanted to wish you luck in your new apartment," a man said.

"Who is this?"

"Because you're gonna need it, devil worshipper."

Although he had an unlisted phone number, he began receiving the calls at his apartment after he moved in.

His tires were slashed again, all four this time; the following week, someone painted a red cross on the hood of his car.

He decided not to buy a pet.

Roger drove nightly to Studio City where he spent a few hours writing over coffee in Tiny Naylor's. He was unable to spend much time in his apartment; the clamber from Tiny's kitchen and the chatter of the waitresses was comforting and preferable to the confinement of his apartment.

He got to know several other writers who frequented the coffee shop for the same reasons. One was a screenwriter who interested Roger in writing for the movies and even arranged a couple of meetings so Roger could pitch some ideas. Neither meeting was successful, but Roger told himself it was good experience if nothing else.

The pain returned with a vengeance and brought with it horrifying nightmares. Roger remembered little of what happened in those nightmares except for two things: looking at his hands and seeing, instead, hideous blood-soaked claws and the burning sensation of his skin changing its texture.

He began to renew his relationship with alcohol, which had gone ignored during his months with Denise.

When the calls increased in spite of the fact that he'd changed his number, he spent more and more time at Tiny's, never looking forward to going home.

One morning, Roger awoke to find his apartment door open a crack. The lock had been broken during the night and the contents of his open closet were scattered on the floor. With his head pounding from a hangover, Roger went to the closet and fell against the wall suddenly, afraid he would be sick.

His clothes were splattered with blood; clots of it clung to shirtsleeves and had dribbled into small puddles on the floor.

But it wasn't blood. It was red paint.

All but the clothes in his hamper were ruined.

As he stared in disbelief at the closet, the phone rang.

"Most people have *skeletons* in their closet," a man said. "You've got *blood* in yours. And we want *you* to know…that *we* know."

Roger hung up.

Later that day, he bought new locks and an answering machine.

From then on, he went out only to buy groceries or go to the post office. Even then, he tried to make his errands as brief as possible; sometimes he got the unshakable feeling that people were staring at him, maybe even whispering about him behind his back. The pain in his gut became a companion that clawed his insides at the most unexpected moments, doubling him over, sometimes sending him retching to the nearest bathroom. Sometimes he lay in bed waiting for the pain, afraid of it.

Tony came over one afternoon and pounded relentlessly on the door until Roger let him in. Tony looked around the messy apartment and stared at Roger like a stranger, muttering, "Shit, man, what's wrong?"

Roger tried to smile. "Caught me on a bad day, I guess."

"Bad day my ass. You need help."

Tony insisted Roger see a therapist and, reluctantly, he agreed.

Her name was Dr. Yee—"But please, call me Laurie"—a softspoken Asian woman in her thirties whose interest turned to confused shock as Roger told her of the harassment and threats he'd been receiving.

Shortly before the end of the session, she frowned and said, "Tell me more about this pain in your stomach."

"Well, it has no pattern that I can see, it's not brought on by food or—"

"Stress? Anxiety?"

"Maybe, but I'm not sure."

"Tell me again what it feels like."

"Like...like a claw scraping out my insides."

"Picture the claw in your mind and describe it to me."

"It...it has long, bony fingers...knobby joints...coarse, leathery skin and...and..." He stopped, afraid that talking about it would stir it up, bring it to life. "Razor-sharp talons are growing out of the ends of the fingers."

"Is it always there?"

"No. Sometimes it...well, it's like it curls up in a ball and just...waits."

"For what?"

"I don't know."

"What is it trying to do, Roger?"

"Well, it...Jesus, this sounds crazy."

"Go on."

"Sometimes I feel like it's...trying to get out. Like it will tear right through my stomach."

He saw Laurie again that week and she continued asking him about the pain. After searching his face for a long thoughtful moment, she said, "What is it about yourself that you're afraid of, Roger?"

"I'm sorry?"

"Look at the way you're sitting. Arms folded in your lap, hunched forward, like you're covering something up. Or...holding something in."

"I don't understand."

"What do your Adventist friends think of you now, Roger?"

"They think I'm evil. That I'm some kind of monster."

"Do you agree?"

"Of *course* not."

"But Roger, you were raised to believe that the things you're doing now are wrong, *very* wrong. This was pounded into your head from birth. Aren't you just a little afraid that maybe the Adventists are right?"

He didn't respond.

"I'm not saying they *are*. But you can't just throw away more than two decades of being taught what's right and wrong. Especially when you've still got people *telling* you how evil you are. You know what I want to do here, Roger? I want to help convince you that what's inside of you—the real Roger Carlton—is *not* an evil, clawed monster. Because I don't think you're too sure yet."

She assured him he would not see immediate results, that it would take some time, and that he should be patient. But patience did not come easily. He wanted whatever was wrong with him to go away now.

When that didn't happen—when the pain grew worse and the calls continued and someone left a large dead rat at his door with a crucifix on a chain around its matted neck—Roger bought a gun.

He told himself he was just buying it for protection, but when the man in the store told him he couldn't have it for two weeks, he suddenly knew the truth.

"Why two weeks?" Roger asked.

The broad black man behind the counter flashed two rows of bright teeth and said, "California law. We call it a cooling off period. Say you get really pissed at the wife, decide to blow her head off, and buy a gun. Two weeks later, maybe you'll be cooled off. But then again," he chuckled, "maybe not."

"Two weeks," Roger muttered, thinking, *That'll give me plenty of time to decide how to do it.*

Two weeks later, Roger knelt over his bathtub and eased the trembling barrel of the .25 caliber automatic pistol into his mouth as rain thrashed against the windows.

He stayed that way for a long time, feeling disoriented, wincing at the jagged-edged fragments of thoughts that cut through his mind.

The phone rang three times—three long meandering rings—

and the answering machine picked up; it was Barry Leese, one of his writer acquaintances from Tiny's.

"Hey, Rog," he said, "if you wanna try your hand at screenwriting, I think I can get you something. It's just a cheap-shit horror flick, but maybe it'll get you out of your cave. Give me a call tonight."

All Roger heard was, "Maybe it'll get you out of your cave." He heard it over and over as his sweaty palm slid against the butt of the gun.

Something about the call jarred him and he sat up and pulled the gun away. His stomach was hurting and he realized he'd shit his pants.

He called Laurie.

By mid-afternoon the next day, Roger was admitting himself to Sylmar Neuropsychiatric Hospital.

"I really think it's the best thing for you now, Roger," Laurie told him. "You can't be alone, and you know that. It's entirely voluntary, so you can spend a night there and if you don't think you'll benefit from a stay there, you can leave. Anytime you want. I promise."

Laurie was unable to keep her promise. She was called out of town shortly after Roger was admitted. "A personal emergency," her service said. "She's turned her caseload over to Dr. Stanwick until she returns next month."

Next month.

Roger repeated those words to himself as he waited to see the chief of staff, Dr. Lyle Abbott, who said, "A voluntary admission means nothing if you're still suicidal, Mr. Carlton. And I'm not so sure you've passed that stage yet."

He repeated them as he waited to see Dr. Stanwick, a short, stern, gray-haired woman who told him, "You've only been here two days, Mr. Carlton, and I sense no sign of improvement over the symptoms described in these records."

He repeated them silently to himself as he was questioned by Dr. Abbott:

"What do you think of when you see the color black?

"What does 'a rolling stone gathers no moss' mean to you?"

"Do people talk about you behind your back?"

Next month, next month, he thought, wishing Laurie could hear the words.

She returned almost seven weeks later. Roger was polite and reserved when she came to see him; he smiled a lot and answered all of her questions positively, hating her all the while. Pleased with his disposition, Laurie authorized his release. He made an appointment to see her later that week at her request but had no intention of keeping it. He returned none of her calls; he couldn't even bear to listen to her messages on the answering machine. Her voice was no longer pleasant and sincere; now it seemed the very sound of deceit and conspiracy. It was the voice of a used car salesman or a carnival barker and, because he once trusted it, he could no longer listen to it.

As before, he spent most of his time alone in his apartment trying to write, drinking, and thinking a lot about that gun in the closet…

14

Leo had been dead for more than a week. Betty did not come into the deli; she slept until one or two in the afternoon and drank until she went back to bed.

"Should I be worried about you?" Roger asked her one evening.

"Probably. But don't be. Give me just a little more time."

Each night, Roger went to the deli after watching *The Tonight Show*. There he would write, listen to the radio, and sometimes sip a little scotch. He found it easier to work at his table in the Munch Room where he used to, even easier at night when it was quiet and dark except for his small lamp. The novel was beginning to unfold and draw Roger into its pages. It was called *Personal Sacrifices* and was about a frustrated young man who, as an act of rebellion against his strict religious upbringing, joins a satanic cult, never for a moment taking it seriously. The cult members, however, are *very* serious and he is drawn into an underworld of human sacrifice and ritualistic child abuse.

One afternoon, Roger took a break from the deli and drove to the bookstore in Napa where he used to work; there he picked up eight books on devil worship and satanism, hoping to give his novel as much authenticity as possible.

He immersed himself in his work each night and usually lost track of time, sometimes looking up to find it was four a.m. when just a moment ago it hadn't even been one. He usually left the deli about the time Sidney, the bread man, delivered the day's supply from the bakery in Rutherford. Sidney let himself into the storeroom in back, usually whistling a tune, and greeted Roger as he left the deli with, "Hey-hey, still at it, huh?" Roger would get a couple hours sleep, then shower and go back.

Although he was not accustomed to a nine-to-five routine, he didn't mind getting up in time to open the deli. He tried to tell himself that he even looked forward to it; secretly, he knew he looked forward to seeing Sondra.

Roger found her very attractive, but knew better than to try starting something. Still...there were times when he had to clench a fist to keep his hand from touching her face, her hair, her slender neck.

For God's sake, Roger, he remembered Betty saying. *She's only seventeen.*

While she still seemed very guarded, Sondra had relaxed somewhat over the past week. Her smile came easier and she held her head a bit higher; more than once, she quickly turned away when Roger caught her staring at him from across the deli.

They talked during her breaks; she asked questions about him and his writing and he ended up doing most of the talking. He was unsuccessful in his attempts to get her to talk about herself; although she no longer looked as afraid or guilty when he asked about her as she had before, she still remained closed to him.

But something was coming. Roger wasn't sure if he was imagining it or not, but he sensed that she was slowly developing trust in him, that soon she would take him into her confidence. He didn't know if that was a good idea, but, against his better judgement—which, in this case, was speaking in a very hushed voice—he welcomed it; he wanted to get to know her. Spending time with Sondra was like spending time with himself as he was ten years ago, like having a conversation with his own past.

Except Sondra was much prettier.

Frequently she asked, cautiously but with great interest, about his background in the church. She seemed especially curious about his reasons for abandoning his faith, about his initial feelings of doubt toward the church. He wondered if Sondra were beginning to ask herself the same questions he'd once asked himself:

If there are so many different Christian denominations, how could only one be the true church?

What kind of God would slaughter everybody except the members of one little group?

What kind of God would slaughter any of His children?

He *hoped* she was asking herself those questions, because they were the only things that could save her from a life of confusing guilt and oppressed dreams.

It wasn't until the second week after Leo's death that his suspicions were confirmed.

Roger and Sondra were sitting in the Munch Room during her break on a slow Wednesday afternoon; she'd asked him about his two years at the Adventist boarding academy in Healdsburg and he was telling her about the time he and a friend played an AC/DC tape over the chapel P.A. system during services, when she interrupted him.

"Did you ever think there was something…wrong with you back then?" she asked. Her fingers were tangling nervously on the table and she sounded near tears.

"Sure," he said, puzzled by the sudden change in her behavior. "All the time. I didn't fit there. I used to think it was my fault, that there was something wrong with me. But I eventually realized the only thing wrong was that I didn't fit. And the only thing wrong with *that* was that I was pretending I *did*."

For a moment, Sondra's big eyes darted all over the room as if searching for words, and her mouth worked to find a voice, but she said nothing. She finally nodded, as if in agreement.

Roger leaned toward her and whispered, "Are you pretending you fit, Sondra?"

Her nostrils flared and tears glistened in her eyes as she nodded. Through her tears, the golden flecks in her eyes seemed to grow a fraction larger, as if the gashes were opening to reveal what lay beyond.

"I know how that feels," he assured her. "I went through it and it can really hurt."

She shifted in her chair, turning away from him, and wiped her face with a palm, trying to compose herself.

Roger ached for her then; he ached with sympathy and, he was half-ashamed to admit, desire. He wanted to hold her, tell her she was going to be okay in a few years, maybe a couple decades, *if* she could get out from under whatever cloud the church had put over her.

"Look, Sondra, I realize this isn't the place for it, but if you ever need someone to talk to—" He took her hand. "—I'm always willing to—"

"Stay away from me," she hissed, pulling away.

Roger blanched, shocked.

"I'm sorry, but…you really should. Stay away from me. I'm bad. For you. For everyone." She quickly left the Munch Room and went back to work.

Sondra did not speak to him again all day.

15

Roger taught his first class that night. It was small—only nine people—but after twenty minutes of talking about writing with his students, Roger decided they were all genuinely interested and not just taking creative writing to avoid a standard English class.

Then Marjie walked in.

Roger felt a surge of vertigo and had to check his surroundings to make sure he wasn't back in college standing in the biology lab where he and Marjie had dissected so many frog and cow eyes together.

She stood in the doorway a moment, wearing a rust-colored skirt and brown sweater, a notebook cradled in her arms, a denim bag slung over one shoulder. Her hair was longer now, but otherwise she looked exactly as she had the last time he'd seen her. When a breeze whispered through the open door from behind her, he realized she even wore the same perfume.

Her smile seemed big enough to swallow her whole head as she stepped inside and said, "Sorry I'm late, but I was held up at work and..."

They stared silently at one another long enough to make the students fidget at their desks.

Marjie finally seated herself and Roger spent a few minutes stammering through the course outline, then dismissed the class early for the first of its three hourly ten minute breaks.

The students headed for the restrooms and smoking areas except for Marjie, who remained in her seat smiling at Roger.

"I can't believe you're taking this class," he said, sitting on the edge of his desk. He did not return her smile.

"Oh, it's not for the grade or anything. I've always wanted to take a shot at writing." She stood. "And I wanted to see you." Moving toward him, she said, "Don't I get a hug?"

"No."

Her smile went away.

"I can't believe you're doing this, Marjie."

"Doing what?"

"Acting like you're glad to see me, like we're old friends."

"I *am* glad. And we *are* old friends."

"We *were*."

"Please, Roger," she said softly, her eyes becoming sadly apologetic, "that was a long time ago."

"Six years is not my idea of a long time, but even if it were *twenty*-six years, this would be a surprise. Your...*convictions*—" He spat the word. "—seemed pretty firm back then."

"Oh, you know how it is, Roger, you've been through it. They hold a Week of Prayer on campus, get some loud, charismatic guest speaker to give two sermons a day and call everybody to the altar to surrender themselves to Christ and burn their novels and rock albums and get re-baptized. You get...well, you know, on fire for the Lord and try to clean up your life, read the Bible every day. It's like...like *brainwashing*, almost. Except it doesn't last."

"There was no Week of Prayer then, Marjie."

"I know, but...well, it's the same principle. I was going through one of those stages."

"Did you chase off any other friends during that stage?"

Marjie sighed and moved closer to him. "I tried to find you, Roger. I called your parents, but they wouldn't tell me anything. I wrote a letter to your publisher, but they never wrote back. You just disappeared."

"I *had* to disappear, and don't act like you don't know why."

"I know, there were some people who...overreacted."

"*Overreacted*? Jesus, I'm glad they didn't get *pissed*, they probably would've firebombed my car."

"A lot of people were...disappointed in you, Roger. I don't condone what they did, but they didn't know how to handle it."

"Well, they still don't know how to handle it because they followed me all the way down to L.A."

"I'm sorry," she whispered. "But I promise you...I had nothing to do with any of that. I...I've missed you."

When she was finally close enough to put her arms around him, Roger could not resist. Six years quickly melted away as he held her, smelled her, heard her sigh against his ear.

"I've missed you, too, Marjie," he said, startled by how good it felt to say her name aloud again. He whispered, "But you really hurt me."

"I always prayed—"

...it would go away...

"—I'd get to apologize to you for that." She moved back and placed a hand to his cheek. "You're—"

...sick...

"—still very important to me. Hey, you're—"

...sick sick sicksicksick...

"—my childhood sweetheart. You don't just forget your childhood sweetheart, you know."

Roger lost his feeling of comfort when he heard the old echo of her words and remembered how much they'd hurt; he gently pulled away from her. Suddenly, he couldn't even look at her and he felt a twinge of pain in his side.

No, no, he thought, *not now, please not now.*

He put a hand over his stomach, preparing to double over, waiting for the claw inside him to emerge from its sleep and tear at his organs. It never came.

The students began to file back into the room and Roger tried to continue his class without looking at Marjie. Afterward, she approached him again and put her denim bag on his desk, removing a hardcover and paperback copy of each of his books. With a grin she asked, "How about signing them?"

«« — »»

Roger told himself he would not see Marjie outside of class. He did not give her his phone number or address and asked her no personal questions, hoping she would do likewise. The very thought of renewing a friendship with Marjie made the claw stir ever so slightly...

But he had to admit, it was sure good to see her again.

16

Sondra called in sick the next day. Roger was considering calling her to see what was wrong when Marjie breezed into the deli and kissed him on the cheek.

"It's my day off," she said. "I thought I'd come for lunch and see if you still hang out here."

"I work here now."

"I heard about Leo. I'm sorry. I know you were friends."

Over lunch, Marjie told him she was now living in Napa, working at a property management firm where she was quickly climbing the ladder.

As Roger listened, thinking, *I'm doing exactly what I told myself I wouldn't do,* he noticed tiny studs glistening in Marjie's earlobes.

"What's this?" he asked, pointing to them.

"Oh, yeah," she chuckled, covering her ears with her hair. "Guess I'm gonna burn in hell, huh?" She blushed like a child caught smoking. "I even have a sip of wine now and then. I'm a big girl now."

But, Roger noticed, she was not so big that she didn't keep toying with her hair self-consciously to make sure her pierced ears were covered.

She gave Roger her number on a napkin, saying she wanted to get together for dinner soon. Before she left, Marjie glanced around the Munch Room bashfully, then leaned forward and gave Roger a long kiss on the mouth; he didn't respond, but neither did he resist.

"I *really* want to see you," she whispered soberly, touching his neck.

After she left, Roger realized she was going through the opposite of what he'd experienced. Just as he had tried for so long to fit into Adventist circles, she was now trying to fit in with her co-workers by wearing jewelry and having "a sip of wine now and then". Judging by her self-conscious behavior, she was not succeeding.

Fine, Roger thought with a touch of gleeful bitterness. *See how you like it.*

He tossed her phone number into the trash.

17

Shortly after four the following morning, Roger sat in the Munch Room squinting at the notebook before him. The radio was playing and the deli was dark except for the pool of light shed by the small lamp on the table. His writing was getting sloppy and the scribbled words were doubling before his bleary eyes. He realized he'd been drinking more than his usual occasional sip and it had gotten the best of him.

Roger decided to quit for the night but, before he could close his notebook, someone banged on the back door.

He found Sondra shivering in the misty alley.

"Sondra, what's wrong?" he asked, closing the door as she came in.

She stumbled past him, crying and out of breath, and fell into a chair in the Munch Room. Her tall, shapely body was swallowed by a huge wool coat and she sat forward with her arms over her stomach as if in pain.

"Are you all right?" Roger asked, sitting across from her.

"I'm scared."

"Of what? What's happened?"

"Something's wrong with me, something *horrible*." Sondra shook with sobs and rested her forehead on the table.

Roger figured it was probably finally hitting her. She was beginning to realize all the things she could never do or be if she remained entombed in her faith. She'd begun to question the logic and fairness of such a senselessly restricting lifestyle and now, because of her doubts, she probably thought there was something wrong with her.

That's how it works, he thought. *That's how they want it to work.*

He poured a couple swallows of scotch into his glass and put it before her.

"Drink this," he said.

"No, I really shouldn't."

"It'll calm you down. Come on, drink it."

She took a sip and coughed a few times.

"How did you get here?" Roger asked.

"My bike."

"Does anyone know?"

"They were asleep when I left." With less reluctance than before, Sondra tipped the glass and finished the scotch. She was still sniffing, but her sobs had calmed.

"Now, will you tell me what you think is wrong with you?"

Her face twisted as she whispered, "I don't know," then she pounded a fist on the table, crying, "I don't *know*, I don't *know*!"

"Hey, whoa." He poured another shot of scotch and she drank it with a scowl that slowly relaxed. "Take off your coat."

"I can't. I'm…I didn't change. I'm still in my nightgown."

"Okay. If you'll tell me what's wrong, Sondra, maybe I can help."

"I don't even know what it is, I don't understand it. But I know it's not gonna go away. It just keeps coming back again and again."

"Have you talked to your cousin?"

"She won't do anything."

"What *could* she do?"

"Take me to…to a doctor."

"You're sick?" He remembered the sound of her vomiting in the restroom a few weeks ago and noticed she was still holding her stomach; he wondered if it was something more serious than just a strong period.

She nodded, pouring a bit more scotch.

"Hey, maybe you should go easy on that stuff," he said.

"Just a little more, please." Her hands shook as she drank and a small tremor passed through her afterward.

"Sondra, if you're sick, maybe you should go to a doctor right now. I can take you to—"

"*No.*"

"But don't you want to—"

"No, I can't. I shouldn't even be telling you any of this."

"Yes you should. I *want* you to."

She started crying again. "You'll…you'll have me…put away."

That scared Roger. He suddenly realized this was more than just a physical illness or a self image problem; this was serious.

"Why would I want to do that?"

"Because I'm dangerous."

"Why do you think that?"

"I *know* it. So does Annie, but she doesn't talk about it. Neither does Bill."

"Her husband?"

She nodded. "They're scared of me. They *hate* me."

As she began to cry again, Roger wondered if he really wanted to hear any of this; he'd planned to keep a very low profile in the Valley this time and not get involved with Adventists in any way. But Sondra looked so lost, so hopeless. Her tear-filled eyes were heavy from the scotch and she rested her head in her palm. Roger could not bring himself to turn his back on her.

"Why are they scared of you?" he asked.

She scrubbed her face with her hands, then reached for the bottle again.

"That'll make you sick if you're not used to—"

"I've drank before. A little," she said—but not without guilt—taking another swallow.

Roger was surprised.

She sucked in a deep breath, as if for courage, and began:

"When I was a little girl, I wanted to be a dancer. I had this friend, see, a neighbor girl named Rosa who wasn't an Adventist. She was a little older than me and so pretty. I worshipped her. She took ballet classes and every week after her lesson, we'd go into her garage and she'd teach me what she'd learned. Her mom—she was such a nice lady—bought me a pair of ballet slippers and some leotards. I had to leave them at Rosa's house so my parents wouldn't find out. I was so scared they'd discover I was learning to dance...

"Well, they *did*. Mom came to the house one day while I was in the garage with Rosa. The look on her face when she saw me dancing...I thought she was gonna hit me. 'You're lucky Christ didn't come while you were prancing around in there,' she said when we got home. 'You looked like some kind of a...a *pagan* doing that.' The thing is—" She stopped to swallow some tears. "—I thought I was doing so *well*. I was getting *good*. Even Rosa's mother said so.

"Mom and Dad wouldn't let me leave the house for weeks after that, except for school. They stood in my room each night to make sure I studied my Sabbath school lesson and said my prayers. They...they took my bedroom door off so they'd be able to see if I danced in my room at night.

"I hated them for that. And I hated the church for saying dancing was wrong and I hated Mrs. White for writing all those books and...and most of all, I hated myself for feeling so much hate. I prayed for God to take away my love for dancing, but the more I bottled it up inside, the more I wanted to do it.

"Then I got sick. My stomach started hurting once in a while. Not my stomach, really; it was more in my side. I'd get such awful pains, sometimes I couldn't even *walk*. A few times, I even threw up and...and there was blood in it."

Roger chilled, feeling the fear he could see so clearly in her eyes as she spoke.

It's something else, he thought. *She's talking about something else. It* can't *be the same thing.*

"The doctors couldn't find anything," she went on. "They said it was all in my head. Mom and Dad said it was a punishment from God because I was so preoccupied with worldly things. Like dancing.

"The worse it got, the more they ignored it. Sometimes I'd be sitting at the dinner table saying grace and it'd hit me so hard I'd fall out of my chair and run to the bathroom and throw up. After a while, I figured they must be right—I was being punished. I still wanted to be a dancer. I read books about it, I dreamed about it. No matter how hard I tried to change, I couldn't.

"The pain—" She held her stomach and her eyes tensed as she talked about it. "—was like—still *is*—like something's inside me. Moving. Cutting me."

Roger moved back from the table as he listened, not really wanting to hear anymore but unable to ask her to stop.

"It's like there's something inside me...trying to get out," she said.

Something with a claw, he thought, vividly remembering the claw he had imagined, so many times, to be ripping through his insides.

"It kept getting worse and worse until…about three years ago…" She poured another drink. "It got out."

Roger didn't protest this time; in fact, he was considering having more of the scotch himself.

"I had a pony," she went on. "Three years ago, almost four, it was killed. I had this nightmare, see, this horrible, bloody nightmare. It didn't make any sense at all, but when I woke up—" Her face lost its color and her voice cracked; she seemed about to be sick. "—I was covered with blood. In my hair, in my mouth. My nightgown was torn up on the floor. And I could smell my pony.

"I cleaned up and threw my sheets in the wash before Mom and Dad woke up. That morning, Dad found my pony in pieces, partially eaten. They said a wild animal had done it." She stared into her drink with distant eyes; the flecks of gold among the brown seemed on fire and about to spread. "A wild animal," she whispered.

When Roger found his voice, he asked, "What—"

What…is she?

"—are you telling me, Sondra?"

She shrugged. "I *said* I don't understand it."

"Well, I'm sure you had nothing to do with the pony," he said, certain of nothing.

"Or the neighborhood dogs? Or the little boy down the street who was always offering me his allowance if I'd show him my pussy?"

He could not reply.

"After every one, I woke up the same way, from an awful dream. Covered with blood. When my mother found one of the pillowcases, I think they started to suspect. They became afraid of me. I think they thought I was possessed. When they died, then I knew." She squirmed in her chair, clutching her stomach hard with one hand, in pain. "I'd hear them whispering when they thought I wasn't around, talking about how maybe I should be exorcised or annointed by the pastor, or something. Then they found my dancing books. They went crazy. Mom started screaming at me for bringing the devil into their house, Dad started praying, and all of a sudden the pain hit me like a train and I passed out. Sort of. I...I remember hearing screams. Seeing lots of blood. Then...then when I came to...they were all over the walls...on the floor in pieces...and there were police at the door."

Roger was feeling light-headed. He tipped the bottle to his lips and took a swallow.

Some kind of accident, I think, Betty had said of the death of Sondra's parents.

"There have been other times," Sondra said. "Each one's worse than the last. And now they're not just worse, they're...different."

Roger's fingers toyed with the bottle and scotch sloshed in his burning gut as his mouth worked to ask her *how* it was different; his throat felt tight and the question came out with effort.

"It used to happen just when I was angry," she replied. "But now...well...remember the day Leo died?" Her voice caught and she didn't go on for a moment. "I...I was talking to you in here and...you told me I was pretty and you took my hand and...I wanted so much to touch you," she whispered. "I *wanted* you. But then it started and I ran to the bathroom. I was so sick I forgot to lock the door and...I was on the floor and it was happening to me, the change, and I was fighting it...then Leo walked in. And saw me. And...and he..."

Sondra started to cry again and Roger wanted to comfort her but could not. He could only stare at her, wondering if he should help her because she was crazy or fear her because she was telling the truth.

"Sondra, have you talked to anyone about this?"

"Only you. I thought...well, after all you've said...about thinking there was something wrong with you...I thought you'd understand."

Roger pressed a hand to his stomach, thinking of the horrible pain, the claw, the blood he used to spit into his toilet, the awful nightmares...the bloody, sickening nightmares.

"You need help," he said. "You know that."

"Who's going to help me? I'm...I don't know *what* I am. What could anyone do?"

"What do *you* think you are?"

"A…a monster. Like Mom and Dad said. Maybe I am evil. Possessed. Maybe, when I kept wanting to dance so much, maybe God just…turned His back on me. Maybe…" She couldn't continue.

Roger took her hand as she cried, quickly checking his watch; Sidney would be delivering bread in about twenty or thirty minutes. It would not look good for him to find Roger alone with Sondra at that hour, and with a three-quarters-empty bottle of scotch on the table, particularly if Sondra's problem, whether real or imagined, later came to light. He felt he should call someone but knew of no one but Betty. As much as he hated to wake her at such an hour, he decided he had no choice.

"You sit right here, Sondra, okay? I'll be back in a minute."

He went to the phone behind the register and called Betty. It rang a dozen times before she answered.

"Betty? This is Roger. Sorry to wake you, but I've got a—"

She made a deep, gargled noise into the phone.

"Betty?"

"Whum?"

"Betty, this is Roger. *Please* wake up."

"Rah? Whum."

"Listen, Betty, I'm at the deli and Sondra's here with me…Betty?"

She'd hung up.

Roger dialed again, certain she'd been drinking all day and didn't know what she was doing.

"Betty, *don't hang up!*" he shouted. "Listen to me. Sondra is here with me and—"

"Hoozis?"

"It's Roger. Look, can you get up and—"

She hung up again.

"God*damn*!"

As Roger was dialing again, he felt two arms slide around his waist and firm breasts press to his back.

"Don't call anybody," Sondra whispered huskily.

Her breath smelled heavily of scotch and her words were slurred; when he turned around, he looked into her big, heavy brown eyes and knew she'd finished the bottle.

"Sondra..."

"C'mon, let's go back here."

She took his hand, leading him back to the Munch Room; he followed without protest partially because he knew he'd never get through to Betty and partially for reasons he did not want to think about.

Her coat lay over the back of a chair and she wore only a powder blue nightshirt that didn't quite reach her knees and was slit up the sides to her waist.

Before he could take a seat, her arms were around him and she was trying to kiss him.

"Hey-hey, Sondra, *wait*—"

"It's okay," she said, her voice thick as honey. "I've seen the way you look at me. I *know*."

"Uh, uh, no, just—"

Her mouth was on his and his eyes, wide with surprise, slowly closed as her tongue lightly traced his closed lips and—

It feels sooo good...

—it was only seconds before his tongue met hers—

It's been sooo long...

—and his arms slid around her, his hands moving over her back. Sondra's mouth opened and closed over his, drew his tongue in and sucked on it hungrily. One hand clutched his neck and the other squeezed his buttocks, pressing his hardening crotch to her. Their breathing grew frantic as they bumped the table.

Fighting the warmth that was growing inside him, Roger gently pushed her away but she moved forward again, kissing his throat and face, mumbling, "Don't you like it? Huh? Don't you?"

"Look, Sondra, we can't do this."

"Why not?"

"We...we *shouldn't*. We've both had too much to drink and—"

"Not *too* much. Is there any more?"

"Sondra, *stop*."

He firmly held her at arm's length as he tried to regain his composure.

"You *do* like it," she purred drunkenly, closing her hand over the bulge in his jeans. She stroked it as she kicked a chair aside and sat upon the table, hugging one knee to her chest and gathering the nightshirt around the waist.

"Sondra..." Roger's voice lost some of its forcefulness as his eyes traveled up her long smooth thighs to the small thatch of sunset-colored hair that glistened with moisture. "Put your coat back on," he whispered.

She leaned back and tried to pull his head down between her legs.

"*No.*"

"Do you want me to suck this then?" She squeezed his erection. "That's what Benny wanted."

"Buh...Benny?" Roger stuttered, his mouth dry.

...I don't think he ever really jogged...

"You were with Benny?" Roger whispered.

"Just once." She leaned her head back and slid her fingers through her long full hair.

He especially liked Sondra...

"Just...once..." She frowned and gently rubbed her hand in circles over her stomach. Her face seemed to have less color than a few moments before.

Roger knew he had to get her out of there and back home to bed, but didn't know how to do it without getting himself into trouble. He cursed himself for giving her the scotch.

"Come on, Sondra. I'm taking you home."

She turned desperate eyes to him and gripped his collar. "No, please don't do that. Fuck me. Right here. Nobody'll know."

"I can't do that."

"Why? You *want* to." There was a desperate pleading in her voice and her eyes welled with tears. "Is there something wrong with me?"

What...is she?

"You said, you said—" Her words were nearly lost in sobs. "—that I was *pretty*, you *said* that."

"You are, Sondra, but I can't—"

"*Please!*" she shouted, clutching his shirt. "I want to so bad—"

With her other hand, she unbuckled his belt—

"—so *bad*, I *need* to—"

—unbuttoned his pants—

"—please let me know what it feels like—"

—and reached underneath to touch him.

"—before it happens, *please!*"

"Before what happens?" Roger's voice cracked when her fingers closed around his cock, pulled it from his pants, and began stroking it tremulously.

She didn't answer, just gasped and sobbed.

Roger gently pushed her arm away and said—

It feels sooo good...

—"No, Sondra."

She began touching herself as she reached for him again, whimpering between words as she frantically said, "Please put it in me, puh-*please*, before it's...before it's..."

Her body stiffened, she bucked a couple times, and Roger thought she was coming, but then she made a sound that changed his mind.

She slapped a hand over her stomach and let out a long wretched groan, turned over on her side and vomited onto the table, knocking over the small lamp and tossing light over the walls like dancing ghosts.

Blood speckled her nightshirt and was smeared over her lips and Roger panicked, reached out to support her so she wouldn't fall off the table, but she faced him as her eyes rolled back in her head and her body curled into a ball as if cramped and she grunted, "Too late."

The lamp rolled back and forth over the table throwing light wildly.

Sondra's head craned back and her throat worked, making dry clicking sounds, as her tongue began to flap rapidly in and out of her mouth. Strands of blond hair writhed like tentacles as her head thrashed from side to side and she began to tear the collar of her nightshirt as if it were a tightening noose.

Roger leaned over her shouting, "Sondra, what's *wrong*? What can I *do*?" and her arm sliced the air, hitting the side of his head like a club and sending him against the wall and to the floor.

Pain throbbed through his skull like a drumbeat and he lay facedown for a moment, blinking his eyes and trying to see clearly again.

Sondra made the ragged, throaty sounds of an animal in pain as Roger raised himself to his hands and knees; he heard the nightshirt rip as he got to his feet.

His first thought was to go to the phone and call an ambulance, but Sondra fell from the table and landed in a crouch between him and the door and Roger stumbled backward in horror.

Sondra's teeth—now jagged and tapering to deadly points—protruded from her mouth, pushing her lips outward into a kind of snout. Bloody saliva dribbled from her mouth, glistening in the still-shifting light. Her nightshirt hung from her bare body in tatters; her knees jutted upward on each side of her body and her hands scraped the concrete floor between her sneakers, making a harsh sound.

Something was wrong with her fingers.

They were longer and knobby, as if arthritic, and—

—clawed.

A curved, razor-like talon protruded from the tip of each finger.

A *claw*...

As they scraped over the concrete, sparks flashed and died in the shadows.

Like...like a claw scraping out my insides...

Sondra sounded as if she were strangling, her chin jutting forward, eyes clenched in pain. Her lips writhed over her hideous fangs, her tongue squirmed in her mouth like a pink dying worm—

—and she seemed to be trying to say his name.

"Raaaw...Raaaw...juuhhh..."

Roger could not speak, felt cold and paralyzed with fear, numb...

He groped for something to hold on to as Sondra moved backward into the funnel of light that spilled from the toppled lamp.

Her skin was horribly mangled now, as if burned, and tufts of thin hair had appeared in patches over her body. Her breasts were withered tubes of useless flesh that dangled between her arms as her tortured body quaked.

What...is she?

When he was finally able to move, Roger stepped backward, knocking over a chair as he babbled, trying to find his voice. There was no other way out of the Munch Room and he couldn't bear to get closer to Sondra.

Or what had once been Sondra.

He thought of the knives lined up in cutlery boards by the sink and tripped around a table to get to them, afraid to take his eyes off the creature that was now on all fours before him.

Roger was turning toward the sink when a distant sound froze him in place and made him sob with a combination of relief and dread.

Whistling.

The door to the storeroom in back clattered open and Roger could hear the engine of Sidney's bread truck idling.

"Oh, God," Roger groaned, "oh dear God, *Sidney*!"

The whistling stopped.

"Sidney, get help!"

"Mr. Carlton? That you?"

"Get *help*! Call the *police*!"

"What? Can't hear you. Where are you?" His voice was closer, inside the deli now.

Roger screamed the words again so loudly that his chest hurt.

The beam of Sidney's flashlight cut through the darkness beyond the Munch Room doorway and his feet scraped heavily over the floor.

Sondra's eyes opened then and she was suddenly alert. The golden flecks had spread like fire through her eyes and glowed with hunger in the darkness.

"Don't come in here!" Roger screamed, his knees weakening. "Get *help*, Sidney, don't come—"

Sidney stepped into the Munch Room, sweeping his flashlight

in an arc before him, holding it on Sondra, who turned toward him with a throaty growl.

"What in the fuh—"

She was on him.

Warm blood spattered Roger's face and his legs gave way. He leaned against the wall, swallowing his gorge as bones snapped and gristle tore.

The wet smacking of Sondra's lips was the last sound he heard...

18

He heard Sondra crying before he opened his eyes.

Roger had no idea how long he'd been unconscious and, for a moment, wasn't even sure what had happened.

Light from the lamp and flashlight on the floor fell on black puddles and soggy lumps.

Warm moisture clung to Roger's face and hands.

Trembling, he struggled to his feet and limped to the light switch, his shoes slopping over the wet floor.

When the fluorescent lights flickered on, Roger wanted to scream but could only murmur like a frightened child.

Pieces of Sidney lay scattered about the floor. Patches of tattered skin were indistinguishable from the shreds of his blood-soaked clothes. One limb—Roger couldn't tell if it was an arm or a leg—remained attached to the torso, which lay open like a huge misshapen melon. His head was propped against the wall two feet away from the body, the face a mask of blood, mouth yawning, only one eye remaining, wide and glazed.

Roger took a long deep breath, fighting to hold on to his consciousness as he thought to himself, *It's not a person anymore, it's not a person, not a person...*

It didn't help.

Sondra was huddled, naked, bloody, and shaking, beneath a table, hugging herself and rocking, sobbing then laughing in turns.

Blood dribbled down the face of the Mickey Mouse clock on the wall, which read three minutes to five.

The bread truck idled faithfully in the alley outside.

The room reeked of blood and excrement.

Sondra's huge eyes were frightened and strangely innocent in spite of the tears of blood that trickled over her now smooth cheeks. The flecks of gold were invisible from where Roger stood and her eyes were once again a deep brown. Although she was staring at him, Roger knew she was not seeing him.

"Sondra?" he called hoarsely. "Are you hurt? Sondra?"

She whispered something unintelligible, something that was not directed to Roger.

He moved closer and realized she was singing softly to herself. It was a song he remembered singing as a child in Sabbath school.

"Jesus loves me…this I know…"

Careful not to step on anything, Roger went to the table, bent down, and cautiously reached for her.

"…for the Bible tells me so…"

He took her arm and gently tugged.

"…little ones to Him belong…"

"C'mon, Sondra," he whispered, and she let him pull her out, but kept whispering the song.

"…they are weak…but He is strong…"

He seated her in a chair and told her to stay put, although he knew she wasn't hearing him.

"…yes, Jeee-zus loves me…yes, Jeee-zus loves me…"

Roger surveyed the bloody mess again, then looked at Sondra, who rocked in the chair like a retarded child, and knew he had to help her. For her sake as well as his own.

"…yes, Jeee-zus loves me…"

He began to look for cleaning supplies and garbage bags as the bread truck continued to idle outside.

"…the Bible tells me soooo…"

19

By the time the girls began to arrive at the deli to prepare for another day of work, Roger was exhausted but buzzing with acid-like adrenaline.

His fear that he'd overlooked something that one of them might notice was so great he was barely able to speak when they greeted him.

"Hey, Roger," Michelle called as she came out of the Munch Room tying her apron, "what happened to the Batman and Robin poster?"

"What?" He felt his heart moving up his throat.

"It's gone. The Batman and Robin poster. Did you take it down?"

"Oh, that. Yeah. Betty wants to start replacing all that stuff in there." He'd had to throw it away; it was the only wall hanging that had been irreparably bloodied.

"She's gonna remodel the Munch Room?"

"I guess so." Somehow, he would have to cover for that lie. Among others...

«« — »»

After a few minutes of agonizing over where to start, Roger had filled a garbage bag with the remains of Sidney the bread man and stuffed it into a bin at the south end of the back alley. He made sure Sidney had delivered the day's bread in the storeroom, then, wearing a pair of Playtex gloves, he drove the bread truck to the north end—the direction in which it had been headed—and killed the engine. He wanted to give the impression that Sidney had simply left his truck and decided he might be more successful if he didn't leave the keys. He dropped them into his coat pocket.

Once Sondra was coherent, Roger led her to the big sink in back, took a cloth soaked in warm soapy water, and gently began to clean her up; he slowly moved the cloth around her neck, over her face, across her breasts and belly, speaking soothingly to her, trying to hide the horror and disgust he felt at the sight of her beautiful young body covered with blood and strips of human flesh. When he had her rinse her mouth with water, she gagged and spit up a hunk of Sidney's hair.

After using cold water to remove the few streaks of blood on her wool coat, Roger put her bike in the backseat of his car and drove her home, following as many back roads as possible. He stopped the car half a block from her house to drop her off.

"Now, you're sure you're okay?" he asked.

She nodded and when she spoke, her voice was hoarse and strained. "I may not come to work today."

"Sondra, you *have* to come to work. *And* go to school. Do *nothing* unusual, do you understand?"

"But I'll be so tired." Her casual, weary tone suggested this had happened before and she'd simply walked away from it, just as she'd said. It gave Roger a deep, profound chill, as if he'd stepped through a door and suddenly found himself standing on the edge of the Grand Canyon, naked and cold in the middle of the night. He heard no regret in her voice, not even a hint of understanding of what she'd done.

"I promise you, Sondra, you won't have to do much. Just look busy, that's all."

Roger watched her walk the bike down the sidewalk until she turned into the drive, then returned to the deli where he spent the next few hours vigorously scrubbing the Munch Room.

When he was finished and everything was put away, he stood in the middle of the room and scanned the walls and floors, searching for the slightest telltale sign.

Then he went to the bathroom, kneeled over the toilet, and threw up until he could barely stand.

«« — »»

Now, as he sipped his coffee, having gone home for a shower and a change of clothes, he thought about what he'd done and the fear began to eat into his bones like termites into wood.

The keys to Sidney's truck were in the back corner of his bottom dresser drawer, about a dozen of them splayed from their ring like the stiff, barbed legs of a metal spider waiting to pounce on the next person to pull the drawer out.

Roger knew that, had he called the police, there would have been no way to explain the killing. They would not have believed the truth—*Roger* still did not believe it—and he had the feeling that the blame would somehow fall on him.

But there was another reason he helped her, one he could not pinpoint; it seemed to hover on the edge of his thoughts, unwilling to be discovered.

It had something to do with the claws that Sondra's hands had become, with the talons that had grown from her fingers.

He'd seen them before in his imagination; he'd watched them, with his mind's eye, tearing through his insides as he lay curled in his bed, clutching his abdomen in agony.

It had something to do with the fear he'd felt as Sondra spoke of her mysterious illness, described the painful symptoms and the equally painful circumstances under which they'd arisen.

He'd felt an unsettling bond with Sondra when he saw her huddled beneath that table splattered with blood, a sort of empathy, as if he had been in the same situation himself once.

That, of course, was ridiculous.

But when he thought of those claws and of the pain that used to cut through him until he bled inside, when he thought of the way he used to dream of changing, his skin burning as it writhed and squirmed into something that was not human, he wondered if he'd been close—perhaps *very* close—to experiencing the same thing...

20

Late that morning, a man from the Rutherford Bakehouse called to ask if Sidney Nelson had made his delivery that morning. When Roger said that he had, trying to hide the dryness in his throat, the man said Sidney had not yet returned; he was going to call the police and they might come by and ask Roger a few questions. Roger said that was fine, hung up, then went to the back and quickly drank a glass of wine to calm his tattered nerves.

A police officer did indeed come in that afternoon—officer Chuck Niles, a boyish, freckled man—and asked if Roger had spoken to Sidney, if the delivery man's behavior was in any way unusual, if he'd been angry or mentioned quitting his job, if he'd been alone.

Roger answered the questions calmly and with assurance, saying that Sidney had simply come in, said hello, made his delivery, then left.

When the officer left, Roger had more wine, only because there was no more scotch.

Sondra came in a few minutes late looking weary and pale, just as she had the day Benny Kent's body had been discovered. The confidence she'd developed over the past weeks, however small, was gone; she would not look at Roger.

Although he had not slept, Roger was not tired; instead, he was jumpy and irritable and could not think straight. He dropped things and bumped into things and once looked up at the sign over the Munch Room doorway and began to giggle uncontrollably; remembering the sound of Sondra's wet, sloppy chewing early that morning gave new meaning to the Munch Room sign and he found it horribly funny.

Shortly before closing time that evening, Roger spotted Sondra going into the bathroom with a broom and followed her.

"Did you get caught this morning?" he asked quietly, half-closing the door.

"No. They were asleep."

"How do you feel?"

"The way I always feel afterward. Tired. Shaky." Her eyes never met his.

"How many times has this happened?"

"I don't know."

"How often? What brings it on?"

"*I don't know*," she hissed.

"You killed Benny Kent, didn't you?"

After a long moment, she nodded and began sweeping as if he weren't there.

"What happened?"

"He wanted to...to...be with me. We met that night by the footpath? Between here and Manning? And we started to...you know..."

"Did you want to?"

"*Yes*, I wanted to. Just like with you. But when we started...I...like always, it happened."

"Sondra, you've go to do something about this. I know you're scared, but you've got to see someone or—"

"Forget it."

"What? What do you mean, for—"

"Thank you for helping me, but...you have to forget it because...I'll be looking for a new job now."

"What? Why?" He was speaking in urgent whispers now, fists clenched at his sides.

"They don't want me to work here anymore."

"Annie?"

"And Bill. I shouldn't even be talking to you like this. She could come in any minute and—"

"Because of me? They want you to quit because of me?"

She started for the door but Roger stepped in front of her.

There were heavy footsteps in the Munch Room, obviously not those of one of the girls.

"What do they know about me?" Roger asked.

"I have to go, let me *go*," she snapped, moving around him and leaving the bathroom.

Roger followed her into the Munch Room where he froze when a familiar voice said, "Sondra, you ready?"

Bill Dunning stood before them leaning on a cane.

A silence as solid and cold as stone fell over the room.

Sondra stopped, folded her arms protectively over her breasts, and stared at her shoes.

A second, minute, or hour could have passed as Roger stood in the doorway, his eyes locked with Bill's; he wasn't sure and didn't care.

Bill's face was solid now, the boyish roundness it had in college replaced by a stern, jaw-clenched look of bitterness. It might have been because he was looking at Roger, but Roger didn't think so. The look was not a temporary one; it was chiseled into the bones beneath his skin, carved into his jaw. He was thicker; stubble sprinkled the lower half of his face.

And his right leg was gone.

The leg of his black pants was filled out but stiff, and when he shifted his weight once, the leg clicked. It was a prosthesis.

"Come on, Sondra," Bill said, his voice low and level, his eyes still on Roger. "Let's go. Annie's waiting."

Sondra was hurrying for the door before Bill was finished.

Bill remained for a moment, eyeing Roger warily.

Swallowing a clot of felt in his throat, Roger tried hard to smile, to sound congenial when he stepped forward and said, "Well, hey, Bill, it's been—"

"Sondra won't be working here anymore," Bill said. "Thought I'd let you know." As he turned and walked out, leaning heavily on his cane, Bill's right leg clicked softly with each step and he muttered, "Getting a job someplace else."

Roger listened until he heard the front door rattle shut behind them, then he sent the others home and closed up for the night.

21

A thin mist crept into the Valley that night and spread itself through the vineyards like a blanket of cobwebs. The stars were hidden by gathering clouds and the air had fangs of ice.

When he turned down his street, he noticed a car pulling up in front of his house.

Roger suddenly felt sick.

It wasn't a police car, but it was unfamiliar.

As Roger pulled into his drive, the driver's door of the car opened and a woman got out.

Marjie.

"*There* you are," she called happily as he got out of his car. "I was afraid I'd come up here for nothing. Hope you haven't eaten yet." She lifted two grocery bags from her car.

Hiding his annoyance, and the fact that eating was the *last* thing on his mind, Roger helped her carry them inside.

"Spaghetti sound good?" Marjie asked as she emptied the bags on the kitchen counter.

"Sure, Marjie, but I really don't—"

She held up a bottle of wine. "Do you want this before, during, or after dinner?"

"Right now, please," Roger sighed, sitting at the table. "How did you find me?"

"I've got a friend in payroll at Napa College. She looked your address up for me. Why, did I come at a bad time? You look terrible, are you sick?"

"No, just tired," he yawned.

She opened the wine and poured two glasses, then busied herself with the groceries, preparing dinner.

It wasn't until he'd finished his first glass of wine that Roger realized how beautiful Marjie looked.

She wore a tight black skirt, a red-and-black top with a scooped neckline, and a dark gray blazer. Her hair was up in the back and gently curled strands of it fell to the sides of her face.

"You look nice," he said, pouring more wine. "What are you all dressed up for?"

"For you," she said, sounding disappointed that he would think otherwise.

As she darted around the kitchen, chatting about work and her two cats, Roger watched her and realized this was not just a friendly visit; this was a *very* friendly visit. She meant to start something. Roger thought it might be nice to spend the night in her arms—*God, it's been so long*, he thought—and forget about everything else for a while. But he wouldn't; he couldn't. He knew he shouldn't even be having dinner with her, but he couldn't very well tell her to take her spaghetti dinner and go home. Things had happened between them that no amount of explaining or apologizing could erase and, knowing that the average back-slidden Seventh-Day Adventist could undergo a spiritual about-face at any time, he didn't want to open himself up to more of the same.

Over dinner, Marjie brought him up-to-date on some of their former schoolmates.

Clearing his throat, Roger asked, "Whatever happened to Bill Dunning?"

"Oh, what a sad story *that* is. He's married now, you know. Married some girl from Michigan just out of college. Annie something. A little wallflower. He got *really* religious and was planning to go right back to school—the seminary—and become a minister. Then he had an accident on his motorcycle. Lost his right leg, couldn't work. Annie's a receptionist somewhere in Manning. And if Bill was religious before…well, he and God are on a first name basis now. The accident…I don't know, I think it maybe made him a little, you know, wiggy. Annie's cousin from Michigan is living with them now. She's got a job somewhere in St. Helena and helps pay some of the bills."

"Not anymore."

"Oh?"

Roger told her about Bill's visit to the deli that day.

"Then you know the girl," she said.

"Not very well." He suddenly felt uncomfortable with the subject.

"I met her once. I hear she's a real troublemaker."

Roger swallowed a black, morbid chuckle.

"A horny little devil, I understand."

"I…wouldn't know."

There was a pause filled with the clatter of forks against plates, then Roger asked, "Are you sure Bill lost his leg in a motorcycle accident?"

"Yeah. I mean, there aren't too many ways to lose a whole leg, you know. Why?"

He shrugged. "Just wondering."

"No, really, tell me why you asked. You seem…I don't know, troubled. Did Bill say something today that—"

"Nevermind, Marjie. I really don't want to talk about it."

After dinner, they had ice cream and Marjie turned on the television and cuddled up beside Roger on the sofa, after opening another bottle of wine.

Roger stiffened, forcing himself not to respond.

"What?" Marjie asked, puzzled. "What's wrong?"

"I...don't think it's such a good idea, Marjie."

She pulled away from him, smiling, and removed a baggie and a small pipe from her purse on the floor.

"You just need to relax, that's all," she said, waving a lump of marijuana under his nose.

Roger had tried to get her to smoke pot with him the summer of their senior year in high school, but she'd refused politely, saying she had no intention of ever trying it.

"Like I said before, Roger, I'm a big girl now," she whispered conspiratorially, as if reading his thoughts.

They each took a few hits and began laughing at some vapid sitcom on television until Marjie spilled some wine on herself.

She stood, giggling. "Shit, oh shit," she said as she brushed at the spreading stain. "Do you have a robe, or..."

"Sure." Roger went to his room.

"Where's your washer? Do you have one?"

"In the garage, through the kitchen."

Roger returned to the living room with his bathrobe and was about to sit down again when he remembered his blood-splattered clothes stacked on the washer and he bolted through the house after her.

"Roger, what *happened?*" she asked as he stepped down into the garage. She was holding up the shirt splashed with Sidney Nelson's blood.

"Oh, that," he said, trying to calm himself, thinking fast. "I hit a, a—um deer last night. I had to, you know, move it out of the road." His hands were trembling and he was beginning to perspire as he took the shirt from her and tossed it aside along with the pants. "It was, it was a mess. A mess." When Marjie had her shirt off, Roger handed her the robe and quickly started the wash, then led her back into the house.

"That must've been awful," she said. "Hitting a deer. I did that once and thought I'd never stop crying."

On the sofa once again, Roger suddenly felt giddy at having succeeded with his lie.

They smoked some more, drank some more, and kept laughing at the television show, but now Roger's laughter was deep and heartfelt and not in response to the sitcom they were watching. They leaned on one another as they guffawed with the laughtrack, her arm around his shoulders, his arm resting across her thighs.

Then they were kissing.

Minutes later, they were in bed.

Laughter continued from the television set, blending with their sighs and whispers, and with the sound of the rain that had begun to fall gently outside.

«« — »»

When Roger closed his eyes, holding Marjie's body beneath him, beside him, above him, moving his hips in crescendoing circles, it was not Marjie who filled his mind.

It was Sondra.

22

When Roger woke the next morning, Marjie was gone. She'd left a note. *It's still as good as before. Soon—M.*

Over coffee in the deli, Roger searched the paper for any mention of Sidney Nelson. A small article said only that the delivery man's truck had been abandoned in the alley; a tiny smear of blood hinted at foul play and a check was being run to see if it matched Sidney's type.

Roger grew faint for a moment, but was relieved to read that the police suspected Sidney had been attacked and robbed and was perhaps wandering around, injured, lost, and confused; they expected him to turn up within twenty-four hours.

Roger called Betty, woke her, and told her Sondra had quit and she would need to hire a new girl. He was not familiar with the procedure and said he would be more comfortable if she came in and did it herself.

"Oh, sure, honey," she said, groggily. "You've been awfully good to me. I should've come back before this. I'll be in this afternoon. Why don't you go home and relax."

He did. He watched a Godzilla movie on television that afternoon, munching on pretzels; he read through some of the books on Satanism he'd bought and leisurely wrote pages of helpful notes; he finished a chapter that had been stumping him for days.

Marjie called him from work and said she wanted to see him again that night.

By the time she arrived, Roger had set up a tray of take-out Chinese food in the bedroom, and they took turns eating off one another between courses.

The next week was smooth as glass, and so were the days following it. Roger enjoyed teaching his classes; he had regained an old friendship—and then some; and he was thinking hardly at all of Sondra. He was able to enter the Munch Room without seeing Sidney the bread man scattered over the floor and walls. He began to feel as if it had never happened.

For the first time in years, Roger's life was good. He would even go so far as to say he was happy.

That worried him.

It had been so long since Roger had felt happy that he began to wonder what would happen to end it; surely it could not last long.

It didn't.

23

Roger tore himself from a nightmare—

Sondra was peeling a bloody sheet of skin from the back of Sidney the bread man, who was convulsing on the Munch Room floor and who had an enormous set of antlers growing from his skull.

I hit a deer last night...

—He sat up in bed, gasping in the dark.

"What is it?" Marjie pressed warmly against his back and her breath was hot on his neck.

"Night. Mare." He was still out of breath.

"Get you something?"

"No." He lay back down and Marjie curled up beside him, kissed him, and whispered. "Be right back."

She went into the bathroom and he heard her urinate, flush, wash, then go to the kitchen for a drink.

After a few moments of silence, Roger started to doze.

"Roger, what are these books?"

He opened his eyes and saw her standing in the rectangle of soft light spilling in through the door, holding a book in each hand.

"*The Satanic Bible*?" she said in a tiny voice. "*Satanic Invocations?* Roger, what are you—"

"Research." He rolled over.

"Roger," she whispered, "this is...these are...I can't believe you—"

"C'mon, Marjie, it's just research for the book I'm writing, that's all."

"But why so many? You've got *more* out there. What are you *writing*?"

"Another thriller," he mumbled into his pillow. When she didn't return to bed for a while, he sat up and saw her still standing in the doorway looking at the books. "Marjie, it's just research. What's the problem?"

Still she did not move for a while, then put the books on his dresser, turned off the hall light, and slowly returned to bed. They were silent for a while, then, her voice cautious and just a little afraid, touched with a nervous chuckle, she asked, "Roger, that...that blood on your shirt the other night..."

But Roger was asleep.

24

At noon the next day, Roger was hunched over his notebook in the Munch Room when some of the high school students began to crowd into the deli for lunch. The noise level rose as they took up the tables around him, laughing, swearing, and constantly smoking.

Roger hardly looked up from his work; it was going too well, he was in too deep—

—until he hit bottom. It happened even when he was on a roll: A line of dialogue that didn't ring true or a description that was murky, sometimes even something as small as a single word that didn't fit.

He leaned back in his chair with a sigh, chewing on the end of his pen and, as if drawn to the very spot where she sat, his eyes fell on Sondra.

She saw him, too, apparently at that very moment because she was half-smiling at something someone at her table had said and the smile froze for a moment, then slowly chipped away until it was gone.

She looked weary; her beautiful bright eyes seemed dimmed and had puffy half-moons beneath them. She looked just like she had the day Benny Kent's body had been discovered.

Their eyes remained locked like the bumpers of two cars that had collided and Roger became deaf to the voices in the room. He was suddenly afraid that if he were to look around him, he would see Sidney's blood splashed on the walls and he tried hard to keep the memory of that night from seeping into his mind. But it wasn't easy. He hadn't seen Sondra—had hardly even thought of her—for nearly two weeks, two wonderfully comfortable, content weeks that had passed mercifully slowly. Seeing her now brought it back, reminded him how she'd touched him that night...how her breasts had felt beneath his hands as he washed the blood from them...how much—how very achingly much—he'd wanted her...

Movement twitched over her face, as if searching for a hold, then her lips curled upward at the ends. The smile warmed slowly, grew, and for a moment Roger thought she was going to cry.

Then she stood and quickly left.

25

His writing didn't take off again that day. He pieced together a few more paragraphs, then gave up.

When he got home, the red light on his answering machine was winking lecherously and he played his messages.

There were three hang-ups.

He called Marjie at her office and invited her out to dinner that night.

"Um, I don't think so, Roger," she said. "I'm kind of, you know, um, tired."

"We have been pretty active the last few nights, haven't we?" he laughed, but she didn't respond. Silence hissed over the line. "Is anything wrong?"

"Things are kind of hectic here today, really busy, you know? I'll probably have to work late, and…"

She didn't finish.

"Well, if you change your mind," he said, "give me a call."

"Yeah, sure, that's a good idea. I'll call you if not tonight, then…well, maybe tomorrow. But…things look pretty thick here for the whole week. I don't know…"

"Whatever. I'll see you in class tomorrow night, though, right?"

"Yeah. Sure."

He stood by the phone for a while after hanging up, puzzled; Marjie sounded as if something were definitely wrong.

The phone rang and Roger picked it up immediately.

"Hello?"

"Leave the Valley."

It was unfamiliar, a low male voice, so low it was almost a growl.

"You didn't learn your lesson the first time, demon-lover. Don't make us teach you another one."

The voice hung up.

Roger slowly replaced the receiver. He turned on the stereo and found a San Francisco station that played hard rock and roll—none of that middle-of-the-road cotton candy—turned it up loud, and started doing some housework.

He didn't let himself think about the phone call. He didn't let himself wonder if it had anything to do with Marjie's odd behavior, if the three hang-ups had been the caller, waiting for Roger to answer. Each time he started to think, *It's happening again,* he stopped himself by singing loudly with the radio or dancing hard to the beat as he vacuumed.

He decided he would ignore it.

He would ignore it if it killed him.

26

The phone didn't ring again until shortly before two o'clock the next morning as Roger was typing.

He'd spent the entire evening cleaning and the house was immaculate. After a few hours of television, he'd gone back to work, having pushed the phone call far into the back of his mind, deciding it was an isolated incident.

Before the third ring, he'd gone through all the possible reasons someone might be calling him at such an hour and decided to let the machine get it, just in case...

By the fifth ring, he realized he hadn't turned the answering machine back on...

By the ninth ring, he decided perhaps it was important and answered.

"Your lights are on. Don't you ever sleep? Or *can* you sleep?"

Roger slammed the receiver down so hard the phone gave a started little *ding*! sound, then he went to the front window and pulled the curtain aside, peering out at the early morning darkness.

The streetlamp across from his house was out and he could see nothing.

He turned off his porch light and went out front, walked down the drive, shivering in the cold. The street was silent and lifeless.

Roger tried to remember if he'd heard a car drive by earlier, but couldn't.

When he got back inside, he was still shivering.

But not from the cold.

27

Betty was miraculously herself again. She bounced around the deli hugging the regulars and treating new customers as if they had reservations.

Roger heard her before he saw her when he went to DiMarco's late the next morning. She gave him a big hug, then frowned.

"Jesus Christ, Roger, you look like *death*," she said.

He stroked his sandpapery chin. "Forgot to shave."

"Is that all?"

"I didn't get much sleep last night. I was up working." It was true, he hadn't slept a moment. He had not, however, gotten any work done after the second phone call; he'd sat before the television watching movies.

"Well, comb your hair and look sharp," Betty said. "The law's waiting for you in the Munch Room."

"Huh?" Roger felt his jaw drop and smacked his mouth shut again.

"Chucky Niles. He's waiting for you."

"Niles," he murmured as a block of ice exploded in his chest.

Officer Niles was seated at Roger's table, sipping coffee. He nodded his greeting, meeting Roger's eyes for only an instant.

Roger put his notebook on the table and seated himself, forcing a smile.

"Something I gotta do, Mr. Carlton," Niles said hesitantly, almost shamefully.

Roger willed his heart to keep beating, willed his eyes not to tear up.

"If I don't," Niles went on, reaching under the table and bringing up a heavy brown paper bag. "I'll be sorry, believe me."

He removed hardcover editions of three of Roger's novels and plopped them onto the table. "I *said* I didn't want to bother you, but since I told her I met you a couple of weeks ago, my wife talks about nothing else. She's a fan." He offered a pen to Roger and sheepishly asked, "Would you?"

Warm relief spread through Roger's body like urine spreading through his pants and he grinned. "*Would* I? I'd *love* to." He'd never enjoyed signing anything more than he did those three books for Ellen Niles. He felt so good as he scribbled in them that he was able to ask the next question without losing his smile. "Have you found Sidney yet?"

"Um, no. Not exactly."

"Oh? What do you mean, 'not exactly'?"

"I'm, uh, not at liberty to discuss it."

"Then you *do* know something."

"Well, not myself, exactly, but...yes, they have made some progress. They say..."

Roger finished, put down the pen, and saw Niles's face squirm uncomfortably.

"...I really can't discuss it. I'm sorry."

Keep the smile, Roger ordered himself with dread.

"Well, I hope he's okay."

Niles shook his head hopelessly.

After the officer left, Roger stared at the tabletop a long time, wondering how much they knew.

27

Roger held up his class for five minutes waiting for Marjie to arrive. When she didn't, he clumsily began the first hour's discussion on characterization, glancing now and then at the door, hoping to see Marjie sheepishly peering through the window.

He ended up letting the class go early, unable to shake the feeling, the *fear*, that something was terribly wrong. He suspected that something more than an unusually busy day or a flat tire had kept Marjie from the class. After her behavior on the phone yesterday, he wouldn't be too surprised to find she'd dropped the class.

As he pulled into his drive and his headlights passed over the front of his house, he saw what looked like a small sack on his porch with two short sticks protruding from the top.

He got out of the car and headed up the walk, his pace slowing as he neared the object. In the glaring yellow glow of his porch light, there seemed to be two glistening marbles stuck to its sides and something dark and wet was puddled around the bottom of what Roger no longer thought to be a sack.

The puddle dribbled over the edge of the top step and onto the next.

Roger moved closer, squinting in the poor light, and when he was certain what it was, small clicking noises sounded in his throat as he swallowed dryly again and again. He gingerly touched the toe of his shoe to the severed goat's head and it fell heavily to one side, the freshly hacked neck pulling away from the concrete with a gentle moist sound.

Light glinted off the yellowed teeth revealed by curled back lips and the eyes were comically wide and bulging, a morbid caricature.

Roger stepped over the head, avoiding the blood, sucking cold air deep into his lungs. He turned his back on the front door and kicked the head onto the front lawn. It hit with a heavy thunk and rolled over the grass.

Inside, he poured himself a drink and finished it in a couple gulps, then poured another. He leaned on the kitchen counter, waiting for the liquor to soothe his trembling.

"No," he said quietly, flatly, as the pain in his side returned for a moment, just an instant, then disappeared. He took another drink, then spit it into the sink, crying out like a child when the pain hit again, the worst since his stay in Sylmar, chewing through his insides like a ravenous demon, silently screaming at him in a mocking nails-on-a-blackboard voice:

I'm back, you jelly-assed motherfuckerrrrr, I'm back and it's been TOOOOO LOOOOOONG!

29

When Roger shuffled into the deli the next day, exhausted from lack of sleep, Betty stared at him open-mouthed for a moment, took his hand, and led him into the Munch Room and sat him down.

Roger fidgeted as she watched him, chewing her lip.

"What's wrong, honey?" she asked somberly.

"I didn't sleep well last night. I was working on—"

"Don't jerk me around. What's wrong?"

Roger tried to look puzzled; he lifted his brows high over his eyes and when he saw she wasn't buying it, he smiled. "C'mon, Betty, I'm just tired."

"Roger, you look like *hell*. You're pale, you're...you're..." She chewed a thumbnail nervously. "A police officer was just in here. It wasn't Chucky, it was someone I don't know. He was asking...questions about you."

Roger's stomach twisted.

"I'm not sure," she went on, "but I think it has something to do with Sidney."

"Well, that makes sense. Apparently I was the last one to see him."

She shook her head. "It sounds like more than that, Roger. Please. Tell me. Just between us. Did something happen here? Is there something I should know? Do they...*suspect* you of something?"

"Jesus, Betty," he laughed, "what *is* this? The guy came, said hi, delivered the bread, and *left*. That's it."

She tugged at her lower lip, searching his face.

"Betty, I'm telling you, there's nothing to—"

Glass shattered out front and someone screamed.

"*Jesus!*" Roger blurted as he dashed out of the room, Betty close behind.

There was a jagged hole in the window facing Main Street. Michelle stood frozen behind the register, both hands over her mouth. Broken glass was scattered over the floor and on the front table, which was fortunately unoccupied.

A brick lay among the pieces of glass; attached to it with a rubber band was a crumpled piece of paper.

"Is everyone okay?" Betty called.

No one was hurt.

Except Roger, who felt a needle-like squirming in his side as he stared at the brick, afraid to pick it up.

Betty did before he could. She took the paper off and straightened it out. Her eyes scanned it, then looked at Roger.

"What is it?" he asked.

She handed it to him.

In crude block letters, the note read: ROGER CARLTON IS EVIL. HE BROUGHT DEATH HERE.

He couldn't look at Betty, at *anyone*. He wadded the note in his fist, spun around, and went back to the Munch Room and gathered up his things, feeling sick.

Betty followed him, calling his name. In the Munch Room, she said, "Roger, we'll call the police."

"No."

"Where are you going? We should report this to—"

"I'm going home. Don't report it to anyone. I'll pay for the window."

"Roger, *wait!*"

He didn't wait. He had to get out. The pain was coming.

30

When he got home, he began to drink, pacing the house like an expectant father, chain smoking and muttering to himself under his breath.

What had happened to bring it all back? Everything had been going so well…

He wondered what the police had asked about him, what they knew, what they'd found.

He couldn't have felt more confined, more enclosed, if he were hunkering in his closet.

The drinks started to hit and he started getting sloppy drunk, crying like a barfly, sitting on the sofa, elbows on his knees, hands hanging between his thighs. He got sick of his own company, decided he had to get out of the house and talk to someone, and cleaned up, then drove to Josh's.

The cold day smelled sweet, which made the odor of death in Josh's house even more overwhelming.

Roger had spoken with him on the phone twice since their last visit, but the dying man's voice, although weaker and more hollow, could not have prepared him for the visible progression of Josh's illness.

His face seemed to be collapsing, his skull deflating like a balloon with a slow leak. He walked with two canes now. When he walked.

The shock Roger felt showed on his face and Josh chuckled—it sounded like someone slowly wadding a sheet of waxed paper—and said in his trembling, pencil-thin voice, "I'm dying, for Christ's sake, what'd you expect, the cover of *GQ*?"

Josh nearly fell in the living room and Roger quickly reached out for him, felt the skeleton beneath the robe, the ribs and fragile joints, the sticks that would serve as limbs for only a short while longer.

Later, Roger would remember the clothes—a long-sleeved shirt, pants, a heavy sweater, and an overcoat—neatly laid out on the sofa. He would even remember seeing Josh's car keys on the coffee table. But his eyes passed over them blindly at the time; his head was too crowded with his own problems for him to realize the significance of what he saw.

"Did Betty get my flowers?" Josh asked.

"Yes. She wanted to thank you, but—"

Josh held up a twig-fingered hand. "I understand. So. What brings you here?"

"Haven't seen you in a couple weeks. I thought I'd drop by."

"And I appreciate that. But what's *wrong*?"

Roger laughed and said, "You sure are..." He was going to say *sharp for a dying man*, but a great muddy sob sprang from his center and snatched the voice from his throat and he put his face in his hands and bawled...

SLIVERS OF BONE

«« — »»

Roger had never discussed his problems with Josh; their conversations had always been limited to movie trivia and Hollywood gossip, talk that Roger hadn't gotten from his other friends and which—having been a movie fan long before he ever mustered the courage to risk his soul to hellfire by entering a movie theater—he craved. Roger had always talked to Josh to forget his problems, not stir them up or work them out, so Josh knew nothing of his ordeal with the church.

Roger told him; he covered everything up to the time he left Sylmar.

"After that I did some screen work, sold *Ledges* and wrote a draft of the screenplay. I kept busy and made quite a bit of money, but...nothing changed. It went on. Phone calls, vandalism. Finally, I just sort of disappeared for a year," he sighed. "Didn't even go home for Christmas. I spent New Year's Eve watching Dick Clark on a black-and-white television in some roach-eaten motel outside Kansas City. I told no one where I was. I put my parents in charge of my finances—they were very understanding—and had them wire money to me as I needed it. I wanted, *needed*, to be away from everyone, everything. I needed to be unreachable. I got no more obscene phone calls because I had no phone. I found no surprises in my closet because I had no closet, just my suitcases in the trunk of my car. I just drove and stopped and looked and ate and slept and drove. It was nice, a relief. For a while, anyway."

"After all that happened," Josh asked, "why in God's name did you come back here?"

"I love it here. I missed the Valley. It made me angry that I'd allowed myself to be chased out of a place I loved. And I got sick of being alone. I wanted to prove to myself that it was over—I figured it *had* to be after all that time away—and to prove to the people here that there's nothing wrong with me. I guess I came back to clear my name."

"Is the pain gone now?"

Roger shook his head. "It's...come back."

"Then it's not over."

After a long moment of thought, Roger decided to tell Josh everything. He knew it would go no further than the room and Josh would take it with him to the grave—probably sooner than most.

He told him about Sondra, about Sondra's parents and Benny Kent and Leo and Sidney Nelson, and Josh was silent for a long time.

"You're afraid I don't believe you," Josh finally said.

"What sane person would?"

"Listen to me, Roger. All my life, and without even realizing it, I have lived, thought, and acted as if I would never die, would live forever. Well, now I'm sitting here at Death's table and we're having a drink. I mean, I'm *dying*, here. It's no longer just a distant possibility, a *myth*. It's real. And suddenly, a lot of other things are beginning to seem real. Suddenly...flying saucers don't sound as silly. Bigfoot and the Loch Ness Monster seem to be possible, even likely. Things don't seem as...as *absolute* as they used to. If *I* can die, then I guess *anything* can happen."

"Then...you *do* believe me?"

"Go to the bookcase. Third shelf, far left, the black one."

Roger removed a trade paperback titled *Lon Chaney, Full Moons, and Lycanthropy*. There was a picture of Lon Chaney as the Wolfman on the cover.

"I bought it because I thought it was about movie werewolves," Josh said. "You know, 'Even a man who is pure of heart and says his prayers by night...' That sort of thing. It is, in a way. But it's more than that. It turned out to be much more serious than I expected."

"Really?" Roger thumbed through it quickly.

"Did I ever tell you I was a Mormon, Roger?"

Sitting down again, Roger shook his head.

"Well, I was. A good one, too. I loved my church, grew up in it. But when I got to junior high...ah, those were hellish years. I knew I was...different than the others. I went to a church school so everyone was Mormon and everyone was pretty much alike. Except me.

"When all my friends started noticing girls, I started noticing all my friends," he chuckled, "the *guys*, you know. I got so scared. I didn't understand what was wrong with me, and I didn't dare tell anyone.

"I was taking piano lessons then from Mr. Coswell. A kinder, gentler man never lived. He knew something was wrong and started to pry a little. Didn't take him long to figure it out. He was gay, too, see, but no one knew. God forbid. He would've lost his job, been cast out of the church. It was a while before he gathered the courage to tell *me*. We became very good friends. Not lovers, though. He wasn't like that. Mr. Coswell was in his forties when I knew him, and I don't think he'd had a lover since high school. No, he was only gay in his head, not in his pants." Another chuckle. "He helped me understand myself and accept myself. Yes, he was a good man." Josh's eyes looked past Roger, past the walls of his house, and focused on something far away.

"Anyhow, Mr. Coswell helped me to believe that there was nothing wrong with me. I wasn't a pervert, a monster. And the...the summer before I went to college...I told my parents.

"Have you ever heard of the Doctrine of Blood Atonement, Roger?"

"No."

"It's Mormon. A lot of people deny it, some have left the church because of it and formed little offshoot churches. Very controversial. Some people take it very seriously.

"It's like this: Some sinners have committed a sin *so* heinous, or have sinned unrepentantly for *so* long, that they cannot be forgiven. Their only hope for salvation is death. Their life must be ended, their blood spilled, in order for them to be accepted into the Kingdom.

"So, I told my parents. We'd always been so close...I guess I thought they would accept me unconditionally. But no. My father went insane. Tried to kill me. Chased me out of the house with a knife. Destroyed all my belongings. He even called the college I was planning to attend—a Mormon college—and told them I was a homosexual. I was not accepted, of course.

"I lost all of my Mormon friends and the church—the church I loved and had actively contributed to all my life—no longer wanted me." He smiled. "I don't have to tell *you* how that felt, do I?"

Josh carefully shifted in his chair and took a deep, labored breath.

"I was the same person I'd always been," he went on, "but suddenly everyone in my life—including my family—felt differently about me, was rejecting me. I was bitter for years. I hated God and Christianity and any organization that vaguely resembled a religion.

"I feel a little better about it now. Mostly because of that book, silly as it may seem. There's a section in there—you'll know it when you find it—that made me think long and hard about all this, and I found some answers to my *whys*. I'm at peace with them now.

"People like you and me, Roger, we're the lucky ones. We went through hell, and yours isn't over yet, but we're *still* lucky. There aren't many like us."

"I don't understand," Roger said, "why are we lucky?"

"*They* are being controlled, those people. So, in turn, they try to control others. It's like a sort of pecking order. Ever since their childhood or since some other vulnerable time in their lives, they were led to believe in the importance of a list of rules. Some of the rules are contradictory, some are impossible to follow, but they have become all-important to these people, whether they're Adventist rules or Mormon rules or Catholic rules. So they are under the control of this list and the people who enforce it.

"Then along comes someone like you or me who very innocently breaks one of those rules. You wanted to be a writer, I learned to accept the fact that I'm gay. It doesn't matter how innocently we broke them—we *broke* them. These other people—Adventists, Mormons, whatever—see that we're not following the rules that control *their* lives, so they try to enforce them. They try to scare us, or *hurt* us, into keeping those rules. They try to control us as they are controlled. They do this by convincing us we're sick, evil monsters.

"Do you know why that so often works, Roger?"

Roger shook his head.

"Because if you tell someone he's a monster long enough, he *becomes* one.

"And if you claim it's evil to be gay, then gays have to find their companionship in a dark, secret place and it *becomes* dirty. Evil.

"If you tell a writer it's evil to write stories because stories that aren't true make people ill, depress them—I believe Mrs. White says something along those lines, doesn't she?—then harass him and tell him he's going to burn in hell for doing something he loves, well, pretty soon it affects his work. The stories become bleak tales of doom, stories of pain and violence. Evil stories, if you want.

"You see, Roger, their little plan is really quite beautiful. With all those rules, they *create* their own monsters. Otherwise, they would have nothing to fight or control.

"But they didn't get me," he smiled. "That's why I'm one of the lucky ones. And they haven't gotten you yet, even though they're still trying. But this girl, Sondra..."

Josh shook his head and his eyes darkened. His sunken face soured into an expression of bitterness. It was so bitter, in fact, that Roger asked, "What's wrong? I thought you said you're at peace with them."

"Oh, no-no. I'm at peace with my *whys*. I'll never truly be at peace with the Mormons. Or *any* of them, actually." He paused a while, resting his face against a palm, then said, "My father called about six months ago, when he found out I had AIDS. I hadn't heard his voice since the day he chased me out of the house, but I knew it immediately. He laughed at me and said, 'God always finds a way to spill the blood of the sinners.' See...*that's* what bothers me the most. He thinks I'm being punished for my wicked life. *I* don't; I just happened to get this horrible sickness that gave me five to seven years and I got the short end of the stick. But after I'm dead, he'll smile, and all his friends will smile, and all the people who used to be *my* friends...and they'll think they are victorious.

"I'm at peace with myself in spite of how they tried to make me feel. The truth is, I'm *right*. But there are only a few like me. Most people are controlled, or are controlling others. The only truth to them is that list of rules. So...nobody ever believes the truth.

"In the end, they always win." He thought about what he'd said and turned to Roger with a warm smile. "Don't get me wrong, I'm not saying every single Seventh-Day Adventist or Mormon is like that. They're not. In fact, there's a young Adventist couple who visits me every week. They bring books and magazines—regular ones like *Time* and *People*, no religious tracts—and just talk. *Most* people are scared to walk on my side of the *street*; not them. They're good people.

"But it doesn't matter. The good people are outnumbered.

"In the end, *they* always win."

Roger sat in confused, overwhelmed silence for a while, drained by what Josh had said. He thumbed through the book, glancing at the black-and-white stills from old werewolf movies, the sketchy illustrations of bodies writhing through hideous transformations.

Josh said, "Take it."

"I'll bring it back."

Josh laughed dryly and said, "Keep it, Roger, I have no use for it."

"Are you sure?"

"Positive." He stood with effort, as if his frail body were several times its actual weight. "I think there are some things in that book that you'll find interesting. I wish I could be of more help."

"You listened."

"Happy to."

"Sorry to dump on you like—"

"Hush." He struggled away from the chair. "I don't mean to be rude, Roger, but why don't you take off now. I'm very tired..."

Roger closed the book and said, "Oh, sure, Josh, you gonna be okay?" He realized, even as he was speaking, how stupid the words were.

"No," Josh laughed.

"Jesus, I didn't—"

"Don't *worry* about it." He hobbled toward Roger, his shoulders rising and falling slowly above his stiff arms like the pistons of a dying engine. He stopped, lifted his arms, swayed slightly, and lowered them around Roger's shoulders, embracing him as he said, "Thank you for coming by, Roger. You take care."

Roger felt a sliver of the realization that would later stab him and make him feel so stupid, so selfish. He cautiously returned Josh's embrace, afraid he might break, and said, "Well, I'll come back in a couple days and let you know what I think of the book."

Josh smirked as he pulled away. "You do that."

It was the last time Roger would ever see him.

31

Roger went home, made some coffee, and sat down to read the book.

It was poorly written and not even bound very well, but once Roger skimmed through the first three chapters—all of which dealt with the Hollywoodized myth of lycanthropy—he began to find passages that rang chillingly true.

There were several different theories behind the physical transformation that allegedly plagued victims of lycanthropy.

Some attributed it to supernatural curses: a gypsy's hex, a witch's spell.

Others claimed it was a rare disease that caused hair to grow over its victim's body at regular intervals, made him unable to walk upright, and caused him to crave raw meat.

It was a subheading in bold print near the end of the chapter that fully captured Roger's attention: LYCANTHROPY AND RELIGION. He read the section slowly, then reread it again and again.

A psychiatrist in Boston had linked religious repression to a mental and physical aberration that resembled lycanthropy.

"Often, one who is raised in the confines of a fundamentalist faith," Dr. Regis Maine said at a 1978 psychiatric conference in Washington, D.C., "will, at some point, begin to doubt or reject the doctrines of his church. This independent thinking is inevitably met with severe negative reinforcement from family and friends who try, through various means of exclusion and harassment, to convince the subject that the fault is with *him* rather than the church."

"No shit," Roger muttered as he read.

Dr. Maine claimed to have several patients who, after extensive counseling, admitted that they were "werewolves" and were physically transformed with increasing regularity—some at times of anger, others with feelings of sexual arousal or even simple happiness and contentment. He even claimed to have *witnessed* one of these transformations.

"While the physical alterations were nothing like those seen in films or on television, they were, without doubt, complete and inhuman—animal-like—and the patient became extremely violent and exhibited a drastic increase in physical strength."

With continued therapy, Dr. Maine learned that each patient, all of whom were raised in ultra-conservative fundamentalist homes, had been the subject of what he called "intense reconversion or ostracization campaigns" designed to either woo the backslidden, wayward patient back into the fold or shame or frighten him into rededicating himself to Christ. During this process, the patients became convinced they were in some way monstrous or even possessed, that they were indeed evil and deserved the treatment given them. It was during this time that they began to experience mysterious physical ailments—usually severe abdominal pains—all of which escaped the diagnosis of doctors, even after extensive tests. These eventually developed into the physical **metamorphosis** which Dr. Maine suggested had, for centuries, been identified by the superstitious and fanatically religious as a demonic curse that turned its victims into ravenous wolves.

"It was not a curse at all," Maine said, "but quite likely a severe mental *and* physical condition imposed upon its victims by the very people who feared it most."

Dr. Maine proposed a treatment: if the patient were convinced that the desires and aspirations considered to be so evil and monstrous—artistic goals, sexual longings—were perfectly natural and healthy, if they were encouraged and ultimately acted upon, the patient would come to accept and love himself and learn to reject the harmful accusations and teachings of the religious zealots surrounding him.

No one took Dr. Maine seriously. In fact, according to the author, by the time Dr. Maine went public with his theory, he was exhibiting some rather bizarre behavior himself. He'd lost a great deal of weight, his hands shook as he stammered through his address, and his fellow psychiatrists speculated that Dr. Maine was nearing a breakdown.

They were right.

Only weeks after the 1978 conference where Maine shocked his colleagues into an embarrassed silence with his "findings," he was forcibly admitted to a mental institution, hysterical and violent, after being found running naked down a city street babbling wildly about monsters, "horrible flesh-eating monsters."

32

Dr. Maine was a small man with wiry hair the color of a silent film and, because it seemed appropriate to Roger's subconscious, he spoke with a stereotypical German accent. He sat facing Roger in a Naugahyde chair, hugging himself in a straitjacket and clamping a sweet-smelling pipe between his teeth. A strip of perspiration glistened like jewels above his wide, darting eyes.

"Sumzink is vorryink you, no?" the doctor asked through clenched teeth, puffing smoke. "Ze monster, perhaps?"

"Yes."

"Yours or hers?"

"I'm sorry?"

"*Your* monster or *Zondra's* monster?"

"I don't understand."

"Vell, zat *is* ze problem, no?"

"The problem?"

Dr. Maine began rocking in his chair. "You und ze girl, you are zo much alike, no? Und your symptoms are zo much alike, no? You *vant* her, und yet you *fear* her. She brings you too close to *zem*. You fear zat, had you not fought zem, *fled* zem, had not continued to exorcise your demons on paper, ze pain vould have continued. Vould have come *out*. Like *hers*."

"Come out?"

"Like *zat*," Dr. Maine laughed, nodding toward Roger's stomach.

Roger looked down to find he was naked and his belly was bulging, leaking blood as it tore open and a hideously gnarled claw ripped its way out of him, dangling bracelets of viscera...

《《——》》

When he woke from the nightmare, he was sitting up, holding his belly and grunting; the pain was snacking on his guts again.

Roger had reread the section titled LYCANTHROPY AND RELIGION until he knew it by heart, and then had run it through his mind again and again.

It seemed as if that section of the book had been written specifically for Roger, *meant* to be read by him.

Meant to frighten him.

And frighten him it did.

He tried to go back to sleep and did drop off a couple more times, but his sleep was shallow and diseased with nightmares he'd thought long gone...

He heard the thunderous footsteps of a giant raging messiah destroying the neighborhood as He bellowed, "Where's Carlton? Where *is* that little shit?"...

He hid in black filthy corners—a child again, weak and terrified—as the Adventist hunters stormed around him with bright flashlights and powerful guns, shouting, "There's one over there!" and "Hah—I got another one!"...

He writhed in bed as he dreamed his skin was moving over his body, changing, twisting...

And the claw. He saw it when the pain came in his sleep, its curved nails dark with blood...

He finally gave up and sat at his bedroom window with a drink, watching the sun rise behind a thick veil of raining clouds that glowed a dull steel gray. As he watched the day begin, he imagined Sondra waking, showering, eating breakfast as Bill limped silently around the house on his clicking leg. She would go to school, go from class to class, eat lunch with friends, acting like just another high school senior, a shy and silent teenager.

Acting as if she'd never hurt a soul, ended a life, or tasted blood. Until it happened again.

And when will that be? he wondered.

Roger decided he had to talk with Sondra soon.

Today.

33

Roger parked outside the high school and waited for thirty minutes. Shortly before three o'clock, students began to spill down the front steps and scatter in the parking lot to board buses and speed away in cars. When he spotted Sondra, he honked his horn and called to her out the window.

She approached the car warily.

"We have to talk," he said.

"I can't. I've gotta go to work."

"I'll drive you. Get in."

"Roger, I'm not even supposed to—"

"Get. In."

Once she was in the car, he turned to her and asked how she felt.

"I'm...fine, I guess."

"You look tired."

She shrugged.

"Has it happened again?"

"Roger, I told you to forget it."

"I *can't*. And neither can you. It's only going to get worse unless you try to do something. Look, I think I know what's wrong. What's causing it. It's not your fault, Sondra. It's—"

"I have to go to work." She opened her door and Roger reached across and pulled it shut, then started the car.

"Where?"

"Vintage Video."

Jesus, he thought. *First they let her work in a deli serving food they'd never let her eat, then they let her work in a store that rents movies they'd probably never let her watch. They may say I'm evil, but at least I'm consistent.*

As he drove, he told her what Niles had said about Sidney.

"They know something," he said. "I'm afraid maybe they've found him."

She seemed not to hear.

He parked the car in front of the video store, getting angry.

"Goddammit, Sondra, quit acting like nothing's wrong, like nothing's happened!" he snapped. "I think I can help you. I need to know if Bill knows about—"

Sondra gasped, looking out her window.

Bill stood outside the video store glaring at them.

"Oh, no," she breathed, closing her eyes, "oh no, no, no…"

"Jesus," Roger hissed. The dread in Sondra's face made him ache for her. He reached over and squeezed her hand as Bill began to hobble toward them. "Listen, Sondra, *listen* to me, you can get my number from Betty and call me anytime, I want to help you. Is there anything you should tell me?"

She looked at him with terrified eyes and whispered, "You should be very careful. Be careful of—"

Bill opened the door.

"C'mon," he said, his voice low and ominous.

Sondra quickly got out and Bill leaned into the car.

"I *had* to talk to her, Bill," Roger said quickly, "please believe me—"

"You've got nothing to say to her."

"Bill, *we've* got to talk, it's important, *very* important, it's about Sondra and I'm afraid that—"

"You've got nothing to say to me, either. And if I ever…*ever*…see you with Sondra again…" His lips trembled with quiet rage.

"Listen, Bill, we *have* to put our differences aside and talk about—"

"Just don't let it happen again." He stared at Roger with stony eyes a moment, then shook his head and said, "You were stupid to come back here." He slammed the door so hard the car shook.

As he drove home, Roger pounded the wheel with his fist, furiously cursing God, the church, and Bill Dunning.

34

When Roger got home, he was useless; he was angry and afraid and exhausted. He searched his bedroom, hoping to find a little pot to go to sleep by; he finally found a pipeful in his closet—

—along with his gun.

It was in its box, wrapped in a red cloth, where it had been since he'd lived in North Hollywood. He stared up at the closet shelf where it lay under a stack of books and, a few moments later, took it into the living room.

As he filled a pipe, Roger stared at the gun lying on his coffee table. He took a few hits, then picked it up, hefted it.

The phone rang and Roger had the urge to aim the gun and stop the noise with one shot, but the gun was empty.

The answering machine picked up.

A dial tone hummed into the recorder.

It would be nice to end his problems with a single gunshot, but shooting the phone wouldn't do it; they'd find another way to contact him. He could shoot *them* until his trigger finger fell off, but there would always be more to replace them.

There was only one person he could shoot to end it all.

God always finds a way to spill the blood of the sinners...

One person...

He returned to his closet and got a box of bullets, then started loading the gun.

Before he could finish, Roger heard someone crying outside his door. The bell rang and he recognized Sondra's voice calling his name.

He went to the door, pulling his robe closed and tying it.

She was covered with blood and her left eye was nearly swollen shut. Her clothes hung in tatters on her otherwise naked body and she was hugging herself, shaking violently. She looked very much like she had after killing Sidney Nelson, and Roger wondered who had died tonight.

"I'm cuh-cuh-cold," she whimpered, falling into his arms.

The blood was cold and sticky, clinging to Roger's bare chest when his robe fell open. He kicked the door shut and carried her into the bathroom.

The remnants of her clothes peeled from her body easily, like tender meat from the bone, and he tossed them onto the floor.

"What happened?" he asked, holding a washcloth under hot water.

"I...I'm really not sure."

"Are you hurt bad?"

"Just my face."

"How?"

"Bill."

"He hit you?"

She nodded.

The dirty copper smell of blood was turning Roger's stomach and he flipped on the fan, then began to gently dab the blood away with the cloth.

"He beat up on you often?"

"Never this bad." She flicked her tongue over a loose tooth and muttered, "I think I'm gonna lose that one."

"And the blood...where did it come from?"

"Some...man, I think. Out in the woods."

"The woods? Where?"

"Off Silverado Trail."

"Jesus Christ."

Once her face was clean, Roger hunkered down in front of her, took her bloody hands in his, and spoke softly.

"You've gotta let me try to help you, Sondra. You can't keep doing this. And it'll *never* stop if you don't at least let me try."

With a slight shake of her head, she said, "That's why Bill beat me up. Because he found me with you."

"Why was he waiting for you at work?"

"To catch me doing something wrong." She pushed a blood-caked strand of hair from her eyes. "He was afraid you'd try to see me because...well, he's been worried about you, because..."

"About *me*? Why?"

She looked away from him and said, "I want to wash."

Roger let it pass. He handed her the washcloth, pulled back the curtain, and turned on the faucet. Pouring some bubblebath into the water, he said, "I'll leave you alone. Is there anything I can—"

"Don't leave me alone," she whispered, standing and pressing herself against him, crying softly. "Please don't."

Roger helped her into the tub, sat on the edge, and began passing the cloth over her back.

"Why is Bill so concerned about me?" he asked.

"He has been ever since you came."

"I didn't tell anyone I was coming. How did he know?"

She shrugged, then laid back in the tub, wetting her hair.

The same way somebody always managed to learn my phone number even when it was unlisted, Roger thought, *and the same way they always knew where I lived no matter where I went.*

Roger averted his eyes when her nipples broke the surface of the water and rose through the foamy suds, erect as pencil erasers atop her pale breasts.

The marijuana had made him uncomfortably loose, just loose enough for the sight of Sondra's wet and soapy body to give him an erection despite the fact that the bathwater was brown with the blood of a dead stranger.

"I'm not going back," she whispered as Roger shampooed her hair. "I won't live with them anymore. With *him*."

"Where will you go? What will you do?"

"I don't know, but I can't live like that anymore." After a long silence, she said, "Can I...could I stay with you?"

He wanted to say yes immediately, say it without a second thought, but he couldn't.

"How about if we go see Bill together and I'll talk with him."

"Oh, God, no," she gasped. "No, he'd...he'd...no. You can't do that." She turned to face him, her head crowned with bloody suds.

"They've been talking about you. A lot. Bill and some of the men from the church, elders and deacons. Especially lately."

"Why lately?"

"Marjie's been coming over."

"*Who?*" he asked, certain she wasn't talking about Marjie *Shore*.

"Marjie Shore. She told him...she said you had some books."

He remembered Marjie's reaction to his research books; he realized that was when things had changed between them, when she found the books, and he cursed his stupidity.

"She said you had some bloody clothes and...well, they all figured you were, you know, doing it again."

"Doing *what* again?"

"The rituals. Worshipping Satan."

"Jesus H. *Christ*, Sondra, I've *never* worshipped—"

"I know that. But they're convinced. That's why Bill was so upset with me. See, my whole family...all of them...have always thought there was something wrong with me, that I was evil, 'cause I've always been such a black sheep. Then...when *this* started...you know, the *change*...they figured I was possessed, like I told you before." She laughed humorlessly. "So now they figure you and I are gonna get together, y'know? Have demon parties and maybe give birth to the Antichrist, or something." Another laugh.

Roger was still shocked about Marjie. If she really thought he was serious about satanism, why didn't she *say* so? Why didn't she confront him with it so he could defend himself instead of going to Bill—especially after talking about Bill as if he were crazy and she'd written him off—and stirring up ridiculous stories that weren't true.

You asshole, Roger thought to himself, *you knew the risks, you knew what might happen if you got involved with her again, you knew, Goddammit!*

"Do you love her?" Sondra asked.

Roger blinked his eyes rapidly, shaking off his thoughts. "Uh, no," he said. "Well...we used to be close, but..." He didn't finish; he kept thinking, *How could she? How could she when things were going so well?*

He finally stood and said, "I'll get you a towel."

Slivers of Bone

«« — »»

Roger put her in his bed.

"Do they know where you are?" he asked, pulling the covers up around her.

"No."

"Should I call them? Let them know you're all right?"

"No, *please* don't!"

"Okay, okay. We'll wait until morning." He went to the door and turned out the light. "If you need anything, just call."

"Roger?"

"Hm."

"Please…stay with me."

He sighed at the temptation, turned it over in his mind, but decided he'd already made one mistake too many.

"Get some sleep," he whispered, closing the door.

35

Roger made himself a drink, sat down in front of the television, and chewed on what Sondra had told him about Marjie until his feeling of betrayal had become a smoldering anger.

Two drinks later, the doorbell rang and Roger somehow knew that it was Marjie.

"Is she here?" she asked when he opened the door.

"Who?"

"Please, Roger, don't play with me. If she's here, let me take her home. If you know where she is, *tell* me. Please."

"I don't understand why it's any of your business, Marjie."

"I'm doing this for your own good, Roger."

"Oh? Running to Bill and telling him I'm worshipping *Satan*, for Christ's sake—was *that* for my own good, too?"

With a frustrated sigh, Marjie bowed her head and said, "Bill told me what happened today, and I thought—" Her words caught in her throat and she gasped, "Oh, my God!"

There were bloodstains on the cream-colored carpet.

"What have you done?" she breathed.

"Nothing, it was—it's just—she—"

"Sondra?" she called, scared now.

"She's fine, Marjie, she's sleeping."

"Get her." She was trembling, apparently from anger as well as fear.

"I'm going to take her home in the morning, don't worry. I'm going to talk with Bill about—"

"You *can't* take her home in the morning, Roger, *dammit*, will you listen! Right now Bill is getting some men together to come over here looking for Sondra and if they find her with you...please, won't you just let me take her home. It'll save a lot of trouble."

Roger was livid. "They're coming over *here*? Jesus, like some fucking holy posse! And what will they do, *lynch* me? Hang me in a public place, maybe?" His voice was raising slowly to the level of a shout. "Very *Christian* of them, and certainly in keeping with everything else they've been doing, like the goat's head on my porch and the brick through DiMarco's window. Were you in on that, Marjie? Did you play along, huh? Maybe the goat's head was *your* idea. Inspired by my books, were you?"

"I had nothing to do with that. I didn't even know about it."

"Uh-huh, sure." He stepped toward her and she moved back, frightened. "I don't suppose you mentioned to Bill that you've been *fucking* the neighborhood Satanist, did you? Because if you did, the son of a bitch'd probably be throwing things through your window, too, you ever think of that? *Huh?* Did it occur to you that you're dealing with a very sick person here?"

"Roger, h-he's a f-friend," she said, trying to hold in her tears. "We...*all* of us used to be f-friends."

"And what brought that to a screeching halt? I never had any friends, Marjie. For the first twenty years of my life I never had any friends. Jesus, and to think I let you...all over again, I let you..." Anger constricted his throat and he could say no more. He kicked the ottoman and it slid over the carpet and slammed into the coffee table, knocking off a full ashtray. "Get out of here."

Moving back toward the door, Marjie shook her head and said, "No, Roger, I'm not—"

"Get the fuck *out* of here!"

Wringing her hands in front of her, she tried to sound calm and reasonable. "I'm not leaving without—" She looked over his shoulder. "Sondra!"

Roger spun around to see Sondra standing in the hall holding his robe before her.

"Sondra," Marjie pleaded, "please come with me. Bill is furious."

She stepped back into the shadows, shaking her head.

"Sondra, *please!*" She turned to Roger, her face red with anger. "She's only seventeen, for God's sake, how could you...how *could* you?"

"How could I *what*? You think I'm fucking her? Well, I'm not. I'm trying to help her. No one else will. Maybe you've heard of it, it's called decency. You could use some." He turned toward the hall. "Go back to bed, Sondra." Stepping past Marjie to open the door, he said, "And you—go."

"I will not."

He grabbed her elbow and jerked her toward the door but she pulled away, screaming. "Let *go* of me! What's wrong with you, Roger, don't you see I'm trying to help you? I'm thinking of *you*." Her face twisted and tears rolled from her eyes as she massaged her elbow. "You act like I hate you or something, b-but I duh-*don't*." Her words garbled by sobs, she lowered her voice to a raspy whisper. "I've never for a second stopped loving you. And *admiring* you. You weren't afraid to do what you wanted to do even though everyone was telling you it was wrong. I...I never had that kind of strength. I'm a...conformist, Roger, a weak, spineless conformist. I've always admired your independence. I never *really* believed all that Satanist stuff, not back then, but I was...concerned about you. I was different back then, I bought it all, the whole philosophy, being saved, *all* that. And because you were breaking the rules...I wanted to *save* you. I'm not that way anymore. Well...not quite. But when I saw those books here...I looked through them and they're *awful*. I got scared. I thought maybe…maybe it *was* true. And those bloody clothes out in the garage…it made sense, sort of. I started to worry again and I talked to Bill. You say he's crazy—and he *does* have problems, I don't deny that—but he is a sincere Christian, a good Adventist and…I thought he could help, could tell me what to do. I was worried about you, Roger, that's all."

"Worried? That I was committing some great sin? Breaking a few commandments? Not following all of good old Sister White's rules? Is that what you were worried about while you were sipping wine like a *big girl*?" He spit the words mockingly, hurtfully, and Marjie's pain bled from her eyes; Roger enjoyed it. "Were you worried about that while you were smoking *pot*? Or sucking my *cock* out of *wedlock*?"

She pressed a fist to her chest and released an agonized cry.

"*You* were worried about *me*?"

"I was, I was wrong," she cried. "I was tuh-trying to, to *fit*, Roger, I *told* you I'm a conformist. I was trying so hard to fit into an environment that's still new to me. I don't really believe in that kind of life. I don't believe in…in…I don't know *what* I believe in. I'm always trying so duh-desperately to *fit*."

"You fucking hypocrite," he growled through gritted teeth just an instant before the pain tore through his guts. He doubled over, fell, tried to get up but fell again, groaning as it wrenched his insides.

"Roger?" Marjie sputtered.

He rolled over the floor, retching.

"Roger, what's wrong? Roger?"

"Go," he grunted. "Get out."

"Roger, what…what should I do? What's *wrong*?" Her tears were subsiding and the pain in her voice was replaced by urgency.

"Go…away." He tried to sit up but curled into a ball instead, releasing a high-pitched wail of misery.

It had never hit him so hard, had never been so intense. The pain exploded in his abdomen, sending shrapnel upward into his throat and downward into his testicles, down his arms to the very tips of his fingers. He screamed a shrill jagged scream, opening his eyes to see Marjie and Sondra standing over him, their mouths working soundlessly, and he realized he could no longer even hear his own voice, just a bone-deep throbbing in his ears, a powerful liquid rush that threatened to send his eyes shooting from their sockets.

He tried to speak, to plead for help, but he had no control over his tongue; it was a thick, numb chunk of meat and his teeth were gritty pieces of stone that sliced at his lips like razors and his hands—

Sweet merciful Jesus my haaaaands! his mind screamed.

—were cracking open, the fingertips splitting to make way for deadly hook-like claws.

When he looked up, Sondra was smiling as if she'd found a long lost friend, smiling and crying at once, and Marjie was pressing her fists to her mouth, shaking her head as she stumbled backward—

—and as the pain reached a crescendo, Roger felt a hatred for Marjie, a hatred so heavy and thick he felt he could vomit it up like a steaming lump of half-digested food and he swung his arm through the air clutching at Marjie's leg.

She turned to run but her foot struck the ottoman and she fell, arms and legs splayed as she hit the floor.

A thin veil of red covered Roger's vision as he crawled on all fours toward Marjie, the throbbing growing louder in his skull, the pain in his center turning into a deep, engulfing hunger. The red darkened to a rust...

...then to brown...

...then black...

36

Laughter.

High, musical, crystal-clear laughter.

Roger's vision returned slowly, rising from a dark sludge to a soft glow, from blurred light and colors to a slowly growing clarity.

The drumming pain in his head began to subside as physical sensations returned.

The floor beneath his back...

The carpet against his palms, strangely wet and warm...

And something else...

Something wonderful...

Roger moaned and slowly lifted his hips from the floor—

What's happened?

—sliding his cock deeper into the warm sucking mouth that held it.

Why am I here? On the floor? Doing this?

The sensation stopped, the laughter rang out again, then the sucking continued, the voice humming warmly, hands cupping his testicles and stroking his thighs...

"You're like me," the voice said, breath hot on his genitals. "We're the same..."

He tried to lift his head but was too weak, drained, empty...

"We're alike, Roger..."

It was Sondra.

Her hands moved over his stomach, his chest, up to his shoulders as she crawled up his body like a cat. Her fingers wrapped around his cock and she impaled herself on him, crying out in gleeful pain.

He tried to speak but only made a hoarse, clogged sound in his throat—

—and tasted the blood.

It slicked the inside of his mouth like oil and he coughed, retched, turned his head and spit as she moved on him.

"Aaahhh, yes, just alike...you and meeeee."

She leaned forward and placed her open mouth on his throat, licking and sucking, nibbling gently, her heavy breasts brushing his chest and abdomen.

Sitting up again, she reached behind her and held his testicles, squeezed, tugged...

There were spots on the ceiling, dark red spots that had not been there before, but he noticed them only peripherally because of the powerful warmth growing between his legs, spreading upward slowly...

Must be drunk, he thought, because he remembered nothing and didn't know how this had started. But he didn't care.

He found the strength to lift his head just enough to see her towering over him, grinding herself against him, her body covered with dark wet smears, one hand stroking a breast…

Her left hand…

On her right arm…

What's happened?

He blinked, squinted, certain his eyes were not seeing what he thought they were seeing…

Sondra held the left arm in her right hand. It was torn off at the elbow, the skin pale, the fingers splayed and slightly bent just enough to cup her breast, lift it, press it hard against her ribs…

"What…what's…" Roger croaked.

"We're the same," she breathed through a smile, eyes half-closed, hair flowing over her shoulders…

Roger turned his head to the right, groaning when he saw the splash of blood on the side of the recliner…

The other arm beneath the coffee table…

The leg not far from that, a lump of bone protruding from the tattered glob of black-red meat above the thigh…

And the head…

Marjie's head rested on its side, mouth open in a scream, tongue hanging from the corner…

Roger screamed as he came, but it was not a scream of pleasure.

37

Sondra slid off him and curled up beside him on the bloody carpet, nuzzling his neck, purring like a kitten.

"No, no, no," Roger hissed, rolling over and getting on his knees, looking around at the scattered gory mess that used to be Marjie Shore, his first kiss, his first date, his first girlfriend. "I…I *did* this?" he cried. "Did *I* do this?"

Sondra embraced him from behind. "Mmm-hmmm. You're like me, Roger."

"No," he croaked, stumbling to his feet, "no, I…I couldn't

have." But he knew he had. Marjie's blood was in his mouth; bits of skin and hair were stuck beneath his fingernails. If he thought about it, if he were to close his eyes and concentrate on it, he knew he would remember doing it in the same murky way he might remember a bad dream.

He limped into the bathroom and splashed cold water on his face, then began to clean himself off so he could decide what to do next.

38

"We have to clean this up," he said, his voice unsteady, standing in the hall and facing the mess.

Sondra stood at the window staring at the night, twisting a strand of her hair around a finger.

"They'll be coming soon," she muttered softly.

A burst of adrenaline surged through Roger because he knew she was right and he clapped his hands together sharply and said, "C'mon, *c'mon*, get cleaned up, let's *go*."

Roger felt a crank-like rush as he dashed to the window and looked out to see Marjie's car parked on the street. He paced the room as Sondra slowly made her way down the hall.

This would be much more difficult than Sidney the bread man...

The phone rang and Roger ignored it.

"Roger?" It was Betty and she sounded very upset. "Roger, if you're there, *please*—"

"Oh, Roger, Roger—" He could tell she'd been drinking. "—it's the police, they're *everywhere*! Running around with their chemicals and little brushes and—"

"Betty, what are you talking about?"

"The police! They're here at the deli going over *everything*! They called me, got me out of bed, said they had a search warrant and that they, they've brought some men in from San Francisco, *lab* men, they said. It sounds like they're looking for *blood*!" she hissed, lowering her voice. "They're in the Munch Room, talking, whispering to each other, and Roger, they keep talking about *you*, Roger, they keep saying your *name*! I'm scared, Roger, what's going *on*? What have you *done*?"

Roger clutched the receiver so hard, his knuckles ached and he was struck with the urge to laugh, to throw back his head and guffaw; it was so *absurd*, all of it.

"Look, Betty, just…just…"

"You're keeping something from me," she said. "What *is* it? Does it have something to do with what happened here? With the brick through the window?"

"No, no, that's something…that's a…Jesus. Oh, Jesus." He did laugh then, a giggle at first that built to a deep belly laugh, and he had to sit down, holding his sides with one arm, his eyes filling with tears as Betty spoke his name again and again.

And then he heard the voices.

There were several of them outside, all male; first one spoke, then another, then all of them at once, as if in disagreement.

Then silence.

Footsteps.

Roger stopped laughing in time to hear one of them say, "I still think we should call the police."

Another said, "Well, as long as you don't *use* that gun, we'll be okay."

Gun?

"Betty," Roger whispered, "hang on a sec." He put down the receiver with Betty's pinched, insect-like voice still coming from the earpiece. Pulling the curtain aside slightly, Roger peered out the front window and saw five men coming across the lawn toward the house. Bill was leading them with a shotgun cradled in one arm. "Christ," Roger hissed, returning to the phone. "I'm sorry, Betty, but I've gotta go."

"You *can't*! I don't know what's—"

"I'm sorry," he said again before hanging up and rushing to the bathroom. Sondra stood naked before the mirror brushing her hair, her eyes heavy-lidded and distant as she whistled tunelessly through her teeth. "C'mon, we've gotta go," Roger said.

"Hm?"

"Get *dressed*, we have to—shit, you don't have any clothes." He led her to his bedroom where he took a pair of sweats from the closet; they were baggy on her, but there was no time to be choosey.

The doorbell rang.

Sondra turned to Roger with panic in her eyes.

Roger put a finger over his lips. "The back door," he whispered.

The bell rang again, three times in rapid, impatient succession.

After putting on his coat, Roger went to the living room and got his gun from the coffee table, loaded it, and stuffed it in his pocket, got his car keys, then led Sondra through the kitchen, out the back door, and around to the side of the house. A drizzle was falling and an icy breeze made Sondra's teeth chatter.

As they rounded the front corner of the house and approached the car, Roger could hear Bill's deep, unfriendly voice:

"Roger? Open up. I've come for Sondra."

Sondra took Roger's hand and squeezed fearfully.

He quietly opened the door on the driver's side and waved Sondra in. Behind the wheel, he softly clicked the door shut and slid the key into the ignition.

Someone pounded on the front door and Bill shouted, "Roger? Sondra!"

"Let's go, Roger," Sondra whispered frantically, "please, please, please hurry, let's *go*, if he takes me home he's gonna be so mad..."

Roger started the engine, punched the car in reverse, and sped out of the drive.

Even in the car, Roger could hear the burst of voices from the porch. The men turned and jogged to a pick-up truck and an old Pinto parked across the street. Bill hobbled behind them on his cane, glaring at Roger as he put the car in gear and drove away.

"He has a gun," Sondra said, frightened. "He means business. We have to go to the police, Roger, we have to—"

"No. Not the police."

"Why *not?*"

"I just killed somebody, remember? And now they think I killed Sidney Nelson, too." He quickly told her about Betty's phone call, glancing in the rearview mirror to see the truck and Pinto turning around to follow him. "If they've got a warrant to search the deli and they've brought a bunch of lab guys in from San Francisco, *they* mean business, too."

"Then...then what're we gonna *do*?"

Roger took a sudden left off Beekman, then another left on Watson.

"First, we've got to lose them," he said, taking yet another turn, zigzagging past warmly lit houses with smoke rising from the chimneys. "Then we've got to get rid of this car."

Then what? he thought. *Leave town? Hide out? Take a minor across the state lines and up your sentence?*

Headlights appeared in the rearview mirror.

"Damn!" Roger barked, hitting the wheel.

"Where are we going?"

He rounded another corner, increasing his speed, making his way toward Silverado Trail. He thought about that, going over his options, which didn't take long, then said, "To see my friend Josh."

39

Josh lived in one of a row of small bungalow-like houses on the south side of town, behind which ran a narrow alley.

Roger parked his car in the alley where it would be invisible from the street, went through the gate that opened onto the small rectangle of grass that served as a backyard, and knocked on the back door. When there was no answer, no sound from inside at all, he knocked again and called for Josh.

"Maybe he's gone," Sondra whispered, shivering as she looked around them nervously.

"No, he's very sick." Roger knocked again.

They'd managed to stay far enough ahead of Bill and his friends to get to Josh's without being tailed, but now Roger began to think perhaps they'd gotten there for nothing.

When he tried the door, it opened easily.

"Josh?" Roger called, taking Sondra's hand and going inside. He checked all the rooms, but the small house was empty. When he looked out the front window, he muttered, "His car's gone. But where could he…" Then he turned to the sofa where he'd seen the neatly placed clothes the day before—

—and he knew.

I'm going to disappear…

Roger slumped onto the sofa and scrubbed his hands over his face, hating himself for being so blinded by his own problems that he didn't see what Josh was about to do—even after Josh had *told* him what he was going to do.

"My…God…" Sondra whispered.

Her voice startled Roger; he'd forgotten he wasn't alone. She stood across the room looking at a row of pictures on the wall.

"What?" he asked.

"Him." She pointed at one of the pictures, backing away slowly, crying.

Roger stood and looked over her shoulder at the picture; it was Josh at Disneyland, a much healthier Josh but still quite obviously ailing, standing between Mickey and Minnie, arm in arm, grinning like a thrilled little boy.

"It was him," she whispered. "The man. In the woods. Tonight. It was *him…*"

40

Roger stumbled backward and fell onto the sofa again, his arms loose at his sides.

"He's…the one…you killed?" He weakly lifted an arm and pointed at the picture. "That was his blood?"

Fingertips covering her mouth, tears sparkling in her eyes, she nodded. "He looked really sick, but yeah, it was him."

"He was sick," Roger breathed. "He had AIDS."

Sondra turned to him slowly, very slowly, her jaw slack, face blank, eyes disbelieving.

"Whuh..." She swallowed dryly, leaning against the wall. "What did you say?"

Roger repeated himself.

They looked at one another for a long time, their eyes speaking for them, both thinking of the same things—the blood that had covered Sondra when she arrived at Roger's, their lovemaking on the floor earlier—then Sondra crossed the room, her steps small and clumsy, and knelt before Roger, lips trembling.

"I'm sorry," she rasped.

"You couldn't have known."

She took his hands in hers and made a futile attempt to smile.

"We're gonna die anyway," she said.

"I know."

The gun resting heavily in Roger's coat pocket suddenly felt comforting, not as a means of defense, but of escape.

They held each other for a long moment until they heard engines slowing outside and Sondra pulled away from him and said, "That's Bill's pick-up."

41

When Roger looked out the window, Bill was limping toward the house. He met Roger's eyes with a smile as cold as a tomb and called, "I figured you'd be here with your fag friend," his voice padded by distance. He still held the shotgun in his arm, but appeared to be alone now.

Roger dropped the curtain and turned to Sondra.

"Let's go!" He grabbed her arm and rushed her back out to the car. She got in and slammed her door as Roger hurried around the front of the car—

—and staggered to a halt.

The left front tire had been slashed and was now flat and useless.

So was the right.

And the two in the rear.

"Out, out," he stammered, waving her from the car, "they've slashed the tires."

"What?" she cried, panicked.

"C'mon." He pulled her out and, holding her arm, led her toward the north end of the alley—

—where two men were headed toward them taking long rapid steps. One of them carried a baseball bat, the other a flashlight.

Sondra backpedaled, gasping, "No, no, no, no…"

"Just give us the girl," one of the men said.

They walked with such purpose, such force, that Roger wanted to cringe, frozen in place. Instead, he steeled himself and led Sondra in the opposite direction; his heart battered his ribs as he broke into a jog.

For an instant—a terrifying, brain-searing instant—he was a child again, the child of his nightmare, weak-kneed with fear, the debilitating fear of a hunted animal looking for a place to hide.

He reached into his jacket pocket and clutched the cold, heavy gun, holding it like a lover in a last embrace.

Sondra began to cry, coughing sobs that made her stumble against Roger and nearly fall; he held her up and dragged her with him until they reached the cross street.

"This way," he gasped, pulling her to the right—

—and scrambling to a stop when Bill rounded the corner before them.

His stiff leg clicked as he neared them, hefting the shotgun threateningly.

Once again, Roger and Sondra began to walk backwards, clinging closely to one another.

"Sondra!" Bill shouted. "Come here. Now. Annie's worried sick."

Roger said, "Bill…Bill, you've gotta listen to me."

"No. No, I don't." He aimed the shotgun at Roger.

"You don't want to do that, Bill."

"Maybe that'd be good. You're both as evil as the night is dark."

Roger thought with chilling certainty, *He's insane.*

"Listen, Bill, Sondra is *sick*. What you're doing is only making her worse. She needs help. She needs—"

"She needs to get away from you, that's what she needs. She's always been a problem, but you've only made it worse. She needs to get down on her knees and plead for God's forgiveness. Isn't that *right*, Sondra?"

Digging her fingers into Roger's arm, groaning miserably, Sondra leaned forward, clutching her stomach, and Roger put an arm around her shoulders to support her.

"No, Sondra," he whispered, "hang on, don't let it happen now."

There were hurried footsteps behind them; the other men were closing in.

Roger remembered the baseball bat and, holding Sondra close to his side, he drew his gun, spun around, and leveled it at the man who was holding the bat over his head, preparing to strike.

The bat clattered to the sidewalk.

The yellow sodium glow of the tall streetlights above them cast deep shadows over the shocked faces of the two men; they were both large, like lumberjacks or truck drivers, but they backed away cautiously, keeping their eyes on Roger's gun.

"Stay back!" Roger barked, waving the gun suddenly. Both men were startled and one fell backward into a patch of bushes growing along a fence.

Sondra struggled in Roger's embrace as he turned toward Bill. She hid her face against his shoulder, her voice a muffled growl as she began to chew on his jacket.

"Why have you done this, Bill?" Roger cried, his voice strained. "Why do you—"

Sharp teeth broke through his jacket and pierced his flesh; Sondra writhed in pain against him and Roger felt blood trickling down his arm beneath his clothes, felt her teeth gnaw deeper into his arm, and—

—he felt something else: a blade-fingered fist of pain closing around his entrails, squeezing, crushing...

No, Roger thought, *no, not now, please not now!*

The pain raged and Roger dug his elbow into his side as hot bile rose in his throat. He swallowed, coughed, and continued:

"Why do you *keep* doing this?"

Bill started toward them as they staggered backward, the shotgun aimed at Roger's midsection; an icy smirk broke the surface of his hard face, but he said nothing.

"It's gone on too long," Roger gasped, trying to conceal his pain. "It's time to stop now, time to…to just…leave me alone."

Still no response.

Roger screamed, *"What do you want from me, a fucking apology?"*

A door slammed somewhere on the block and a voice shouted, "Take it home or I'm calling the cops, asshole! People are tryna sleep!"

Bill spoke softly: "It's too late for repentance now, Roger. You're too far gone and you've taken too many souls with you." His prosthetic leg clumped as he walked: the rubber end of his cane made sloppy kissing sounds on the wet sidewalk. In a monotonous droning voice, he began to recite: "The books you've written, Roger…they're evil. 'Developed by agents of Satan.' Recognize those words, Roger? Know what that makes *you*, Roger? An agent of Satan. Bewitching the minds of your readers 'with theories formed in the synagogue of Satan.' Recognize *those* words, Roger?"

Roger was crying now, overwhelmed by the pain as he stumbled into the street with Sondra leaning on him heavily, her cries garbled against him, her fingers digging into his chest now, tearing his shirt.

"They were written by Ellen White. God's prophet. Heaven's scribe. Leader of the Remnant Church. She used her gifts for *Him*, for *His* glory. But you…*you've* used yours for the Prince of Darkness. *You* are an agent of Satan. *You* have put his words into every bookstore and supermarket in the country and you have trampled on the Truth to do it! You've rejected God's word and His plan for you in favor of leading precious souls to the lake of fire!" His voice was rising, trembling with righteous indignation. "Every person who reads one of your books is a step closer to eternal damnation and you are responsible for their loss!" He kept coming steadily: step...*clump*...step...*clump*... "You're a disease, Roger, and you're spreading, infecting minds, turning thousands—maybe *millions*—away from the plan of salvation by corrupting them with the Devil's dictations!"

The man who had fallen into the bushes struggled to his feet and warily approached Bill, saying, "Bill...c'mon now, Bill, that's enough, don't you—"

"Back off, Matt!" Bill snapped, then turned to Roger again, lifted his cane, and pointed an unsteady finger at him, bellowing, "*You...have* to be...*stopped!*"

Sondra pulled her teeth from Roger's shoulder; he couldn't feel the bite because it was eclipsed by the pain that was spreading inside him, digging its way into his testicles and down his arms as it had earlier that night.

Bill dropped his cane and lifted the shotgun to his shoulder.

"Run!" Roger cried, pushing Sondra across the street toward the alley that continued on the other side.

"No, Bill, wait!" one of the men shouted, afraid now, apparently unaware that Bill would go to such an extreme.

Roger ran after Sondra in a half-crouch, the intensity of his pain making him unable to stand upright. He felt spittle dribbling down his chin, felt himself quickly losing control over his own body.

He cried Sondra's name but it came from his mouth a thick and mangled sound: "Shon-daaahhh!" As he reached the alley, he heard the shotgun explode...

42

Time slowed to a heavy crawl after the gunshot.

Roger tried to run fast when he heard the shotgun go off, hoping to round the corner and duck into the alley for protection before he was hit, but he felt the burning sprinkle of buckshot over his back and legs and he fell, skinning his palms on the ground. His skin felt like fire and his clothes clung to his small bloody wounds.

He didn't stop moving; Roger crawled for a bit, sobbing as he looked down at his hands scrambling over the ground below him and saw the black claws scraping the pavement.

"No. *No!*" He fought the pain and the changes that were quaking through his body, tried to hold them off by biting his lower lip until he tasted his own blood, trying to use one pain to battle another.

On his left was a tall brick wall and on his right a cyclone fence that separated a row of backyards from the alley. He hooked his clawed fingers into the fence wire and pulled himself up. The fence was crawling with ivy through which webs of soft light from the houses on the other side cut into the murky alley. He pushed away from the fence and staggered on toward Sondra, who was even farther ahead of him now.

Every few yards, a garbage bin hunkered against the wall like a giant metal toad patiently waiting for a passing morsel; a cat dove from the top of one of the bins and shot across the alley in front of Roger.

Up ahead, Sondra careened back and forth down the alley like a pinball, slamming into the fence, then the wall, her arms joined over her abdomen and her miserable cries echoing in the night.

Roger called her name again, more clearly this time, gaining on her in spite of the flames of pain licking his back and legs.

The sound of a scuffle broke out behind him.

"Go then!" Bill shouted. "Don't take part in the Lord's work! *Let* evil spread like a—"

"This is not what we came to do!"

"No," a third voice insisted, "Bill's right, he *is* evil, he's—"

"It's what *I* came to do," Bill growled. "It's what I'm *supposed* to do. It's part of His plan for me…"

Roger glanced over his shoulder but could not see them; they hadn't reached the alley yet. He wondered where the other two were.

Sondra collided with a corner of one of the bins, spun like a top, and sprawled onto the ground face down.

Kneeling beside her, Roger rolled her over.

Bits of gravel clung to her forehead and her left eyebrow was bleeding from a deep gash and she was shaking like a junkie in need of a fix.

Her skin was moving over her face, shifting into a leathery distortion, then smoothing again; her chin jutted as her mouth snapped open and shut, open and shut, like a deadly trap, spitting and snarling.

Roger put the gun back in his pocket and helped her up; she couldn't stand but was able to sit up, leaning against him. Her eyes seemed to notice him for the first time and she clasped his wrists in her hands.

"Roger, Roger!" she gasped, speaking as if through a mouthful of barbed wire. "Make it stop, please, make it go away!"

Her fingers tightened painfully on his wrists and her knuckles became knobby and purple before his eyes; at the same time, Roger realized that his hands were *his* own again—the claws were gone.

"Please make it stop, Roger, kill me, kuh-kill me now before I—" Her head fell back and she gurgled in her throat; her teeth ground together loudly as they lengthened, sharpened, splitting her gums—then they returned to their normal shape and size. She began to thrash and pummel Roger's chest with her fists—which were once again dainty and pale and smooth-skinned—hissing, "I hate them, I *hate* them, oh God, *howIhatethem*!"

"Stop it, Sondra!" He tried to hold her but she was too strong and broke away—

—as voices neared them from ahead.

"The shot came from over there," a man said.

"Yeah," another replied, "maybe through that alley. Bill? That you?"

"Jesus, stand *up*, Sondra!" Roger had her by one arm and jerked her to her feet. "Be quiet," he hissed, looking around. He could see no one at either end of the alley but the voices were near and he knew they would be trapped in seconds. Holding tightly to Sondra, he searched frantically for an exit, a refuge.

He might be able to get over the fence, but he knew it would be impossible for Sondra.

"Over here," he whispered into her ear, dragging her to one of the gates that opened onto a backyard. He pushed and pulled on it, groping for a latch—

—and a flash of yellowed fangs and pink-black gums burst from the darkness, barking viciously, and Roger dove away from the gate as a Doberman slammed itself against the mesh.

A porch light came on, illuminating the yard, and a woman shouted from inside the house: "Hush, Julius, shut *up* right *now!*"

From one end of the alley, Bill shouted, "Damn, now I've lost them! Where'd they go?"

From the other end: "Bill? Where are you?"

"John? That you?"

Sondra's knees buckled and she whimpered, "Kill me, please, before he finds me…"

Roger jerked her over to the nearest garbage bin, lifted the lid and leaned it silently against the wall. With a gush of breath, he lifted Sondra in his arms and dropped her into the bin, climbed in after her, and pulled down the lid.

The stench of rotten vegetables and cat shit and leftover food and old cigarette butts and a dozen other odors stung Roger's eyes and nostrils and made him gag.

Sondra immediately tried to climb back out, hacking dryly, and Roger pulled her back down, slapping a palm over her mouth.

"Don't move, Sondra! Be very quiet!"

She mumbled into his hand and he pressed her head to his chest.

Footsteps clopped on the wet pavement outside.

"You get him?" John asked.

"He was hit," Bill replied, "but not bad. Not bad enough."

Roger closed his eyes and tried to calm his raspy breaths. Surely someone in the neighborhood had called the police about the gunshot; Roger didn't care to see them arrive either, but they were preferable to *this*.

"I thought they came down here," one of the voices said.

More footsteps, then Bill said, "Maybe they did."

There was a thunderous *gong* that bounced the length of the alley, lingering for several seconds.

Bill shouted, "You in there?" After several of Bill's limping steps, the gong sounded again. "Where *are* you, Roger? You can't hide from God, you know. He'll find you."

Gaaawwwnngg...

"And so will I."

Roger realized what Bill was doing: walking down the alley hitting each of the bins with his cane.

"Come on, Roger." *Gaaawwwnngg...* "Your probation is over. Judgement Day is here."

He's gonna find us before the cops get here, Roger thought with sickening dread.

Sondra's hands groped over his jacket and he grabbed her wrists, trying to make her stop. Her fingers were black with blood; he wondered if it was hers or his.

"Please," she said, her voice less than a whisper. "Please kill me." She pulled her hands loose and reached for his pockets. "Kill me, Roger. Please..."

She opened her mouth and vomited loudly, slapping her hands over her face, clawing at her eyes—

—which were filling with an evil, golden glow beneath eyebrows that were becoming sharp ridges.

"No-no, Sondra, don't let it—"

She joined her hands together in a doubled fist and swung upward, catching Roger under the chin and knocking his head against the wall of the garbage bin—

—and firecrackers went off in his skull and voices whispered in his ears.

The next echoing gong was not the sound of Bill's cane whacking one of the garbage bins but a footstep, a huge monolithic footstep followed by another, and another, accompanied by the roaring voice of an angry messiah that only Roger could hear:

Where's Carlton? Where is *that little shit? Where—*

"—*are* you, Roger?" Bill shouted.

"Look, Bill," one of the men said quietly. They were very close now, just a few feet from the bin. "Maybe you should give this up, you know? I mean, there's—"

—one over there! a loud male voice echoed off the inner walls of Roger's skull.

The pop of a gunshot was followed by laughter.

Got him!

Running feet and panting lungs sounded all around Roger's hiding place.

There's another one! someone shouted enthusiastically. *It's a woman! Quick, get—*

"—off my back, Matt," Bill ordered. "I *have* to do this. It's my purpose. It's His will."

Roger squeezed his head between his hands as if trying to put it back together. He opened his throbbing eyes and, dark as it was, could see Sondra's claws tearing at her clothes as she gagged and tried to gulp air, growling, "Raaaaw-juuhhh! Kuuhhh maaaayy! Peeeeeze! Kuuhhh maaaayy!"

She slammed her bulging knuckles into the wall of the bin and the metal made a thick wrinkling sound beneath the force of the blow.

"There!" Bill cried. "Hear that?"

Roger's hands began to fumble over his coat pocket, one holding the pocket open while the other clutched at the gun, getting a grip on the butt and pulling it out—

—but not before Sondra's arms flailed spastically in the dark, hitting Roger in the face, clawing his cheek, and knocking his head against the metal wall again—

—and he was on his back on the bloody carpet, naked, with Sondra sliding slowly up and down his cock.

Josh stood over them; he was healthy again, smiling, arm-in-arm with Mickey and Minnie. Mickey giggled as he scratched his back with one of Marjie's arms.

"What...what is it a-again?" Roger stuttered.

Josh said, "Five to seven years. Maybe sooner. Who knows? But think about it. Even if you've got seven years of health left, what kind of years will they be? I mean, *listen* to them!" From somewhere in the distance, Roger could hear Bill shouting his name in a voice filled with hatred.

Slivers of Bone

"And if it's not *them*," Josh said as he and the two big grinning mice slowly began to dissolve, "it'll be the cops, right? And they won't believe the truth. Nobody ever believes the truth."

Yeah, Roger thought, hearing the far-off wail of a siren steadily drawing nearer, *the cops...*

"And what kind of life will *she* have?" Josh muttered sadly, nodding toward Sondra, who bucked and writhed on top of him, her skin shriveling, breasts collapsing like large draining boils, fangs shredding her own lips. "Providing she lives at all, that is." Josh was a faint glow now, fading to a mist. "Remember, Roger...in the end, they always win..."

...they always win...

...always win...

The echo of his words dwindled as he became little more than a shadow...

Mickey waved goodbye with Marjie's arm as the three of them disappeared...

The gun.

It was in his hand.

Heavy.

Almost too heavy for his weakened fingers to grasp.

He lifted it—

I'm so sorry...

—and fired.

The sound was deafening in the small space and in the white flash of gunshot, Roger saw the small hole bloom like a flower in Sondra's left cheek and felt lumpy warmth splatter his face.

Sondra's body convulsed a few times, then grew still.

Through the ringing in his ears, Roger heard Bill cry, "Over here! In this one over here!"

The lid of the bin flew up and hit the wall with a loud *clang*.

A beam of light shined in Roger's eyes.

Bill screamed.

The siren grew louder.

In the light, Roger saw his hands: the claws sticking from his fingers, the patchy hair and mottled, crusty skin.

Has it happened again? he wondered. He hadn't noticed the pain or the sickness...

"Oh dear *Lord!*" Bill shrieked. "Oh, Father in Heaven!"

The flashlight slipped from his hand and fell in Sondra's lap.

Beneath the blood that ran down her cheek like tears, her face was smooth and unblemished once again.

Lifeless...but beautiful.

The monster was gone.

Roger's eyes filled with tears, his heart with loss, and his gut with hatred, and he shot to his feet in spite of the dizziness brought on by loss of blood. He slapped a hand aside Bill's head and closed his fist on a clump of hair, pulling Bill close to his face, pressing the barrel of his gun to Bill's throat.

Forming his words with effort, Roger screamed, "Look... what...you've...done!"

The other men stood around the bin like statues of ice.

Bill's pale face quivered like Jell-O, his eyes impossibly wide.

A deadly silence fell over the alley, broken only by the siren, which was just blocks away, and by the soft hissing trickle of Bill's urine spilling down his leg as he pissed his pants.

"Look...what...you've done...to uuuussss!"

Roger wasn't even sure if they could understand what he was saying; his words were garbled by the mouthful of needle-like shards that his teeth had become...

But it didn't matter.

In the end, nothing mattered because—

—they always win.

Roger stuffed the gun into his own mouth, bit down on the barrel, and leaned into Bill's face.

In the half-heartbeat before Roger squeezed the trigger, his mind screamed, *I only wish I could live long enough to see my blood splash all over your fucking head you Goddamned worthless hypocritical son of—*

«« — »»

43

AUTHOR'S PAST REVEALS
SATANIC CULT CONNECTIONS

Napa Police have been busy sorting through the past of best-selling author Roger Carlton, who killed himself, seventeen-year-old Sondra Nivens, and at least four other people over the last eighteen months, including Nivens' parents, Paul Nivens, forty-nine and Georgia Nivens, forty, Sidney Nelson, a forty-four year old bakery delivery man from Rutherford, and Napa resident Marjie Shore, twenty-eight.

According to police reports and people close to the author, Carlton, who twice hit the best-seller lists with his novels of murder and sexual obsession, was an active member of a Satanic cult, although the specific cult still remains a mystery. Books on Satanism and the occult were found in his St. Helena home, along with keys belonging to one of Carlton's victims.

The FBI took up the case in a surprise turn two weeks ago when it was learned that Carlton "just dropped completely out of sight for about eleven months last year, during which time Paul and Georgia Nivens were murdered in Berrien Springs, Michigan," according to FBI agent Garson Petrie.

Although some questions still remain unanswered, investigators believe Carlton met Sondra during those eleven months, while she was living with her parents, and involved her in his Satanic practices. After the death of her parents, Sondra moved in with her cousin Annie Dunning and her husband Bill in Manning, California. Investigators believe she participated in the murders that took place shortly after Carlton returned to St. Helena, a neighboring town, where he had lived six years earlier.

Bill Dunning, who attended college with Carlton, was the last to see the writer alive and witnessed his suicide. Minutes later, he was found by police, running down an alley in St. Helena. According to attending officer Brian Spottaford, Dunning was screaming, "Jesus help me! Jesus help me! I've seen the face of Satan!" That night, he was admitted to the psychiatric ward of St. Helena Medical Center.

When asked what he meant by "the face of Satan," Dunning said, "Naturally, I was upset. I'd just seen a man die. But he *was* evil. Roger was always evil. I've been saying that for years, but nobody's believed me. I guess they believe me now."

In the end, they always win...

Hair of the Dog

He opens his mouth before opening his eyes, and it makes a sound like sweaty flesh peeling off Naugahyde. The sound is only slightly louder than the one he expects his eyes to make when he opens them, so he does not. Instead, he becomes preoccupied with the thick, rusty ax someone drove into the top of his skull while he was sleeping. Pain radiates from it, pressing his eardrums and the backs of his eyes, threatening damage. In fact, that pain spreads through his entire body, gnawing at his muscles as if he'd spent the night engaged in exhausting physical labor. Even patches of his skin hurt, stinging as if rubbed raw.

Jeremy Culp opens his eyes slowly. Although the motel room is a dim gray, he flinches and groans with pain at the light, squinting as he lifts his head from the pillow. He sits up and clumsily slides his legs out from under the tangled sheet and over the side of the bed. He isn't sure what annoys him most, the hangover itself or the fact that he let himself get so drunk the night before. As he massages the back of his stiff neck with one hand, he winces when his hand rubs over one of the sore spots. There are others here and there, as if he was attacked by fire ants in the night.

He can't remember getting drunk. He can't remember *anything*, not at first. It takes a moment.

The digital clock on the nightstand reads 3:14 p.m., its big red numbers glowing accusingly. He croaks the time aloud, rubs his eyes, and mutters, "Middle of the afternoon, for crying out loud."

The air in the motel room is slightly cloying and redolent of perfume, liquor, dead cigarettes, and sex. It is that smell combined with the sight of two mostly empty liquor bottles on the dresser that make Culp remember the two women.

He eases himself to his feet, dipping a bit when the room seems to lurch to one side, and turns around to look at the bed. It's empty, and when he looks around the room, turning his head with stiff-necked caution, he sees no clothes, no purses, nothing. They are gone, though he does not remember them leaving.

They probably had the good sense not to get themselves hammered, he thinks as his stomach cramps and roils. But then, as he thinks about it, he doesn't remember drinking much himself, certainly not enough to justify a hangover of such proportion. Culp isn't much of a drinker, never has been, and he can't remember having a hangover since college, and never one quite like this.

Three despondent balloons hover halfway between floor and ceiling over by the dresser, and confetti and noisemakers litter the ugly copper-colored carpet.

"Happy New Year," Culp mutters as he lifts his robe from the floor and slips it on. His feet barely clear the carpet as he makes his unsteady way to the bathroom. The flesh between his legs is sore and burns as he walks.

The face in the mirror is an unfamiliar one: pale and long, with shady crescents beneath the puffy eyes; his brown hair, thinning on top, splayed around his head; lips cracked and pallid.

After splashing some cold water on his face, he leans both hands flat on the sink and lets his head hang low as the tap runs. He thinks about the two women. The events of the night before come to him in jittery, disjointed images, just vivid enough to make him smirk and shake his head in disbelief. He cannot believe what he did. Where did a doughy, married, forty-nine-year-old high school English teacher find the energy to do such a thing, not to mention the nerve?

Culp thinks that perhaps he is not suffering from a hangover alone; perhaps he is feeling the aches and pains that come from indulging oneself in something as silly and ultimately embarrassing as a midlife crisis.

Culp walked out on his wife on the first day of his Christmas vacation, and ever since then, every time he thought of himself as a married man, he amended that, considering himself instead to be a soon-to-be-divorced man. He knew that after twenty-two years, it was going to take a while to make the mental adjustment, but he intended to make it as soon as possible.

Culp had spent the first afternoon of his Christmas vacation preparing an elaborate dinner while Norma was at a UFO seminar. The meal was to be an effort to breathe some life back into their marriage before the death rattle sounded, to create a little romance… to remind her that he was there.

In their second year together, Norma had taken up the harmless hobby of macramé, which led to crocheting, which led to knitting. She went from one hobby to the next, like a hummingbird in a flower garden. Culp did not object, although he found hobbies to be impractical and had none himself. But over the years, Norma became more and more consumed by her hobbies; by the time their kids were in school, she was juggling three at once. She went from rock collecting to Middle Eastern cooking, from learning Esperanto to growing roses, from collecting Tarot cards to birdwatching, and more, so many more. After the kids left for college, conversation no longer seemed necessary at the dinner table. He stopped trying to keep up with Norma's hobbies, and she stopped trying to include him in them. Over the intervening time, a chasm opened up slowly between them.

Nearly a year ago, Culp had realized that he was lonely in spite of the fact that the kids visited frequently and he was happily married. That was when he realized that he was no longer happily married. Not exactly unhappy, and certainly not miserable…just married. The revelation panicked him, and he began to make an effort to scale the wall that had been constructed, one slow brick at a time, between himself and Norma.

He tried talking to her more, asking about her hobbies and

fellow hobbyists, none of whom he knew. Norma talked, but with an air of distraction about her, as if there were someplace else she'd rather be. Sometimes when he spoke to her, she'd look at him with surprise, as if startled to find a total stranger in her house. Culp tried to take her to dinner, to movies. She usually didn't have the time, but the couple of times they did go out were very awkward; she was always running into people she knew from her UFO watching club or from the Crystal Society, and Culp would stand around while she talked with them about sightings or about the metaphysical properties of crystals. It was awkward because Norma never introduced him, and it made him realize he had no friends of his own.

The candlelight dinner he'd prepared for her on the first day of his Christmas vacation was to be his final effort, although he didn't know it at the time. Norma arrived home just as Culp was lighting the candles and turning down the lights. But she arrived with eleven other members of the Crystal Society. She sniffed the air and said pleasantly, "Oh, you cooked dinner. Is there enough to go around?" Culp said, "Sure," then went into his bedroom, packed a couple of suitcases, and left the house while Norma and the girls chatted in the kitchen. After a dinner at Lulu's Café, he went next door and checked into the Thunderbird Motor Lodge, then started thinking about what to do with the next thirty years or so. Just like that, as casually as if he were rearranging the furniture in his office rather than his entire life. His only regret was that he'd let the relationship with Norma, which once had been so intimate and joyous, just slip through his fingers.

He'd gone home early Christmas morning, because he knew the kids would be showing up and he didn't want to ruin their holiday. Peter came with his wife and baby, and Beth brought her boyfriend. It was a noisy, festive gathering, and none of them seemed to notice anything unusual. Seconds after the kids left, Culp was on his way out when Norma stopped him at the door. With genuine curiosity but no emotion whatsoever, she asked, "So, have you found a place?"

«« — »»

After splashing more water on his face, Culp turns away from the mirror, sick of the sight of himself. The thought of a shower is just too much. He prefers to come slowly back to life; coffee first, then a shower. Culp decides to go over to Lulu's.

As he goes to the closet, he notices his clothes from the night before scattered all over the room. He remembers tossing them. They took turns removing articles of clothing, Culp and the two women, almost as if they did not want to separate even long enough to undress, touching and kissing and licking. The memory amazes him, but he is shamed by the fact that he must think a moment to remember their names: Pam and Valerie. They were so oral, both of them, their mouths all over him. And they were less than half his age, probably younger than his kids. But they were so beautiful, so carnal, as if they'd been fantasized rather than born. They looked like they could make him forget he was ever married, happily or otherwise. They almost did, too. Almost, but not quite.

He puts pants and a shirt on the bed, takes a clean pair of socks from the dresser, then mounts a search for his shoes. On hands and knees, he finds one beneath the chair beside the dresser, then gropes beneath the bed for the other.

His hand slaps onto smooth, cold flesh, and a gasp catches in his throat as he jerks his hand back, crawling backward quickly. He doesn't move, doesn't even breathe as he stares slack-jawed at the dark space beneath the bed. For a moment, his confused mind ceases to function properly as it claws for some shred of logic to hold on to. But it finds none. That was flesh he touched under there, and it does not, it simply *does not,* belong under the bed, not cold naked flesh, no way.

His breath comes in tremulous bursts as he lowers himself very slowly until he is lying flat on the floor, head turned to look into the darkness beneath the bed. There is a shape of some kind in the murky space, but it takes a moment for his eyes to adjust themselves, to bring the thing into focus…to see the hair. Valerie's lovely red hair.

«« — »»

Culp and Norma had never paid much attention to New Year's Eve. Another holiday a week after Christmas seemed like overkill. But a celebration of some sort was in order. After all, it wasn't just another year that was beginning; his whole life was starting over. Besides, he'd spent the last week looking diligently and unsuccessfully for an apartment. He deserved a few drinks, maybe a few games of darts if there was a board. Whatever he did, he decided he wasn't going to sit in that motel room and watch Dick Clark rock in the new year; he'd done that with Norma too many times.

Outside, the Shack was just a flat, nondescript building attached to the side of a coffee shop; inside, it was mostly the same, only darker and smokier. Country music was playing on the jukebox. Normally, Culp hated country, offended by its feigned, self-righteous wholesomeness, but he figured if he was going to start a new life, he might as well try new things, and he gave the song a chance. By the time he reached a barstool, he decided his new life wasn't *that* new and simply ignored the twangy music.

A small, exhausted Christmas tree twinkled halfheartedly, and balloons floated among festive streamers, all of it draped in a veil of cigarette smoke.

Culp perched at the bar, ordered a vodka gimlet, and looked around. It was busy, as Culp had expected it to be on New Year's Eve. There were only two empty stools, all the booths were full, and just one of the cocktail tables stood unoccupied. There was no dartboard, but two video games and a pinball machine stood against the back wall. Beneath the country music, there were voices, laughter, the vague sound of ice clinking against glass.

As the bartender put the gimlet on the bar, the song ended and the voices became louder. Culp took his drink and walked to the jukebox over near the games. Taking a sip, he read over the patchwork of country, blues, and pop as he jingled change in his pocket. Another country song started as Culp put in a couple of quarters and punched up some blues, preferring B. B. King's guitar to Merle Haggard's. He took another swallow of his drink as he headed back to the bar, and that was the first time he noticed them.

They were sitting in a booth leaning over their drinks and

smoking. And they were watching him. He nearly tripped over their gaze, immediately wondering what was wrong. Was his fly open? Had he put on a stained shirt? Suddenly nervous, he returned to the security of his stool and took another swallow.

The bartender set a bowl of peanuts on the bar, and Culp popped a couple into his mouth. Slowly, he sneaked a look over his shoulder to the booth where the two women were sitting. They were still watching him but looked away the moment he caught them.

One was facing away from him. She had hair the color of raw honey that fell in luxurious waves to her pale bare shoulders; he followed the line of her arm down to her hand, where the tips of her unpainted nails rested on the scarred tabletop. The other woman was facing toward him and had long, thick, straight red hair. They wore tight clothes, party clothes, the kind of clothes you'd wear to a nightclub, not to the Shack. The redhead wore a simple, short black dress, and Culp looked at her bare legs beneath the table, shapely ankles crossed. But he did not stare. He was already embarrassed enough by their stares; he didn't want to get caught gawking at them.

The long-faced bald man on the next stool watched Culp watching the women and finally chuckled. "You oughtta buy one a them a drink," he said. "I saw 'em checkin' you out over at the juke. Shit, buy 'em *both* a drink, maybe you'll get lucky. Write a letter to *Penthouse* about it."

Culp had been caught. He was reaching his embarrassment threshold. He laughed it off and ate some more peanuts. A minute or so later, the man sitting next to him was chatting with the bartender. Culp snatched another cautious look.

The redhead was leaning forward, smirking as she said something to the blond. She was staring directly at Culp, but she didn't look away this time. Instead, she leaned back, tilted her head to one side, and stretched a leg beneath the table as she shifted position, giving him a good look. Then she returned her attention to her companion.

Culp's face became very warm, and he almost laughed out loud at himself, sitting at a bar on New Year's Eve staring at a couple of beautiful young women and blushing like a shy teenager. It was laughable, no doubt about that.

A noisemaker squealed somewhere in the bar, and another quacked in response. The man beside Culp pulled a disgusted face and shook his head as he slowly got off the stool, leaving Culp between two empties.

"That's my cue to go home," he said. "The later it gets, the louder it gets, and I'm all holidayed out." He put some money on the bar, nodded at Culp, and walked away.

Culp turned on the stool and watched as the man went to a coat tree by the door and slipped on a rumpled overcoat. He let his eyes wander from the man to the women in the booth, but he felt an immediate shock of embarrassment and turned back to the bar quickly.

They were *both* looking at him, hunched forward and chattering intently over the small round candleholder in the center of their table.

Culp frowned at his drink for a moment, then took a sip, wondering why they kept looking at him like that. Did they know him? Maybe they were former students. The possibility made him consider going back to the motel to watch Dick Clark after all.

The country song ended, and a moment later, Culp's first song began to play. He tapped the bar to the beat and scooped up some more peanuts, leaning his head back and dropping them all into his mouth. He nearly choked on them when he looked over his shoulder to see the women coming toward him with their drinks and purses, smiling and walking like they were in a music video or something. He gulped the peanuts down and wet his mouth with a sip of the gimlet.

"You look awful sad for New Year's Eve," the blond said. She didn't speak very loudly, but he could hear her plainly above the music and voices, and he watched her lips form the words, moist and smooth as rose petals.

"Yeah," the redhead added. "You look like you need a little help."

Culp felt his mouth working independently and fought to control it. "Uh, help? Doing what?"

"Having fun," she said, and they both eased onto the stools flanking him.

Hookers, Culp thought, feeling a little better. That explained a lot. But why were they targeting him? He certainly wasn't the only man in the crowded bar. Did he look *that* needy?

The bartender stood before them, smiling. "Pam? Valerie? Anything for you?"

"No thanks, Phil," the redhead said. "But another for our friend here." She put her hand on Culp's shoulder and squeezed ever so gently.

The bartender grinned at Culp, winked, then went to make the drink.

"That's very nice, thank you," Culp said, nodding, "but you didn't have to do that. I haven't even finished this—"

"People who only do things they *have* to do are not happy people," the blond said.

With her hand still on his shoulder, the redhead added, "In fact, they're usually pretty miserable." She touched his earlobe with a fingertip. "You're not from around here, are you?"

Culp almost said he was, that he'd lived there for nearly twenty years, but thought better of it. Instead, he just said, "No, not…really."

The bartender brought his drink and winked again.

"And you're all alone on New Year's Eve," the blond said.

"That's how it's turned out," Culp replied, finishing his first drink.

"Well, you aren't alone anymore," the redhead said, touching the fingertip to his hair. "I'm Valerie."

"And I'm Pam. Who are you?"

"Steve." He spoke the name without a second's hesitation, surprising himself.

"Well, Steve, you've certainly got better taste in music than most around here."

"Thank you."

Pam put her hand on his knee. It was cool through the material of his pants as it inched upward along his thigh.

"What's a tasteful man like you doing alone on New Year's Eve?" Valerie asked.

Culp started to give some inane response but stopped, thinking that it was a very good question. Why *was* he alone on New Year's Eve? He wasn't married, not *really*. He had no intention of purchasing the services of the two lovely women, but he might as well enjoy their company until they realized he wasn't interested and moved on to better prospects.

"I was just wondering that myself," he said, sipping his second drink.

"Well, you don't have to wonder anymore," Pam said, running her nails over his crotch.

The touch sent shockwaves through Culp's body, and his back stiffened. So did his penis.

Valerie leaned over and pressed her breasts to his arm, lightly touching his ear with her lips. "Now you've got us, Steve. Wanna dance?"

"Uh, ho, no, I'm afraid I don't dance. I've never had any rhythm. My wuh—" He almost said "wife." He almost told them how his wife had laughed at his dancing when they'd first met. He corrected himself quickly. "My wuh-worst, um, memories are of, um, high school dances."

"You don't have to be embarrassed," Pam said, cupping him in her hand and massaging his erection through his pants. "We can go someplace else. Someplace where it's just the three of us. We won't laugh at you. Promise."

"Yeah, we'll find your rhythm," Valerie said. "It's in there somewhere, you just gotta—" She flicked her tongue over his ear. "Pull it out."

His face hot, Culp knew he had to bring an end to this or he was going to break out in a sweat and stain his shirt. "Look, uh, ladies, I'm…flattered. Really. But I'm afraid you're not, uh…within my budget."

The women laughed. It was a beautiful sound, their laughter, and it held no cruelty or condescension.

"You're too hard on yourself, Steve," Pam said.

"Yeah, we aren't ladies of the evening." Smiling, Valerie bit his ear and hissed, "We're ladies of the *moment*!"

"And at the moment, we wanna teach you to dance," Pam said, stroking and squeezing his erection. "So why don't we go someplace where nobody's watching us?"

"Uh, like I said, I'm not—"

"We don't charge, honey," Pam said, leaning close as she scraped her fingernails over his balls. "We *want* to teach you how to dance. Just dance your little heart out."

"Don't worry," Valerie said. "Your wife will never know."

He looked at her, startled, about to ask how she knew.

"Unless she's got your ring bugged," she added with a throaty laugh. Her fingers teased the back of his neck and she nuzzled his hair with her nose.

Culp looked down at the wedding band still on his finger. He hadn't thought to take it off; he'd forgotten it was there. He'd gained some weight, and it was squeezed into the flesh. He figured he'd probably have to have it cut off and thought he wouldn't be surprised to find the skin beneath it black with moist rot.

The women smelled of alcohol, of course; who in a bar on New Year's Eve did not? But they'd probably had too much to drink. If they weren't prostitutes, that was the only explanation Culp could think of. Pam's restless hand between his legs and Valerie's lips against his ear were going a long way to convince him he should take advantage of their drunkenness.

"You staying near here?" Pam asked, brushing her smiling lips to his cheek.

"Next door," Culp replied. He regretted it immediately and squirmed away from them. "Thank you for the drink, but I think—"

"*I* think you're a sad case," Valerie said, smirking as she pushed herself against him again, ignoring his squirms. "You've got two women coming on to you, and you're wiggling like a boy in church. I thought that was every man's fantasy."

Pam went back to what she was doing as well. "Most men can't handle having their fantasies come true. Did you know that, Steve? They can't. Too much for them. They talk a good game, but when the cards are on the table, all bets're off. You're not gonna be like most men, are you, Steve?"

Slivers of Bone

He looked first at Pam, then at Valerie, back and forth. They were beautiful...and they were driving him out of his mind. His hands trembled as he took a few healthy swallows of his gimlet, then asked, "You're not prostitutes?"

"We're missionaries, Steve," Valerie said, and her words were slightly garbled because she was sucking on his earlobe and sending an electrical current straight to his groin. "We spread the word. And tonight, the word is *legs*...or maybe *lips*."

"We wanna do this because we *want* to," Pam assured him. "For free. No strings attached. In fact, we'll even buy you another drink." She turned away from him. "Hey, Phil. Another one for Steve, here." Then, to Culp, she said, "We're gonna hit the ladies' room, Steve. You enjoy your drink. When we come back, we can go to your place, and I can make you dance. With my tongue. My tongue'll make you dance, Steve, I promise."

Suddenly, they were gone, and once again, Culp was sitting there alone with his drink. The music and voices had faded out before, but they came rushing back from all around him.

He could still feel them on him—Pam's hand, Valerie's lips, and he could still smell their perfume. But they were gone. He shifted position on the barstool, reaching down to surreptitiously adjust his erection in his pants. It was a powerful erection, hard as brick and almost painful, and he was struck with the certainty that it would never go away. Not unless Pam and Valerie came back. Not unless he left the bar with them that night. His erection would not go away unless they made it go away, he felt sure.

It was absurd, of course, but he was feeling his vodka, and Pam and Valerie had been feeling *him,* so he was worked up; he allowed himself the silly thought, then dismissed it. But it would not go away. And neither would their ghostly touches, still on him, teasing him, making him feel things he hadn't felt in years. He tipped the drink back, finishing it off as Phil brought another.

"Looks like you've made a couple friends," Phil said with a harmless leer.

"Do you know them?"

"Not really. They come in here maybe three times a month."

"They're not prostitutes?"

"Wouldn't let 'em stick around if they were. They're just real friendly. You're new here. From outta town, are you?"

Culp nodded vaguely.

"Yeah, they seem to like outta-towners. But they're not hookers." He chuckled, shook his head, and started down the bar saying, "Just real friendly."

His hands were trembling so hard he used both of them to lift his drink. It was his third, and it didn't live as long as the first two. The alcohol warmed him, made him feel a bit giddy, but it could not numb the hunger he felt for the two women in the restroom.

They were on him again, their hands and lips, and Culp was elated that they had come back, that it hadn't been a nasty joke with blue balls as the punchline.

At that moment, Culp decided he couldn't think of a better way to start a new year and a new life than doing something about which he could write to *Penthouse*.

«« — »»

Culp does not know how much time has passed since he crawled crablike away from the bed, as far as he could get, until his back was against the wall. Maybe an hour, maybe thirty seconds, he doesn't know. His mind is too busy to keep up with time, too busy going over the night before, trying desperately to remember everything. Sometimes, as he stares at the space beneath the bed, his thoughts slip out of his mouth.

"A witness," he says, his voice high and soft and breathy. "They've got a witness. He'll identify me."

He is thinking of the bald man who sat beside him at the bar. And the bartender, of course. Who else? Who else in the bar will remember him, the last man to see those two beautiful young women alive?

"I didn't do it!" he gasps, pulling his knees up, hugging them. "I didn't, I couldn't, I—"

—can't remember, he thinks. *I can't remember, so I don't know what I did!*

He stands suddenly, winded, feeling panic in his throat. He can't see them while he's standing, but he knows they're there, flat on their backs, arms and legs straight, almost as if positioned that way.

It occurs to him that they might not be dead after all; maybe they were just still passed out. But he remembers that white skin, cold as marble.

"No," he says, moving decisively toward the bed, "they can't be dead. Can't be." Moving with erratic, jerky motions, he slides the bed to one side, until the two women are unhidden.

Their clothes are balled up between their feet with their purses on top. Their eyes are closed, and their hair is pooled about their heads. There is no blood, none that he can see. But they do not move as he watches them closely, not even to breathe.

With nerves humming just beneath his skin, Culp gets on hands and knees and crawls to Pam's side. He presses a hand over his mouth as he reaches down and touches two fingertips to her neck, feeling for a pulse. The roiling in his stomach worsens when he feels no sign of life. He touches her face reluctantly, rolls her head back and forth, holds his palm over her mouth and nose. No breath.

"Oh my God," he whimpers. "Oh my God, oh my God, oh my God." He says it over and over again, realizing after a moment that he is crawling on hands and knees in a small circle. There is movement inside him, and he scrambles to his feet as he heads for the bathroom. His insides explode just before he reaches the toilet, and some of it splashes onto the tile floor. He hunches over the toilet for a few minutes, groaning into the bowl. He wants to keep vomiting, to heave up the fear in his gut, the terror filling his chest and smothering his lungs.

Culp staggers out of the bathroom and goes to the dresser, grabs one of the bottles, and tips it back, taking a couple of gulps. It scalds his raw insides, but he takes a couple more. He is beginning to sweat as he turns and looks at them again.

The clock on the nightstand reads 4:03; more than forty-five minutes have passed, but it feels like seconds. Culp is shocked that so much time has gone by. If he could let nearly an hour pass without realizing it, what *else* might he do without realizing it?

"No," he says, shaking his head. "I didn't. I couldn't." His cheeks are moist, and he realizes he's been crying. "*I couldn't!*"

Then who did? he wonders. *Did somebody get into the room, kill Pam and Valerie without waking me, then hide them under the bed? How would*—why *would somebody do that?*

He looks at Valerie's purse, then Pam's, and kneels down at their feet. He opens Pam's first. It appears nearly empty at first, its black lining clean as if it were new. There is a billfold, a checkbook, some keys, and a black notebook. He opens the billfold and looks at her driver's license. Pamela L. Gleason. She is twenty-one years old.

Was twenty-one, Culp thinks.

There are foldout pockets with credit cards and photographs in them. There is a black-and-white snapshot of Pam with her hair in a beehive; it looks old, its white border yellowed with time. He finds sixty-eight dollars and change in the billfold. The black notebook contains phone numbers, addresses, shopping lists, meaningless reminders. She hasn't been robbed. That would make it too easy, a robbery-killing; he would call the police, and after the initial suspicion blew over, everything would be fine. Although he is certain she has not been robbed, either, he opens Valerie's purse anyway.

The inside of Valerie's purse is almost identical to Pam's: perfectly clean and mostly empty. Culp frowns. He has never seen a woman's purse so neat and tidy. Norma's purse is always a pocket of chaos, with chunks of lint and old breath mints and bits of tobacco from stray cigarettes clinging to the lining. His mother's purse was always a mess. His sister's, too. But these purses look freshly shoplifted.

There is a folded-up manila envelope in Valerie's purse, bulging with its contents. He pulls it out, unwinds the red string from the tab, and opens it. The envelope is filled with what look, at first, like business cards. But they are not. Some are driver's licenses, some are credit cards; there are a number of Social Security cards, and in the bottom he finds half a dozen passports.

Each driver's license has a picture of either Pam or Valerie on it, each under a different name and with a different address. So many identities...and just two people.

The envelope slips from Culp's hands, and the licenses and cards and passports spill onto the carpet. He is paralyzed by fear, unable to move, even to blink. Although he thought it impossible, the situation has just become worse somehow. Two women with an envelope full of identities? Good ones, too. Those driver's licenses must be fake, but they are *great* fakes, professional. So who are they *really*, these two gorgeous women who, one New Year's Eve, just suddenly get the urge to team up and seduce a middle-aged man with a puffy paunch and an occasional problem with gout? That sort of thing doesn't happen in real life, not even in the real lives of people who write letters to *Penthouse*. Culp begins to think there is something else going on here, something much stranger and more ominous lurking beneath the already horrible surface.

Culp feels sick again but does not vomit. The poison stays inside and tries to eat its way out. He stands and paces, his body prickly with sweat beneath the robe. The sweat is stinging him in places.

Stinging the wounds, he thinks, only vaguely wondering what wounds he might have. Were they *that* rough last night?

The light outside the drawn curtains is dimmer. The first day of a new year is winding down. Culp can hear traffic outside. And rain, it is raining.

I'm going to have to go out there, he thinks, staring at the door. *I'm going to have to call someone...the police, an ambulance, someone. And they're gonna come and take me out there in handcuffs.*

He hurries to the bathroom, wets a washcloth, and dabs his face and neck with it, then continues pacing, thinking now, trying to remember everything. There are blank spots...gaps in his memory...images that skip a beat, jump ahead in time, like those old damaged black-and-white movies on television in the middle of the night. Those skips get bigger, more jarring, until the memories stop. But he goes over them again, and again...and again.

Once inside the hotel room, Pam and Valerie were at him like two cats on a scrambling rodent. They'd bought two bottles of whiskey at a liquor store on the corner, and Culp dropped them in their brown bag onto a chair. He felt a panicky moment of claustrophobia as they closed in on him, kissing him, groping him, removing his clothes, their own, and each other's. He was still wearing his underwear, socks, and unbuttoned shirt when they pushed him onto the bed, faceup. Valerie pinned his arms to the mattress, and Pam straddled his legs.

Culp's shirt was the first sartorial casualty of the night. Valerie's fingernails ripped into it and began peeling it off him as she sucked hard on one nipple, then the other. When she kissed him, he feared she was going to suck his tongue out of his throat by its roots. She chewed on his lips, nipped his flabby chest, teasingly at first, then harder, almost too hard.

Pam pressed her mouth to his cotton briefs and wrapped it around his erection, which was straining the material. She gnawed on his cock, her tongue wet through the cotton, and pulled at the shorts as her fingernails clawed teasingly at his balls.

Culp's heart was hitting his ribs like a police battering ram, but very fast, and he suddenly regretted not sticking to that diet he'd started about five years ago, because he feared he might have a heart attack and die beneath these women. A blissful way to go, yes, but not so soon. His heart continued to hammer without consequence, and he soon became too lost in the things Pam and Valerie were doing to him to worry about dying.

He heard the sound of material ripping again, his underwear this time. He tried to lift his head, but Valerie wouldn't let him. Pam tore the briefs away from him and took him in her mouth.

Someone in the room made a sound like a deer in pain, and Culp was shocked to realize it was *his* voice, that *he* was making the sound, but he had no control over it, over anything. *They* controlled him, completely, as surely as if they possessed his soul like demons. And that sound coming from Culp's throat was one of delirious joy. He reached out his hands and felt delicious flesh, soft round breasts, and rigid nipples. Their skin was cool, and he found the sensation of it exciting.

Slivers of Bone

As Valerie kissed and licked and sucked her way around his neck and over his abdomen, Pam's tongue licked around the base of his cock, then down, over the wrinkled flesh of his scrotum, then down even further as Valerie reached over and stroked him while she kissed and chewed his belly.

There was another sound in the room: lusty, throaty laughter. Pam and Valerie were laughing as they devoured him, laughing in a buoyant way, with relish.

Culp felt heat rising inside him, between his legs, growing thick and unbearable, and he was going to come, he knew it. But he did not. Valerie stopped stroking him and squeezed his erection in a fist, then let go of him and—

—that is where the first skip occurs.

Culp folds his arms on top of the dresser, drops his head onto them, and groans as he goes over it again and again, that one moment that just seems to blink out in his memory, one second on his back and the next—

—he slid in and out of Pam, his movements slow, controlled by Valerie, who clutched his ass with both hands, guiding him as she pressed her face between his legs and licked and sucked his balls.

And they never stopped laughing. Sometimes they even talked to him, and each time they pressed him for a response.

"You enjoying this, Steve?" Valerie asked, and when he didn't respond, just kept grunting, she said, "C'mon, Steve, you enjoying this? We're not boring you, are we?"

"No, no, yuh-you're not," he gasped.

Pam smiled up at him and said, "You look so serious, Steve. How come you're not smiling? Fucking is *fun!*"

After a while, when he was beginning to feel the heat rising again, Valerie pulled him off Pam, her voice trembling slightly as she said, "My turn, Steve. On your back, baby, it's my turn."

Once he was flat, she mounted him, fell forward on him, engulfing his face in her long red hair as she kissed his face and throat, licked and sucked on his ears, and humped viciously. She sat up straight as her fingernails dug into his doughy flesh, and her bucking grew faster and faster. Culp turned his head to the right and saw Pam lying on her side, her grinning face inches from his. She ran her left hand through his hair as her right nested busily between her thighs.

Valerie became frantic and cried out as she came. She said something. It startled Culp because it was in a foreign language. French, or maybe German, he wasn't sure. He had other things on his mind. She kept moving on him, grinding, her head back, lips open on clenched teeth, and—

—he cries out in frustration, pounding a fist on the dresser. He empties the bottle and lets it thunk to the carpet as he begins pacing again.

His memory decays rapidly from that moment on, and there's no way he can fill in the blanks. The sex is just a series of disjointed images that simply end.

He remembers, at one point, being on the floor. He was on the bed, then—*skip!*—he was on the floor with them, rolling around, limbs entwined, rutting like animals, their cool, smooth skin rubbing frantically against his. One of the women—he couldn't remember if it was Pam or Valerie—opened one of the bottles and poured some whiskey over his head. Valerie drank some, then kissed Culp and spit it into his mouth. He drank some from the bottle, too, but he doesn't remember drinking much. Maybe two or three swallows. Not enough to have blackouts, not nearly. Unless he'd become very sensitive to alcohol without realizing it over the years; after all, he isn't as young as he used to be.

Just flesh, that is mostly what he remembers, tongues and breasts and moist lips hidden in thatches of kinky hair. And the laughter, of course. They never stopped laughing, and Culp joined in after a while, enjoying himself as if for the first time in his life.

He stops pacing to look down at Pam and Valerie, wondering how long before they will start to smell. He steps over to Pam's side and looks down at her throat.

Like Valerie's, it is unmarked. If he *did* kill them, how did he *do* it? Strangling would leave bruises, and there is no blood, so he didn't stab or bludgeon them to death.

Feeling sick again, he hurries to the bathroom, just in case, but nothing comes up. He stands over the toilet a moment, staring at the puddle of vomit on the floor. The sobs surprise him in their suddenness and intensity. He puts the lid down, sits, and cries until his lungs ache. With his tears comes resignation.

Culp stands, getting himself under control, wiping his eyes. He walks to the phone bolted to the nightstand, picks up the receiver, and punches 9-1-1.

On the second ring, a female voice says, "Nine-one-one operator, what is your emergency, please?"

His voice fails him at first, and he coughs a few times. "I've, uh, found…there are two, um…"

"What is the emergency, sir?"

"I'm at this motel, and…when I woke up…there were two dead bodies…under my bed."

"You found…excuse me, sir, did you say you *found* them under your bed? When you woke up?"

"That's right."

"Who are these two people?"

"Two women. Young women."

"Do you know them?"

"I did…sort of."

"How did these women die?"

"I don't know, I… didn't do it. Really. I don't re—" He coughed again. "I didn't do it. I don't know. They're just dead."

"What is your name, sir?"

"I'm at the Thunderbird Motor Lodge. Room Twelve. I'll wait here until they come." He hangs up the phone.

The room is very dark now, and Culp turns on a lamp. It lends a garishness to the two corpses.

Sweat clings to him like honey, burning in his wounds. He frowns as he wonders again how he got cut in so many places. He feels sweat dribble down the middle of his back and down his sides from his armpits, and he drops the robe and goes straight into the shower, swinging the bathroom door shut behind him out of habit, although the door only closes halfway. He turns on the cold water and begins to rub a bar of soap over his skin halfheartedly as he stands beneath the stream.

He winces as he passes the soap under his left armpit; something stings sharply. Reaching under his arm, Culp feels a few small puncture wounds. He inspects every spot on his body that stings as if raw: behind his neck, in back of his ear, between his legs just behind his scrotum, and between the folds of flesh where his legs join his groin.

Culp's insides turn cold. He feels a dread that he cannot quite identify.

Who were they, really? What had they done to him?

He turns off the shower and steps out, grabs a towel, and begins to dry himself, his mind numb, perhaps beyond repair. He is unable to concentrate enough to think of what he will tell the police. He freezes with the towel over his head.

There are voices in the room. Quiet, sneaky voices.

Culp jerks the towel from his head and looks at the half-open door, his eyes gaping as he wonders if the police have already arrived.

But they are female voices. Two female voices, chattering in hurried whispers, giggling mischievously. There is movement as well. Culp sees shadows flitting over the dresser and hears whispers of fabric. His throat begins to close, and, to prevent it, he makes a startled sound.

The movement stops, and the voices are silent. A hand pushes the bathroom door all the way open, and—Pam and Valerie stand in the doorway, smiling. They are all dressed and carry their purses. And they are still beautiful. But something is different. They look much paler than he remembers.

"Well," Valerie says hesitantly, "this is an awkward moment, isn't it?"

"Sorry, Steve," Pam says. "We don't usually do this sort of thing. Stay over, I mean. We just stayed too late and had to crash here till sunset."

Culp backs away from them, saying, "You...you're both...you were..."

Valerie steps forward and reaches out to touch his face, but Culp throws himself backward, slamming painfully into the aluminum towel rod on the wall. She places a hand to his cheek, and it is very cold. It's as cold as they were just moments ago while lying dead on the floor.

"You don't look so good, baby," she says. "You look like you could use a little hair of the dog that bit you."

"Unfortunately, we've gotta go," Pam says.

Culp tries to speak, but his mouth moves silently.

"Don't worry, Steve," Valerie purrs, leaning forward to kiss him. Her lips feel repulsive on his. "You'll only remember the good parts, I promise. And you *were* good." She turns and steps past Pam and out of the room.

Pam licks her lips and winks. "You were *real* good, Steve." Then she, too, leaves the bathroom.

Culp realizes he is shivering. The punctured flesh on his neck and behind his ear and under his armpit and between his legs stings cruelly as he hears the door of the room open, then close.

With his mouth hanging open, he staggers out of the bathroom to the window and pulls the curtain aside. Just cars in the parking lot and traffic in the street outside. Pam and Valerie are nowhere in sight.

Culp turns around and stares a few minutes at the empty space on the floor, the place where, just minutes ago, two corpses lay still and naked. The unidentified dread he felt earlier is replaced with a sickening fear as the dimly lit room becomes bathed in the pulsing red-and-blue glow of a police car. He turns to the window again and looks at the light bleeding through the frayed curtain as three hard knocks sound on the door.

Punishments

I arrived in Manning the day after I read of Jayne's death in the paper. It was front-page news across the country, the kind of story the press wrings dry.

**TEENAGER KILLS CHURCH ORGANIST
IN BIZARRE SEX SLAYING**

I wouldn't have read it if I hadn't seen Jayne's picture, her big tortoiseshell glasses perched on her small nose, dull brown hair gathered in the back, her usually timid, fleeting smile opening brightly for the camera. It was a recent picture and she'd changed little in the last ten years.

I immediately arranged to take a day off work, saw that my pet, Clarissa, had plenty of food and water, and left Los Angeles for Manning.

I was raised in Manning, a small Seventh-Day Adventist village in Napa Valley. My parents still lived there, but when I arrived, I went straight to the boy's house. It was easy enough to find; reporters were gathered on the sidewalk waiting for a glimpse of the killer. I parked my rented car across the street and stared at the house, wondering what the boy was like, how he'd met her. And if she'd done to him what she did to me…

When I was sixteen, I thought of Jayne Potter only as the woman who, each week, placed a square brown cushion on the church organ bench, sat down, and played for services. I didn't find her attractive; she had fair skin, dressed plainly, and always wore her hair in a bun or braided. She didn't wear makeup, but, because that was against Seventh-Day Adventist rules, neither did any of the girls at the Adventist prep school I attended. *They,* however, were the stars of my fantasies; although restricted by dress codes, they somehow managed to dress in ways that accentuated their curves and angles to the fullest. Repression is the mother of creativity, I always say.

Miss Potter attended every church function and gave more than her share of time to its causes. At a bake sale or potluck, she was impossible to distract, so great was her concentration on her duties; she seemed driven, as if she *had* to participate in church activities, as if she were repaying an important debt. But in spite of her sizeable contributions to the church, the congregation seemed to ignore her; sometimes I even thought they were *shunning* her. Most people that participated were quite popular socially. Not Miss Potter. She smiled and nodded a lot but spoke little and was seldom, if ever, spoken to.

It wasn't until she came down with a summer cold and my mother had me take her some homemade cream of vegetable soup that our relationship began. I drove to her place in my mom's car. Miss Potter lived on the north side of town in a mobile home nestled by itself at the foot of a shady hill.

It was a hot summer day, but she came to the door wearing a heavy white terrycloth robe. I didn't expect to be invited in, but she did so immediately. Once inside, with the glare of sunlight out of my eyes, I could see that she wasn't wearing her glasses and her hair was down, full and wavy on her shoulders and back, and I discovered something. It wasn't an instant discovery; it took a while to sink in and wasn't fully absorbed until after I'd left her. I discovered that Miss Potter was beautiful.

She didn't seem sick. Her eyes were puffy, but that might have been from crying. I would later realize that she had been. I lost count of the times I found her crying when I came over for my visits. In fact, I lost count of the visits.

Inside, her trailer was dimly lighted; only one small lamp was on on by the sofa, but its dark gray shade shed little light. It was sparsely furnished and the walls were bare except for the most hideous portrait of the crucifixion I've ever seen; blood, dark and viscous, poured from Christ's head, hands, and feet, and from the gaping hole in his side. His face was a long, cadaverous nightmare.

She thanked me for the soup, took it to the kitchen, then sat on the sofa with a smile, gracefully folding her legs beneath the robe. She patted the cushion beside her and I sat, but there was nothing graceful about *my* movements. I was a clumsy and shy teenager, particularly in the presence of females. Especially ones wearing robes. Miss Potter managed to put me at ease, though; we made small talk about school and the upcoming church picnic. As she spoke, she frequently patted my shoulder, hand, and knee—innocuous conversational gestures, but ones I'd never noticed in her before. She was somehow...different.

After insisting I call her Jayne, she discovered my interest in reptiles and softly said, "Ah, then, I have a book you'll enjoy." She scooted forward and leaned across my lap toward a small bookcase against the wall.

My heart quivered like Jell-O. A shadowed valley plunged between the lapels of her robe and flesh shifted slightly; her skin was white as summer clouds and a faint green-blue vein meandered over the curve of her left breast, disappearing in the shadows. I wanted so badly to follow that vein down her robe that my fingers actually twitched to reach out and pull the lapel aside. I blushed furiously and stood when she moved, preparing to leave.

At the door she gave me the book, gently touched a cool hand to the back of my neck, and said, "This will give you an excuse to come back and see me." As I stepped out, something brushed my behind; it could have been a shifting wrinkle in my jeans or the corner of the end table by the door...or her fingers.

Of course, it *was* her fingers, but I couldn't bring myself to believe it then. I did, however, masturbate my way through variations of that fantasy for the next few nights in the secrecy of my bedroom. Masturbation is, of course, another no-no among Adventists, but I've often attributed any stability I may now possess to my refusal to stop masturbating even after my biology teacher told the class it could cause a nervous breakdown.

Slivers of Bone

I wanted to talk about this fantasy, as boys do, with my best—and nearly *only*—friend, Gary Sigman, but Gary wasn't saying much to anyone that summer. The previous fall his parents had divorced; both were teachers at the Adventist grammar school in Manning, and lost their jobs because of it. (The church cannot prevent divorces, but it does punish those involved for allowing their marriages to fail.) Gary became pale and withdrawn. Everyone attributed his subsequent sullenness and weight loss to the upset of the divorce. Everyone but me. I knew something *else* had happened to Gary; he looked older and didn't laugh much anymore. But it was out of my reach, so I decided to let him make the first move to open up. If he had, we might have spent those summer evenings on my back porch whispering about Miss Potter. But he didn't.

When I returned the book three days later, Jayne met me at the door wearing that same robe. I thought that was odd; it was midafternoon and surely she was no longer ill. She greeted me pleasantly and led me to the sofa where she presented me with another book. It was huge and full of color photographs of rare and exotic reptiles.

"I don't want to loan it out," she said, sitting close to me and opening the book on our laps, "but you're welcome to look at it here if you want. Anytime."

As we paged through the book, her leg rubbed slightly against mine; beneath the book, my crotch began to bulge. I realized I had imagined nothing three days before but didn't know what to do; dry-mouthed and trembling, I stared blindly at the book, aware only of the burning friction between her leg and mine. When she unexpectedly pulled the book away, I found myself staring down at my erection. Jayne was staring at it, too. Smirking. She *slowly* reached over and touched it. Caressed it. Squeezed it slightly. My lungs convulsively sucked in a breath.

"Do you like hot fudge sundaes, Paul?" she whispered, leaving the room to clatter around in the kitchen a moment. "I do. Would you like one?"

I think I shook my head.

She returned with a bowl of ice cream, chocolate syrup, nuts, and a cherry, and said, "*I* would." Placing the bowl on the coffee table, she knelt before me and began to undo my belt.

I was paralyzed. I imagined my mother's horror should she walk in and find me. I remembered Pastor Helmond's recent sermon in which he declared, "Sex is a sweet-tasting poison which will surely *kill* your *soul!*" I remembered my Bible teacher at school telling the class, "Sex is such a dangerous, unhealthy diversion that, when faced with sexual desires, even married couples should take a cold shower or run around the block instead of having intercourse unless, of course, it's done only to reproduce." Long before I even knew what it was, I was told sex was a moral crime, the most treacherous curve on the road to heaven. But when Jayne took me in her hand, I lost all fear of the lake of fire that I had so long been warned about. Placing the bowl on the floor between my legs, she turned off the lamp, spooned ice cream and chocolate onto my cock, sprinkled nuts over it, placed the cherry on the head, and hungrily, lovingly, and oh-so-deliciously devoured her sundae.

Her sofa converted into a bed, which we put to great use that afternoon. I was clumsy at first, but soon lost my self-consciousness as she covered my body with nibbles and kisses. I wanted to see her, touch her, *taste* her, but when I tugged at her robe, she refused to remove it. I rolled on top of her, but she pushed me away and gasped, "No, no, like *this*," and rolled onto her knees and elbows. I knelt behind her, she guided me in, and immediately began to groan. It wasn't a sound of pleasure, it was a *groan*, and I feared I was hurting her somehow. When I started to pull out, she snapped, "No, do it! Hard!"

My thrusts were uncertain at first, but I soon lost myself in waves of new sensations. The robe's hem gathered between us, but when I tried to slide it up so I could stroke her back, she quickly pulled it back down again and began uttering garbled words between her gasps.

I leaned forward and whispered, "What? What'd you say?" but she spoke into her pillow after that. It would be weeks before those words became clear to me.

I went home on weak knees, saying little to my parents on the way to my room. I remained in a stunned silence until the following afternoon when, at her request, I returned to Jayne's trailer like a somnambulist returning to bed. Once again she was wearing that robe; once again she seated me on the sofa. There she stripped me and licked every inch of my body except my cock until I put her hand on it myself and breathed, "Please...please..." She opened the bed and, as before, left her robe on and cried out as we writhed together, her sobbed words buried in her pillow.

There was only silence afterward; although we exchanged small talk before, we never spoke after. We *never* spoke of what we did. As we lay side by side that second time, I tried to stroke her hair, her neck, but she pulled away and curled into a trembling ball. Finally she whispered hoarsely, "Come back at three tomorrow."

Her strange behavior was lost on me at first; I was too overwhelmed by the fact that I was HAVING SEX. On top of that, it was with an OLDER WOMAN. And I suppose I got a charge from the fact that my lover was timid Miss Potter.

Church became a new experience altogether; each time I saw Jayne mount the organ bench after carefully putting her cushion in place, I immediately grew hard—right there with Mom and Dad in our usual pew. I covered my erection with my leather-bound monogrammed Revised Standard Version Bible. I watched her throughout the sermon; sometimes her hips squirmed on that cushion, and I wondered if she was thinking of me.

She wasn't.

In the middle of our third week together, Jayne went into the kitchen to make lemonade when I arrived. I spotted her cushion on a chair against the wall and, knowing that her firm ass squirmed over that cushion during church services each week, I couldn't resist sitting on it myself. I gulped the cry of pain that came from what felt like hundreds of tiny needles puncturing my behind. I shot to my feet, grabbed my ass, then picked up the cushion. It was made of heavy brown corduroy and was flat and hard on the bottom. But it was not cushiony.

It was stuffed with tacks.

When I heard her coming, I dropped the cushion, spun around, and tried to return her smile. She leaned forward to put the tray of lemonade on the coffee table, and I stared at her ass, thinking of how she always kept it covered when we fucked, realizing that perhaps it wasn't as smooth and touchable as I'd thought...

For a while my thoughts were on that cushion and the questions it raised. But as we began to fuck—and that's what we did; I preferred to think at the time, in a naive sort of first-love way, that we were MAKING LOVE, but that simply wasn't the case—she started calling out again and I listened carefully to her words.

"I'm sorry...punish me...I'm so sorry I made you hard...p-punish me, Daddy, *punish* me!"

I stopped when the words registered, but she reached back and gripped my thigh, dug her nails in, and cried, "Don't...*stop*!"

I think she tried to hide her words after that, but I knew what she was saying. I know now—and probably knew then, to some extent—that I should have realized something was very wrong with quiet, timid Miss Potter and I should have stopped seeing her immediately. But she was my first lover and my first addiction. I never allowed myself to consider ending our relationship; I knew I couldn't. But her cries for punishment—from her *father!*—stayed with me and echoed in my dreams.

Jayne told me to return on Sunday, three days later. It was our longest separation yet and made me realize how attached I'd become to our visits.

I fidgeted a lot as I watched her in church that Saturday. After services there was a potluck lunch and I went to the car to help Mom carry in the food she'd brought. I asked her what she knew about Miss Potter, but she obviously didn't want to talk about her, so I dropped it. After lunch, as Dad and I were bringing the freshly washed dishes back to the car, he said, "Your mother said you asked about Miss Potter. How come? You hear something?"

I got a little nervous. "No. I just wondered...well, she's so involved in the church but has no friends, no family. Just wondered, that's all."

"Well, I'll tell you. Get in." We got in the front seat and he chewed on a toothpick as he spoke. "Miss Potter's a good woman.

She's devoted to the church but gets no thanks for it. Your mom doesn't like talking about her because...well, she just doesn't think it's right. There's a lot of people in this church could take a lesson from her. Anyway, when Miss Potter was a little girl, her father, Hudson Potter, was pastor of this church. One night when she was nine or ten, Jayne left her house, walked to the St. Helena police station, and said her daddy was...molesting her. Sexually." He cocked a brow. "Know what I mean?"

I nodded, feeling a chill coming on.

"There was a big scandal. Pastor Potter was suspended for nearly a year. Stopped coming to church and just stayed in their little house by the grammar school. Nothing was done, really. It was all hushed up. One Sabbath about eighteen months later, Jayne asked to speak before the congregation. Said she made it all up after having an argument with her daddy. The evil had taken hold of her, but now the Holy Spirit was moving her to make amends. Everyone nodded and clicked their tongues like they'd suspected as much and offered to return Potter to the pulpit. But by then he'd become a recluse. Most said his daughter had broken him. Ruined him with her cruel lies. He died at home about a year later. Jayne's never been forgiven even though most of the people here don't even know what happened."

"Do...do you think she was telling the truth?"

He chewed on his toothpick a moment. "That's between her and God, son."

It was another warning I should have heeded but didn't. Five deadly words occurred to me after Dad's story: *Maybe I can help her.*

After sex the next day, when Jayne once again refused to let me touch her, I said, "But I want to. You...you do things to me that feel so *good*, but...you won't let me touch you...make *you* feel good."

"Is that what you want?" she whispered, smiling.

"Yes."

"You'll do anything I want?"

I smiled. "Of *course*."

God, I was such a babe in the woods.

"Then come back on Tuesday at three and you can."

My next warning came Tuesday morning when I went grocery shopping for Mom. As I left the store hugging two brown bags, I saw Gary Sigman leaning against the car. He looked horribly pale and thin in the bright sunlight. Before I could greet him, Gary said, "I saw you leaving her place, Paul. Twice."

"What're you—"

"*You* know. Stay away from her. She's sick." He stared at me silently for a moment, whispered, "She'll make you do bad things," then hurried away, leaving me with my groceries.

It bothered me, yes. I gave it careful thought, yes. But did I do what he said?

No.

Jayne had the bed open when I arrived, and immediately began to undress me, whispering, "You promised...anything I ask...anything that will make me feel good..." She had me lie on my back, reached under the bed for something, then put it on the bed beside me. Hiking the robe up only slightly, she turned her back to me, straddled me, and sighed as I entered. She moved on me slowly for a moment, then pointed to the object on the bed, rasping, "Take that."

I did. It was a three-foot-long whip with three strips of braided leather sprouting from the handle, each knotted at the end.

"Now *whip* me!" she hissed.

When I stuttered for a moment, she repeated the order firmly. My first strike was weak and uncertain, and she cried, "Harder!" I brought the whip down again—"*Harder!*"—and again—"*Harderrr!*"—until it was smacking loudly against the taut terrycloth on her back. "Yes!" she cried, bucking furiously on me. "Punish me! I'm sorry I made you hard, Daddy, sorry I told, sorry, *sorry, sorrysorrysor*ry! *Punish* me!" Her laughter was breathy and high, void of humor but so full of *joy*. I think that's what did it to me, what shattered my initial fear of and disdain for the act: her joy. She loved it.

We were both out of breath afterward and neither of us spoke. As she lay panting on the bed, moaning with each exhalation, I slowly dressed, then left.

SLIVERS OF BONE

At home I went to my bed in a daze, thinking of everything—my household chores, a phone call I had to make, maybe driving down to Napa tomorrow—except what I'd just done...

My visits to Jayne's became a blur after that. The whip always awaited me on the bed. She never removed her robe. We fucked in various positions, and with each blow of the whip she cried out with delight. After a while so did I. Although I never admitted it to myself then, I came to enjoy those whippings. Part of it was the pleasure she derived from her pain. But there was something else, something I couldn't have identified back then if I'd tried or wanted to, something within me that remained hidden and dormant until I took the whip in my hand; then it crawled from its lair, suddenly in command, and swelled with pleasure at each strike. While most of those visits are hazy memories, even after only ten years, I vividly remember the day she finally took me to her bedroom.

It was a small trailer, so I assumed she slept on the sofa bed. Not so. Jayne had simply *been preparing* me for her bedroom.

In the living room she opened my pants, knelt down, and began licking my cock. "This is our secret," she whispered, attacking my erection voraciously with lips, tongue, and hands. "I'm sharing it with you because you're...so...good to me." She brought me to the edge quickly and when she saw my trembling she mumbled, "Come. Come on my face." I did and she laughed, rubbing my semen over her face and neck. She stood and kissed me tenderly. I was startled to realize it was our first kiss. Staring intensely into my eyes, she breathed, "I...*know*...you'll be so...*good*...to me." Then she led me to the back of the trailer.

Just as a church is a house of God, Jayne's little bedroom was a house of pain. The window was blackened and dim light bled through the red shade of the room's single tiny lamp. It was a garden of chains and straps and pullies all tediously connected and threaded through eyelets in the walls and ceiling. Visually, it made no sense. One wall was covered with whips of various lengths and designs. Paddles and manacles and small insect-like clamps hung from hooks. Mounted above them was a long, barbed, harpoon-like object. I wanted to be horrified by it all, and perhaps I pretended to be at first; but as that creature inside me began to awaken, teasingly flicking its black tongue, I shivered with anticipation.

Then I saw the oddest, most incongruous thing of all hanging on the wall above the bed: a large framed photograph of a man with thick black-and-silver hair, narrow glistening eyes that seemed to bore into my head, and a craggy face as cold as steel. Pastor Hudson Potter, I was certain.

As I began to undress, Jayne dropped her robe and quickly turned off the light. But in that instant I saw the scars and calluses on her body. All *over* her body.

She lit a candle and took some of the accoutrements from the wall: a short whip, manacles, clamps, spherical weights on thin chains...and the barbed rod. She attached the clamps to flaps of skin between her legs, then the weights to the clamps, groaning through clenched teeth. The tender flesh of her pussy hung impossibly low, like the flabby sinking skin of a very old woman. Climbing onto the bed, she put the manacles on her wrists and ankles and had me attach them to the chains hanging from the ceiling. At her request, I turned a crank on the wall, and she slowly rose a few feet above the bed, weights dangling from her rubbery labia. I was trembling as I flipped the latch that locked the crank.

"Now," she whispered, "whip me. Punish me."

I started slowly, like the first time, whipping her legs and sides as I knelt on the bed.

"No, *no!* My cunt! Whip my filthy, sinful, evil *cunt!*"

"Juh-Jayne, I can't—"

"Do it!"

I did.

She writhed and laughed and cried obscene apologies, her head hanging back so she could look at her father's icy face. The weights bobbed and she began to bleed as the teeth of the clamps bit into her flesh.

That was when I began to laugh and whip her harder. My cock stood at attention, and I began to stroke it with my free hand, breathing faster.

"Now, Paul, *now!* Put it in me!"

I stopped, confused. "What—"

"The *rod*!" she growled. "Drive it in! All the way in! *Fuck* me with it! Punish me!"

I hesitantly lifted the pointed rod from the bed; the barbs curved like small evil grins. Something happened to me then. A clean bright light inside me went out and a ragged hot flame spat up in its place. I think I smiled as I eased the rod into Jayne—

"Fuck me with it Daddy Daddy I'm sorry—"

—a bit deeper—

"—Daddy sorry I told sorry I made you hard sorry Daddy punish meee!"

—until the first barb was touching her vagina. I think it was the blood that stopped me. One of the weights plopped onto the bed taking a piece of flesh with it and I caught some blood on my face. I realized what I was about to do and gasped, pulled out the rod, dropped it, and ran to the bathroom to vomit. It wasn't because I was horrified or disgusted by what I was doing, but because I wanted—wanted *so badly*—to do it.

Jayne screamed obscenities at me as I lowered her to the bed, unhooked the manacles, and dressed. As I left her for the last time, I heard her crying, "I'm sorry, Daddy, so sorry…I need to be punished…punished…"

Gary Sigman committed suicide two years later. Had Jayne done that long before, things would have been very different for us all—especially for the boy who finally did what she wanted. But suicide is a sin.

Despite my parents' disapproval, I drifted away from the church; instead of attending an Adventist college, I went to UCLA. There I met Roz, a beautiful business major. One night while we were making love, I began to pound the mattress with my fist, lost in passion. When I finally heard her screams, I realized it wasn't the mattress I was pounding. I expected her to press charges, but she didn't. I paid her dental bill and never saw her again.

I tried prostitutes for a while, but they weren't safe. One night I left a motel room in Hollywood and met the girl's pimp in the parking lot. When he saw the blood on my hands and shirt, he beat me senseless. He hurried in to check on his girl, and I limped to my car and left, certain he would kill me if I didn't.

I remained parked before the boy's house for two hours, watching the reporters surrounding the front yard.

I considered visiting my parents, but they would want me to stay a while and I couldn't. I had to get back to my pet, Clarissa. Sometimes, if left alone, she stops eating, just out of spite. Sometimes I have to force her.

I found her on Sunset Boulevard. In the right light she even looks a bit like Jayne. She's about seventeen or so and says she has no family. I keep her in a box in the spare bedroom.

I guess I forgot what I was waiting for; I started the car, drove away from the house, and left Manning.

Weird Gig

Bill Wyatt stood up suddenly behind his desk when Travis Block walked into his office unannounced. Wyatt's quick smile faded when only two other members of the band sauntered in behind him.

"Where's Elmo?" Wyatt asked with urgency in his voice as the three men seated themselves before his expensive cherrywood desk.

J.J. White spoke in his usual slow, quiet drawl. "Across town. He's doin' one of them anti-drug TV spots."

"Son of a *bitch*!" Wyatt snapped, pounding a fist on his desk as he dropped back into his chair. "That means he'll be coked out of his fucking mind by the time he gets here, and I wanted to make a good impression on this guy."

"What guy?" Travis asked.

"The guy I called you here to meet. When is Elmo gonna be through over there?"

Buddy Flatt shrugged. "You know what happens when he gets together with those anti-drug guys. Party-party-party."

"Shit. Okay, here's the deal." Wyatt stood, walked around his desk, and leaned back on the edge. "There's this guy, Leverett—um, uuhhh, *Malcolm* Leverett, yeah—called me a couple days ago and said he was interested in hiring you guys for a gig. Private. I mean, you can't buy tickets, okay? This isn't like a regular concert or anything. He has a client—clients, actually, a bunch of people—who want—"

The door opened and Elmo Carr hurried in, grinning broadly

and tossing his bushy brown hair. He hopped into a chair and fidgeted for a moment before saying, "Hi, guys, how's it hangin'? Sorry I'm late, but we ended up doin', oh shit, I don't know *how* many takes, and then the—"

"Are you fucked up, Elmo?" Wyatt asked.

"Fucked up?" He laughed nervously, bouncing in the chair. "I'm not fucked up, hell, no. I'm not fucked up, shit, we spent the whole day doin' one take after another and then we—"

"Shut up, Elmo," Wyatt said firmly. "I want you to just shut up, sit still, and try to make a good impression."

"Good impression, a good impression on who—who'm I s'posed to be makin' a—"

"Just *listen,* dammit. This guy, Malcolm Leverett. He's got these clients, some big group of—I don't know—maybe a club or something. He didn't tell me. Anyway, they want you for a private concert. You. Understand? He said they aren't even *interested* in anybody else."

"Aw, c'mon, man," Travis sneered. "What, are we back to playing dances now? What *is* this? After fourteen albums and about a dozen hits, we're doing some fuckin' convention?"

Wyatt held up his hands. "Just listen. This guy says—are you listening?—he says money is no object. *No object.*" He folded his arms and cocked a brow confidently. "So I kind of think this is more than just some fuckin' *convention,* okay?"

"Where is it?" Buddy asked.

"I don't know yet."

"Who are these people?" Travis asked.

"Look, I don't know *anything* yet, okay? Leverett wanted to meet with you guys. Personally."

The four musicians exchanged glances.

Still bouncing in his chair, his fingers dancing over an invisible keyboard on his lap, like a graying, hyperactive teenager, Elmo rattled, "Well, shit, man, it sounds good to me 'cause, y'know, it's not like we're booked up to our asses these days and I mean, y'know, we've gotta—"

"Sounds like some kinda bullshit to me," J.J. drawled, pulling a handful of pills from his pocket. He picked out a few, popped them into his mouth, and put the rest back as he walked slowly to Wyatt's liquor cabinet, filled a glass with Jack Daniels, and drank them down, finishing the glass in three big gulps.

Wyatt glared at him for a moment, then shouted, "Now, dammit, J.J., if you do that while he's here, I swear I'll kick your ass up around your shoulders and you'll walk outta here on your fuckin' *hands!* And you!" He stabbed a finger at Elmo. "If you don't stop crawling all over that chair like a fucking circus monkey, you'll get the *same!*"

Travis leaned forward, frowning. "Correct me if I'm wrong, Billy, but...don't you work for *us*?"

Wyatt closed his eyes and rubbed them, nodding.

"Then how come *you're* doing the yelling here?"

"Okay, okay. You're right. I'm sorry for yelling. I *do* work for you. For almost twenty years. We've been through a lot of shit together, right? You think I'd be with you that long, after all we've been through, if I didn't really *love* you guys? Huh? I'm asking you. No, I wouldn't. I'd be out spending all my time digging up new bands, *hot* bands. You're right, Travis," he said, pacing, "Jagged Edge *did* cut fourteen albums and you *did* have a dozen hits and you *were* hot shit on a silver platter for a lotta years. But you notice something about what I just said?" He stopped and faced them. "It's all in the past tense. Now, I know your slump began when Johnny OD'd, that's a given, because we all know that Johnny was everybody's favorite. Sexy Johnny, sensual Johnny, the kids loved him, the press loved him, *everybody* loved him. But when Johnny died..." He shrugged and shook his head. "Then all those kids overdosed at that concert, and six months later a bunch of them were crushed to death against the stage at another. And what about that kid who blew his dad away with a shotgun because his dad was taking away his Jagged Edge albums, huh?"

"C'mon, Billy," Travis said, "we didn't have anything to do with—"

"I know, I know, you guys didn't do it, but the media had a heyday with it because the kid was a rabid fan of yours and his mother claimed he'd been going down the shitter since he started listening to your music and when he finally did his dad in, he was so full of drugs the cops needed a prescription to question him. And, of course, you guys were always getting arrested. Hell, I was bailing you out every time I turned around. You were making the papers twice a month, maybe more. And pretty soon…nobody cared anymore."

Wyatt seated himself behind his desk and rubbed his eyes again. "Yeah, I work for you guys because I love you and I want you to come back. I want the old days back. When you guys couldn't take a crap without all of America wanting to know how big the turd was. But you know what? They're not coming back, those days. Things are different now. Look around you, watch the news for a change. Listen to that man in the White House. There *is* a new breeze blowing and it's blowin' you guys away! Why do you think I keep telling you to write new songs? I mean, different songs! Last year, *Time* magazine called you 'the band that killed a generation.' Drugs, man. That's all you were back then and that was fine. You read *Us* last week? Your *Wild Horse* album was number three on the list of top ten all-time favorite rock albums, guys. You know that? But that was back then. This is *now* and you haven't changed. You keep writing about drugs and singing about drugs and doing drugs and—"

"Hey, man," Elmo said, a little angered, "you know what I just *did,* man, I just did a fuckin' anti-drug statement on national fuckin' television, and I'm not gonna sit here and—"

"You doing an anti-drug statement is like a Christian going on TV and saying Jesus Christ was a clown, Elmo. You *had* to do it because you got busted three months ago, so don't give me *that* song and dance. It's the third one you've done and you're still bouncing around here like a fucking Ping-Pong ball. And you—" He pointed at J.J. "You're a fuckin' *zombie,* popping downers like they were breath mints. And you two guys probably have livers harder than your dicks'll *ever* get. Hell, we're all about the same age, but you guys look ten or fifteen years older than me. But none of you stop. And you're poison out there now, do you hear me? *Poison.*" He scrubbed his face and groaned hopelessly.

"Look, Billy," Travis said, standing, "if we have to sit here and listen to a sermon about—"

"Don't you see I'm trying to save your asses?" he shouted. "I'm your agent and manager, not your mother, but if I can't save your lives, maybe I can at least breathe a little life back into your career. Now, you've got a guy here who says money is no object. You know what that means? How long has it been since you've done a gig? I mean, a really big one, not some dive in a bad part of town, but a real gig! And how long has it been since you've gotten any positive press? Something without the word 'arrested' in the headline? This could do it. This could make people notice you again. This could—"

The intercom on Wyatt's desk buzzed, and he punched the button. "Yeah?"

"A Mr. Leverett is here to see you, Mr. Wyatt," his secretary said.

Wyatt licked his dry lips and whispered, "Please, guys. Just...shape up for a few minutes here and give me a chance to put you back on the map. Okay?"

More glances were exchanged; then Travis nodded.

Malcolm Leverett looked like a giant, shaved hedgehog. He was round, slightly hunched, had no neck, and looked rather sweaty. His eyes were magnified by the thick lenses of the round, rimless spectacles that rested on his shiny, pointed nose. With his briefcase tucked under one arm, he introduced himself in a pleasant but very quiet, tremulous voice, then took a seat and folded his puffy hands delicately on the briefcase on his lap. There was a smell about him: faint, rather sweet, moist, and slightly unpleasant.

"As I'm sure Mr. Wyatt has explained to you, gentlemen," he said in his feathery voice, his words sounding rehearsed, "I have a client who wishes to enlist your talents in a private performance. My client represents a large group of people who have unanimously chosen Jagged Edge for their entertainment. They have no interest whatsoever in any other performers and have authorized me to approve of whatever fee you wish." He cleared his throat again, wriggled his interlocked fingers, and twitched his nose as he sniffed. His brows rose high above his magnified eyes, and he waited.

"Who's your client?" Travis asked, looking unimpressed.

"It is my policy to maintain the anonymity of all of my clients."

"And what do your clients hire you to do? What are you, a lawyer? An agent? What?"

Wyatt stiffened behind his desk and took a deep breath, closing his eyes.

Leverett removed a card from his breast pocket, leaned forward, and handed it to Travis. It read, simply:

MALCOLM LEVERETT Intermediary

"It is my job," Leverett said, "to intermediate between two or more parties attempting to reach an agreement or make a deal. And I assure you that this deal is entirely legitimate." He blinked slowly, tilted his head back, and pursed his lips for just an instant. "All you need do is name your price."

Elmo was making an effort to remain still and calm in his chair, but some part of him was always twitching—his feet, his hands, his shoulders or legs—and he stuttered when he spoke. "You muh-m-mean we can ask fuh-for…any-anything?"

"I have been instructed to meet your fee, gentlemen, whatever it might be."

"Where's this private concert going to be?" Travis asked.

"The Chase Coliseum."

"Huh-hey," Elmo said excitedly, "we played there once, yeah, we played there."

"Burned down," J.J. said sleepily.

"Yes. But it has been restored."

"I didn't hear anything about the Chase being restored," Travis said suspiciously.

"The restoration was completed very recently and took place over a very short period of time. My client, uh…financed it." Travis leaned forward in his chair, inspecting the odd man through narrow eyes. Turning to Wyatt, he said quietly, "I'd like to talk to you in private for a second."

Wyatt stood and went to the front of his desk, grinning. "Oh, no, Travis, I don't think there's any need for that. I think we ought to—"

"No, wait a sec, here, Billy. Something's not right about this. I don't want to go into anything blind, know what I mean?" Then he turned to Leverett: "What *is* this group? Are they political? Are they a club? A lodge? What?"

"As I said before, it is my policy to main—"

"Well, it's *our* policy to find out what we're getting into before we—"

"Tra-vis," Wyatt interrupted firmly, "Mr. Leverett is just trying to make us an offer and I think you're being—"

"No, no, Mr. Wyatt," Leverett said, almost whispering, never taking his eyes off Travis. "I understand Mr. Block's feelings. I think it is very wise to know all there is to know about a transaction before becoming involved. But you must understand my position, Mr. Block. I simply cannot reveal the identity of my client. I can, however, assure you that this group is neither political nor officially organized. It is nothing more than a great number of people who admire your work tremendously and have missed your presence in the limelight. They wish to express their admiration by offering you whatever sum of money you ask to perform for them. I myself have followed your work over the years—not to the extent that these people have, I must admit—and I am aware of the problems you've had. The deaths, the bad publicity, your association with drugs, and the subsequent arrests. The difficulty in maintaining your audience."

"Hey," Travis said, sounding angry, "don't come in here telling us—"

"Please." Leverett held up a sweaty palm. "I do not mean that as an insult. I simply mean to say that, considering the path of your career over these past several years, I would think this offer—this opportunity—would be difficult to turn down. You are being offered the chance to perform for a large audience of devoted, adoring fans for whatever fee you choose." He folded his hands on the briefcase again, paused, then added, "There will be a down payment, of course. In cash." He patted the briefcase daintily.

"I think the problem the guys are having with this," Wyatt said soothingly, tossing a warning glance at Travis, "is that it usually doesn't work this way, see what I'm saying? I mean, it's not customary for someone to come up and say, 'We'll pay you whatever you want.' It's a little...startling, if you know what I mean."

"Ah. I see. Well, perhaps a suggestion would help. Would, say..." He pursed his lips and stared at the ceiling for a moment. "...two million dollars be an appropriate start?"

All five men in the room turned to Leverett and stared silently. Even J.J. cocked one brow over a heavy-lidded eye. After a long silence, Wyatt said, "We'll take it."

«« — »»

Their footsteps resonated as they walked across the expansive stage of the Chase Coliseum.

Their instruments were set up, microphones were ready, the stage lights were on, but there were no seats down on the darkened floor.

"I'm tellin' ya, man," Elmo said, bouncing to a silent beat, "this is, like, I mean, y'know, this is fuckin' bizarre, y'know what I'm sayin'? This place is like new and I didn't hear *shit* about—"

"Yeah, I know," Travis said. "Something's not right about this." He pulled a flask from his back pocket and took a healthy swallow of whiskey, then turned to Wyatt. "Billy. There's something you're not telling us. Who are these people that they can restore a whole auditorium—I mean, the fuckin' *Chase*—without it even getting in the paper?"

"I'm telling you, Travis, I don't know. And frankly, I don't care."

"And these are ours," Travis said, waving at the instruments. "How did—"

Wyatt said, "Mr. Leverett wanted to have everything ready for you when you arrived, so I took the liberty of—"

"You what? This is—I don't even know if—"

Footsteps sounded down on the floor. As they grew louder, Mr. Leverett materialized slowly from the darkness, his pudgy hands joined together before him.

"I'm assuming," Leverett said, "you'll want to...well, to do whatever it is you do before a performance."

"Weird gig, man," J.J. drawled quietly, shaking his head.

Travis simply stared at Wyatt for a moment, his eyes burning. Wyatt shrugged.

To Leverett, Travis said, "Look, we got here at the time you told us to be here, right? We don't even know when this thing's supposed to start because you won't tell us shit, and I don't—"

"The concert will begin whenever you're ready," Leverett said calmly.

Buddy gawked at Elmo. Travis's jaw was slack as he stared at Wyatt. J.J. shook his head and muttered, "Weird gig, man, weird fuckin' gig."

"There aren't even any seats!" Travis snapped at Leverett. "Are these people in fuckin' wheelchairs, or what?"

"They do not wish to be seated," Leverett said. "I believe they plan to do a good deal of dancing."

Elmo said, laughing, "So where, I mean, like, when're they-um, where *are* they, man?"

"When you play, they will come."

Travis's bitter laughter rang through the auditorium as he whipped the flask from his back pocket again and drank more than a swallow. Then he turned to Wyatt and said, "*Field of Dreams,* right? I saw that. Can't fool me. Tell you what, Billy, why don't you and the penguin down there entertain the Shriners. I'm outta here."

Wyatt stepped in front of him and grabbed his arms. "C'mon, Travis, don't do this, don't—"

"I assure you, Mr. Block, they *will* come," Leverett said, raising his voice. "But not until you begin to play."

Elmo jumped in front of Travis, poked him in the ribs, and jittered from side to side as he rasped, "What the hell, man, you know what I'm sayin'? I mean, you know, like...if they wanna pay us a couple million to play for, like, y'know, dustballs, then...what the hell?"

"Weird fuckin' gig," J.J. said, picking up his guitar. He sent a grumbling bass riff into the darkness. "Sounds good, though," he said to Travis over his shoulder.

SLIVERS OF BONE

"But there's—" Travis turned to Leverett again. "Where's the crew, the sound—"

"Everything is taken care of, Mr. Block. All you need do is play."

Travis shook his head, glared at Wyatt, then picked up his guitar, saying, "We end up on *Totally Hidden Video,* I don't want to hear any bitching from you guys, because I *warned* you." He bounced a few riffs off the walls as Buddy went to the drums and Elmo ran his fingers over the keyboards.

"Okay," Travis said, "let's try, um… 'Snakeskin.'"

They went into the song and Wyatt's shoulders sagged with relief as he sighed. He gave the okay sign to Mr. Leverett, who nodded stiffly.

Halfway through the song, Travis stopped singing and turned to the others, waving an arm vigorously. "Whoa, hey, *hey!*"

They stopped.

Travis said, "Dammit, Elmo, you're dragging behind on the—"

Applause broke out in the darkness. What sounded like a small group of people cheered and whistled.

Shocked, Travis spun around so fast that the neck of his guitar hit the microphone stand, making it wobble back and forth, and the sound thunked through the darkness.

The *empty* darkness.

The band stared silently out at the floor, but saw no one behind Mr. Leverett.

"I *told* you," Leverett said quietly, then turned to his left and began to walk away. He stopped and said, "Well? Continue." In a moment, he was out of sight.

Elmo muttered, "But we were just, like, y'know, rehearsing."

"I don't see nobody out there," Buddy said, squinting under the shade of one hand.

"C'mon, guys," Travis said, "let's give 'em 'Needles and Whims.'"

J.J. said, *"Weird* fuckin' gig, man."

The song began with a single chord, then a long shrieked note from Travis, whose raspy voice tore into the darkness like a barrage of rusty fishhooks.

Wyatt backed away from the band quickly, out of sight of the audience...although he still couldn't see the audience. Their voices sounded young and their number seemed to grow gradually as the song—which Wyatt had always thought their ugliest, although it was one of their biggest hits—played out.

Then they began to appear slowly. Then disappear...then reappear...dancing in and out of the darkness almost beyond the reach of his vision. He caught glimpses of lanky arms snaking upward and jerking to the beat, of legs kicking and feet stomping the floor as they came closer. But he couldn't see a whole person. Not yet.

The song ended and the crowd, now much larger out there in the dark, went wild. Wyatt watched the band soak up the applause, saw them swell with the praise. Travis tossed him a glance that, for the first time in a lot of years, was not darkened by anger, bitterness, or pain. He actually looked, for that moment, happy...still wrinkled and ravaged by his own addictions and excesses, but happy.

They waited for the cheering applause to die down, but it didn't. It grew as the audience grew. The movement in the darkness became more dense, and Wyatt squinted from the wing but still had no idea what kind of people made up the audience.

Travis spun on the band, shouted something, and they broke into "Purple Streak in a Night Sky."

The audience grew out of the darkness, their arms vines that led them to the stage, their faces pale blossoms, mouths opening and closing, shouting, singing...

Young people, mostly, it seemed. High school students, maybe? College students? Some appeared to be adults, but it was difficult to tell; they were still very hazy. Overall, they seemed to be the same kind of audience the band used to get back in those long-ago days before MTV and talk radio.

They continued to come forward into the light that bled from the stage and their voices grew even louder, so much louder that Wyatt looked up in the direction of the tiered balconies. He couldn't see them, but he knew they were loaded. And they'd filled up suddenly.

No echoing voices from the lobby...

No footsteps pounding in on the concrete floor…

Just instant audience.

The song ended. The auditorium trembled with the cheers and applause, which let up only a bit as Travis raised his arms above his head and screamed, "It's great to be here!"

The roar was deafening.

Travis grabbed the mike and screamed something else into it, but Wyatt couldn't understand the words. The band went into its cover of "Baba O'Riley."

The crowd was too loud, and it bothered Wyatt. He looked around for Leverett, hoping to ask him where they had all come from so quickly, who they were, but the old man had disappeared.

He looked down at them again as they reached up toward Travis, as if they could pull him down from the stage, and Wyatt frowned. The more he looked at the crowd, the more he realized that it was *exactly* the kind of audience they used to get. He saw a lot of long, stringy hair out there, even some beads dangling around necks and wrapped around heads. There were ratty blue jeans with bell-bottoms and patches sewn onto the denim: peace symbols, flowers, ankhs, and the word *love* with the "LO" on top of the "VE". And was that long-haired kid wearing a…it looked like…yes, it was—

"Nah," Wyatt grumbled doubtfully to himself—

A nehru jacket.

As the band played, the voice of the crowd began to unify into a pulsating chant. Wyatt tried to make it out, but couldn't. Not yet.

Travis was having the time of his life—all *four* of them were—and it showed in every movement, every note. They were stars again, not has-beens, not black-and-white faces in a where-are-they-now article or in some magazine's disdainful look back at the drug culture. They were on top once more.

But Wyatt didn't feel good about it. Something wasn't right, something more than just the mystery that surrounded Leverett—and where the hell *was* he, anyway?— no, something wasn't right about this crowd.

He looked for Leverett again, jogging into the murkiness off the stage and shouting the man's name. No response.

The chant was clearer now. The crowd was shouting, " 'Wild Horse'! 'Wild Horse'!"

Wyatt hurried back to where he'd stood and saw something happening down on the floor. The crowd was splitting down the middle. Opening right up like the Red Sea in that old Chuck Heston movie. A narrow path was forming down the center of the auditorium, disappearing into the solid darkness as the chant continued.

"'Wild Horse'! 'Wild Horse'!"

It was their biggest hit, the title cut off their biggest album, and the song for which they would always be remembered...a song the media now referred to as a "drug anthem" or a "love song to mind-altering substances." And this crowd was determined to hear it.

"'Wild Horse'! 'Wild Horse'!"

"Baba O'Riley" was nearing its close. The chant was growing steadily louder. And Wyatt was feeling tense. A corkscrew was working its way through his guts and his tense fists were hitting his thighs nervously. He spun around, walked a few yards into the darkness, and shouted, "Dammit, Leverett, where the hell *are* you, you son of a bitch!" then told himself to knock it off because they were, after all, making two million dollars and the man had arranged it...

But Wyatt couldn't shake the feeling that something was coming, something bad, something—

The song ended.

Travis shouted to the band, "Let's give 'em what they want!"

They did "Wild Horse." Wyatt felt the crowd's voice in his bones. He turned to them again and his eyes followed the path that had opened in the center of the mass and saw that a figure was making its way out of the darkness and toward the stage, moving without hurry, arms dangling loosely in a familiar way. Wyatt felt like he was about to vomit and his neck and shoulders were aching from tension as his heart was pounding faster and faster against his ribs and the figure drew closer and all heads in the crowd turned to follow it to the stage.

Travis moved like the kid he used to be, and saliva sprayed from his mouth as he sang and made sweeping motions with both arms, beckoning for the figure to come down and join in the dancing and singing.

Without knowing why, Wyatt whispered, "No, Travis, no, don't do that, Travis," and he spun around, sucking in a breath to scream for Leverett.

But Leverett stood just two feet away from him, hands joined in front, face calm and expressionless. Wyatt rushed him, pressed his face close to Leverett's, and said, "What's going on?"

"A concert."

"No, I mean *out there*. Who are those people? Where did they come from? So quickly? Why are they dressed like that? And why are they all stepping out of the way for that—that—for whoever that is?"

"I don't know them, Mr. Wyatt. I'm just a mediator."

Frustrated, Wyatt turned back to the crowd as the figure began to move into the light.

Tall and thin and shirtless, long black hair that fell in thick curls around the bare shoulders, tight black jeans.

"Oh, God," Wyatt breathed, shaking his head, confused.

Elmo hit a sour note on the keyboard, stopped playing, and stared.

Travis's voice cracked; he stopped playing his guitar and J.J. and Buddy followed.

Their mouths hung open as they gawked down at the floor.

Wyatt spun, clutched Leverett's lapels, and shook him, spitting, "What the fuck is this, a joke? Some sick fucking joke?"

"Take your hands off me." Leverett's voice was surprisingly loud in the sudden silence.

Wyatt lowered his hands slowly, then jerked around when he heard Travis's dry, ragged scream.

"Johnny?"

"Hey, Travis. Long time, huh?"

It was Johnny's voice, his movements, his face and body…Wyatt rushed to Travis's side and said, "C'mon, guys, let's go, we're outta here, this is fucked, this is bullshit, we're gonna—"

"Hey, Billy."

Wyatt froze and stared down at the impostor.

The last time he'd heard his name spoken by that voice, it had come from a dying man.

The man smiled, spread his arms expansively, and said, "Some crowd, huh?"

The crowd stared at him from the dead silence.

Wyatt said, "C'mon—all you guys—we're leaving."

Travis stared at the man beneath them dumbly, the way he sometimes stared when he'd had too much of everything.

"But you haven't finished the song yet," the man said.

Wyatt thought, *It's not Johnny, it's not, it's—*

"That's our favorite song."

No, it can't be Johnny, he's gone, he's—

"It's why we wanted you to come."

Dead, he's dead, I saw his body. I saw it!

"So we could hear our favorite song."

"Johnny," Travis groaned, "God, Johnny, Johnny, what're you—you're supposed to—I thought—"

Wyatt grabbed Travis, groaning, "Let's get outta here, this is just some kind of—"

Travis pushed Wyatt away and tried to take off his guitar but tangled his hands in the strap, dropped it, and hit the microphone stand, knocking it over. Feedback whined through the auditorium. Travis got on his knees to get closer to the man as Buddy, Elmo, and J.J. stared from behind their instruments, frozen, stunned, and confused.

"Who are you?" Travis rasped.

"C'mon, man, I'm Johnny."

"What is this? Who *are* all these people?" He waved at the darkness.

Johnny laughed. "Your fans. *Our* fans. The people who bought our albums, came to our concerts. The people who followed us all over the country from one gig to another, man, our...they're our followers. They followed me. But, hey, what'm I alone, huh? I need a band, man. That's why you guys're here." Travis's eyes swept over the faces, young and gaunt, with their long hair and beads. He slapped Wyatt's shin and hissed, "Houselights, turn up the fuckin'—"

"No, Trav, you don't wanna do that yet," Johnny said soothingly, the way he used to talk to the groupies who came backstage as he ran a long narrow finger along the curve of a breast. "Why don't you just play s'more. You want, I'll come join you."

Travis laughed, but it was cold and tremulous and edgy. His features looked stretched to their limit as he looked up at Wyatt, then clamored to his feet, screaming, "Fuckin' lights, man, turn on the fuckin' lights!"

He brushed by Wyatt and ran off the stage, where Leverett stepped before him and said, "Mr. Block, you might want to—"

Travis pushed him aside, shouting, "Outta my way, you fuckin' maggot!" He found a bank of levers and began throwing them at random.

Leverett rushed over to Wyatt and said, "May I have a word with you outside?"

"What the hell's going on here, what's—"

Leverett grabbed Wyatt's elbow and squeezed hard. "Outside, Mr. Wyatt."

Light began to fill the auditorium, first in a far corner, then just over the stage, then in the center.

Buddy's voice rose in a shrill, laughing shriek and his stool toppled; a cymbal crashed as he kicked it going down.

Elmo staggered in circles, crying, "Get me outta here, I wanna get outta here. How the fuck d'ya get outta here?"

J.J. simply stared.

Wyatt jerked his arm away from Leverett and looked out at the audience. As the lights came up, endless faces appeared, all staring up at the stage. As the light grew brighter, the features of those faces changed.

Skin whitened and some of it disappeared. Lidless eyeballs stared out of deep sockets. Hair gave way to peeling scalps. Necks thinned. Lips frayed.

And they were everywhere. Below the stage and above it.

Johnny smiled up at Wyatt, skin a bluish-white, shiny black hair gone, toothless and gaunt. "Oh, God!" Travis screamed. "Oh, Jesus! God, oh God!"

Johnny spread his arms as he looked over at Travis and said, "Play for us!"

The crowd raised its hands, and long narrow bones tore through fleshy sheaves as the fingers curled into fists and the skeletal arms began to pump, pounding the air as the crowd chanted again: "'Wild Horse'! 'Wild Horse'! 'Wild Horse'!"

Wyatt's stomach was roiling and whatever was in there would be coming out soon, as the auditorium was filling with an awful stench, a thick, throat-closing stench that made Wyatt think of fat, buzzing flies.

Leverett grabbed his arm again and, with surprising strength, pulled him off the stage, past Travis, who was crawling on his hands and knees, face wet with tears as he stared out at the ocean of corpses calling for another song.

Wyatt was led forcibly down narrow concrete stairs, at the bottom of which was a metal door with an exit sign over it. His mouth had been hanging open in wordless shock, but now he turned to Leverett to demand some explanation, but instead—

Wyatt cried out in horror.

Half of Leverett's skull was gone. The left side of his face was raw meat. Only one eye was left in the white, puffy face.

Wyatt blubbered, "Whuh-what—I don't, I-I don't—how did you—"

The good half of Leverett's mouth smiled and he said, "My son did it. With a shotgun. When I tried to take away his Jagged Edge albums."

Leverett turned Wyatt around and threw the door open. "There's no place for you here, Mr. Wyatt."

Wyatt felt a foot on his ass and was kicked hard into the night. His face landed in dry, cool dirt.

He heard traffic.

A plane went by overhead.

The door didn't slam behind him…and yet he couldn't hear the chanting voices.

Slivers of Bone

Wyatt stood. He turned.

He stared for a long time at the charred and skeletal remains of the old burned-down Chase Coliseum.

The Other Man

My wife's body was empty again.

She lay beside me in bed, eyes closed, breathing so shallowly that when I placed a mirror beneath her nose only the faintest vapor appeared on the glass. Even the small twitches and tics her body usually went through during sleep were absent. The muscles of her face were so flaccid that her cheeks seemed to sag, as if about to run fluidly off her skull.

I lifted her arm, then let go; it dropped heavily to the mattress like the arm of a corpse and she did not stir.

I pinched the back of her hand hard. No response.

I clutched her shoulders, shook her violently, and shouted her name. Nothing.

Sharon was not there.

I sat on the edge of the bed for a while, holding my head in my hands, thinking thoughts that made me doubt my sanity, absurd thoughts that had haunted me for weeks, seeming less and less absurd as time passed.

Putting on my bathrobe, I left the bedroom, made myself a drink, and started a fire in the den's fireplace. With only the light of the small lamp beside my chair and the flickering glow of the flames, the den became a ballroom where shadows danced with light all around me, mocking me, making light of the cold fear that grew in my gut.

There were three books stacked on the lamp table. They were *her* books. There were others like them scattered all over the house. I reached for one, stopped, then jerked my hand back as if burned.

Slivers of Bone

I stared at the book warily, as I might have stared at a poisonous snake coiled to strike. To open one of those books and begin reading would be to admit that my idea might not be absurd at all. I wasn't sure I was ready to admit that yet.

The room grew cool as the fire waned and I finished three drinks, all the while sitting in my chair staring at the top book on the stack. The liquor made me tired, but I knew I wouldn't be able to sleep.

Finally, I opened the book and began to read...

The first change I noticed in my wife was her silence in the evenings. After twelve years of marriage, I had grown fond of our conversations at the end of the day, our dinner table banter and discussions of the day's events. But eight months ago, I ate dinner alone for the first time I could remember. When I asked Sharon why there was only one place set at the table, she said she'd already eaten and left the dining room. After dinner, I found her in the den curled up with a book before the fire. I asked her what she was reading, but had to repeat my question again before she was even aware of my presence.

"Oh, I'm sorry, Jim," she said, distracted. "Just a book I picked up." She continued reading.

She picked up a lot of books over the next few weeks, some of them dusty and dog-eared used copies, others brand new and all of them about the same thing: astral projection.

I had always known Sharon to be an extraordinarily rational, levelheaded person who was so uninterested in sensationalism that she didn't even glance at the tabloids at the supermarket checkout stands. Even more odd than her new interest was the growing distance between us. There was less and less conversation between us; we never made love anymore; and when she was reading one of her books—which she seemed to be doing all the time—I felt completely alone in the house.

When I tried to get her to talk about whatever was wrong, she would only smile, maybe laugh and swipe a hand through the air gently, and assure me that *nothing* was wrong, she was just *reading*, that was all.

"But why are you reading *that*?" I asked one evening.

"This? Because it's interesting."

"But you've never been interested in that sort of thing before. People floating around outside of their bodies? Come *on,* Sharon."

"So I'm interested now. What's wrong with that? I had no idea there was so much written about the subject, that there was such a large pool of knowledge. It really is fascinating, Jim. You oughtta give it a chance."

She went back to her book and I walked away frowning.

I finally decided it was nothing more than a passing preoccupation and tried to bury myself in my work...until she started talking in her sleep.

I began to wake up in the early hours of the morning to the sound of Sharon's voice. I couldn't understand her words the first time, but she spoke urgently. Then, after a few moments, she sighed, rolled over, and was still.

It happened again the next night. And several nights after that. And it was always at about the same time—shortly before four a.m.—and only for a few moments. Then she would roll over and fall silent. Sometimes I was able to make out a few words—"It's coming...I'll help you...I promise...it's coming...hurry, hurry... it's coming..." But nothing that made any sense to me. And always, even in the grogginess of sleep, her voice sounded so urgent and passionate and...so very *secret*...

On one of those dark early mornings as I listened to Sharon's unconscious ramblings, it struck me: she was talking to another man in her sleep...a man she'd no doubt been seeing for some time...the man who had put such a chill in my once warm life...

I was unable to face her the next day and was grateful, for once, that she was somewhere in the house reading when I got home. The day had been long and painful; unable to work, I'd agonized over my suspicion, wondering what I might have done—or might *not* have done—that would turn Sharon's eyes to another man. Was I boring? Had I grown stagnant? Did she even *love* me anymore? I even found myself wondering if I loved *her* anymore. I was unable to eat dinner and, instead, vegetated in front of the television. I waited until long after I knew she was asleep before I went to bed—

in fact, it was about three-thirty in the morning, maybe a little later—knowing that I wouldn't sleep but willing to try. I slid carefully into bed, not wanting to wake her, and reached for the light when I noticed something...*different.*

The room was completely, utterly silent.

My hand froze halfway to the lamp and I listened. Nothing.

Sharon had never been a silent sleeper—who is?—and I had spent twelve years falling asleep to the rhythmic sounds of her slumber: the throaty breathing, the occasional snore, the sniff or cough that was usually followed by a change of position under the covers. I heard none of those sounds as I sat up beside her, arm outstretched toward the bedside lamp.

I turned, leaned toward her.

She lay on her back, arms outside the covers, hands resting one atop the other on her abdomen. Her lips were parted slightly, her hair pooled about her head. But her breasts did not rise and fall as she breathed; there were no facial tics, no sleepy stirrings. Even her eyes did not move beneath her eyelids, subtly shifting the thin flaps of skin as they usually do during deep sleep.

I felt a jolt of panic and touched her hand.

Her skin was cool. *Too* cool.

"Oh, God," I hissed, leaning down and pulling the covers back so I could put my ear to her breast. I heard nothing. And when I pressed two fingers to her throat, I felt no pulse. "Oh, my God, Sharon? *Sharon!*" I clutched her shoulders and began to shake her vigorously; I lifted her into a sitting position and shook her some more, making her head loll back and forth like that of a rag doll.

I dropped her back onto the mattress and stared at her stupidly; I found myself unable to breathe, to move for a moment. Then I bounded for the telephone to dial nine-one-one. My fingers suddenly had no feeling and punched the wrong buttons repeatedly. I don't know how many times I hung up and tried again before I finally made the connection. The *burrrr* of the phone ringing at the other end seemed eternal and I felt myself beginning to hyperventilate, suddenly having forgotten the possibility of Sharon's infidelity, and—

—I heard a sound and stiffened, spun around.

Sharon's head was rolling back and forth slowly on the pillow. Her mouth was moving. She began to speak very softly.

"...Coming...it's coming...I'll...be back...promise...I'll help you..."

I dropped the receiver back in its cradle as I stared at her, dumbfounded.

After a few moments, she smacked her lips a few times, then rolled over and began to snore softly.

I plopped onto the bed, jaw slack, my body weak with sudden exhaustion. "Sharon?" I asked, my voice hoarse. I touched her shoulder. "Sharon? Are...are you all right? Sharon?"

She stirred, muttered, "Fum? Shebble carf?"

"Are you all right, Sharon?"

Her eyes opened slightly. "Corsham. Gosuhleep."

I did not sleep, though. As I sat there, I found myself staring at the book on Sharon's nightstand. It was a new one. The title was written in shimmering gold letters on the cover: *Going Solo: Adventures Out of the Body.* For the rest of the night, I couldn't get that title out of my mind.

It happened again the following night, but I was waiting for it. When all signs of life left her at about one-thirty a.m., I began trying to wake her. I shook her, I shouted at her, I pinched her—*hard*—and even, much to my shame, gave her a solid slap in the face. Nothing worked. I finally gave up and just watched her until, shortly before four o'clock, she began to stir, mumble, and then snore.

The next day, I noticed her books around the house more than ever before. They were on the coffee table, in the kitchen, in the dining room, the bedroom, the sewing room...there was even one in the bathroom. The titles caught my attention, held it, and wouldn't let go: *Astral Travel...Leaving the Body: A Personal Memoir...Outside the Earthbound Carriage*...and more...so many more...

With each book I saw, I remembered Sharon lying in bed, still, lifeless, cold, *empty,* and I began to think thoughts...consider possibilities…that made me ashamed of myself, that even made me doubt the state of my mind.

That night it happened again, at the same time, in the same way. Except on this night, I got out of bed, went to the living room, opened the closest book and, against my better judgement, began to read.

I was still reading when it came time to go to work and found it difficult to put the book down. Not because it was such a great book, but because I was finally getting a glimpse of what had been holding Sharon's attention in such an iron grip, and it read like a long, elaborate gag. And yet, after my initial reaction, I began to realize that there was a certain kind of logic to it all—a bizarre kind of logic, granted, the kind of logic one might find between the covers of a complex, well-thought-out fantasy novel, but logic nonetheless—and I began to play a sort of connect-the-dots game with it all, connecting the bits of information I found in that book and the others on the lamp table with the strange things I'd witnessed over the past several nights.

I put two of the books I hadn't opened yet into my briefcase and took them to work with me, leaving shortly before I knew Sharon would be waking up.

With the help of a lot of coffee and a couple No-Doz, I managed to stay awake that day, but I got little work done. I worked in a small tax consulting firm but did not hold a terribly important position, so I was able to postpone my one appointment, lock myself in my little office, and read.

I read until my eyes watered. I read until I'd finished both books, then went back and read over sections that were particularly interesting.

According to the books, the best time for a beginner to try leaving his or her body was during sleep. In fact, the author claimed that many dreams were not dreams at all but memories of out-of-the-body journeys experienced during sleep; the sensation of "falling awake," as the author called it—the sudden feeling that one is falling, and then waking abruptly, startlingly—was actually caused by the spirit "falling" back into the body of the sleeping traveler. Both of the books I'd taken from the house included long chapters giving explicit instructions for preparing oneself, before going to sleep, to leave one's body during the night. It read like self-hypnosis to me, but neither book used that term.

The most disturbing thing I found was a single paragraph under the heading, *Soulmates:*

> It is almost unheard of for one to find one's true soulmate in the physical plane, but not so on the non-physical planes, although it is rare. There have been passionate romances between out-of-the-body travelers who have never met physically. In the physical plane, both parties have been involved with other people. According to those who have experienced them, out-of-the-body soulmate romances eclipse anything they've experienced in the flesh, but, in the end, they remain unconsummated and, therefore, they remain unfulfilling.

That single paragraph gave me a flesh-crawling chill and made me want to read more on that particular aspect of out-of-the-body travel. Unfortunately, that was all I could find in the two books I had. So...

When I went home that night, I avoided Sharon—which, of course, was easy—and gathered a few more books together, took them to the den, locked myself in, and began poring over them like an adolescent hunched over his father's girlie magazines.

I found little more information on soulmates meeting outside their bodies...just enough to feed my suspicions that perhaps I'd found the man to whom Sharon had been speaking in her sleep for a few minutes each morning.

I was shocked by my own thoughts, shocked to learn that I was even capable of taking such a fanciful idea seriously. But somehow, it felt right. The idea that Sharon had been seeing another man—actually having an *affair*—simply did not ring true to me; but the idea that she was meeting with someone *outside* her body...

Slivers of Bone

I was growing so tired that I was unable to continue reading. Sharon was fast asleep in bed. Before joining her, I read once again the instructions for preparing for out-of-the-body travel during sleep and, once I'd committed them to memory, went to bed.

As I lay in the dark staring at the ceiling, unable to sleep at first despite my weariness, I felt a bit nervous, like a schoolboy about to give an oral report in front of the whole class, a report for which he was not prepared.

Part of my unrest was due to the silliness of what I was about to try. But when my hesitation went on too long, I turned to my right and watched Sharon for a moment as she slept, her head tilted toward me, lips almost but not quite smiling. I wondered if that look was caused by some whimsical dream she was having or the knowledge that she would soon be with her ethereal lover...if in fact he existed. As I watched her, I felt a jealous ache in my chest and found myself unable to doubt the existence of the other man.

I looked up at the ceiling again, closed my eyes, and began taking the slow deep breaths that the book said were necessary to start my journey. I relaxed each and every part of my body, felt myself sink into the mattress as if it were shifting sand.

Following the book's next instruction, I visualized a gentle blue light glowing softly inside my body from head to foot. When the image was clear in my mind, I began to concentrate on the very center of my body, pulling that blue light into a single throbbing globe in the pit of my abdomen.

As I continued breathing deeply, slowly, eyes closed, body limp, I began to drift off.

The last image I remember before falling asleep was that of the blue globe rising slowly out of my body.

I awoke suddenly with my body stiff, hands clutching the mattress.

I'd been startled from my sleep by a falling sensation, as if I'd been thrown from the bed.

Almost ninety minutes had passed, barely enough time for me to dream. But I *had* dreamed. I remembered a vague but unsettling image from my sleep; I'd seen *myself* from above—my body lying beneath the covers, lifeless—as if a part of me were hovering over the bed...

The next morning I awoke with unexpected enthusiasm. I left the house as if to go to work but called in sick and rented a cheap motel room.

Not wanting to raise Sharon's suspicions, I didn't take any of her books from the house. Instead, I went to a local bookstore and bought half a dozen books on astral projection.

In my motel room, with the DO NOT DISTURB sign on the door, I spread the books out on the bed, opened them, and went from book to book, reading them urgently, like a knowledge-hungry student. In fact, I was exactly that.

I read and meditated, as the books directed; I underlined and took notes, memorized and recited. I hadn't worked so hard since my last college final exams.

As the shadows lengthened in the late afternoon, I grew tired and hungry, but couldn't bring myself to stop yet. I hadn't really done anything; so far, I'd just studied the books, inhaling information like fresh air.

Finally, I stacked the books on the floor, took off my shoes, and lay down on the bed. It felt good; my neck was stiff and my shoulders ached. It would have been so easy simply to go to sleep, but I couldn't.

I closed my eyes and breathed deeply.

I visualized the cool blue light inside me and willed it to merge into a fist-sized sphere in my center.

As the sphere began to rise from my body, I allowed myself to drift off...

Soon I began to dream of floating. I was floating above my body, watching it lie motionless in bed. I moved around the motel room, inspected the dirty corners where the walls met the ceiling, saw the dead insects that lay inside the opaque cover on the overhead light.

When I woke later, rather suddenly, I tried to tell myself that it had not been a dream, but I couldn't. It had possessed the vague soft-focus of images that came during sleep and had looked no different from any other dream I'd ever had.

I'd slept for less than an hour and decided to take advantage of the fact that I was awake. I got up, opened the books again, and continued reading.

It was getting late and I knew I would be getting home much later than usual, but couldn't stop yet. I continued studying…underlining…reading aloud to myself…memorizing.

I skipped the sections of the books that seemed irrelevant or silly, but absorbed everything else.

Soon I was nodding off even as I read.

I put the books aside once again.

I went through the steps once again.

And, once again, I slept…

In the dream that wasn't really a dream, I opened my eyes and saw the motel room's stained ceiling. The ceiling began to lower and the stains grew larger as the room seemed to tilt back and forth. But the room wasn't moving at all and the ceiling was where it had always been.

I was rising.

I could feel nothing; I was weightless and no longer felt my own body. Slowly, unsure of myself, I turned over. Normally, what I saw would have made me gasp, but I no longer had breath.

About four feet below, I saw my body lying on the bed. It was exactly like the dream I'd had the night before, but much more vivid.

I continued to rise; my body grew smaller and smaller until—

—I felt an odd feathery tingling sensation and—

—I was outside, rising above the motel. I saw my car in the parking lot, the 7-11 across the street, the mini-mall on the corner, all of them shrinking until they looked like toys.

My first reaction was one of amazement and wonder, but it was quickly replaced by fear as I passed up through vaporous clouds, higher and higher until the evening light began to fade and I was moving through a vast, utterly empty blackness. When I began to shoot through the darkness at lightning speeds, I tried to control my direction, hoping to turn back, but failed. I wanted to scream, but had no voice.

Specks of light began to rip silently past me like tracer bullets trailing iridescent streaks that lingered for a few seconds before fading. More and more passed by me—or was *I* passing by *them?*—and the blackness around me began to dissolve slowly. I sensed that I was approaching something and, for no reason I could see, I began to slow down.

There was light ahead...no, *below*...the light was *below* me. Was I...*landing?* Once again, I passed through clouds, but they were unlike any clouds I'd seen before; there were layers and layers of them, each layer a different color from the last, and tiny pinpricks of blue light—like small jolts of electricity—shimmered through them this way and that, crisscrossing and zigzagging.

I knew, although I'm not sure how, that I was suddenly no longer alone. Somehow, I sensed the presence of others. A moment later, I sensed the *communication* of others. And shortly after that, I sensed an end to it as something else approached. Whatever it was, it was not yet in sight, but there was a new feeling in the atmosphere...a throbbing feeling...a distant pulse that was growing rapidly...growing more intense and closer...closer...

The sparkling pinpricks of energy in the multicolored clouds around me stopped, remained still a moment, and I felt a final communication. It was not in the form of words, it was literally a *feeling,* but unmistakable in its urgency. Had words been spoken, they would have been, *it's coming...it's COMING!*

I remembered what I'd heard Sharon say in her sleep: *It's coming...I'll help you...I promise...hurry, hurry...it's coming...*

What's coming? I thought as the shimmering clouds around me began to disperse as if blown away on a strong wind.

The throbbing grew louder. I could somehow *feel* it now. And it felt...bad. Wrong. *Malignant.*

Without having seen the source of the sound, I sensed its strength and enormity, and suddenly I feared that an arm—perhaps a long, tentacle-like arm ending in a hideous claw—might shoot from the surrounding darkness, perhaps *several* arms, all of them attached to the same black, throbbing mass of a body. I willed myself away from the approaching entity and found myself moving suddenly back the way I had come. In a blurred rush, I passed back through the darkness, down through the clouds and toward the small buildings below, which grew larger and larger as I fell toward my motel, down...down...until—

—I sat up in bed with a startled yelp.

I sat there for a long time, staring at the opposite wall, holding my breath and listening to my heart. It throbbed loudly in my ears, making a sound not unlike the one from which I'd just fled in my—

"No," I said to myself, getting off the bed. "That was no dream."

I searched through the stack of books until I found one in which I'd skipped over a section titled, *Dangers of the Non-Physical Planes*. I'd skipped it because it seemed unimportant; I did not yet believe in a non-physical plane, so how could I possibly feel threatened by the dangers to be found there?

Now I felt differently. Whatever it was I had fled from in that strange cloudy place, it had been dangerous...malicious.

I flipped through the pages until I found the section I wanted.

> Just as it is in our physical existence, the astral planes hold their share of evil. However, there are two differences. First of all, the evil is far more powerful, infinitely more consuming than any evil *we* know. Secondly, it cannot be hidden; if an evil entity is nearby, it will not—it *cannot*—hide its intentions, and you will *know* that you are in danger. In such a case, it is essential that you flee, and the only safe place to which you can flee is the physical plane—your own body. Waste no time in doing this, because if you are taken by such an entity, *you will NOT return to your body*.

There was more, but I read no further. What else did I need to know? My body chilled for a moment at the thought of what I'd just done, at the realization of how much danger I'd been in, however briefly. But more than that, I realized that Sharon was exposing herself to that same danger every night.

I thought of her sleepy words once again: *It's coming...I'll help you...I promise...hurry, hurry...it's coming...*

What was coming? And who had she promised to help again and again every night?

Whatever it was that had been rushing toward me in that dark place, it was something so evil, so unimaginably deadly, that its malevolence had preceded it. I shuddered at the thought of it, and I groaned at the thought of Sharon being taken by it.

I couldn't let that happen. To prevent it, I might have to face that thing again, but even so...

...I could *not* let that happen.

It was dark outside. Dusk had come and gone long ago. I gathered up the books, checked out of the room, and hurried home.

When I got home, Sharon was busy writing letters—or so she said as she sat at the desk in the kitchen—and did not even ask why I was nearly four hours late from work.

I made a sandwich in the kitchen and ate it quickly as I continued reading in the den. I learned nothing new, but reviewed everything I had learned.

I did not look forward to repeating the experience I'd gone through earlier; my skin crawled at the very thought of coming within range of whatever hideous, filthy thing had been pulsing its way through the darkness.

It's coming...

But I knew it was necessary.

...I'll help you...I promise...

I was willing, if necessary, to meet it face-to-face in order to keep it from Sharon.

...hurry, hurry...it's coming...

I read late into the night.

Sharon went to bed without saying goodnight.

I joined her later, hoping I would be able to leave my body at, or close to, the same time she left hers.

I slid under the covers and visualized, once again, the soft blue light...

When I left my body for the third time that day, I felt no amazement or wonder as before; instead, I focused my attention on Sharon to see if she was still there. Her body did not move; there was no sign of life; I knew she had gone before me.

I rose from the room, out of the house, above my darkened neighborhood and into the black sky. I passed quickly through the darkness that had so frightened me before, until pencil-thin streaks of light were shooting by me, until I found the shimmering clouds I'd seen earlier.

I moved among them, sensing the wordless conversations that passed between them, listening without ears, eavesdropping not on conversations but on feelings, until I picked up something that made me stop. There were no words as such, but I recognized the emotion, the sensations that passed through my non-physical body.

I'll help you, I promise. It's only a matter of time. Just a matter of time.

It was Sharon. But there was someone else, someone whose emotion was just as strong...

But how can you be sure it will work?

Because I know. Trust *me!*

Trust you? I love *you!*

When that sensation reached me, I ached. Although I had no blood, I bled.

The sensations were strong and I searched for the closest entities. I found them: Two nebulous clouds shimmering with energy, both of them a soft yellowish-green.

The unfamiliar entity continued:

And even if I didn't love you, I have to trust you. I have no other choice. I've been here so long. I've been running for so long! I can't run any longer.

I love you, too. And don't worry. I'll help you.

I was devastated. But I had no fists to clench, no teeth to grind, and no voice with which to protest.

How did they communicate? There had been nothing in the books about communicating on the astral planes. I was mute, a helpless observer. I waited for more, bracing myself for something even more painful.

Then it happened.

The throbbing.

It was distant at first, even more distant than before, but coming closer. I sensed Sharon then; had she been speaking, she would have recited the words I'd heard her speak in her sleep so many times.

It's coming. It's coming!

Yes, coming again, I know. But we've had so little time.

You have to go. I'll help you. I promise! It won't be long now.

The two yellowish-green clouds began to move along with all the others. They were whisked away from me as if blown on a breeze.

I followed.

The throbbing grew louder, closer.

Hurry, hurry, please...it's coming closer...

I followed them into the darkness, deep into the black nothingness that lay between me and my body. I waited for the familiar sight of clouds, of my neighborhood far below...

But it did not come.

Instead, a vast, unfamiliar landscape appeared below. I followed them downward. The ground below began to take on shape. It was clay-red, the flat ground webbed with great jagged cracks from which rose tall peaks of all heights—some short and stubby, others tall and needle-like.

The two clouds before me moved low to the ground and headed for a dense group of peaks and hills. I tried to follow them closely—all the while trying to ignore the horrendous pulsing behind us—but they increased their speed and began to zigzag between the hills and mountains, moving so quickly that, in a short while, they were nothing more than green streaks ahead of me that appeared in flashes as they shot out from behind the mountains ahead of me, moving back and forth, back and forth, until...until—

—they were gone.

I stopped, positioned between two towering mountains that rose high above the others on the alien landscape. Below, I no longer saw the dry, cracked ground I'd seen before; there was only darkness, as if the mountains rose up from endless nothingness.

And somewhere behind me, the throbbing continued. It grew closer, louder...

If my voice had been with me, my scream would have echoed through the darkness, bouncing off the dry clay walls of the peaks and hills, continuing endlessly downward in the depths that fell below me.

I fled.

Behind me the evil drew closer.

I tried to move faster through the blackness, but wasn't sure if I was successful. In the darkness, it was impossible to tell.

For a short time, I passed through familiar surroundings; once again, the specks of light shot past me, leaving behind their colorful tails.

Then they were gone and I was once again blind.

Until I found the clouds.

Although the throbbing continued behind me, I felt relieved. It wasn't long before I saw the familiar sight of lights below.

Streets.

Houses.

My house.

I moved faster.

The throbbing grew more and more distant. The feeling of danger—the sensation of being pursued by a black, cancerous mass—subsided.

I was in my bedroom.

I saw my bed. I saw my body, lying peacefully beside Sharon, who was equally motionless.

I fell as fast as I could, unable to reenter my body fast enough. But something made me freeze.

Sharon moved. She jerked, stiffened beneath the covers, then sat up, her eyes wide. Her head turned and she stared at my body with an odd expression on her face.

I dropped lower and lower until I was mere inches from my body and—

—I froze once again.

My heart would have stopped if I'd had one.

I saw my eyes open. I watched my shoulders jerk. I saw my body sit up. Its head turned to face Sharon.

She seemed tense for a moment, squinting as she asked, in a breathy voice, "Is...is it *you?*"

My face smiled. My head nodded. My voice said, "Yes. It's me. I'm here."

Sharon's face split into a grin and she shrieked like a happy child. "It worked! It worked, just like I thought! Just like I promised!"

My arms lifted slowly and my hands touched her shoulders.

Sharon's arms embraced my body and she laughed, "My God, we're finally together!"

My own laugh filled the room, deep and heartfelt.

They kissed passionately, hands moving intimately over one another's bodies.

"I told you," Sharon said, kissing her way down my neck, "I *told* you it would work." Kissing...kissing...like she hadn't kissed me since the early years of our marriage. "I knew if I left the books around the house...he'd read them sooner or later." They disappeared beneath the covers, their bodies nothing more than jostling lumps. "I knew he'd get suspicious," she went on, her words interrupted by loud wet kisses. "I *knew* he'd try it after a while...I *knew* he'd follow me...you're safe, my love...*safe*...it can't find you here...it can't chase you anymore."

It...

There were no more voices for a while. Only labored breathing and squeaking bedsprings...moans of pleasure and wet smacking sounds...

The movement of their bodies became very familiar; they were moving in ways that Sharon and I had not moved for a long time.

They were making love.

Her moans and sighs stabbed me like hot knives.

I watched helplessly, hovering above them, as Sharon began to speak, her voice growing louder and louder.

"Yes...oh, God, *yes*...don't stop...more...*more...*"

The sounds that came from beneath those covers were wet and rhythmic. I wanted to be sick...but, of course, I couldn't.

Then I heard it.

The throbbing.

It was far above me at first, nothing more than a *feeling*. But it was growing closer, growing louder, more intense.

"Oh my *Gaawwd*," Sharon hissed.

It came closer, that malignant thing that had pursued me through places known only to the disembodied spirits of the living and the lost souls of the dead. The throbbing became louder and louder, as if it might surround the entire house and swallow it whole.

"I'm coming," Sharon whispered, "My God, I'm *coming!* I'm—"

—*coming, it's coming, it's*—

"—*coming,* I'm, I'm, oh God, I'm—"

—*coming, it's coming, hurry, hurry, it's*—

"—*coming,* I'm *coming!*"

There was nothing to do but go. I rose from the bedroom, up and up until I could see the entire house below me. And yet I could still hear her.

"I'm *coming,* my *God,* I'm—"

—*coming, it's coming, it's*—

"—*coming,* I'm *coming!*"

It was close, so close that I could sense its form, the lumpy, pustulous surface of its massive flesh, and I fled. I shot upward into the darkness as the throbbing grew louder behind me. I envisioned its limbs—numerous and writhing, reaching outward for the nearest life force, the closest source of energy to feed its insatiable hunger—and I continued upward.

My cry, if I'd had voice, would have been endless. My fear was beyond description.

I fled, screaming silently, into the vast and endless blackness…

The Picture of Health

Caryl Dunphy was no longer a virgin. At the age of twenty, she had finally done the deed, as the girls used to say in school; she'd lost her innocence, popped her cherry, become a woman. But she had not done it with just *anybody*. Caryl had done it with *somebody*.

Hawk.

He stirred next to her beneath the covers, smacking his lips in his sleep and sighing as he rolled away from her, taking his hand from her breast, pulling his moist cock away from her thigh.

Caryl propped herself up on one elbow and just stared at him in the dingy light of the dressing room.

His face was so finely sculpted, its complexion so perfect, that it did not look real; it more closely resembled a beautiful mask. His shoulder-length hair spilled over the pillow in wavy reddish-brown strands. Long lashes rested on his high cheekbones and full lips parted slightly with each exhalation. His broad shoulders spread above a smooth muscular chest which rose and fell rhythmically with his flat, rippled belly.

Caryl touched his hair gently with two fingertips and her stomach fluttered with excitement.

I'm actually here! she thought. *With him! With Hawk! My first time...and it's with the biggest rock star in the world...*

He'd first appeared about twenty years ago as the lead guitarist and songwriter for a band called Birds of Prey. Back then, he was Darren Hawke. When the band broke up in 1980—after only two top-forty hits—Hawke continued to perform on his own, mostly in nightclubs and small auditoriums, but only for a while. He disappeared for three years—the equivalent of a death certificate in the music business—and rumors blew around like the wind: Darren Hawke, the sexiest and most-admired member of the Birds of Prey, had died; he was in hiding because he had AIDS; he was in a drug-induced downward spiral; he'd had a sex change operation and would soon reappear as a *female* rock musician.

But no one really knew what had happened to Darren Hawke during those three years of invisibility. Then, suddenly, as if he'd never been gone, he reappeared as, simply, Hawk. He had a band, but its members were incidental. Hawk was the only star of *this* show. There was an album from which four songs became number-one hits. A series of steamy videos on MTV just fed the flames of his popularity. The music was at once dark and uplifting, romantic and shamelessly sexual. Suddenly, Hawk was the favorite target of gossip columnists and tabloids. A week did not pass when he was not paired with a new woman: a movie star, a recording star, a model, writer, or television actress. Sometimes the tabloids even paired him, both subtly and blatantly, with other men. But his career flourished and his popularity only grew. His reputation as a man who never spent more than one night with the same woman only helped his career.

And Caryl had followed it all. She'd savored every picture of Hawk in every paper and magazine that featured one. And then he'd come to San Francisco. In spite of the limitations of her budget and the complaints of her mother, she'd bought a ticket. She'd gotten a seat in the third row and was shocked when Hawk had pointed at her several times during the concert, smiling and winking. Afterward, as she was making her way out of the auditorium, she was approached by a man in a black leather jacket who gave her a backstage pass and told her that Hawk wanted to see her. At first she thought it was a joke. But when the pass got her past the guards and into his dressing room, she knew it was for real.

Caryl was led down a long, poorly lit corridor with doors on either side. *Dressing rooms,* she thought. Some of the doors were open and Caryl couldn't keep herself from peeking into a few as she passed. Three half-naked bodies writhed on the floor in one room; in another, a man with long platinum hair injected something into his bony arm as a girl's head bobbed up and down on his lap. Caryl didn't look into any more rooms, but she could hear sounds: muffled laughter...crying...sucking..."Now lick my ass, bitch!" was snarled through clenched teeth. Caryl became frightened and, for a moment, considered running back the way she'd come.

"Right here," the leather-jacketed man said, opening a door.

Hawk was shirtless, barefoot, and sweaty as he sat on the edge of a narrow bed drinking from a flask. Smiling, he offered her a drink, but she declined. What was her name? Did she like the show? Did she come alone? Did she need a ride home? Or maybe she'd like to go out? Go to his hotel for a late dinner?

Dinner with Hawk, she thought, her jaw slack. "Yuh-yeah. Sure. That would be nice." Her mother would never have to know; Caryl could say she went out with friends. And that wouldn't exactly be a lie, would it?

"Lemme get dressed." He put the flask aside and stood, removing his tight black pants in one graceful sweep of movement, and Caryl spun around with a gasp, her heart pounding like a jackhammer in her chest.

Hawk chuckled. "What? You never seen a naked man before?"

She closed her eyes but the image would not go away: his perfect body, smooth skin, firm muscular thighs and...and *that*...smooth and cylindrical...not too big, not too small...at least, as far as *she* knew. And what did *she* know?

"A-a-as a muh-matter of fact," she said, her mouth dry, "no, I haven't." She kept her back to him, head bowed, afraid to turn around, and stiffened when she heard him coming toward her.

Hawk stepped in front of her, completely naked and smiling, and said quietly, "Really? Never?"

She just stared at his bare legs and feet, but when he hooked a finger under her chin and slowly raised her head, her eyes traveled the length of his body and her breath caught in her throat. She stopped at his eyes—sparkling and slightly narrowed—and there her gaze held.

"Really?" he asked again, stroking her cheek with a finger, and she nodded; her mouth was too dry to speak now, "Well, you got one right here. Look all you want." He held her hands lightly and, grinning, took one step back so she could look him over.

Her face burned, but, as if of their own will, her eyes moved down his body slowly, lingering on his muscular torso, passing over his hairless, unblemished skin to the patch of hair surrounding his penis. It moved. Twitched. Began to grow. Caryl thought her heart would jump out of her mouth.

His hands were on her shoulders and she found herself moving backward and sitting when her legs bumped the edge of the bed, where her purse dropped from trembling fingers. He knelt before her, closed his eyes, and pressed her hands to his face, his hair, moved them down his neck, over his shoulders, down his chest, holding her fingertips to his nipples, and—

—Caryl felt weak, felt a warmth in her middle that she'd never felt before, growing warmer, *hotter*, and—

—Hawk moved his hands up her arms and began removing her clothes smoothly, gracefully, until she was in nothing but her underwear, and—

—she knew there was something she had to say, something she had to do, to make *sure* of, but she couldn't remember *what*, until—

—he pushed her down on the bed gently and laid down beside her, pressing his erection to her bare thigh, and then—

—she remembered. Caryl's mother, Margaret Dunphy, was a devout Christian and disapproved of premarital sex. But, unlike many others who shared her belief, she condemned no one who felt otherwise and always knew Caryl might choose to live her life differently than Margaret had. For that reason, she'd told her daughter to make sure she was prepared and never to engage in sex without protecting herself, not only to prevent pregnancy but also to prevent the transmission of diseases. "The Bible doesn't condemn promiscuity just because God didn't want us to have fun," she'd told Caryl once. "It just took a few thousand years for the reasons to become painfully obvious." It was not Margaret Dunphy's belief that AIDS was God's punishment to the sinful; it was, quite simply, she thought, the result of man's lack of common sense. "Whether you're married or not," she'd said, "screwing around is just *not* common sense. Right?" So, because of her mother's concern, and with her approval, Caryl kept a few condoms in her purse at all times. And if this was *it*, if this was going to be her first time, she was going to use them.

"Wait," she whispered hoarsely, the frantic pounding of her heart making her voice hitch rhythmically. "Just a second."

"What?" He raised his head, frowning.

As she reached for her purse, the only thing she managed to say was "Pruh-protection."

He chuckled and wrapped his fingers around her wrist, pulling it away from the purse. "We don't need that."

His words broke through her hypnotic stupor and she pushed herself into a sitting position. "Oh, I think we do. *I* do, anyway."

He leaned close and gave her a little kiss. "Have you ever heard the phrase, 'It's like taking a shower with a raincoat on'? That's what it's like for a guy. And besides, you don't have anything to worry about."

"Buh-but I know about your repu-reputation," she breathed. "I've heard the stories. All those women…some say men, too…"

He laughed loudly this time. "And you *believed* them? They're just *stories*. Anybody in my position has to put up with that. I don't even pay attention to them anymore. It comes with the territory. I just wanna make music. Jeez, you think I'm screwin' around as much as they say? I'd be in an AIDS ward by now if I was!" He stroked her breasts, slipped his fingers under her bra while tugging at the strap with the other hand and kissing her shoulder gently. Electric tingles shot down through Caryl's body from the spot touched by Hawk's lips. "We don't need one of those things," he whispered, kissing her again. "We want skin, right?" Another kiss. "Flesh against flesh." Another. "Our juices mixing with nothing in between." He had the bra off and was working on her panties now as he sucked on her breasts and rubbed himself against her.

But she didn't feel right about it, couldn't enjoy what he was doing to her because her stomach suddenly welled up with fear at the idea of having sex without any protection and her mother's calm, rational voice echoed in her mind:

Whether you're married or not, screwing around is just not *common sense. Right?*

Right? Right? Right?

His tongue was on her nipple and his hand was between her legs, fingers making their way between her lips, which had grown so wet and—

—she reached down and grabbed her purse with one hand, trying to push him away again with the other, gasping, "No! Wait! A second! No!" but—

—he straddled her, held her head between his hands and massaged her temples with his fingers as he looked into her eyes and whispered, "We're going to make love…and it's going to be beautiful."

Caryl's muscles relaxed. Her legs loosened and she allowed him to remove her panties completely and lower his head between her thighs. His lips made her arch her back; his tongue made her whimper like a child; his fingers made her cry out. He moved up her body, licking all the way, and hiked her legs over his shoulders. Slowly, carefully, he slid his erection into her, staring into her eyes during every moment of it. Caryl bit her lower lip so hard she tasted blood and her hands clutched at the bedsheets as if for life. Her breasts rose and fell with piston-like speed as Hawk began to move inside her, and after a few moments of stinging pain…it was wonderful…

And now she lay beside him, stroking his satiny skin and watching him sleep. His eyes opened suddenly and he turned to her, smiling, as if he'd never been asleep.

"I'll get a car for you," he whispered. "You can go home and get anything you need. I want you to come to L.A. and live with me. Our plane leaves in three hours."

«« — »»

Caryl let herself into the apartment quietly. Something by Mozart was playing softly on the stereo in the living room, and the lamp by the recliner cast a shaft of light into the hallway. Caryl braced herself, hoping that her mother had fallen asleep while reading in her chair so Caryl could just leave her a note, but she suspected otherwise. She suspected correctly.

The recliner creaked as Margaret Dunphy stood up, and her footsteps sounded on the hardwood floor; Caryl's back stiffened as her mother appeared in the hallway.

Margaret Dunphy was tall and slender with graying brown hair and a soft face. She wore a long bathrobe of maroon velour and smiled at her daughter warmly.

"So, how was the concert?" she asked, folding her hands.

Caryl felt herself blushing and turned away, whispering, "It was...guh-good."

"Did you go out afterward?"

"Uh-huh." She nodded.

"What did you do?"

Caryl's gut tensed into a knot. "No," she breathed, "I didn't. I-I'm sorry. I can't lie to you. I didn't actually...go *out* afterward."

"Oh. What did you do?"

Tears burned the back of her throat as she spoke, trying to control her voice. "I, um...Hawk? The singer I went to see? He...invited me backstage."

"Really?" She smiled as she said it, with no sign of anger, as if she were happy about the honor given her daughter.

Caryl had expected that; although her mother was a Christian, she was neither a Bible-beater nor a tyrant. But that only made it worse, because Caryl knew she was going against her mother's wishes, and that hurt.

"So you got to meet him," her mother said.

"Uh-huh."

"Well, that must have been nice. I know how much you admire him. What was he like?"

Staring at her feet, Caryl said, "Nice." There was a long silence, so long that Caryl could not bear it any longer and suddenly, unexpectedly—

—she told her mother everything. *Everything.*

The next long silence was even worse. Her mother's smile disappeared, but slowly. And it was not replaced with an angry glare—only a raised eyebrow.

Finally, Margaret said, "I hope you were...careful. You know what I mean, don't you?"

"Yes. I know what you mean." Caryl couldn't bring herself to tell the whole truth about *that*.

"So, you've decided to go? And live with this man?"

Caryl nodded.

"Do you think it's serious? I mean, do you think there's, you know...marriage in the future? Or is this just...oh, I don't know...an affair?"

Still not looking at her, Caryl said, "I don't know. I only met him tonight. I mean, really *met* him."

"Well." Margaret put her hands on each side of her daughter's face and smiled. "You know what you want. I just hope what you *want* is what's *best* for you. You might think I'm a fuddy-dud, but I'm aware of this Hawk's reputation, you know. I read magazines and papers. I watch television."

"Yeah, we talked about that and...he said they were just rumors and he's not like that at all. He said...well, he told me that...oh, Momma, I don't want you to hate me. I know you think this is wrong and...well, I just don't want you to hate me."

Embracing her daughter, Margaret sighed. "Oh, I could never hate you, Caryl. I just want you to be happy. That's all."

«« — »»

Hawk's three-story house in Bel Air was spectacular. The yard was like a green shaded field with a pond and ducks and so *many* singing birds, and inside, the rooms and hallways were endless. Secretaries, assistants, butlers, and maids attended to Hawk's slightest whim and they all treated Caryl as if they worked for *her* as well as for Hawk.

She was given free reign of the house and Hawk encouraged her to look around as much as she liked; he would be busy with meetings for the next few days, then he had three weeks free and they could do whatever they wanted, spend all of their time together, stay in bed for days at a time if they felt like it.

So Caryl looked around.

She went from room to room and floor to floor, staring in awe at framed pictures of Hawk with The Who, the Rolling Stones, Elton John, Led Zeppelin, Joe Walsh, Roxy Music, Peter Frampton and more, all of them signed. She admired his Grammys and American Music Awards and People's Choice Awards, all on dustless shelves behind spotless glass. She went from room to room, finding giant blowups of his *Rolling Stone* magazine covers and his album jackets, paintings of Patti Smith and Stevie Nicks and Joan Jett, framed gold and platinum records. The halls were lit by wall sconces—white ceramic hands that held glowing globes—but on the top floor of the house at the end of the hall, the last few globes were dark and the shadows were long. Caryl reached for the knob of the very last door and a hand touched her shoulder. Starting, she spun around.

Barnes, one of the butlers, a tall, balding, black-haired man, pulled his bony-fingered hand away and smiled, inclining his head slightly as he said, in a low, quiet voice, "Mr. Hawk prefers that this room remain closed. It's locked anyway."

"Oh. Oh, sure. Okay, sure, I'm sorry." Embarrassed, Caryl nodded as if her head were about to bob off. As Barnes walked away, she asked, curiously but timidly, "Um, what's in there?"

Barnes turned slowly, his thin face still smiling. "Just some dusty old personal items. We aren't even allowed to clean in there," he added with a soft chuckle.

Caryl nodded and smiled and said, "Ah, I see," and Barnes headed back down the hall. But before following him, Caryl turned back to the door and stared at it a moment. Above the knob was a second lock, a deadbolt. She tossed a glance back to make sure Barnes was gone, then tried the doorknob. It was, indeed, locked.

But something was wrong.

There in the shadowy end of the hall, Caryl could see the faintest orange glow seeping from beneath the locked door.

Slivers of Bone

«« — »»

The next few days were like a wonderful hazy dream to Caryl. She only saw Hawk for a few minutes in the morning and then in bed after he got home, when they would make love so furiously that a couple of times they actually ripped the sheets. Hawk still refused to wear a condom and it terrified Caryl just as much as it had during their first time in his dressing room. She was scared of picking up any diseases, of course, and she most definitely did *not* want to get pregnant. Not yet anyway.

"You don't have to worry about that, babe," Hawk told her one night as he moved inside of her. "I can't make babies. I've been fixed."

Caryl thought that was kind of sad, but they were too busy to talk about it then. In fact, they were always too busy to talk about much of anything. When they were together, they were either making love or sleeping, or Hawk was just on his way out. And he went out every day, long after his promise that he'd be busy for just a few days. Caryl was still so overwhelmed by the fact that she was actually living with Hawk that she was able to ignore the inadequacies easily. At first. One morning after breakfast, as Hawk lit up a joint before leaving, she asked him why he was gone so much…every *day,* in fact.

He kissed her, pulled a wad of cash from his jeans pocket and pressed it into her hand. She shuffled through it and, shocked, discovered twenties, fifties, and hundreds. "Whuh-what's th-*this* for?"

"I'll have Kelsey drive you into town. Go shopping. Beverly Hills is great for shopping. Get some clothes. Some jewelry. Go over to Gucci and get yourself a nice leather outfit. Have lunch. Baby yourself a little. And don't come back till you've spent all of that." He kissed her again, slipped his tongue into her mouth, and squeezed her ass as he held her close for a moment. "I've got a few meetings to go to. Some asshole video director wants to tell me his ideas for the new song. Then I'm going to the studio for a while. I'll see you tonight." And then he was gone.

Caryl was afraid she would stick out like the proverbial sore thumb in Beverly Hills, but riding through the immaculate streets in a black limousine with tinted windows made her blend in like a chameleon.

She did buy a leather outfit at Gucci, just as Hawk had suggested, along with a gorgeous pair of shoes. At Tori Steele, she bought two dresses (one of which she wore out of the store) and a coat, and at Tiffany's she got a beautiful diamond necklace and a pair of ruby earrings. She'd felt guilty at first and was hesitant to spend so much of Hawk's money, but he *had* told her to spend it all, so she decided to find someplace quiet and elegant for lunch. Maybe Kelsey the driver would have a suggestion.

On her way out of Tiffany's she stumbled to a halt with a startled gasp when a woman stepped in front of her suddenly, stopping just inches away. She was tall but stooped, leaning on a cane in her left hand; her right hand held the collars of her heavy ragged coat tightly together, although it was a warm, sunny day. Both of her trembling hands were skeletal and blotched with scabrous sores, as was her long, flour-white face. Her scalp was visible beneath her dark greasy hair, which fell in thin strings around her skinny, frail neck, where more sores disappeared beneath her collar. The worst of it was that in spite of the pasty skin and the horrible wounds all over her and the stick-thin wrists and the pasty eyes, she looked young...and she looked as if she might have once been beautiful.

"Excuse me," Caryl said, going around her, but the woman stepped in front of her again.

The woman's mouth opened, and a few slow seconds passed before she finally spoke. "Have you been with him yet?"

Caryl flinched and stepped back, but the woman just stepped forward, her cracked lips curling up in a rictus grin around darkening teeth as she nodded knowingly. "You have."

"I'm sorry, but I don't think I—"

The woman leaned even closer, so close that Caryl smelled her putrid breath when she hissed, *"Have you been tested yet?"* Then she turned and, as quickly as she could on unsteady legs, hurried away, disappearing in the crowd of pedestrians.

Caryl had lunch at a small sidewalk cafe. She ordered a glass of white wine before her cobb salad; the woman had shaken her up. She was obviously some hopeless street person who appeared to have reached the end of her drug-addicted rope and probably had no idea what she was saying. But that didn't make it any less upsetting. What she'd said had been so...so frighteningly appropriate.

Don't be stupid, she thought, sipping her wine. It was warm in her stomach; she wasn't used to alcohol.

She nibbled on a bread stick as she waited for her order, wondering how her mother was, reminding herself that she *had* to call her soon before she started to worry.

A metallic squeaking behind her made her look over her shoulder. A well-dressed but frail-looking man was walking into the café, slowly pulling a green oxygen tank on a dolly at his side. A thin transparent hose stretched from the tank's nozzle to the man's face where it wrapped around his head just beneath his razor-thin nose. Although he walked slowly, he took short, labored breaths. He glanced at her, and she saw the dark gray circles under his shadowy eyes, the blue veins in his skull-thin temples, and the gray patches of skin on his sunken cheeks. His blond hair was cropped short and his hairline receded halfway back on the top of his head. He looked at her and smiled, and the taut skin of his face looked ready to split and peel back over his skull; there were dark gaps between all of his upper teeth, which were small white beads.

Caryl jerked her head away so quickly she almost spilled her wine.

The man wound his way around the tables to the far corner of the short wrought-iron fence that surrounded the cafe; he seated himself so that he was facing her. Caryl diverted her gaze by reading the small dessert menu. As she sipped her wine, she tossed a casual glance toward the man's table. He was just sitting there without a menu or a glass of water or any food in front of him. But he was still watching her with a hint of a smile on his cadaverous face. Caryl returned her eyes to the dessert menu and studied it as if it were fascinating until her cobb salad and croissant arrived. As she ate, she tried to cheer herself with the thought of all the wonderful things she'd bought that day—the beautiful clothes and jewelry—and with thoughts of what she might buy for Hawk to surprise him when he came home, but she could not shake the feeling of being watched by that gaunt balding man at the corner table with the oxygen hose under his nose.

Finally, she heard the squeaking again. *He's leaving,* she thought with relief.

She took a bite of salad.

The squeaking stopped beside her. She could hear his ravaged lungs fighting for air. His voice was soft and tremulous.

"He wouldn't wear a condom, would he?"

Caryl gasped, and a few chunks of lettuce caught in her throat, making her choke. She grabbed her ice water and took a few swallows. "Have you been tested yet?"

She coughed again and water shot from her nostrils. She dropped the glass, and it shattered her salad plate and knocked the wine over. She coughed and fought for air. A waiter approached her in an instant with another glass of water. She drank, caught her breath, and looked up but—

The man with the oxygen tank was gone.

"Where did he go?" she gasped.

"Who?" the waiter asked.

"The man. With the tank. The oxygen tank."

The waiter looked confused. "Oxygen tank?"

"Yes. He was just *standing* here a few *seconds* ago *talking* to me!"

He shook his head and looked at her somewhat suspiciously. "Sorry, lady. I didn't see nobody."

After the waiter had calmed her, Caryl left and went straight home instead of buying Hawk a gift. She decided to fix him dinner instead, but once in the kitchen, she realized her hands were too shaky to cook, so she had another glass of wine and sat in front of the television for a while and watched Oprah and Dr. Phil.

When Hawk got home that night, she was still upset; she'd spent the day trying to keep those two thin voices out of her head...

Have you—
He wouldn't use—
—been tested—
—a condom—
—yet?
—would he?

Slivers of Bone

When Hawk came into the bedroom to find her trying to read a magazine, she smiled with relief and sat up to embrace him, but he wandered around the room distractedly, undressing, mumbling to himself. Then he said, "Gonna take a shower," and went to a dresser, opened his bottom drawer, removed something that jingled metallically, and left the room.

Caryl thought that was odd. They had their own bathroom adjoining the bedroom; why would he leave the room to take a shower? And what had he taken from the bottom drawer of his dresser?

The wine had made her sleepy and she felt even worse than she'd felt before. She put the magazine aside, turned off the light, rolled over, and went to sleep. She dreamed of walking corpses that whispered of tests and condoms...

When she woke the next morning, suddenly, drenched in sweat brought about by the visions in her sleep, Hawk was already gone. He'd left a note on his pillow that read, *See you tonight, babe. Think dirty thoughts and have your legs spread when I get home. We'll fuck till our gums recede.*

The note depressed her so much she skipped breakfast. She wanted only to get out of the house. Instead of a limousine with a driver, she took one of Hawk's cars, a Corvette, and drove herself into town with no idea of where she was going. As she drove out the front gate, she saw a woman standing across the street near a patch of bushes. She was very thin, wore a sweater, and had her arms folded tightly over her breasts as if she were cold. She stood as still as a mannequin, just staring at Hawk's house with deep-set shadowed eyes.

Caryl tried to fight back the shudder that passed through her and just drove. She found herself in the village of Westwood near UCLA and looked for a restaurant where she could have brunch. When she spotted one that looked good, she parked the car and walked back toward the building, strolling past a police officer who was writing a ticket for an illegally parked car. A woman walked toward her on the sidewalk. She was black and, although Caryl didn't think it was really possible, she looked rather pale. Her hair didn't look real; she was obviously wearing a wig. Just as they were about to pass, the woman stepped in front of Caryl and asked, "He's using you, isn't he?"

Caryl stopped and, suddenly angry, fed up with questions from strangers, she snapped, "Who *are* you? What do you—" She swallowed her words when she saw the woman's throat. It was bulging with hideous lumps, as if a number of small rocks had been slid beneath the skin. "—want from me?" Caryl finished in a breath.

The woman looked deeply into Caryl's eyes, frowning, and asked quietly, "What does he keep in the room upstairs?"

"*What do you want?*" Caryl shrieked. "*Why are you asking me these things?*"

"What do you suppose he keeps up there?" the woman whispered. Then she stepped around Caryl and walked on.

"No!" Caryl shouted. "You *wait!* You wait *just* a second, lady! Who *are* you? Why did you *ask* me that? What do you *want?*" She broke into a run and almost fell when—

—a police officer stepped in front of her, a ticket book in one hand, a pen in the other. "Excuse me, lady. Can I help you? Do you have a problem?" His voice was firm.

Caryl fought back tears, closed her eyes, and whispered, "Thuh-that woman. That woman I was just talking to."

"What woman?" the officer asked, frowning.

Caryl pointed down the walk. "That wo—"

She was gone.

The officer shook his head, trying not to smirk, and said, "I'm sorry, ma'am. You *look* sane enough. But I'm afraid you were just, um, talking to yourself."

Caryl felt dizzy for a moment, scrubbed her face with a trembling hand, turned, and walked away.

Two hours later, she was still wandering the sidewalks of Westwood, staring blindly into store windows, trembling in the warm sunlight as she rounded the same corner she'd rounded just a little while ago.

What does he keep in that room upstairs?...What do you suppose he keeps up there?

Slivers of Bone

Staring at her reflection in the window of a small dress shop, Caryl began to think she'd made a horrible mistake in coming to Los Angeles with Hawk, although she wasn't quite sure why she felt that way. Surely the people who had been accosting her on the street knew nothing of her personal life. It was *impossible!* She'd never seen them before. They never mentioned any names. They never said anything specific.

What does he keep in that room upstairs?

Well...nothing *too* specific. And just because other people hadn't *seen* them didn't mean they hadn't *been* there. It had to be some incredible coincidence.

But she couldn't shake the feeling that she'd made a dreadful mistake. Maybe her mother had something after all.

The reflection of a woman standing behind her and to her left appeared in the window beside her own, slightly blurry and undefined. Another appeared on her right. And behind that one, a man with a gauze patch over one eye stopped, also facing the window.

A hand touched Caryl's left shoulder and she gasped, started to spin around, but a woman's quiet, weak voice said, "Don't turn around."

"Just listen," the man rasped.

"We want to help you," the other woman said.

"He's doing to you what he did to us."

"Making you feel so important," the man said. "At first, anyway."

"But he's just using you. Someone to come home to."

"Someone to come home to and *fuck,*" the man added.

Caryl took in an unsteady breath to speak, but the woman said, "Just listen."

The man said, in his gravelly voice, "What he *really* did to us was far worse than that."

"It's what he does to everyone," the second woman whispered.

"He doesn't go to the studio," the first woman said. "He doesn't go to meetings. He goes to see his lovers. All day long. Sometimes prostitutes."

"Sometimes bathhouses and gay bars," the man said. "He's insatiable."

The second woman: "And they're always nobodies. Never celebrities."

The first woman: "He saves the celebrities for parties and concerts and premieres, when he knows the press will show up. And the *celebrities* he never *touches*."

"Otherwise his secret would be out." The man chuckled.

"Secret?" Caryl muttered, staring at the glass.

The man: "People would find out what he's doing."

The second woman: "He would be destroyed."

The first woman: "Now we come to all of his lovers—"

"His *conquests,*" the man interrupted.

"And try to warn them, stop them before it's too late," the first woman continued.

The second woman whispered sadly, "But it's always too late."

"What're you—" Caryl breathed, her gut swelling with a sick fear.

"Shhh," the first woman hissed reassuringly, patting her shoulder. "You can stop him."

"Get into that room," the man said.

"The room upstairs. Get into that room and stop him."

"And whatever you do," the first woman whispered ominously, "don't let him touch you again."

"At least," the man added, "not without a condom."

Her fear began to melt away and was replaced with the same anger she'd felt toward the black woman earlier. With teeth clenched, she spun around to shout at them, tell them to go away, *threaten* them if necessary, but—they were gone.

That night, Caryl pretended to be asleep when Hawk got home, hoping he wouldn't try to wake her so they could fool around. He didn't. Instead, he paced the room and mumbled, as he'd done before. She could hear liquid sloshing in a bottle and, after a moment, caught the stinging odor of whiskey. He chuckled, mumbled some more, then opened the dresser drawer again. She heard the same jingle she'd heard before and he left the room.

Caryl threw the covers back, slipped into her robe, and peered out the door cautiously. At the end of the hall, Hawk was just rounding the corner, still mumbling; she heard his feet clump up the stairs as she hurried down to the corner. As soon as she heard him walking down the third-floor hallway, she glanced around to make sure no one was nearby and started up the stairs silently. As she reached the top step, she heard the door at the end of the hall close with a muted click, followed by the sounds of two locks being turned in succession.

Walking on the balls of her bare feet, Caryl went to the end of the hall, where the light was dim, and approached the door carefully. The soft orange glow still flickered through the narrow crack beneath the door, then disappeared...flickered some more, then disappeared...

Hawk was pacing inside. She heard his voice, soft and indecipherable but frantic, breaking occasionally into a soft, breathy laugh, then falling back into sibilant mutterings. Caryl flinched when she heard a loud thump, as if Hawk had fallen heavily to his knees, and his voice rose, but only slightly. She leaned closer to the door, until her ear was almost touching the wood, but could only pick out snatches of what he was saying.

"...am thankful once again...fair and just and...be transferred to my image on this...for you in return..."

Caryl's brow wrinkled so hard that it hurt, and she realized her white-knuckled fists were pressed together between her breasts. She wasn't sure of what she'd just heard and thought she might have misunderstood his words altogether, but for some reason it sent an icy blade of fear into her gut and twisted it.

Keys jingled.

Footsteps approached the door.

Caryl thought her heart would stop as she turned and ran down the hallway as quickly and quietly as she could, and her feet tangled together for an instant as she turned to rush down the stairs, and when she reached the bedroom, she couldn't get the doorknob to turn at first because of the cold, clammy sweat that coated her palms, and when the door finally opened, she fought the urge to slam it behind her and tore a seam in her robe as she ripped it off her body and tossed it aside and threw herself onto the bed, pulled up the covers and turned on her side as—

—the bedroom door opened again and Hawk came inside.

Caryl closed her eyes and tried to breathe normally, tried not to let her chest heave, tried to calm herself so he wouldn't be able to hear the drumming of her heart.

Please don't let him try to wake me, God, she prayed silently. *I'll leave tomorrow and never do anything like this again, I swear, I swear, I will, just DON'T LET HIM TRY TO WAKE ME!*

The drawer was pulled open again, the keys dropped inside, and she could tell he was moving unsteadily, drunkenly, as he undressed. A match was lit, Hawk inhaled deeply and the cloying smell of marijuana filled the room. The bottle sloshed again: another drink. And then a throaty chuckle as he walked to her side of the bed.

He touched her shoulder, shook her gently, then a little harder. He pulled back the covers and got on the bed, straddling her and rubbing his erection on her thigh as he took another drag on the joint.

She didn't stir, tried not to move a muscle, kept her eyes closed.

Hawk slurred, "C'mon, babe, dincha get my note?" He shook her some more, a little too hard this time, and she knew he'd never believe it if she didn't wake up.

She rolled her head slowly toward him, mumbling.

He cupped one breast and squeezed it too hard, then reached down and tried to wriggle his fingers between her closed legs.

"Time t'plaaay," he gurgled through a broad grin. He leaned toward the nightstand, put the joint in an ashtray, picked up his bottle of whiskey and finished it off, then tossed it to the floor, getting off her. He pulled her toward him and said, "Sixty-nine."

Trying hard to feign waking up, she muttered, "Huh? What?"

"C'mon, babe, sit on my face while you suck my cock. S'all nice'n hard for ya."

Her mind raced and her stomach churned. "Oh...oh, honey, I can't."

"What?" He squinted at her, annoyed. "H'come?"

"Oh, honey, I've been sick all evening. Didn't Barnes tell you?"

"Sick? No, he didn't. Wha's matter?"

"Flu, I think. My...stomach." She wasn't lying. Her guts were moving and she felt like vomiting. But it wasn't the flu, it was fear. "In fact..." She sat up slowly. "Well, I don't think I should...oh, no." Caryl slid off the bed, hurried into the bathroom, and leaned over the toilet, emptying herself loudly.

"Sheee-yit," Hawk groaned from the bed.

When she was finished heaving, she remained on her knees, trembling and weak, and whimpered, "I'm suh-sorry. Muh-maybe I shuh-should sleep in, you know, another room, so...so you won't cuh-catch this. Huh? You think?" She stood on wobbly knees, leaning on the edge of the sink, and flushed the toilet. After rinsing her mouth she said, "You think so, Hawk? Hawk?"

When she came back into the bedroom, she found him sprawled over the bed, mouth yawning open, snoring.

"Hawk?" she said loudly, then, even louder, "You awake, Hawk?"

He didn't move.

That room upstairs. Get into that room and stop him...stop him...stop him...

Caryl stared at the bottom drawer of the enormous dresser, then again at Hawk. She didn't know if she could take the stress, the pressure—

Get into that room and stop him.

—but she had to try. With her robe back on, she crept to the dresser and pulled the bottom drawer out slowly, cautiously. It was full of underwear and socks, a couple of dirty old marijuana pipes, a dildo that looked like a real penis only *much* too big (and *that* one surprised her)...Hawk was such a slob.

And there they were, two keys on one little ring nestled in a pair of undershorts in the back corner of the drawer. To keep them from jingling, she wrapped the undershorts around them, put them in the pocket of her robe, and closed the drawer silently. Then she left the room.

Afraid of being caught, Caryl instinctively wanted to hurry; terrified of being heard, she was afraid to move too quickly. As a compromise, she went upstairs and started down the hall. It seemed much longer this time and the far end seemed much darker. And the hands...they chilled her...so patient and motionless as they held up the globe lights. All but the ones at the end that held cold, dead spheres of darkness.

At the door, holding the keys level with the knob, she froze up.

Just go, she told herself. *Just go back downstairs, get dressed, grab some money, and go home to Mom.*

But other voices spoke to her, too: *Stop him...get into that room...stop him...stop him...*

She tried one key, it didn't work, so she tried the next and the knob turned. She unlocked the deadbolt. Taking a deep breath, she opened the door.

Candlelight. That was all she noticed at first as she closed and locked the door behind her. They were everywhere in the room: fat black candles, at least six inches in diameter, dozens of them arranged in no particular order, flames dancing and flickering in the darkness. There were shelves of them on the walls, shelves on top of shelves, and as she looked up, she saw a three-foot-tall crucifix complete with a bleeding figure of Christ painted black and hanging upside down on the far wall.

Caryl staggered backward and slapped a hand over her mouth as if she were about to be sick again.

"Oh, dear Jesus, I'm sorry," she breathed, "I'm so sorry for being here, for, for, for being with *him,* please forgive me, please forgi—"

Her breath stopped when she saw what was beneath the desecrated cross.

It was an enormous painting on an equally large easel, a painting of the most hideous creature Caryl had ever seen, something out of a madman's worst nightmare. Gulping at saliva that wasn't in her dry mouth, she stepped forward, wincing as she got a closer look at the painting.

The creature resembled a human being, but in form only. Its

arms—which dangled helplessly at its sides—and legs—bent at the knees as if they were about to buckle—were reduced to white, brittle sticks. The ribs pressed dangerously hard against the paper-thin skin, as if they were about to slice through and open the entire abdomen to reveal whatever foul things were being held inside. Shadows were dark just above the collarbone where the skin had sunk into virtual canals below the bony shoulders. The neck was painfully thin except for the dreadful bulges like—

Like small rocks beneath the skin, she thought, remembering the black woman she'd seen in Westwood.

And all over the flour-white body there were sores, dark scabrous sores that glistened and ran, some of them small, some of them huge, as if they'd grown and were still growing, intent upon covering the entire body, devouring it as if it were food. They even covered the face. And the *face*...

It was nothing more than a skull coated with a thin layer of paste. The nose was a razor and the cheeks disappeared into black holes beneath the knife-like cheekbones. The lips were so cracked they looked ready to crumble. The mouth gaped as if in a desperate effort to draw in a breath that would not come, and the teeth inside were dark and rotting away; some of them were already gone. The head was bald except for a few patches of colorless, thin, dry-looking hair. The ridges of the forehead stuck out over two pits, from the bottom of which the eyes stared in pure, hellish agony. The eyes...what was it about the eyes? Or was it something else that disturbed her even more deeply than the decayed thing hunched on the canvas?

Caryl wasn't sure what repulsed her more: the image or that indefinable thing about it that moved her, that...haunted her.

She moved closer to the painting and bumped into a wooden dais on which she found a large leather-bound book that resembled a photo album or scrapbook. There was nothing written on the front, and a strip of leather was snapped onto the cover holding it closed. Hesitantly, she unsnapped the strip, and the cover crackled as she opened the book slowly.

At first she turned the heavy black pages looking only closely enough to see that the book was filled with small newspaper clippings, some of which were accompanied by grainy black-and-white photographs. It took a few moments for her to realize they were all obituaries. Frowning, she stopped and read one. A twenty-seven-year-old woman named Phyllis Browning, who died of complications due to AIDS. The next was accompanied by a photo of a handsome man named Walter McClaren; he also died of complications due to AIDS. She began scanning the obituaries of men and women more rapidly, squinting in the candlelight...

"...died of pneumonia due to AIDS..."

"...of complications brought on by the AIDS virus..."

"...of bone cancer due to AIDS..."

"...due to AIDS..."

"...AIDS...AIDS...AIDS..."

Caryl was finding it more and more difficult to breathe as she read and finally stopped breathing for a long, long moment when she saw one particular picture.

A beautiful, smiling black woman. Twenty-nine years old. It was the woman she'd seen in Westwood. But this was her obituary.

She swept through the book until she found another familiar face.

The man with the oxygen tank in the sidewalk cafe.

And the sore-covered woman outside Tori Steele.

Caryl tried to breathe but couldn't at first as she raised her head slowly, her eyes moving up the dilapidated body on the canvas. The same hideous sores...the same sickening lumps under the jaw...and the eyes...those eyes...

Something else caught her attention. It was a shallow wooden box with a glass top on a three-foot-tall platform between the painting and the dais. A single candle burned brightly in front of the box.

Breathing shallowly now, Caryl walked around the dais and hunkered down to look in the box. It held a single sheet of paper—heavy paper, it seemed—on which was written a lot of indecipherable gibberish in black, beautifully formed letters. Even some of the *letters* were unfamiliar to her. But one word stood out, one word that made her upper lip curl in disgust and made her want, more

than she'd ever wanted before, to be with her mother, to see her face and her smile, to hear her warm, comforting voice:
SATANIS

Caryl made a low, miserable whimpering sound in her throat as she began to stand again and then she froze. There was something else at the bottom of the page. Something that was written differently and not in ink but in what appeared to be a brownish-red paint that had dried to a crust. Something familiar. Something that made the confusing writing above much less confusing...and much more frightening.

It was Darren Hawke's signature.

He goes to see his lovers...all day long...
Have you been tested?

She looked up at the painting, at those eyes that looked so familiar.

...sometimes prostitutes...
Have you been tested?

They were Hawk's eyes.

...sometimes bathhouses and gay bars...
Have you been tested?

She looked at the crusty brownish-red signature again.

"Oh, dear God," Caryl whispered, burying her fingers in her hair and pulling...pulling...grinding her teeth together. "Oh, dear God, dear God."

That room upstairs...get into that room and stop him...stop him...stop him...STOP HIM!

Something stirred inside Caryl, something hot and writhing and angry. She no longer felt like herself. She was a different person now...a person defiled and filthy and—

Oh God no please no don't let it be God please—
Infected.

She wrapped both hands around the fat black candle before her. "Oh..." She stood slowly. "Dear..." She lifted the candle, paused a moment, then brought it down hard on the box's glass top as she screamed, *"GAAAWWWD!"*

The glass shattered into half a dozen deadly sharp shards as her scream went on and on, and when that scream was done, she sucked in a deep breath and let out another as she looked up at the painting, swung the candle back, and threw it with all her strength. It tore through the canvas, ripping a hole in the dying Hawk's chest and knocking the painting over before thumping the wall behind it.

There was another scream, then, from downstairs. A man's scream. It was just a sound at first, but in a moment it formed words: "*What? What? What are you doing? WHAT ARE YOU DOOOIIING?*" A door slammed open and feet pounded the floor, then the stairs, as the scream continued. "*WHAT THE HELL ARE YOU DOOOIIING?*"

Caryl continued screaming, too, as she reached into the box and took out one of the glass shards, holding it so tightly in her hand that it cut into her palm. She threw herself on the painting, attacking it, lifting her arm and bringing it down again and again, ripping through the canvas with the shard, slicing through the emaciated diseased body in the painting as she screamed senselessly, spittle spraying from her mouth.

Footsteps in the hall outside. Screaming. Pounding on the door. "*STOP IT! STOP IT! NO PLEASE NO STOP PLEASE STOP IT YOU'RE KILLING ME YOU'RE KILLING MEEEE!*"

But she didn't stop and the house rang with their screams.

The canvas was little more than shreds, but Caryl didn't stop in spite of the pain in her arm and the heat on her sweaty face. Then her voice became dry and hoarse, and the movements of her arm slowed and she became weaker and weaker because of the heat...the burning heat...and the crackling...

She stopped, heaving for breath, and raised her head.

Flames from the fallen candle were slithering up the wall, licking at the inverted crucifix.

"No, oh-no, no," she croaked, dropping the glass. She ignored her bloody hand as she stood and staggered away from the fire, stumbling toward the door.

There was pandemonium outside, running feet, screams, pounding on the door. Caryl recognized Barnes's voice as he screamed, "Oh my God! Oh my God!" One of the maids shrieked, "What's happening to him?" But Hawk's voice was gone.

Slivers of Bone

Caryl unlocked the door, opened it, and looked into the hall. If she had had any voice left, she would have screamed.

Hawk lay on the floor, his back against the opposite wall. He was naked and he was changing rapidly.

As Caryl watched, black-red sores blossomed and spread over his body, which had turned sickly pale. He convulsed as his skin seemed to shrink around his body. His ribs became more and more visible until there seemed to be almost no skin over them at all. As his neck grew thinner, bulbous lumps swelled on his throat, and he hacked as if he were about to spit up parts of his lungs. His long wavy hair fell away from his head and fluttered around him to the floor. A few teeth fell into his lap. He vomited uncontrollably and his bowels let loose with a sickening sound. The coughing grew worse quickly, as did the convulsions.

In moments, as the fire grew worse in the room behind Caryl, Hawk was a shriveled husk on the floor, motionless, reeking, and dead.

Two weeks later, Caryl knocked on her mother's front door at a little after four in the morning, trying hard to hold in her sobs. She had a key and could have let herself in, but it didn't seem right. Not anymore.

In a few minutes, Margaret Dunphy called sleepily, "Who is it?"

"I-it's me, Muh-Momma."

The door swung open and Margaret cried out as she threw her arms open. "Caryl, oh, Caryl!" she cried. Caryl's purse dropped to the porch as she returned her mother's embrace and began to sob uncontrollably.

"Oh, baby, I was so worried, so scared. I heard about the fire but nobody knew anything about you and I thought maybe...I was afraid you'd...oh, thank God, thank *God,* I'm so glad you're okay, so glad you're home."

But, as she held her mother tightly, all Caryl could say again and again through her tears was, "Positive...*positive,* Momma...positive..."

Screams at the Gateway to Fame

For Cheri Scotch

The young couple was like all the other countless couples that had run together into a smiling, nodding, tale-telling blur in Janine Werner's memory over the years. Except for...something. Something about the couple that Janine had not yet isolated, but she was trying.

Jack and Delia Bellinger sat across from Janine and Tom in the booth, four cups of coffee on the table with the small tape recorder in the middle silently capturing their words as they told their story loudly enough to be heard above the clamor of the diner, but not so loud that others could hear.

"We moved into the house last summer," Jack said. "It was perfect, 'cause, y'know, we couldn't afford a lot of money, and it was pretty reasonable."

"Reasonable?" Delia interrupted with a smirk. "It was a steal. We couldn't believe it. I mean, the place was just *gorgeous*, and the price was so *low*."

Tom nodded slowly, significantly, and said, "That's very common. Sometimes you get more than you pay for."

"Things were fine at first," Jack continued. "It was real nice, y'know? We'd never lived in such a big place before. Then come October, our little boy, Richie, he started telling us about this man." Jack bowed his head a moment, sipped his coffee.

"Richie said the man was real tall and thin," Delia said. "And bald. He wore a black suit. And he'd come into the boys' room in the basement at night and just walk around, looking at things on their dressers, peeking into the closet."

"The boys sleep in the basement?" Tom asked.

"It was their idea," Jack said. "It's real big, a little drafty, but they loved it right off. They even got their own bathroom down there. No shower, but a sink and toilet, y'know?"

"Did your other son see this man?" Tom asked.

Jack and Delia, both thirty-five, had three children: Richie, seven; Wendy, eleven; and J.J. (for Jack, Jr.), fifteen.

"Oh, well, uh, no," Delia said haltingly. "See, J.J. is, uh…kind of a heavy sleeper." She glanced at Jack twice as she spoke.

Janine knew immediately that there was something wrong with their oldest boy, something that troubled them. Something they didn't want to talk about. A violent rebel? A drug problem, perhaps? She picked up nothing specific yet, but knew she would eventually. Perhaps whatever was wrong with J.J. had been the source of that jagged tension, that underslept, wire-taut anxiety Janine had felt when she'd shaken hands with Jack and Delia not twenty minutes ago.

It was present in all of them, that anxiety, in every couple she and Tom had ever dealt with. Sometimes only Janine could pick it up; sometimes they wore it on their drawn faces, held it in their baggy eyes. Of course, the cause of that tension never had anything to do with the reason Tom and Janine had been called. It was usually alcoholism or drug abuse, sometimes a woman or a child cowed by the fists of the violent man of the house, sometimes even incest. It was always something, as Janine's mother used to say. But it had nothing to do with Tom, Janine, and their work.

It had gnawed at her at first, those families and their dirty, ugly secrets. But that had been decades ago. She was fifty-nine now, and Tom was sixty-eight. Just as they had grown accustomed to a certain daily schedule at home, to watching certain TV programs, to eating certain foods, they had grown accustomed to the peripheral peculiarities of their work.

It would come to Janine eventually, the source of Jack and Delia's anxiety. And perhaps she would discover, as well, that one thing that made them different from all the other couples, that single, nagging, ungraspable thing.

"Have *you* seen this man?" Tom asked.

Hesitantly, Jack said, "Yeah. We have. We didn't believe Richie at first. We even punished him for lying to us. Then, one night, I went downstairs to their room to make sure they'd gone to bed and…there he was. Richie was sitting up in bed wide awake, eyes really big. The guy looked right at me. He smiled. Then he went into the floor. Just…sank away into the floor. Like it was quicksand." Jack's hands fumbled nervously around his coffee cup and he glanced at Delia darkly.

"After that," Delia said, "it's like this gate opened up or something. I mean, all of a sudden, things started happening. Just strange things at first. Then they got…well, scary."

The waitress came with their orders: cheeseburger and fries for Jack, chef's salad for Delia, chicken-salad sandwich and raw vegetables for Janine, and a chicken-fried steak with mashed potatoes and gravy and a tiny, obligatory, green salad for Tom.

Janine looked at Tom's plate sadly. She kept trying to warn him. He'd already had one heart attack, and he was at least a hundred pounds overweight. He was a short, gray-haired man with a belly so large it gave his back fits and had decayed his posture over the years. At five-ten, Janine stood three inches above her husband, not counting the tall bouffant of brown-dyed hair on her head, and with the help of some lucky genes Janine had kept her figure and was only a few pounds heavier than she'd been in high school. But she worried about Tom: He had no genes working in his favor, and he did nothing to take up the slack.

"What kind of things happened, Delia?" Janine prompted gently as the four of them began to eat.

"Toys. The kids' toys, um, in the living room, you know how kids leave their toys everywhere. Well, first they started disappearing. I didn't think anything of it, okay? I mean," she shrugged, "kids're always losing their toys, right? Then, uh…Jack lost his job at the factory."

There was an uncomfortable silence then; it was as loud as all the clatter around them.

"Hey, look, I'm a good worker, y'know?" Jack said suddenly. "I mean, I've got problems. Me and Delia…we've had some problems. Who doesn't, y'know? But I've always been a good worker, always on time, always the last to leave, always willing to come in when somebody else was sick. Then one morning, I go into work and my boss and four other guys I worked with corner me and say I been makin' these phone calls to 'em. In the middle of the night. Really foul, obscene calls. They say it was my voice and I even identified myself. I tell 'em, hey, I says, I don't know what the hell they're talkin' about. But they wouldn't listen. I was fired. They practically chased me out."

"The factory's a toll call," Delia said quietly. "We checked our phone bill. The calls were there. In the middle of the night. To the numbers of Jack's boss and four coworkers."

"But I swear to *God,* I didn't make them calls!" Jack insisted.

Tom lifted a hand and wagged his thick fingers at Jack. "Don't worry," he said. "We've seen this before. It's okay. We believe you. Right, honey?" He turned to Janine.

"That's right, Tom."

They could have been following a script, so identical were their words to all the other couples they'd dealt with, who were so identical to Jack and Delia Bellinger. Except:

Janine was feeling that anxiety again, coming to her from Jack now like the wavering heat of a dying fire. It was real. And unlike everything else about the conversation, it was...*different.* She watched Jack's fidgeting hands, saw him fumble with his wedding ring. Janine saw an identical gold band on Delia's finger. Then it struck her. She thought of all the couples they'd met over the years and remembered the crucifixes being worn around necks, the rosaries being caressed during conversation; all of them, every single couple, without fail, clutching their religion in the form of trinkets and icons, there for all to see, to draw attention away from the dark and diseased secrets of their lives.

But Jack and Delia carried none of those icons, wore none of that jewelry.

"Are you Catholic?" Janine asked both of them.

Jack shook his head as Delia said, "Oh, no."

"Any religion at all?"

Delia chuckled nervously. "Not us."

Jack said, "Neither of us come from religious families, and we've just never taken to churchgoing, tell you the truth."

Janine nodded, trying to hide her surprise. It was a first, and she glanced at Tom, but he did not react to it at all.

"After Jack lost his job," Delia went on, "things got really bad. Instead of disappearing, the toys...they started just, um, moving around. On the floor. By themselves. Lots of things in the house moved and were broken. And the voices...the wailing and crying and laughing at night, and other things that, um...well, they're personal, okay? I mean, they're hard to talk about."

Tom cleared his throat and leaned forward as much as his belly would allow. "Are they of a sexual nature?"

"Uh, yeah," Jack said, fidgeting even more, ignoring his burger. "They are. We, uh...well, something came into our bedroom one night. Into our bed."

Delia said something with her head bowed, staring at her salad, her voice too low for the words to be understood.

"I'm sorry?" Tom said. "You'll have to speak up."

Tom was high-strung, his manner coarse, and he was often thought rude by strangers, even when that was not his intention. Janine nudged him with an elbow, a signal for him to lighten up. Tom smiled and added, "If you don't speak up, dear, the recorder won't catch it."

"It touched me first," Delia said. "Something...above the covers. It squeezed my breasts. It even scratched me."

"I saw the scratches," Jack said. "Four of them. Across her left breast. They bled."

"It was a hand," Delia added. "Nothing was there, okay? I mean, I couldn't see anything, but...it had four fingers and a thumb. And it squeezed. And pinched. Hard."

"It bruised her. I saw the bruises."

"Honey, do you think—" Delia turned to Jack reluctantly, placed a hand on his arm, "—do you think you can tell them what it...did to you? I mean, without breaking down?"

Jack turned away from all of them and stared out the window

beside the booth for a long moment. Finally, still gazing out the window, he spoke, voice brittle: "It raped me. One night. I was in bed, lying on my back. It flopped me over. Like I was a rag doll, y'know? Just flopped me over. Onto my stomach. It hurt. I never screamed before in my life, but I did that night. That was the first time it happened. But not the last."

Delia put her hand over Jack's and squeezed.

It never failed. In recent years, there was always sodomy involved in every case, whether the victim was male or female. It puzzled Janine, but it delighted Tom, because he thought it did wonders for book sales and sounded great on the talk shows. On the surface, this sounded like every other story of demonic rape she and Tom had heard, but...beneath the surface, things were different. What she felt from Jack was so upsetting that it withered her appetite and she pushed her plate away.

"Then there were the dreams," Delia said, still holding Jack's hand. "Horrible nightmares. But I mean *really* vivid, okay? Like they were really happening. Horrible. Every night. Pretty soon, we couldn't sleep. None of us."

"Not even the children?" Tom asked.

"No," Delia said. Then she tossed a look at Jack, glanced all around nervously. "Except for J.J. He's...different. He hasn't been bothered by any of this. In fact, he stays away from us. Out of the house. He says we're crazy. See, J.J. is, um...we've been having problems with him. He's been...doing drugs. We've tried everything. Punishing him. Pleading with him. Even turning him in to the police. Nothing works."

Tom closed his eyes and nodded knowingly. "That's not at all uncommon. In every case we've handled where a teenager was involved, there's usually drugs involved."

Janine knew that was true, but this was another first. In every other case, the family tried to hide whatever drug problem existed. Tom and Janine always found out by accident, and the couple always apologized, as if it might damage their credibility, their chances of going on *Jenny Jones*. But never before had anyone revealed the problem during the first meeting.

Tom continued: "We haven't figured out yet whether the drug problems are the cause of the evil presence or the result of it. Maybe we'll be able to pinpoint it in this case."

Janine ignored that; it was the usual prattle Tom had developed over the years, more lines from the nonexistent script they followed while dealing with one ruptured, broken family after another. She ignored it because she was still trying to process the oddities that kept popping up in this particular case: The Bellingers weren't Catholic, or religious at all; they surrendered the information about their son's drug problem; and that...*thing* she kept feeling, especially from Jack, that anxiety, that *fear*. It was not the usual secrets she always felt crawling and writhing around beneath the clean surface of all the other families; it was different, new, and disturbing.

Jack and Delia went on to tell familiar stories: screaming white faces hovering over them at night in the dark; being awakened in the night by the cries of their two youngest children; taking their young son and daughter into their bed protectively as voices and laughter sounded throughout the house all night long. And one more thing that sounded familiar:

"The man in the black suit," Jack said, "he told my son that the house, the ground beneath the house...well, he said that we were living at...the gateway to hell."

"You mean, he said your house was the entrance to hell?" Tom asked.

"Something like that. He used the word gates, or gateway. The gateway to hell was open beneath us, something like that."

"All right," Tom said. "I think we've heard enough to know that we're definitely dealing with a hostile supernatural force, most likely demonic. Tell you what. We're gonna go back to our hotel room, get ourselves settled, then we'll come over to your place in about an hour."

Delia said, "That sounds fine."

"I hope the hotel's okay," Jack said. "We couldn't afford anything really expensive, but we wanted you to be comfortable."

"Oh, it's fine," Tom assured him, "just fine. Uh, one more thing.

Why did you call us? Did you read one of our books or articles? See us on a talk show, maybe?"

Jack shook his head. "We'd never heard of you before."

"Beg pardon?" Tom said, cocking his head.

"Really, we didn't know who you were," Delia said. "No offense, but we'd never heard of you till they told us to call you."

"They? They *who?*" Tom asked.

Jack and Delia exchanged a long look. Then:

"The voices in the house," Jack said.

"And that man in the black suit," Delia said.

"And in our nightmares. They told us in our nightmares."

Delia nodded. "Yeah. All of them. They said to call you."

"Tom and Janine Werner," Jack said. "They said your names. It's all we've heard since this whole thing started. Call the Werners, Tom and Janine."

The tape came to its end and the two depressed buttons on the recorder popped up with a quiet but startling *plick*.

«« — »»

Janine had possessed her peculiar talent for as long as she could remember. She was barely five when she'd first put her secret perceptions into words spoken aloud. She'd been sitting on her mother's lap, her head leaning on her mother's breast, and suddenly she'd said, "Mommy, something's growing in your titty." Her mother had found the remark humorous, had treated it as nothing more than the fanciful babbling of a child. But the breast cancer metastasized, made its way from one organ to another, and she was dead in a little over a year. But Janine had known it was there the whole time. She had felt it with her mind, seen it with her feelings. She had *known* it.

It was something that had been with her so long that she thought nothing of it. So when she met Tom, while she was in high school, she thought nothing of the fact that she was attracted to him when all of her peers saw him as a figure of fun. He worked in a fishmarket in the small northern California coastal town in which they lived, and he always smelled of fish, even though she knew (without having any reason to know) that he bathed and washed constantly to get rid of the smell.

She also knew that inside him existed something that drew her to him, a lifespark, an ambition, a consuming but directionless *desire* that made her say yes the first time he asked her out and every time after that. She knew other things about him, too: He'd dropped out of high school years before to go to work and support his ailing mother and little sister after the death of his abusive, drunken father. But Tom told her none of those things until after she'd married him, right after graduating from high school.

Two years after they married, the fishmarket where Tom worked—where everyone came to ask Tom's advice about which fish was freshest and what was the best way to cook it and which wine would best complement it—closed down. No one wanted to go to a fishmarket anymore when they could get everything they needed at a supermarket, and without the unpleasant smell. After that, Tom went from one job to another, none of which was high-paying, and none of which he kept for long. None of them gave him the feeling of belonging that he'd had while working at the fishmarket; everyone in town had known him then, they'd respected him, he'd been *somebody*. But the jobs that followed were not the same, and Tom began to change. He became depressed, sluggish, and that bright light of ambition and desire that had once glowed inside of him began to dim, until it was nearly extinguished.

Janine knew all these things because she felt them from inside of him. And she knew something else. She knew what was *really* wrong with him, but did not know how to approach it because there was really no way she *could* know; Tom knew nothing of her gift yet, and she wasn't sure how to tell him. After all, she had told no one up to that point. No one at all.

Tom started drinking. He'd stay up all night listening to the radio, then doze off around dawn on the sofa, and by the time he felt like job hunting, it was much too late in the day. Sometimes she caught him talking to himself, sniffling. And when Janine got a part-time job at a drugstore soda fountain, he got even worse.

One afternoon, she came home to find Tom shattering dishes in the kitchen and screaming obscenities. He was drunk, but she knew that wasn't the only cause. He didn't even notice when she came into the room.

"You're only *making* your father's prediction come true, Tom!" she cried, and he stopped, just froze where he stood, both hands holding a plate between them, ready to smash it to the floor. He looked at her with the eyes of a sleepwalker who's been awakened on a street corner, lowered his hands slowly. The plate slipped from his fingers and landed with a dull clap without breaking. He went on staring at her, looking confused.

"You don't have to be the failure he always said you'd be," she said softly. "Not unless you *want* to be. It's up to you. You know I have faith in you, Tom, but you're sick now. You have…an illness. We need to work hard to make you well. Then you can prove your father wrong."

He dropped to his knees then, embraced her legs, and sobbed, "How did you know? How did you know?"

After a hot meal, when he was feeling better, she told Tom how she knew about his father, a brutal alcoholic who'd never held a job for more than two weeks, who'd beaten Tom and his mother relentlessly, but Tom especially. Tom the worthless sissy-boy who would never amount to anything. She told Tom how she knew, and that she'd never told anyone before in her entire life. It would be their little secret, just between them.

Although Tom went to the county hospital the next day and checked into the psychiatric ward—all of his own free will and with promises that he would be much better when he came out—he never quite recovered. The doctor gave him some pills upon his release, but Tom threw them away and became furious whenever Janine mentioned them. He said they made him tired, they didn't work, he didn't need them. He was fine, he said. And for a long while, he was. But over the years, the illness returned, because it had never left. It lolled just beneath his personality, behind his smile and his laugh, behind his eyes, underneath his incredible energy and enthusiasm, and occasionally it would bob to the surface like some bloated, purple, grinning corpse coming up from the bottom of a powerful river, and there would be a dark period of anger and silence and insomnia and drinking, and sometimes—not always, but sometimes—a period when Janine would have to go visit her parents or sister to keep from being beaten.

But Tom did manage to prove his father wrong. He'd made something of himself—of *both* of them. And he'd sacrificed their little secret to do it. It wasn't their little secret anymore.

«« — »»

"This is it, honey," Tom said, slipping his coat off as he plowed into the hotel room like a John Deere. He tossed his coat onto the bed and started pacing, back hunched, head lowered like a bull's, this way, that way, fists clenching, unclenching. "Did you hear what they said? They asked for us. By name!"

Hanging her coat in the closet, Janine admitted to herself that was certainly an interesting twist. She was not surprised by Tom's elation, but she knew it was a lie; of *course* the Bellingers had seen one of their books or articles, or caught them on *Sally Jessy Raphael.* But Tom no longer saw things the way she did.

"Tom, don't you think there's something different about this couple?" Janine asked, making herself a glass of icewater at the sink.

"You're damned right there is. They're gonna get us on the cover of *People* magazine, *that's* what's different about 'em."

"No, not just that business about the spirits asking for us by name. I mean them, the Bellingers themselves. Didn't you notice anything about them that was different from all the others?"

"Nope, 'fraid I didn't, sweetie," he said as he hefted a suitcase onto the bed. It was their prop case, a large Samsonite filled with religious icons, vials of holy water (blessed by a defrocked priest they knew back home), Catholic literature, and Bibles of every size, as well as copies of their books, videotapes of their talk-show appearances, and a scrapbook of newspaper and magazine articles and photographs of "haunted" and "possessed" houses and people they had helped.

"Well, I did. For one thing, they're not Catholic."

"So? That's not a crime. And besides, Evil doesn't care what religion you are or aren't, honey, you know that." He sorted through the contents of the open suitcase carefully.

"Have you ever known a *Protestant* to call us, Tom? *Ever?* Not to mention anyone who has no religion at all?"

He raised his head, cocked it to one side and frowned, as if he'd heard a sound he thought he should be able to identify but could not. "Well, no, not exactly. But," back to work, choosing icons from the case, placing them on the bed, "that doesn't mean anything. Remember that Florida couple?"

Janine remembered the Florida couple, all right. It had been the usual stuff—furniture moving, voices crying in the night, something that looked like blood gurgling up from the sink drains. But the feelings Janine had gotten from the family were *truly* frightening, especially from the teenage girl. Janine told Tom she didn't want to deal with those people, but Tom was quite taken with the case because the house had been a funeral home about eighty years ago and he was sure that would add the kind of color to the story that might get them noticed. So Janine had gone along with it. They'd performed their usual rituals, and minutes after they were done, the family said the house felt different already, and so did they, safer, cleaner, normal again, and they concluded that whatever had been tormenting them was gone, thanks to the Werners.

But Janine knew it was not gone, and she could tell that the silent girl who made eye contact with no one knew it as well. And as she left the house, Janine had given the girl a hug and—

—she got a glimpse of the real evil that lurked within the walls of that house. Daddy. Daddy, who had been touching the girl for as long as she could remember, touching and much worse, and when she could take it no longer and knew she was about to go screaming mad, the girl had gone to her priest for help, and the priest had done the same thing, just like Daddy, and somehow Daddy found out and he beat *her* for it and said they would never go to church again and they didn't, and Daddy still came to her room at night and whatever fragile, whole part of her she'd taken with her to the priest was shattered now because she had nothing left, inside or out, only Daddy Daddy Daddy—

—and Janine could not get away from that family fast enough. She'd cried on the plane all the way home, and she'd tried to tell Tom about it, but he wouldn't listen because the story was too good just the way it was, and it became their first successful book, got them on lots of talk shows and it was their first book to be made into a movie of the week. But Janine couldn't forget that girl, and months later she'd called the family, just to see how the girl was, because she had a feeling, a bad feeling. The girl had opened her own throat with a box cutter and had bled to death in her bed. Janine had not hugged a stranger since, and never would again.

Tom went on: "That Florida couple, they weren't Catholic when they called us. They'd left the church, didn't want anything to do with it. 'Course, they didn't mind having some holy water sprinkled around their house once their beds started floating, but technically, they weren't Catholics. So I guess the Bellingers aren't the first, are they?"

"What about their son?" she asked, ignoring his question, swallowing her frustration with a gulp of icewater. "They told us their son has a drug problem."

"Oh, you know these people, honey, *somebody* in the house is *always* doing drugs."

It always amazed her: One moment, he spoke of their work with the fervor of Van Helsing in pursuit of the Prince of Darkness, and the next he sounded as cynical as a veteran carnival barker. Over the years, the cynicism had been giving way slowly to the fervor.

"But they *told* us, Tom. You know they *never* tell us. The Bellingers offered the information."

"So they offered!" he snapped impatiently as he turned to her. "What's the big deal? What the hell *difference* does it make? This one's got a different angle to it, the demons are actually *asking* for us!"

She nodded, finished her water, then dumped the ice in the sink. She heard him sigh, felt his hands on her shoulders. When she looked into the mirror over the sink, he was looking at her over her shoulder.

"Sorry, honey," he said quietly. "I didn't mean to bark at you like that. It's just that an angle like this...it's really *good*. A house that's the gateway to hell...well, hey, you know, it could be our gateway to fame. The kind of fame that keeps slipping away from us, the real thing, sweetie."

She forced a smile. It took little effort after all these years. When she turned around, he kissed her. Then they got ready to go see the Bellingers.

«« — »»

Tom's fascination with her talent, when she'd first told him about it, had been comical, almost childlike. She'd found it amusing at first. Until he came across an article in the *National Inquisitor* about a family whose house was haunted. They wanted to move, the article said, but couldn't afford it at the moment, but living in the house had become nightmarish because of the sounds of a baby crying and the angry screams of a woman. Janine caught Tom reading the article over and over to himself, having read it aloud to her three times, and she could sense the idea forming in his mind, could feel it solidifying, until he finally told her what he wanted to do. She'd resisted at first, more adamantly than she would think of resisting today; she'd been young then, and so had her disapproval, young and strong. She reminded him it was their little secret, something private and hidden from the world, but he'd broken her down with his energy, enthusiasm, and optimism, then, finally, with his anger and fury. With his illness.

He called the haunted family in Walla Walla, Washington, told them about his wife's psychic powers, and offered her help in ridding their house of the offending spirits if they would only pay for travel expenses to and from and put them up in a hotel. Janine was sure Tom would be laughed at and hung up on, but the family accepted almost immediately and arranged for the flight the next day.

The allegedly haunted house was old and had once been very small, but a number of add-ons had been built over the years. When

Janine went through the front door, her insides shriveled. She quickly learned that she could see and hear things the others could not, and before long, she felt alone in the house, alone with its spirits. Before the afternoon was half over, Janine had communicated with the restless spirit of the woman who had been the first occupant of the house nearly one hundred years before. The woman's husband had not wanted a child, and when she gave birth to their first—and last—he'd drowned it in the sink. Not much later, she'd tried to kill her cruel husband, but had not been fast enough; he had killed her, the murder had been considered self-defense, and he'd lived a long and prosperous life. The woman's spirit would not rest until her baby had received a proper burial. Janine listened as the woman's distant, hollow voice spoke words the others could not hear, watched the woman's wavering, vaporous face, which the others could not see, as it twisted and bent in expressions of long-suffered pain that Janine could feel but the others could not.

Janine led the others down to the small root cellar and told them to dig up the dirt floor, where they found the scant remains of the infant's skeleton. The police were called, the *National Inquisitor* was back on the story in a heartbeat, and Tom and Janine were the center of attention. The baby's remains were buried in a cemetery, the supernatural activity in the house came to a halt, and the story not only made the cover of the *Inquisitor*, but AP and UPI as well. The tabloid paper hired Tom and Janine as full-time "paranormal investigators," and they were flown to "haunted" houses all around the country to report back to the paper.

The case in Walla Walla remained vivid in Janine's memory because, unlike every single other case they handled, it had been real. There had been a real haunting, a real spirit with a solid reason for its unrest. Everything after that had followed a specific pattern, right up to this particular case, the Bellingers...even though there were differences about the Bellingers that bothered her.

Tom and Janine wrote none of the articles for the *National Inquisitor*; they were all ghosted—Janine used to smile at the pun—just like everything else after that, from their articles for legitimate newspapers and magazines to their nineteen books, the covers of which credited them as the authors.

After four years as "paranormal investigators" for the *Inquisitor,* Tom and Janine had enough of a reputation to leave the paper and go ghost hunting on their own, which they did with some success. Their *Inquisitor* articles were compiled in a book, but they got only a fraction of the profits because the tabloid owned the rights. Tom brooded over that for months and vowed it would never happen again; they would own the rights to everything they did, everything they published. That was one of the reasons they were never able to work with the same ghostwriter twice, because the author was paid a very modest flat fee, no royalties. Along with the books came speaking engagements, first for small clubs and societies interested in the paranormal, later at junior colleges and, still later, universities. They told of their experiences, showed pictures of the houses they'd "cleaned," fielded questions about the behavior of evil spirits and warned their audiences against dabbling in the occult with ouija boards or tarot cards, which could possibly attract harmful supernatural activity. Over time, their audiences grew from six or eight blue-haired women gathered in a parlor to university auditoriums filled with everyone from unshakable believers to cold skeptics.

They made their first talk-show appearance six years after leaving the *Inquisitor,* on the *Merv Griffin Show,* and Merv kept making jokes about their work, getting laughs from the audience. One of the assistant producers had told them before the show that it would be a "light conversation" with a few jokes and some good-natured ribbing, but Tom was not prepared for all that laughter, and Janine was not prepared for his reaction. At first, she saw anger growing in Tom's eyes and feared an outburst right there on Merv's stage, with Steve Lawrence and Edie Gormé sitting to their right. As the laughter continued, Tom's anger was replaced by something akin to childlike pouting, but the sadness in his eyes was as real as tears and Janine thought she actually saw his lower lip quiver a couple of times. As Merv began to wind down for a commercial break, Tom launched into a quiet but impassioned speech about their work. Janine had never heard him speak so eloquently about anything, and Merv and the audience and Steve and Edie all fell silent as stones and listened as Tom told them that there was nothing funny about the work he and Janine did, because the people they worked with were hurting very badly, very deeply, their lives were in chaos because of forces not only beyond their control, but beyond anyone's complete understanding, beyond this *life,* and to laugh at that was to laugh at the pain and misery of innocent people who simply wanted their lives back, people whom Tom and Janine helped to heal, and just before he finished his speech there was a small, quiet break in his voice, a hitch of emotion. Then he bowed his head, and after a pause, the audience began to clap, applauding the compassionate, healing work of Tom and Janine Werner as the band began to play softly and Merv promised his viewers that he would be right back after a word from the people at Woolite. During the commercial, Merv was too busy having his makeup touched up to speak with the guests, but Steve leaned over and said to Tom, "That was beautiful, baby." It was during Tom's speech on the *Merv Griffin Show* that it had first showed itself—the fact that the line between the fantasy of their work and the reality of it was beginning to fade for Tom. But Janine thought nothing of it at the time, thinking it was just the showman in Tom coming out unexpectedly at the perfect moment. That very week, they received calls from six other talk shows, four regional and two national, and they had to get an agent. Tom used variations of his speech on the other shows; it was never as emotional, but always convincing, and the only time Tom ever mentioned it to Janine was to say that it probably had something to do with the increase in their book sales.

What had once been just between them, their little secret, had become a full-time career. They went from haunted house to haunted house, sold book after book, appeared on one talk show after another, and Janine avoided touching strangers any more than was absolutely necessary. But she kept smiling, and she nodded sagely when people told her and Tom of the horrible things happening in their homes, and she tried not to pay any attention to Tom's little talk-show speech, which he later incorporated into their lectures, because she knew the only thing they were *really* helping people to do was to sweep their twisted secrets, their *real* problems, further under the rug.

By 1970, business slowed way down. Apparently, people simply were not as interested in ghosts as they used to be. After all, with that party going on in Vietnam and with Nixon in the White House, scares were a penny a gross. But something happened that put their career back on its feet: *The Exorcist*. First the novel, then the movie. Then their phone began to ring at all hours with calls from parents who suspected their children were possessed by demons, from children who suspected their parents were possessed by demons, and from whole families being tormented by demons. Suddenly, ghosts were passé and Satan was the villain of the hour. That was when they had enlisted the help of their defrocked priest friend, Father Bill, who had his own flock of rebel followers who didn't care *what* the Vatican thought of him. Tom and Janine never asked Father Bill why he'd been defrocked, and he never offered the information. And Janine was careful never, ever to touch him, because she did not want to know. They were back in business, more popular than ever, and in the wake of *The Exorcist,* two of their books made the *New York Times* bestseller list, in both hardcover and paperback.

But nothing really changed. As far as Janine was concerned, they had simply recovered from a slump. Some of the words were different—demons instead of ghosts, which needed to be exorcised instead of released—and Father Bill accompanied them on some of their trips, performing exorcisms, blessing houses. And Janine kept smiling, telling the families of the evil presences she sensed in their homes—but never what she *really* sensed, never what she *really* felt as she walked through their bedrooms and bathrooms and kitchens. She never told Tom, either, because she'd tried before and it hadn't worked, so she just followed the game plan, played by the rules.

Many of the people they dealt with really believed they were being tormented by demons. Some even experienced actual poltergeist activity generated by adolescents in the family (she'd done a great deal of reading on the subject). They were all Catholic and took comfort in their icons, and while exorcising their homes or children or spouses of the minions of hell, the families often became emotional and wept copiously, and over the years a few people even fainted. But with the exception of that first experience in Walla Walla, what those people really wanted Tom and Janine to do was to put another big, case-hardened steel lock or two on the door behind which they hid their sins. While gathering fodder for their books and lectures and conversations with Merv Griffin and Mike Douglas, and later Jerry Springer and Montel Williams, Tom and Janine were performing a sort of reverse therapy for those families. It wasn't *real* therapy, because that was supposed to heal, to improve, and what they did was the exact opposite. Each family had a big, smelly elephant in the middle of the living room that they ignored, walked around and refused to look at—booze, drugs, beatings, incest, whatever—and Tom and Janine made them feel better by telling them that it wasn't an elephant at all, it was a *demon*, and it was bringing a piece of hell to their lives through no fault of their own. Tom and Janine threw a Halloween fright wig on the elephant, went through some prayers, maybe had Father Bill sprinkle some holy water on the furniture, wave a cross a few times, say a few things in Latin, and they made the elephant easier for the family to ignore, and much, much harder for outsiders to see. But the elephant remained there between the sofa and the television, shitting and pissing and stinking up the place with foul odors that only the families could smell, and then only if they *let* themselves.

Janine often thought that, although they worked under the titles of "Paranormal Investigators" or "Demonologists" or whatever title might be appropriate at the time, they were really in the insurance business…and they specialized in Elephant Coverage…

«« — »»

The Bellinger house was modest, simple, with a small yard and even a white picket fence. A few toys lay on the lawn. It was in the kind of old neighborhood in which the houses and yards were not identical to one another, a neighborhood once pristine but now rundown, with oaks and maples twisted and hunched with age, branches bare beneath the cloud-streaked autumn sky.

Jack Bellinger came out onto the porch as Tom and Janine walked up the front path, and greeted them with a weary half-smile as he led them inside. Tom carried a leather duffle bag slung over his right shoulder.

"The kids aren't here," Jack said, closing the door behind him. "Richie and Wendy are visiting friends, and J.J.…well, we told you about J.J. He's out. Somewhere."

Something was moving inside Janine. It had started the moment she walked through the door, as if her intestines were shifting, like a bucket of worms squirming over and around one another in a tight, writhing ball.

Delia came into the small, tidy living room, drying her hands on a dishtowel. "We used to keep track of him all the time, but now, with the things that've been going on here…with him being so—"

"You don't have to explain," Tom said, holding up a hand. "We understand, really. Right, honey?"

"Of course we do," Janine said, forcing a smile.

Jack said, "Well, take off your coats, make yourselves comfortable, please."

As they did so, Tom asked, "Anything happen recently?"

"Not today," Delia said.

"Have you noticed if things happen more often when the children are around?" Tom asked.

"Funny you should ask," Jack said. "We looked for that, seein' how it was Richie who first…noticed things. But no, things happen when they happen, whether the kids are around or not."

"I just finished brewing some coffee," Delia said, slapping the towel over her shoulder. "Can I get you some?"

Tom and Janine both accepted as they seated themselves on the sofa, and told Delia how they liked their coffee.

Jack moved toward a recliner, but remained standing, nervous. "I suppose you'll want a tour of the house, right?"

"Not exactly," Tom said. "Please, Jack, sit down, relax. We're not scientists. There's nothing formal about this. It's not like we're from *60 Minutes*."

Jack eased into the recliner.

Tom continued: "The way we do things is like this. Before you take us through the house, Janine likes to go through the place by herself, from room to room. Alone, and without anybody telling her anything about the place."

Jack cocked his head, birdlike. "Really? Well, I mean, y'know, that's fine if that's the way you do…whatever you do. But…why?"

"For impressions," Tom answered. "Psychic impressions."

Jack blinked a few times, but said nothing.

"You knew Janine is psychic, didn't you?"

"Oh." Jack chuckled softly. "No, no, like I said, we never heard of you before. We don't know anything about you. Nothing at all, really. We contacted you because the voices told us to."

"Okay, yes, I understand *that,* but, but—"

Janine pressed her knee against Tom's to let him know he was sounding a bit too harsh.

Tom pressed his lips together tightly, smiled, nodded once, licked his lips, and continued in a softer, gentler voice. "What I mean is, you had to look us up, right? I mean, you had to find out something about us before you could contact us, right?"

"Oh, no. The voices gave us your address and phone number." Jack looked apologetic. "Didn't we tell you that over lunch? I thought we did."

Acidic nausea began to ooze between the squirming, viscous tubes inside Janine.

"No, see," Jack continued, "the voices gave us your address and phone number and at first, we didn't know what it meant, y'know? Finally, we called—well, *I* called the number. I figured you'd hang up on me 'cause I didn't know who I was callin'. But when you answered—" He nodded to Janine "—I asked if you were Janine Werner and you said yes, and I just started tellin' you what was happening. So, no, I'm sorry, I didn't know you're psychic, Janine."

Janine suddenly felt an overwhelming urge to scream at the top of her lungs as the flesh over her back rippled like the surface of a disturbed pond, but Delia came in holding two mugs of coffee and placed them on the scuffed coffee table.

Delia said, "If you want more cream or sugar, just let me know, and I'll fix it. Be right back."

She hurried out and Janine looked at Tom as he lifted his mug to his lips. His brow was etched with deep lightning-bolt lines, all pointing downward in the middle, and his eyes were squinting in that way they did whenever he was worried about something.

Was it finally hitting him? Was it starting to sink in that something was different here? That this was something new, something they'd never dealt with before?

Janine looked away from her husband, lifted her mug of coffee and took a sip, hoping it would quell, with a great splash, the furious activity going on inside her.

In a moment, Delia returned with two more mugs. She handed one to Jack and took hers to the delicate-looking rocking chair that was separated from Jack's recliner by a round-topped wooden lamp table with two coasters, where each of them placed their mugs.

"I guess I'm coming in on the middle of this, huh?" Delia asked, smiling as wearily as Jack had earlier. "So...did I miss anything?"

No one responded for a long moment, and Janine began to get anxious, began to form a response in her mind, even opened her mouth and took a breath to speak. But Tom beat her to it.

Tom repeated what he'd just told Jack.

Delia's eyebrows rose and her smile fell away as she turned to Janine. "You're a...a psychic? Really?"

Janine nodded as she took another sip of her coffee, although it was making no difference in her guts.

"Oh," Delia said quietly. "I didn't know that. Well, we figured you'd want a tour of the place, okay? If that's how you do it, then go ahead and do it."

Tom turned to Janine and asked, "You feel anything yet, honey?"

Janine took another sip of coffee as thoughts spun and toppled in her mind, and all she could manage was: "I feel...discomfort. That's all. So far."

"All right, honey, well, why don't you just start on your little trip through the house. Take your coffee, if you want. I'll sit here and chat with Jack and Delia. You come back and tell us your impressions. When you're ready. Okay, honey?"

Janine stood slowly, as she tried to ignore the wiggly feeling in her knees. She pushed the ends of her mouth up as she said, "Yes, why don't I do that. You three just sit here and talk. I'll be back shortly." And then she left the room, still wearing her stiff, plastic smile.

The fear was everywhere. It was in every room, in every inch of the narrow hall, even in the bathroom. Fear and tension everywhere. Tearing into her like the claws of small rodents. Into her mind, her heart, her flesh.

And something else, everywhere she went in the house, every room, every step. A thick, moist blackness. A diseased molasses. A cancerous syrup. Clinging invisibly to everything, to the furniture, the walls, making her feet stick to the floor, a nightmarish slop that dripped from every surface around her.

Evil. It was evil, that's what it was. It was everywhere and it made her shake so much that she began to spill her coffee, and she finally abandoned the mug on top of the old, battered washing machine in the laundry room, where she encountered the door to the basement. She knew where the door led the moment she laid eyes on it, and she stood there staring at it for the longest of times. The old brass knob made her hand tingle when she touched it, and the old wooden door seemed very heavy when she pulled it open. Beyond the doorway, narrow wooden stairs disappeared into utter blackness.

Janine leaned forward, turning her head to the right, looking for a light switch. It was there. She flipped it. All the steps appeared before her, and a floor, and walls.

Every molecule in her body resisted, but she took the first step. Then the second. And then she was on her way down the stairs, and she was on the concrete floor, and she saw the posters on the wall— a few rock groups, two sexy female TV stars, a couple of comic-book heroes—and the beds, two beds, one made, one not; and two nightstands and two dressers, none matching, cluttered with the things of boyhood, and something else, something, something—

—evil. It moved through every part of her body. It made her

hair shift, made her cuticles itch, made her nipples shrivel into hard nubs. She turned around without hesitation and clasped the banister of the staircase with her right hand, ready to make her way back up quickly, when she heard the voice:

"Hello, Mrs. Werner. I'm so happy you could make it." The voice had a big smile in it.

Janine could not move. Her fingers clutched the wooden banister tightly, until her entire hand became numb. She had no control over her body. No matter how loudly her mind screamed at her body, nothing would move.

"We were beginning to think you would never show up," the voice said. It was a gentle voice, low and oh-so-well-modulated, like some radio announcer from a bygone era, a voice that did not fit into today, into now, perfectly smooth and friendly, so as to conceal the pustular, scabrous reality beneath it.

She couldn't even turn her head. That was all she had to do to see where the voice was coming from, just turn her head, although she knew—in her mind, she could *see*—where the voice was coming from, but she could not do it.

The voice continued: "This one isn't for the magazines, Mrs. Werner. Or the lectures. It's not for your talk-show appearances or your books. This one is just for *you*. For you and your husband."

Her hand trembled as she removed it from the banister.

"You seem troubled," the voice said quietly, pleasantly apologetic. "I'm very sorry about that, Mrs. Werner. You have no reason to be troubled right now. There is one thing, though. Your husband is not here. We need both of you to be here."

Her legs trembled beneath her, threatened to send her to the floor in a heap.

"And please do not take this personally, Mrs. Werner. We are simply following orders. We are following orders from…well, a higher office, so to speak."

Her feet managed to move haltingly over the concrete floor in such a way as to turn her body slowly to the right, toward the boys' bedroom, toward the beds and the nightstands and the dressers…and the voice.

"Like your husband and yourself," the voice said, "we are simply doing...what we do. This is our work. You have yours...we have ours. As far as we're concerned, you have been doing wonderful work, absolutely tremendous. For *our* cause. But there are others who...well, you've had some religious training, so...you understand how things work. We have a boss. But, unfortunately, our boss has to answer to Someone Else. That Someone Else...well, His orders are the ones we are now following. You understand, don't you?"

She tried to move faster, but her body seemed to be trapped underwater, and she turned slowly, so very slowly. But she did turn, and she saw him, the source of that voice, standing there between the beds, where he had not been just an eternal moment before, tall and thin in his black suit, spotted with dust and cobwebs, his white shirt beneath the suitcoat spotted with disgusting stains, hoary hands locked before him at the waist, a stick-like, vein-threaded neck seeming to barely hold up his head, which was bald except for a few yellow tufts of hair, with big ears sticking out on the sides and eyes swallowed so deeply in their sockets that they were little more than shadows as his paper-thin lips curled into a smile, nearly splitting his narrow, hollow-cheeked face in half as it revealed long, brown teeth that had no gums. She saw him, but she knew in her heart that he wasn't really there, that if Tom were there he would not be able to see the man, because the man had the substance of a shadow, a flat shape that could not be touched with human fingers, that was real even though it did not *quite* exist.

"Could you please call your husband?" the thing asked.

And Janine screamed. She stumbled backward until she slammed against the wall, screaming and screaming.

She heard movement upstairs, the hurried footsteps and the yammering voices. But the thing between the beds continued to smile at her, standing as if at attention, as if it were the maitre d' of a four-star restaurant greeting a customer, while the concrete floor began to open up. It opened as a mouth opens, dry lips spreading, clinging for a moment in spots, parting, yawning open silently to reveal a darkness that was darker than dark, a blackness that released a draft so cold that Janine felt her scalp shrink and her throat tighten. It was a darkness like no other, a darkness that lived and breathed and hungered.

There was a thunderous sound to Janine's left and she jerked her head to see Tom leading Jack and Delia down the stairs, all three of them moving rapidly.

Janine held up a hand at them and forced a smile, trying to control her panic and fear. "No, wait. Just Tom. You two stay upstairs. Please." She wasn't in the mood for the explanations she would have to give them. "Everything's fine, we'll be up in a minute, you just go on, now."

When Jack and Delia were gone, Janine's smile collapsed and Tom clutched her arms, speaking to her breathlessly. "Honey, what's wrong, what's the matter?"

She didn't look at Tom. She stared instead at the tall, bony man behind him and the gaping hole in the floor, at the pulsating blackness beneath it. She put her hands on Tom's chest and gasped, "We have to go, Tom. This is n-n-not like the others, not at all, we're in trouble, it's finally happened, everything we've ever done, it-it's all come back on us, Tom, we're—"

He shook her gently, his face dark with worry. "Sweetie, what's wrong, what're you talking about?"

She stopped talking and fought to catch her breath, closed her eyes a moment, then whispered, "Tom, I want you to…turn around very slowly…and tell me what you see."

He turned, but not slowly. His eyes scanned the room, passing right by the tall figure and never even glancing at the hole in the floor. When he looked at her again, his eyes were worried but he wore a gentle smile. "Did you see something? I mean, *really* see something down here?"

Janine watched as the cadaverous man tilted his head back slightly and chuckled.

"You don't see him at all, do you?" she asked, clutching at Tom's shirt.

He glanced over his shoulder one more time, then: "Are you feeling okay, honey? You wanna come back and do this later?"

Then the tall man across the room began to walk toward them, taking long, purposeful strides.

"We have to go, Tom, please, my God, we have to go!" She began tugging on his shirt as she moved toward the stairs, trying to drag him with her, but Tom put his hands on her shoulders and pressed her back against the wall.

"Janine, would you please tell me what's the matter?" he said, rather firmly.

As she watched the grinning figure walk over the large black hole as if it weren't there, her voice became high and ragged: "Tom, upstairs, go upstairs, we've got to go upstairs and get out!"

The man reached out a bony hand as he approached Tom from behind, long fingers curving slightly as he lowered it over Tom's shoulder, and Janine's voice became louder, more frantic, as the hand touched Tom's shoulder and sank into it, disappearing like vapor, and Tom's body stiffened suddenly. His mouth dropped open, eyes bugged, shoulders hunched, and both hands slapped over his massive chest.

"Oh God...oh God," he said, the words barely making it beyond his throat. And then he fell backward, passing through the grinning apparition and hitting the concrete floor with a horrible, thick sound. His chest heaved a couple of times, then he made a rattly gurgling sound...and he became still.

The tall man grinned gumlessly at Janine as she fell to her knees at Tom's side and screamed, "Oh my God, no, no! Tom! *Tom!*"

"Perhaps you should have tried to get him to eat right, maybe exercise," the man said with mock concern. "But then...you prefer not to get involved. Don't you, Janine?"

"Help! Jack, help, please!"

A moment later Jack clattered down the wooden stairs and didn't hesitate to kneel beside Tom and begin administering CPR.

Janine watched as Jack performed mouth-to-mouth, then pumped Tom's chest, back and forth between the two. Every inch of her body grew numb until she could no longer feel herself breathing, and for a moment, she thought she'd stopped. And all the while, standing a few inches away from Tom's head, looking down on it all, was that gaunt, smiling figure. Waiting. For something.

"It's not working," Jack said tremulously, face glistening with perspiration. Over his shoulder, he called, "Delia? *Delia!*" After a moment: "Dammit, she can't hear me. She was afraid, so she stepped outside. Look, Janine, I want you to stay right here. I'm going to call an ambulance and I'll be back in just a second."

Jack turned and rushed up the stairs noisily as Janine leaned over her husband. She knew the ambulance would never arrive in time, because it was already too late. There was no life left in the fleshy bulk on the floor. She reached down and placed a numb hand over his as her tears began to flow, and for that moment, brief as it was, she forgot all about the figure watching her, until:

"Janine."

She looked up slowly, not wanting to see that face again but unable to ignore that icy voice.

"I finally have the two of you together," he said. "It's time."

Sudden movement caught Janine's attention and she looked around the tall man to see hands. They were reaching up out of the impossibly black hole and grabbing hold of the edge, pulling, struggling. Then faces began to rise above the edge of the hole. Familiar faces. Horribly familiar.

The face that rose above the edge of the hole first was the most familiar, but Janine recognized all of them. They were all naked, the women and children…toddlers and teenagers…even a few wide-eyed little babies, pulling themselves up onto the floor with their tiny, pudgy hands.

It was that first girl—the one from Florida whose father had molested her for years until she went to her priest for help, only to receive the same treatment from him—who got to her feet before the others and looked directly into Janine's eyes.

They said nothing; they did not make a sound as they stood and moved forward, the babies crawling without so much as a whimper, and they were led by that girl from Florida, whose name Janine could not remember, but whose face—and whose pain—had haunted her for years.

Janine could not speak. She could only look silently and in horror from one face to another, faces she recognized from cases she and Tom had handled: women whose husbands had beaten them, children whose fathers had beaten them, or molested them; people who had buried their problems beneath tales of supernatural torment and demonic possession, stories of their children being beaten and sodomized by evil spirits and invisible demons.

They closed in slowly but steadily, with great purpose, the Florida girl stopping at Janine's side and staring down at her with an expressionless face while the others gathered around Tom. They leaned forward silently and clutched his arms and legs, his clothes, his head, and began to drag him toward the black, hungry hole. The only sound was that of Tom's body being moved over the concrete floor.

"No!" Janine finally blurted, standing suddenly. "What are you doing? Leave him alone!"

They ignored her and continued dragging her husband's corpse away from her.

"Wait! What are you doing? Where are you taking him?"

The tall, cadaverous man chuckled as he watched the silent, naked figures, then turned to her, his lips peeling back over his long teeth again. "Surely, Janine, you don't think we're only taking your husband, do you? You see, the higher-ups—and when I say that, I do mean *higher,* and I do mean *up*—have ordered us to take you both."

The women and children, even the babies, had reached the hole, and Tom's head hung limply backward over the edge as they continued pulling him, pulling, slowly tipping him into the blackness.

When Janine spoke, her voice was less than a whisper. It was all she could manage, as if she were in one of those smothering, paralyzing nightmares in which movement and speech are impossible. "What...are you talking...about?"

"Well, Janine, you must admit that you are not without guilt in this particular venture to which you and Tom have devoted your lives, am I correct?"

She felt sick, like she might throw up any second. "Please...no," she breathed.

"Not only have you been the driving force," the man went on in his bone-dry voice, "but you've been turning the other cheek like a good Christian, am I right? Yes, you've been turning that cheek...and with it, a blind eye. To all of it. That's why, unlike your husband, you aren't dead right now, Janine."

She watched helplessly as Tom's body slid into the hole, his feet tipping upward, then disappearing into the pulsing darkness.

The Florida girl took Janine's arm in her hand and tugged. Janine jerked her arm away, but the girl simply took it again, her face dead, completely without expression. She tugged on Janine's arm again, harder this time, as the others—the naked women and children and silent infants who had just thrown Tom into that gaping hole—turned and moved toward her, reaching out their hands for her, taking her hands, her arms and legs, tugging, pulling her toward the hole.

"You're not dead because we wanted to make sure you couldn't ignore this," the man said, "as you've ignored so many other things over the years."

"No," she breathed, over and over again, "no, please, no."

She did not have the strength to fight them, even though they were not forceful. She was simply drained of any resistance. And in a moment, she stood at the edge of that hole, staring down into its endless darkness, and then—

—she was plunging downward with their hands on her, holding her arms, her legs, dragging her down as they tilted and spun through the blackness, spinning, spinning.

Janine wanted to scream, but she could not get the scream outside of her body; it went no farther than her gut, no farther than the inside of her head, where it went on and on and on.

She saw the hole above her as she fell away from it, glimpsed the basement ceiling through it, as it closed like a mouth at the end of a yawn.

And the hands did not let go, big hands, small hands, tiny hands, and she looked to her right to see the Florida girl, still expressionless. But the others...the others...

The women and children were gone. They were no longer even

human. Their leathery faces grinned at her around needle-like fangs, and their bat-like wings flapped softly as they dragged her down, farther and farther down, into a darkness that became steadily colder, until it was so cold that Janine feared that breathing the air would freeze her lungs and make them break like ice.

She tried to scream, but her voice was gone, as was any strength that had remained in her a moment before.

Farther and farther down...

«« — »»

"I'm telling you, they were here, right *here,* just a few *minutes* ago!"

"Well, they're not here now," the paramedic said to Jack, flatly. He looked angry.

"But they couldn't have *gone* anywhere!"

The second paramedic said, "Look, buddy, do you know how much trouble you can get into for making a call like this? On false pretenses?"

"It wasn't on false pretenses!" Jack insisted, frustrated. "The guy was lying on the floor, *dead!* I tried CPR, but it didn't work!"

"Maybe he got up and went to the hospital himself," the first paramedic said sarcastically.

Jack was too angry to respond.

The two paramedics started back up the stairs.

"Maybe," the second one said, "they were ghosts."

From that moment on, the Bellingers experienced no further supernatural activity in their house, and after a time, they never brought it up again.

Myiasis

The best thing about the maggots in Kit Shepherd's neck was that he could not feel them. As long as the dressing was on, he could not see them, either, which was fine, because he did not care to look at them. He did not complain about them because they were, after all, eating the malignant tumor on his neck, eating the spot clean and possibly saving his life. But that did not mean he had to watch them do it. He had seen maggots at work once, and that was enough.

Thirty years ago, when Kit was ten years old, his scruffy, Brillo-haired mutt Theodore, Theo for short, disappeared one hot August day. He figured the dog had gotten carried away chasing a squirrel into the woods behind the house, but when Theo didn't show up the next day, Kit went looking for him. He found his dog lying dead in a ditch beside the busy road on the other side of the woods, ripped open and crawling with maggots in the hot summer sun. Theo had been run over, of course, but at first, Kit had thought all those puffy white worms squirming around his poor dog's exposed intestines were responsible. It was something only a kid could think, but it stayed with him, even after he knew better, as if the thought had laid an egg in his mind, where it incubated nicely.

That egg hatched when Dr. Radnitch said he wanted to put a few maggots in Kit's tumor to eat it away. In a vivid flash, Kit saw Theodore lying there in that ditch as maggots—having killed him from the inside out, Kit assumed—ingested his rotting guts. It was not an association he could shake easily, but when Dr. Radnitch explained that maggots could remove the tumor more thoroughly than any scalpel, and that maggot surgery would leave less scarring and greatly decrease the chances of any recurrence, he forced himself. Kit figured Theo would understand.

Against his doctor's wishes, Kit drove to work the day after the maggots had been put into the tumor on his neck. Dr. Radnitch had told him to stay home and rest, take it easy. But sitting around the house during the day made Kit restless and irritable. He was a creature of habit and needed to drop by the store for awhile, if only to check the mail.

The oval, green-and-white F&H Furniture sign was visible long before he reached the store. It rotated slowly atop a tall, white steel pole that had stood in that parking lot since Kit had been a boy. His first job had been loading furniture onto and off of trucks in back of the store when he was seventeen. All that lifting had made him muscular, an added perk, and it was those muscles that had caught the eye of Marla Hendrie, who would become his wife. Eight years later, he was manager. At forty-two, Kit had been a partner in the eight-store chain for almost five years. It was a much easier job than lifting furniture. He traveled often on the job—sometimes he was able to take Marla and the kids—and the pay was far superior. But oh, how he missed having those muscles.

The store where Kit had worked since high school had been the first in the chain. Gordon Fikes, Kit's partner and the "F" in F&H, spent most of his waking hours in his Mercedes, driving up and down the line of eight stores, from Kit's in Napa, California, to the one in Seattle, Washington, and all six in between. Gordo never flew. When asked why, all he would say was, "Because I just don't, okay?" And he did not, ever. His former partner, Bernie Hinkerman, had done all the flying before dying of liver cancer almost six years ago. Since being taken on as a partner, Kit had been doing any flying that needed to be done. In emergencies, Gordo would give him a call and he would get on a plane, fly to one of the stores or the central warehouse, and put out whatever fire had caught on enough to get Gordo's attention.

Kit drove around to the rear of the store, parked in his spot. The green and white F&H logo was on the side of the eighteen-wheeler that had backed into the nearest slot at the loading bay. The second

Kit opened the car door, he heard Mickey's mule-like laugh. The boy stood beside the truck, talking to the driver. Mickey stopped when he saw Kit and his mouth dropped open farther than usual.

"Hey, Kit!" he shouted, surprised.

Kit smiled and waved at the boy, then went inside, past the manager's office, and upstairs to his own office. He peeked between the curtains drawn over the long window that looked out on the main showroom. The parking lot out front was scattered with cars, but the store seemed oddly quiet, almost deserted. Except for Mickey's braying laugh, which bawled up the stairs ahead of him.

The boy was probably laughing at a foul joke someone had told him. The guys in the back and the truckers who made regular deliveries were always telling Mickey dirty jokes, teaching him limericks, giving him dirty magazines. Mickey was 18, a troubled boy who had grown up in group homes and with a string of foster parents, hampered by a childhood of severe abuse and various learning disabilities.

"On top of that, he's a little slow," Kit's brother-in-law Dale had said when he was trying to convince Kit to hire Mickey. "But he's eager, and he learns fast. He's loyal, and a hard worker. He just needs a little encouragement."

Dale was Kit's wife's younger brother, and Marla thought he could do no wrong. It was risky to say anything less than laudatory about Dale within earshot of Marla, and on more than one occasion, she had told Kit she wished he were more like her little brother. Kit had nothing against his brother-in-law personally. Dale worked at Head Start and immersed himself in his work with unfortunate teens, as well as other assorted causes and charities. He lived like a hermit and had little, if any, social life. Kit liked him, even admired him for his selflessness. Dale was a giver, one of that small group of people who focus their entire lives on the welfare of others, even derive pleasure from it. But in the process of living a selfless, giving life, Dale did his share of taking, too—like roping his friends and relatives into donating their money and time to his causes; into hiring, and sometimes even taking into their homes, members of his group of lost kids. It was a group that only continued to grow with time, and some of its members were as dangerous as they were troubled.

Slivers of Bone

"Lemme see it, lemme see it," Mickey said as he lumbered into the office. His big, lopsided grin revealed small teeth spaced apart. He had a single bushy eyebrow that ran all the way across the ridge above his eyes. Muscular, with a mustache half as thick as his eyebrow, and black hair that Mickey apparently cut himself with the aid of a cereal bowl.

Kit chuckled as he dropped the curtain and went to his desk. He lowered himself into his chair and smiled up at Mickey. "Can't take the dressing off, Mickey," he said.

Mickey's grin melted away. "Y'can't?" He went to Kit's desk, looked down at his boss forlornly from his height of six feet and four-and-three-quarter inches. "Y'can't even for a second?"

"Not even for a second."

"How come?"

When Dale had called Mickey "a little slow," he had been very kind. While he was good-natured and eager to please, Mickey had a head full of gravel. Kit was not quite sure if the boy was retarded or just stupid. He was leaning toward a mental deficiency of some kind.

Kit laughed as he picked up a stack of mail and went through it slowly. "If I took the dressing off, they'd fall out."

Mickey's eyes became round beneath his furrowed brow. "They *would*?" he asked as he bent down to get a closer look at the dressing. "They're in there now, them things?"

"Why would you want to see them, Mickey? Even *I* don't want to see them. They're disgusting."

Half of the boy's mouth curved up as he said, "That's why I wanna see 'em—'cause they're disgusting!" He guffawed. "C'mon, Kit, can'tcha take it off for justa second? Just lift it up a little on one side, thassall, know what I mean?"

Everyone at the store liked Mickey. He was a likeable guy. He had a great pair of arms and a strong back when a shipment came in, if he did not get distracted by something else. The problem was, Kit had already had plenty of men working in the back when he had hired Mickey to get his nagging, bleeding-heart brother-in-law off his back.

Kit knew Mickey's muscles wouldn't get him far in life. The

boy could not focus on one task for very long, and he kept forgetting to take the medication that was supposed to correct that problem (and God only knew what *that* was doing to him). Mickey spent little time at the store hefting furniture around, and when he did, he usually did it in a slow, distracted way. Most of his time was spent wandering around in the back, laughing at dirty jokes and fetching junk food for other employees from the 7-11 down the street, or the four fast-food joints up the street. Mickey usually showed up at the store on his days off, too, apparently happy to hang around, shoot the breeze, and make Chalupa runs for free.

Why do I have him on the payroll? Kit thought. It was a sudden, forceful thought that made him blink a few times and stare blindly at the mail for a moment. *Is it really just to shut Dale up? To get him off my neck? My neck? My neck.*

Kit realized he was staring at a large, colorful piece of junk mail—something about business website management—in one hand, while he scratched at the dressing on his neck with the other.

Mickey was laughing, and the upper half of his tall body bobbed up and down as he clapped his hands. "Oh, cool! Y'gonna take it off? Yeah, *cool!*"

Todd walked into the office then, the store's manager. Impeccably dressed in a gray suit, burgundy tie, his short blond hair perfectly in place. One eyebrow rose high on Todd's forehead as he watched Mickey hop from one foot to the other and back, like a little boy with a full bladder.

Kit hardly noticed either of them, because it was itching, the tumor was itching. Or was that a slight tingling sensation he felt beneath the dressing?

Squirming, he thought. *More like a squirming sensation.*

"You won't even know they're there," Dr. Radnitch had said. "They do not eat living tissue. They're not interested. They will only consume the malignancy and keep it from spreading. Don't worry, you won't feel a thing. With the dressing on, you'll forget all about the little fellas."

It was just an itch, nothing more. An itch beneath the dressing, perhaps an irritation caused by the tape. He lowered his hand.

"Aw, c'mon, Kit," Mickey said with a long groan. He slammed both beefy hands flat on the desktop and leaned forward. "I thought you were gonna—"

Kit looked up at the boy and said, "Mickey? You're fired."

Todd's breath caught audibly in his throat.

Mickey froze in that position—hands on the desk, leaning toward Kit—and stared at Kit for a long moment. His goofy grin quivered and melted away, and the center of his eyebrow slowly rose on his forehead. He stood up gradually and his broad shoulders sagged.

"Well, I-I-I'm sorry, Kit," he said. "I didn't mean t'make you mad. I only wanted t'see the—"

"Oh, no, no, Mickey, it's not that," Kit said. He smiled. "I'd show you the maggots if I could, really, but I can't take the dressing off because I don't know how to put it back on. They do that at the doctor's office. So, I was serious, see, when I said I can't take it off."

"Oh." The sadness on Mickey's face tensed into a confused frown for a few seconds. "Oh. Okay." The grin reconstructed itself. "So, like, you were joking. Right?"

"No, I'm afraid not, Mickey. I'm going to have to let you go."

"Whuh...what? I'm really fired?"

"I didn't have any openings when I took you on," Kit said, "but I thought I'd be able to work something out. I was wrong."

Mickey took a small step backward. "So...I'm fired."

"If we have an opening, I'll let you know, I promise. I'm sorry, Mickey."

He took another step backward. Looked as if he were about to say something, but only continued to frown silently. Welling tears sparkled in his eyes.

"Let me take you to lunch, Mickey. We can go to Lucy's Café, or—"

Mickey spun around and hurried out of the office, pulled the door closed hard on the way out.

Todd stared at Kit with slightly widened eyes beneath a frown. "Was that...necessary?"

"Yep."

"But I thought the whole point of hiring him was to give him a—"

"Yes, I know what the point was. He's worked here three months, when I really shouldn't have taken him on in the first place."

"That's too bad. He's a good kid."

"Yes, he is. But he's just dead weight around here. How about you?"

Todd flinched. "What about me what? Am *I* dead weight around here?"

"Lunch, how about you, can I take you to lunch?"

"Oh." He sounded relieved. "Yeah, sure. My break's in an hour."

"Meet me at Celedon," Kit said as he stood. He left the office and looked around for Mickey. Morton, one of the brawnier of the workers, sat on a large crate and opened his paper bag lunch.

"Have you seen Mickey?" Kit asked.

"He left," Morton said. "Looked upset, too. Ran outta here like he was bein' chased. Not sure, but I think he mighta been cryin'. Is the kid okay?"

Fine, Kit thought as he went out onto the loading dock, hopped down to the pavement, and got back into his car. *That makes it easier on both of us.*

«« — »»

When Kit got home that afternoon, Marla was on her knees in the front yard, tending the flowers she had planted around the edge of the lawn. Twenty years married, and seeing her there in blue shorts and a white halter top, blond hair pulled back in a ponytail, stirred him. She still had a nice shape, although she was plumper these days. Kit did not mind—he had been surprised to find that the extra padding beneath Marla's velvety skin was an erotic luxury in bed.

She turned and waved as he got out of the car. "There's chicken salad in the 'fridge!" she called across the lawn.

He waved back, nodded. "Nice ass."

She wiggled it as she went back to work.

In the house, Kit went to the computer in the den and ran a search on Yahoo! for "maggot surgery." He found himself on the Home Page of the Maggot Therapy Project. A cartoon maggot, wearing a long white coat, a stethoscope around its "neck," and a patient's chart tucked under its "arm," stood upright in the page's upper left corner. Kit scanned the page, and followed links to some other pages, looked over those, too. In a couple of minutes, he had the printer spitting the pages into a tray for him.

Kit took the printed pages to the kitchen and made himself a chicken salad sandwich, grabbed a Coke from the refrigerator. Went out on the redwood deck that overlooked the swimming pool, sat at a round white table beneath a large blue-and-white umbrella with fringe, and read.

"You're not working, are you?" Marla asked as she climbed the steps to the deck a few minutes later.

"No, this isn't work."

"What are you reading?" She removed her dirty work gloves, tossed them on the table. Passed the back of her hand over her shiny forehead and removed her round, white-rimmed sunglasses. They revealed pale circles around her eyes that stood out on her tanned face.

"You look like a raccoon," Kit said.

"Oh. Any good? Who wrote it?"

Smiling, he stood and went to her as she rubbed her sweaty hands on her dirty shorts. Put his arms around her waist and squeezed the round cheeks of her ass as he pulled her to him.

"I'm reading about my new pets," he said. "Did you know that the maggot is the wounded soldier's best friend on the battlefield?"

She put her arms around his neck. "Next to the medic, I would think."

"Well, sure, but still, they're the next best thing. Pretty handy little buggers to have around."

"They haven't bothered you at all?"

Kit thought, for just an instant, of the tingling—

Squirming?

—sensation he had felt beneath the dressing earlier. Maybe he had imagined it. From what Dr. Radnitch had told him, and from what he had read, it was impossible to feel the maggots at work, so that had to be it.

"Nope," he said, "not a bit."

She glanced at the pages on the table. "Any pictures?"

"Yeah, but I didn't look at them. If I want to see that, all I have to do is take off the dressing and look in the mirror."

"Don't you *dare* take that dressing off," she said, tweaking his ear and wrinkling her nose. "I don't want to find any of those things crawling around the house."

It was obvious to Kit that Marla had not talked to Dale yet. Her mood was too sweet, her fingers too gentle as they moved through his hair.

He kissed her slowly, then said, "Let's go upstairs and knock some sense into each other."

Marla laughed. "I need a shower. And the kids could be home anytime now."

"Where are they?"

"Peter's at the movies and Emily went to get her hair done with Carmen."

Kit sighed. "I'm telling you, Mar, we've got to do something about that. She keeps hanging out with Carmen DePalma and she's going to end up in juvie. We'll all wind up on *Cops*."

"I talked to her once. That used to be enough."

Kit's voice lowered slightly when he asked, "What about Geoff?"

Marla dropped her eyes briefly. "Haven't seen him. There've been no calls."

"Forget the shower. Let's do it dirty."

Laughing again, she said, "Can't it wait till tonight? What's your hurry?"

The telephone trilled inside the house.

That, Kit thought, *was my hurry*.

"I'll get it," she said, then hurried inside.

When she came back out a few minutes later, Kit was chewing the last bite of his sandwich. Before he turned to look at her, before he heard her speak, he knew her sweet mood was gone. He had no doubt it had been Dale on the phone.

"I can't believe you fired Mickey," Marla said as she sat across from him at the table. She looked and sounded the way she always did at the end of a sad movie.

"I had no choice. I kept him on three months, I think that was pretty generous considering we didn't need him. There's nothing for him to do."

"Dale says he's inconsolable."

"What the hell does Dale have to be inconsol—"

"Not Dale, *Mickey*."

"Oh. Then Dale's not doing his job. He's supposed to be preparing these kids for real life, warts and all. Well, I guess this makes me a wart, and I think I've been a pretty nice wart, so if Mickey can't handle me, then Dale's not doing his job."

Marla looked at him as if he had just suggested he get his .22 rifle and start shooting all the neighborhood's stray cats.

Kit straightened his back, arched a brow. "What? Why are you looking at me like—"

"I thought you liked Mickey."

"Oh, I do. I think Mickey's a great kid, he's—look, let's have him over for dinner tonight, okay? It's got nothing to do with how I feel about Mickey. I fired him because I didn't have a choice."

"I already invited him over. But Dale says he won't come."

Kit raised his voice slightly when he asked, "Who the hell cares what Dale says? What's he got to do with this? I'll call Mickey and invite him myself."

"Dale says Mickey's not coming to the phone, he lets the—"

"Well, screw Dale. We'll cut out the middle man, okay? I'll drive over and pick Mickey up if I have to."

"He had a lot of respect for you, Kit. He thought the world of you."

"Honey, I fired him. I didn't kill him."

"Why? Couldn't you—"

"No, I couldn't, there's no place for him at the store, how many times do I have to say it? Why are you so upset about this?"

Marla sighed. Her fingers fidgeted with each other on the tabletop. "I'm not upset. Just a little surprised, I guess. It's so unlike you."

Kit frowned. "It is?"

"You bent over backwards to squeeze Mickey in at the store." She smiled. "You're always doing that sort of thing, helping Dale's kids. You're very generous."

"That's very sweet of you to say, but did it ever occur to you that I might be helping Dale's kids just to get Dale off my back?"

Marla's mouth dropped open and she stared at him like that for a moment, as if she were experiencing a painful yawn.

Kit was relieved to hear their daughter Emily's voice in the house, rapidly growing louder, closer. He recognized Carmen DePalma's shrieking laugh. His conversation with Marla would have to continue later. Much later, he hoped. He felt too good to go on talking about Mickey and Dale.

The girls ran up on the deck, Emily threw her arms open wide, and they shouted together, *"Tah-daaaah!"*

"Oh my God," Marla said.

That morning, Emily's hair had been long and full, just like her mother's but a darker blonde. The boys favored Kit, but Emily was nearly identical to Marla at sixteen. It was easy to confuse snapshots of Emily with snapshots of her mother in high school.

Her hair had been chopped off and was short and spiky. And hot pink, with a metallic sheen.

Marla stood slowly. "You look like you should be working in a circus."

The girls laughed as they exchanged a secret look of anticipation, then laughed some more. They enjoyed Marla's shock as she approached Emily.

Kit told himself it was no big deal, the kind of harmless, stupid thing kids do simply because they're kids. Maybe pink hair was in vogue that summer. But he could tell by her rigid posture that Marla was not taking it quite as well.

"You're not leaving this house until that's washed out," she said. "And I mean *all* of it, do you underst—" Marla dragged air into her lungs with a loud gasp of shock. "Is that a piercing in your nose?" She spoke quietly—Marla did not raise her voice when she was angry, she became ominously quiet—but the words gushed from her mouth so rapidly, they bumped into each other.

Kit stood and went to Marla's side, saw the tiny sparkling stud in the left side of his daughter's nose. Carmen had a small silver ring in hers, but it had been there for months. He glared at his daughter's friend for a moment—long enough for her smile to dissolve—then turned to Emily and said, "I thought we had a talk about this."

Emily sucked her lips between her teeth to suppress a smile. She tried to hold back her laughter, but it snorted out, anyway. She shook her head several times, then finally said, "No. No, we didn't. Not about this."

Looking at Carmen again, he said, "I suppose you didn't have anything to do with this."

"Hey, don't look at *me*," she said. A second later, she giggled.

"What's next for you two? Gonna put plates in your lips and pose for the centerfold of *National Geographic*?" Without taking his eyes from Emily's, Kit said, "Marla, why don't you take Carmen home, and when you get there—"

"Hey, *wait* a second!" Emily said. Her smile was gone.

"—explain to Mrs. DePalma that Carmen and Emily will no longer be spending time together and that we would appreciate her cooperation in this."

Emily cried, "Daad!" She dragged the word out and gave it two long, whining syllables.

"I think that's a good idea," Marla said. "Let's go, Carmen."

Carmen looked confused and turned. Emily, who stepped toward Kit and, angry and near tears, said, "Dad, you can't just kick her out like this! What do you *mean* we can't spend time together anymore? Carmen's my best friend!"

Kit noticed something odd about the way Emily talked. As if she had something in her mouth, or had burned her tongue biting too soon into a hot pizza. But Kit knew it was neither of those things.

"Open your mouth," he said.

Emily shot a glance at Carmen. "Dad, please don't make her go home and—"

"Open your mouth."

She turned away from him a moment, groaning.

Marla said, "Do as he says, Emily."

When Kit saw the silver ball nestled in the cup of his sixteen-year-old daughter's tongue, he had to take a deep breath and dampen his swelling anger before speaking again. "We did talk about this," he said.

Emily shook her head, smiled. "It was tattoos. You said you didn't want me to get any tattoos." Her eyes narrowed to glimmering slits and her smile widened.

"Tattoos, piercings, it's all self-mutilation," Kit said. He returned her smile. "You knew how we'd feel about it, and you did it anyway. Right?"

Her smile faltered, but only a little.

"Isn't that right?"

"Well…" She shrugged.

"But the tongue…that's more than just a piercing."

With a nervous glance at Carmen, she asked, "Whatta you mean?"

"You know what I mean. You're just surprised that I know it, huh? You didn't think your mom or I would know something like that, did you?"

Another nervous glance, a little longer this time. Looking at Kit, she screwed her face into a forced look of confusion. "What?"

Kit stepped closer to her and said, "It's for oral sex, Emily—"

Marla made an abrupt hiccupping sound, as if her surprised gasp got caught in her throat. Emily's mouth dropped open and she made a series of breathy, "*Ah! Ah! Ah!*" sounds, her eyes open to their limit.

"—and you know it, so don't play dumb. Did you do that for one guy in particular, or for the guys in general?"

"*Kit!*" Marla shouted as her arm swung out and she landed a loud backhanded slap on his upper arm. "That's not going to help."

Still smiling at Emily, Kit said, "Take those things out of your nose and tongue and put them on the kitchen counter. Then get in the shower and start working on that hair."

"Dad, I can't take them out, they have to—"

"Do it, Emily," Marla said. "Now."

Emily sighed and fidgeted with anger, but kept it under control. She turned to Carmen and said, "C'mon, Carm, let's go insi—"

"No," Kit said. "Carmen's going home."

"*Daaad!*" It had three syllables this time, and was much louder.

"Let's go, Carmen," Marla said.

"You can't *do* this!" Emily shouted at her dad. Her small fists clenched at her sides and unfallen tears glimmered in her eyes. Her voice became quiet, but trembled as she went on. "Carmen is my best friend. You can't keep me from seeing her. You can't keep me from seeing *anybody*, I'll see whoever I *want*, and you can't—"

Kit shouted, "That's enough!"

Emily's lips grew pale as she pressed them tightly together.

Marla went to the deck steps, then turned. Carmen was still standing beside Emily, looking very uncomfortable. Marla waggled four fingers at her and said, "Come on, Carmen, I've got things to do."

"Stay here, Carm, this is bullshit," Emily said.

Some of the anger Kit was trying to hold back slipped through his fingers. He pointed a stiff finger at Emily, its tip just a couple inches from her nose, and shouted, "That's it! You're also grounded. For a month. With no telephone privileges!"

Emily squealed like a kicked puppy. "What?"

"The only thing keeping me from grounding you till you're thirty is the law, so don't press me or you'll be locked in your room all summer."

Emily fell silent and Carmen's olive complexion paled.

Groundings never worked during the winter. The kids were in school all day and spent most of their time at home in their bedrooms, anyway. But Kit knew the threat of having to stay inside on long, hot summer days was a serious one. Especially without the use of a telephone.

"Carmen, *please*," Marla said with a snap of her fingers.

Kit knew from the crackling tone of her voice that Marla was furious. There would be a lot more shouting when she got home.

"I don't understand what you guys think *I* did!" Carmen said.

"I'll explain it to you in the car," Marla said over her shoulder as she went down the steps.

Carmen reluctantly followed Marla. "See ya, Em."

Emily sniffled, dabbed her eye with a knuckle. "I'm sorry about this, Carmen. I'll call you later."

Kit propped his fists on his hips as Marla and Carmen went into the house. "You're not calling anybody."

With Carmen gone, Emily suddenly seemed smaller, somehow diminished. Head down, her shoulders hitched as she cried silently.

"Now go in the house and do what I told you," Kit said. "Put those things on the kitchen counter and wash that crap out of your hair, I don't care if you have to stand in the shower all night to do it."

Kit went to the table and gathered up his papers, plate, and Coke can, and headed for the steps. He looked over his shoulder and saw that Emily had not moved.

"Come on, let's go inside," he said. He was about to go down the steps when she shrieked at him.

"Why are you doing this? Carmen is my best friend!" Her face was red and shiny with tears. She rubbed her eyes with the heels of her hands. Her voice was quiet and hoarse when she said, "Maybe...maybe my only friend."

"Then you need to make better friends, Emily." The anger had left his voice, had left him. He could not remain angry when he heard such pain in his daughter's voice. "You've changed since you and Carmen started hanging out together, and not for the better."

"Yeah, I'm changing. I'm a teenager, that's what we're *supposed* to do, isn't it?"

"Not the way you've—"

"I'm gonna change whether I hang out with Carmen or not."

Emily stepped around him and her shoes clumped loudly on the deck as she walked away. "I'm gonna change whether you like it or not."

Kit turned and followed her down the steps. "I'm not trying to keep you from changing, Emily."

She stepped through the back door and turned to him. "Then *why*?"

Kit rubbed the back of his aching neck. He suddenly felt tired enough for a nap. "Because," he said, "I don't want you to end up like your big brother."

Emily stared at him for a long moment. It seemed the more she thought about his answer, the angrier she got. Her arms trembled and her lips slowly bunched together. She stepped back, then turned and hurried through the kitchen.

"Don't go upstairs till you've taken those things out!" Kit shouted. Then added: "I mean it!"

«« — »»

Dinner that evening was more tense than usual, although of late, there had been a lot of tension in the Shepherd household. They ate dinner together at the table in the dining room only on holidays and when they had company. The rest of the time, they took their plates into the living room to watch television, or went their separate ways in the house.

Peter had taken his dinner to the living room where he was no doubt watching the news. He wanted to be a journalist, although he had not yet decided between print and broadcast. Whenever Kit wanted to know what was going on in local or national news, he asked Peter. He probably watched and read more news than any other thirteen-year-old Kit had ever known—more than any adult, as well. But Peter was not the geek he easily could be. Kit was happy to see that his youngest son had friends—decent enough kids, too—and a healthy social life, and didn't sit around all day watching CNN and C-SPAN.

Emily had not come out of her room to eat yet.

Kit and Marla talked quietly over their dinner at the kitchen table.

"I can always heat it up for her later," Marla said.

"Let her heat it up. If she can't eat when dinner's ready, let her do the work. She's not crippled, she's just got a couple new holes in her, that's all."

Marla picked at her food. "She says she didn't know what it was for."

"What what was for?"

"The barbell in her tongue."

"Oh, please. Maybe she didn't at first, but you can be sure Carmen told her. Carmen probably carries around diagrams and photographs in her purse."

"I told Emily I found that hard to believe."

"What'd she say?"

"She didn't argue."

"See?"

With a sigh, Marla said, "I'm not even a little hungry. My stomach still hasn't recovered from Carmen's mother." She put down her fork. "I was very friendly. I mean, it's not like I insulted her, or anything. I just said we didn't want the girls hanging out together and she lost it."

"She raised Carmen, what do you expect? If I'd known she lived in that horrible apartment complex on Laurel, I never would've let you go by yourself."

"Well, it wasn't *that* bad. But it was bad enough. I couldn't help feeling sorry for her. For Carmen, I mean."

"Why?"

"Well, I don't know anything about her father, but I can't imagine life with *Mrs*. DePalma being very easy. If she's like that all the time, Carmen hasn't been raised by a mother, she's been raised by a savage."

Kit chuckled as he spun his fork in his spaghetti. "Don't worry about Carmen. After the nuclear holocaust, there'll be nothing left but cockroaches and Carmen DePalma. She can take care of herself."

He had almost finished his meal, with Marla yet to take more than two bites, when the telephone chirped. Kit got up and answered the cordless phone on the wall above the end of the counter. The winded voice at the other end was Gordo's. More than a hundred pounds overweight, Gordo always sounded winded, but more so than usual on the phone that evening.

"I'm in town a couple days," Gordo said. "Thought I'd give you a call, see if you're well enough to play some golf. Tomorrow morning, maybe?"

Kit frowned as he walked slowly back to the table, lowered himself into the chair. Gordo sounded odd. Rushed, perhaps.

"Tomorrow's no good," Kit said. "I've got to have the maggots in my neck replaced tomorrow."

"Well...well..." Gordo's voice took on the uncharacteristic quality of a whine. He made an abrupt strangled sound into the phone, as if he were gagging. Or trying to hold back a sob.

"Hey, Gordo, you okay?"

He took a deep breath. "Yeah, that's just...it's disgusting, Kit, I'm sorry, but it is."

Kit chuckled.

"Okay, uh, how about drinks?"

"Tonight?"

"Yeah, sure, why not?" He sounded tense. Normally, Gordo's words sounded very wet when he spoke, as if he were sucking on a lozenge, although that was never the case. But now his mouth sounded dry, a little sticky as he spoke. "Let's meet at Chop House in, what...half an hour? That okay with you?"

Forehead still creased, Kit ran a hand through his hair. "Are you sure nothing's wrong?"

"Nah. Fine. See you there, okay?"

Kit did not want to go, but was unsettled by the way Gordo sounded. "Okay. See you there."

《《—》》

A four-piece jazz band played softly and coolly in a corner. It was the kind of music that called for a martini, and it was tempting, but not if he was going to drive home. He found Gordo hunched over his drink in the dim, orange-tinted light of the bar, his big round face glowing in the light of the candle on the table. Kit sat across from him.

"Hey, Kit," Gordo said. "How's the neck?"

"Disgusting as ever."

Gordo wrinkled his broad, lumpy nose. "Does it hurt?"

"Only when they chew through a nerve."

Gordo pulled away from the table and groaned. "*Gawd*, Kit."

Laughing, Kit said, "I can't feel a thing, really."

Leaning forward again, Gordo took a deep breath. His round cheeks bulged as he blew it out slowly. He waved at the waitress as she came out from behind the bar, lifted his glass of ice tinkling in amber, and asked Kit, "Scotch?"

Kit shook his head, smiled at the waitress, and ordered a Virgin Mary. Folded his arms on the table and said, "Gordon, can I ask you a personal question?"

"Sure, what is it?"

"Are you having a heart attack?"

Gordo's thinning gray hair, yellowed by nicotine around the edges, was slicked back, and his pink, perspiring scalp glistened between strands. Tiny beads of sweat on his face reflected the candlelight as he squinted at Kit. "Huh? The hell are you talking about?"

"You look like you're having a heart attack."

"That's ridiculous." Gordo's hand slipped beneath his suit jacket, fumbled around. Came out with a cigarette. He put it between his lips as he searched his pocket for a lighter with the other hand.

"Hey. Where've you been?" Kit asked.

"Just finished a run up the line to Seattle and back."

"Well, you're in California now. You light that cigarette in here, they'll kick you out."

Rolling his eyes, Gordo clumsily put the cigarette back beneath his jacket. Said, "Shit." Gulped the icy remains of his scotch. When the waitress brought Kit's drink, Gordo said, "Another for me."

"Are you sick?" Kit asked. "You look like shit." Gordo had never been the picture of health. He had always looked old and exhausted and had changed little since Kit was in high school.

"Long drive," he said.

Kit knew that was not the reason, but did not pursue it. "How are things in Seattle?" he asked.

"Wet. Only time I feel my arthritis's when I go to Goddamned Seattle."

"Then why do you do it? I mean, when you were still getting the chain off the ground, that was different. But for crying out loud, Gordo, you don't even have to leave your house to go to the office these days, if you don't want to. There's no reason for you to be driving back and forth from store to store; you're the boss, you've got people to do that *for* you."

Gordo often complained about his frequent drives to his chain of stores, but Kit knew he enjoyed them. He shot local commercials for each store and had become a local celebrity in the towns and cities where they aired. In one commercial, he would appear dressed as a farmer and seated on a tractor. In the next, he was a circus clown. In another, a politician running for "town pricebuster." In his most recent commercial, Gordo had appeared as Whistler's mother. The commercials were cheap, amateurish, and silly, and more than a few of the laughs they generated were derisive. But they were wildly popular and gave F&H Furniture a local feel, made each store more a part of its community rather than just another chain outlet.

Gordo removed the cigarette from his jacket again, almost got it to his lips before he rolled his eyes a second time and said, "Shit," again before putting it back. The waitress brought his scotch and he took a couple of generous swallows. "I've gotta ask you a favor, Kit."

"Sure. What do you need?"

"No, you shouldn't be so eager. It's got nothing to do with work. It's personal. I need…I'm having some…" Another good swallow of scotch. "I need a loan. A…a personal loan."

"Is everything all right, Gordo? I mean, I'll be happy to help you out, but is anything wrong?"

After a few moments of fidgeting and sighing and looking hungry for a smoke, Gordo explained that he owed money to a shylock who was not a very understanding man, and soon he would be sending a couple of his large employees to find Gordo and deal with his debt by pounding his kneecaps to pudding with hammers and feeding them to him through a straw.

"Shylock?" Kit said. He leaned forward. "Did you say *shylock*?"

"Yeah. A loan shark. A guy who—"

"I know what a shylock is."

"So what's the problem?"

"That you owe money to one, that's the problem."

Gordo turned his head back and forth and his round shoulders hitched with bitter laughter. His fleshy chins jiggled. "Look, Kit, if you can help me out, I'd appreciate it. But don't expect me to get all weepy and confess my sins to you, okay? Because I'm just too old for that shit."

"Hey, you don't have to get defensive, Gordo," Kit said, arms spread wide for a moment. "I want to do anything I can to help, just tell me."

"I've managed to round up most of it. I just need another eight thousand dollars."

"Eight thousand dollars?"

"I told you not to be so eager."

"*Another*...eight thousand dollars?"

"Don't worry about that."

"Where did you get the rest of it?"

"I said, don't worry about it."

They stared silently at each other for a long time. Kit guessed it was gambling. Gordo had mentioned "the ponies" several times over the years, only casually, in passing. But what else could it be? He certainly didn't have a problem with drugs. Not the illegal kind, anyway. Betting money on the horses felt right to Kit; it was the kind of thing Gordo would enjoy, something he could do without any physical effort.

Kit did not take his eyes from Gordo's as he whispered, "Is it something I should know about?" Almost knocked his drink over leaning closer to Gordo. "Does it involve the company?"

"Don't worry. It's not your problem, Kit."

"It will be when I give you the eight thousand dollars. Is it really to pay back a loan, Gordo, or are you going to bet *that* on the ponies, too?"

Gordo sank into his chair a bit, slowly, as a delayed wince worked its way across his face. His bleary, red-edged eyes turned downward at the outer ends.

Kit felt his mouth drop open as he realized suddenly what he had just said, how cold it had sounded. "I'm sorry, Gordo, that was—"

"No, no." He poured the rest of his scotch down his throat, scooted his chair back, and stood.

"Where are you going?"

"I don't need your money that bad. But you can pay for the drinks."

"No, Gordo, the money's not a problem, I'll give you the—"

"I don't want it," he said over his shoulder as he left the bar.

Out in the parking lot, Kit found Gordo lighting a cigarette on the way to his car. "I'm sorry," Kit said, catching up. "It was a rotten thing to say. I have no idea what you do with your money, Gordo, it was just a stupid guess, and I'm sorry."

At the car, keys jangling in his hand, Gordo said, "Yeah, it was rotten. Especially coming from you. That's not like you, Kit."

"What do you want me to do? I'll give you the money, no problem."

Gordo leaned on the Mercedes, took a pull off his cigarette, and sucked the smoke in deep. "I been playin' the ponies since I was a kid. Never had any problems with it. Till about ten years ago. I let it go too far, and now I'm neck deep. So this is it. No more gambling after this." He opened the car door and clumsily flopped behind the wheel. "Providing I'm still alive after this."

Kit reached beneath his jacket and removed his checkbook, opened it. "I'll write you a check right now. Or, if you'd prefer, I could—"

Gordo slammed the door. Started the engine, slid the window down as Kit tore a check from the black leather book.

"I appreciate it, Kit, but I don't want it. I'll manage." He shifted into reverse.

"Wait a second, dammit, Gordon, this is stupid. Take it!"

"I've known you a long time, Kit. You've always been a good guy. But if you could've seen the look in your eyes when you said that to me…you'd know how I feel."

"What?"

Gordo backed the Mercedes out of its slot and drove away, leaving Kit standing alone in the mostly empty parking lot behind Chop House.

«« — »»

When Kit got home, he went straight to the kitchen, opened a bottle of wine, and poured a glass.

"Dale called again," Marla said as she came into the kitchen. She held a paperback book in her right hand, index finger marking her place. "He'd like you to call him."

"Did he specify *what* he'd like me to call him?"

"He just wants to talk, Kit. You can't avoid him forever."

"Wanna bet?"

She sighed.

"Sorry, honey." He put a hand on her shoulder, kissed her forehead. "I just can't talk about it now. I've got other things on my mind."

"What's wrong?"

In a whisper, he told her briefly about Gordo's problem.

"What are you going to do?"

Kit shrugged. "I have to give him the money. I mean, I can't just let some thug work him over with a tire iron. He should be back in his hotel room by now. I'm going to give him a call." He took the bottle and wine glass with him and went upstairs to his bedroom, put them on his bed stand. Undressed, put on his robe, and stretched out on the bed, sitting up with his back against a couple pillows.

He called Gordo's usual hotel, and although the desk clerk confirmed that Gordon Fikes was registered, there was no answer in his room. He called Gordo's cell phone, but a recorded message informed him the party he was calling was unavailable or out of the area. He assumed Gordo had the cell phone turned off.

Kit sipped wine, watched the news without absorbing a word of it. He was angry at himself for behaving so thoughtlessly toward Gordo earlier, but angrier at Gordo for letting his problem get so big before asking for help. It was infuriating, but not surprising.

Gordo's entire life seemed held together by a glue of personal problems and self-destructive habits. He had a bad heart, yet he continued to smoke and did not lose weight. His liver was in bad shape, but Gordo had not even cut back on his drinking, and was probably drinking more than usual these days. He paid alimony to four ex-wives and child support to two of them, because although he could not stay married—Kit could understand why, now—Gordo married repeatedly. The last six years had been the longest time he had spent unmarried and uninvolved. In the twenty years Kit had known him, Gordo had seemed to spend most of his time either in court dealing with a bitter divorce, or in a hospital being tested or treated for one or more of his chronic, mostly self-inflicted ailments. He was falling apart and seemed to leave bits and pieces of himself wherever he went. Along with most of his money, it seemed.

Kit tried the cell phone again, called the hotel two more times, then left a message for Gordo to call as soon as he got in. He took off his robe, turned out the lights, and slid beneath the covers to watch the rest of the news. He was asleep before Marla came to bed.

«« — »»

That night, Kit dreamed of a monstrous hunger. After awhile, he realized that the hunger was his, and he was eating like a pig, stuffing his mouth with food, chewing so hard and fast that his jaws ached. But the hunger remained untouched, tore through his insides like hot razor wire, somehow made itself felt in every part of his body. He grabbed at his food like an animal and lifted it bare-handed to his mouth. It had no taste. It was a dream, after all—Kit was aware of that—and he did not taste things in his dreams. But it was too dark to see what he was eating, and he was bent over, his face too close to get a good look at it, anyway. He stood up slowly, pulled away from the food, but kept shoving messy pieces of it into his mouth. Suddenly, there was light from overhead, illuminating the meal before him.

His hands were closed around black, oozing flaps of rotting flesh. Gordo lay before him, face-up, dead for some time. His neck and face bloated, eyes puffed shut, lips purple, shirt open. Gordo's mountainous belly, black with rot, was split open to expose his decaying insides. It was from there Kit had been eating.

He opened his mouth and screamed. The sound that came out was not his voice, but a piercing electronic shriek. The overhead light faded as the sound drilled through Kit's temples.

It was the trilling of the telephone on Kit's bed stand. He groped in the dark, lifted the receiver from the base, and mercifully ended that ungodly sound.

"'Lo?"

"Um, is this, are you, um…Mr. Shepherd?" It was a young woman, a teenager.

"Yeah. Who's this?"

"My name's Val. I'm, uh, I'm a friend of Geoff's. His, um, girlfriend." She sniffled.

Kit suddenly felt awake and alert as he dropped his legs over the edge of the bed and sat up. "Is something wrong? Is Geoff all right?"

Marla woke suddenly and sat up beside him.

"That's why I'm calling. He, um, needs you to, um…get him out of jail."

«« — »»

Geoff had been nothing but trouble from the beginning. His birth had been a difficult one—Marla had hemorrhaged and lost a good deal of blood—and he'd cried constantly through his first seven months. As a toddler, he'd been willful and enjoyed testing his parents. One morning, he'd taken from the coffee table a large glass ashtray—Kit had smoked back then—that was so big he could barely handle it. Kit told him firmly to put it down. Geoff glanced back at him, but kept walking away. When Kit repeated himself, the boy stopped walking, but made no effort to return to the coffee table, just stared. "Did you hear me?" Kit asked. Geoff nodded. "Are you going to put it down?" Nothing for a moment, then Geoff had dropped the ashtray. It broke into three pieces when it hit the hardwood floor of the house they'd lived in at the time.

They had repeated endless variations of that scene over and over again, involving more serious things than an ashtray. Vandalism, theft, cigarettes, tattoos, piercings, guns, drugs…and it never got any better. If anything, Geoff had become more problematic as a teenager. Counseling had done no good. Dr. Radnitch had put him on Ritalin, but with no results. When his grades hovered around failing in junior high, Geoff was examined for learning disabilities. None. He simply did not want to do any of the work assigned to him. He was not without intelligence and read voraciously, but never the things he was assigned to read. During his freshman year in high school, he started using drugs—not just marijuana, but more dangerous drugs—and changed, became worse.

It made no sense to Kit. They had raised Geoff no differently than Emily and Peter. In spite of her recent problems, Emily had always been a good girl, had avoided trouble. Peter was exemplary in every way. What had they done wrong with Geoff?

Kit and Marla had neither seen nor heard from Geoff for nearly a week. It was not the first time, and he had been gone longer, but they had stopped calling the police and looking for him when he turned eighteen. At nineteen, he still lived with them, but as he drove to the police station to pick up Geoff, Kit decided it was time for the boy to be on his own. A splash of cold real life in the face might wake him up. But Kit wouldn't be surprised if it did not.

Geoff had been driving his girlfriend's car to a convenience store earlier that night when he was pulled over by a police car. The officer had planned to do nothing more than tell the driver of the car that the right taillight was not working and write up a citation. But when Geoff rolled down the window and the officer got a whiff of the thick smell of marijuana that came from inside, he arrested Geoff. A smouldering joint was found in the ashtray, as well as paraphernalia and some stolen prescription drugs. Val's car and all its contents were impounded.

"How stupid do you have to be to smoke a joint while you're driving around in a car?" Kit muttered to himself as he drove.

He put up bail, which was high enough to make him wince, and walked Geoff silently out to the car. As he unlocked the passenger door, Kit heard sniffling behind him and turned to see that Val had followed them out.

"I suppose you want a ride," Kit said to her.

She bowed her head and sobbed. Geoff put an arm around her and glared at Kit. "Leave her alone. The fuckin' cops took her car."

"That's what she gets for letting you drive it."

Geoff gave Kit directions to Val's apartment building and he stopped to drop her off. As he headed home, Kit asked, "Have you eaten? Are you hungry?"

"Yeah, I could eat."

"When we get home, you can fix yourself a sandwich, or something. Eat whatever you want, as much as you want. And enjoy it. Because tomorrow, you pack your things and go."

"Go where?"

Kit shook his head. "I don't care anymore. We've done all we can. Tomorrow, you're on your own."

After a moment, Geoff laughed. "You're kiddin'."

"Not this time. If you don't pack up and leave, I'll throw you out myself. We'll change all the locks. The phone number, if we have to. You're an adult now, Geoff. Well...you're of legal age, anyway. You don't have any idea what being an adult means. Maybe you'll figure it out when there's no net at the bottom of the next fall. You'll figure it out or die trying."

Geoff laughed again, nervously this time. "Mom won't let you do that."

"You see your mom in this car? She doesn't have anything to

do with this, and you're not going to bring her into it, do you understand? I've got an appointment with the doctor in the morning. If you're not gone when I get back, I'll throw you out the front door and call the police."

"Don't you think she's gonna wonder where I'm going if I just—"

"Tell her you're going out to look for a job and find a place to live. And that had *better* be your plan, too, because you're not getting any more money from us."

Geoff turned in his seat toward Kit. "What the fuck'm I s'posed to *do*?"

"That's up to you."

Kit drove the car into the garage and hit the remote button on his visor to close the door behind them. They got out of the car and faced each other over its roof in the dimly lighted garage.

"Listen to me, Geoff, because I'm dead serious about this." He pointed an index finger at his son and said, "One word of this to your mother and so help me God, I'll knock your Goddamned teeth right down your throat. And remember. Don't be here when I get back tomorrow."

Kit went into the house without waiting to see if Geoff was coming.

«« — »»

"Now, hold still while I take them out," Dr. Radnitch said.

Kit reclined in a procedure chair in Radnitch's lab. It bore just enough resemblance to a dentist's chair to make him nervous.

"Our little friends are doing a wonderful job, here," Dr. Radnitch said.

Kit heard him wheel away on his chair, but did not move.

"Any problems with the dressing, Kit?"

"No, the dressing's fine, but…"

"But what?"

"You said I wouldn't be able to feel them."

"That's right."

"Are you sure about that?"

"Yes. The tumor has no nerves, and that's all they're eating. The tumor."

"I could have sworn I felt them once. Squirming around."

"Probably the dressing. It wasn't the maggots. Remember, they only eat what you don't need. Necrotic tissue, usually, but in this case, the malignancy."

Necrotic tissue, Kit thought. *Malignancy*. They sounded appropriately ugly.

"Okay, hold still while I put these new fellas in," Dr. Radnitch said. He chuckled. "This is an all-you-can-eat buffet for them." The doctor put a new dressing on Kit's neck, then slapped him on the shoulder. "You're good to go. I'll see you again in a couple days."

Kit drove home with the window rolled down and the hot summer air blowing his hair in all directions. He felt good knowing the maggots were doing their job, steadily eating his malignancy before it could spread. Before it could kill him. Too bad they were not big enough to eat away some of the malignancies and necrotic tissue in his life. Gordo and his gambling debt, Carmen DePalma and her bad influence on Emily. Geoff.

He wondered if Geoff would still be there when he got home. If so, he intended to follow through with his threat to throw the boy out of the house. Dealing with Gordo would not be so easy, though. Kit had called his hotel room three times that morning before leaving the house, but had gotten no answer. He hoped Gordo had not left town yet. If he ended up in the hospital after the shylock's men were through with him, that would leave the stores in Kit's hands for awhile. For good, if Gordo ended up dead, which was a possibility. Kit did not know if Gordo's heart could withstand a beating. He liked Gordo, but since learning of his gambling problem the night before, Kit had lost some respect for him. If that was how he ran his personal life, how did he run his business? Had he taken money from the company to pay off his debt? Maybe it wouldn't be such a bad thing if the chain landed in Kit's hands alone.

A slight shudder ran through him as he felt the sensation of movement beneath the dressing. He placed a hand gently over the bandage until the feeling passed.

When he got home, Marla was waiting for him in the living room. She was very quiet.

"I can't believe you told Geoff to pack up and leave," she said. "And you didn't even tell me about it last night."

"Did he go?"

"No, of course not, I wouldn't let him. Kit, he's not ready to go out on his own."

"If we wait till he's ready, he'll be living here till we're old and gray. Last night was the last straw. No more calls in the middle of the night, no more—"

"He needs treatment. He has to get cleaned up before he tries to—"

"Then you do it. I don't want to be involved. How many times have we tried to help him get straightened out? How many times have we—"

"I've been calling around. I've heard some good things about the program at the St. Helena Hospital."

"Fine. Take him. But I'm not trying anymore, because *he* doesn't. Where is he?"

"Out back in the pool."

Kit left the living room and went upstairs and Marla followed.

"Where are you going?" she asked.

"If he's going to stay here another minute, I want to make sure he doesn't have anything illegal in the house."

Marla said no more, but followed him into Geoff's bedroom. He went through drawers, searched the closet, picked through the mess of clothes and magazines on the floor, looked under the bed.

"What exactly are you looking for?" Marla asked.

Kit's hand fell on something cold under the bed. He pulled it toward him, knew what it was before he saw it. A gun. A .38 revolver, also known as a Saturday Night Special. He picked it up off the floor for a closer look, but did not bring it out from under the bed. It was loaded.

"Kit?" Marla sounded irritated.

Was that a tingle? A squirm? Some kind of movement in the tumor on his neck?

He slid the gun back under the bed and got to his feet. "I'm looking for drugs."

"He told me he didn't have any."

"And you believed him? He's a drug addict, Marla. You can't believe a word he says."

Her mouth dropped open and she watched him go through the bed stand drawer.

"I can't find anything," Kit said. He closed the drawer and faced her. "But I reserve the right to search his room any time I want. I'll replace the doorknob with one that doesn't lock. And if I have to, I'll—"

"What is *wrong* with you?"

"I'm just tired of his lies and his refusal to even consider the possibility that he has a problem. We can put him into another program and talk all we want about treatment, but you and I both know he's not going to change. He's lost, Marla. He's gone, he's already out of reach. He has decided to throw his life away and there's not a damned thing we can do about it."

Her head turned slowly back and forth. "I can't believe you'd say that about anyone, but...especially not your *son*."

"You think I enjoy this? It makes me sick. But it's wrong to pretend he's going to wake up one day and be different. He won't. He's always been self-destructive, ever since he was a little kid. He's selfish. He's sneaky and deceptive. He's necrotic, and we've got to be realistic enough to accept the fact—"

"He's *what*?"

"What?"

"You said he's...*necrotic*?"

Did I say that? Kit wondered. *Out loud?*

"Nothing," he said as he stepped around her and went out into the hall. "I've got to get in touch with Gordo."

In the kitchen, Kit called the hotel again. When there was no answer there, he called the store. Gordo had been there earlier, but had left about an hour ago. When he called Gordo's cell phone, it rang only once before he answered.

"I've been looking all over for you," Kit said.

"Yeah, I've been looking for you, too. I wanted to apologize for acting like a jerk last night."

"I'm the one who needs to apologize. That was a shitty thing I said to you. I don't even know why I said it. I'm sorry."

"Okay. Enough of that shit. I'm on my way to play some golf. You wanna join me?"

"Uh, no, I'm going to, uh..." *Going to what?* Kit thought. *I have no plans, I'm supposed to be at home relaxing.* But he knew he had things to do. He simply did not know what they were yet. "I'm going to be busy. But I want to get together. I want to give you that money, Gordo, and I don't want any argument from you."

A dour sigh came over the line, and when Gordo spoke, he sounded drained, beaten. "No, you won't get any argument from me. I really hate to take it, Kit, but I've got no choice."

Kit heard voices from the front of the house. "Don't worry about it. Why don't you meet me at the store tonight. Is, uh, nine o'clock okay with you?"

"Why so late?"

I have no idea, Kit thought as he said, "Well, I...I haven't told Marla about this, and I'd like to avoid having to tell her. So I'm kind of doing it on the sly, understand?"

"Gotcha. Sure you don't want to play some golf?"

"No, thanks. I'll see you tonight."

Kit left the kitchen and walked cautiously down the hall toward the voices. They were coming from the living room. Marla was talking with...Dale. Kit rolled his eyes and hurried up the stairs without making a sound. Went into Geoff's room and closed the door. Got on his knees beside the bed and retrieved the gun, touching it only with a knuckle. He stood and looked around the room, spotted a small brown paper bag on the bed stand. It was full of *Magic: the Gathering* collectible cards. Kit dumped them onto the floor and used the bag like a glove as he put the revolver on the bed. Used a blanket to nudge the gun into the paper bag. Rolled up the top of the bag and carried it at his side as he left the room.

Dale was waiting for him at the foot of the stairs.

"We have to talk, Kit."

"No we don't, Dale." Kit turned to Marla and said, "I'm going to be meeting with Gordo later, so I've got to, uh—" He glanced at Dale, annoyed. "—take care of that problem we discussed last night. If you're going to put Geoff in a program, do it today. I'm serious."

"I will," she said. "You know, the doctor said you're not supposed to—"

"I know what the doctor said, but it can't be helped. I'm sure my life's in no danger." Kit headed for the front door.

Dale followed him, talking rapidly. "Look, I'm serious, too, Kit, we need to talk."

Kit opened the front door, then turned to Dale. "Is this about Mickey?"

"Of *course* it's about Mickey, he's devastated, Kit, he's—"

"I bet he's handling this better than you are."

"What do you mean by that? I'm concerned, Mickey's a good kid. And besides, it's my *job*."

"Then *do* your job and teach Mickey not to be devastated every time he gets fired, otherwise he's got a miserable life ahead of him." He glanced over Dale's head—he was rather short—at Marla, whose face showed discomfort, pain. Kit knew she was probably furious with him for talking to her little brother that way, but she was good enough to keep it to herself. Then he smiled at Dale. "Okay, we've talked. And that's all I've got to say about it." He pulled the front door closed as he left.

Kit smiled as he went down the front steps and across the lawn to his car in the driveway, still carrying the gun in the brown paper bag. That had felt good. His only regret was that he had turned and walked away without getting a look at the expression on Dale's face.

He drove across town to the group home where Mickey lived. Mickey was mowing the front lawn. Kit asked if he wanted to go to lunch, and Mickey said he had to mow the lawn. So Kit waited.

It was a beautiful day and lilacs scented the air. Kit walked up and down the street, a faint smile on his lips. He felt good, healthy. And his maggots were healthy. He did not mind waiting at all.

When Mickey finally killed the lawnmower's engine, Kit asked him to lunch again. Mickey stared at him for a long moment, frowning.

"You're not...mad at me?" he asked.

Kit laughed and slapped Mickey's back. "No! I'm not mad at you, Mickey, I never was. I thought you understood that."

"No. No, I just figured you was mad."

"I didn't want to fire you. But I had no choice."

"Really?"

"Really. It was out of my hands. I'd take you back right now, if I could."

"Well...why can't you?"

Kit shrugged. "My partner."

"Y'mean Mr. Fikes?"

"Uh-huh."

Mickey's frown deepened as he rubbed the back of his neck. "Mr. Fikes doesn't like me?"

"I don't know. But listen, there's a way we might be able to get your job back."

The frown dissolved and Mickey's face brightened. "Really?"

"As long as you can keep it to yourself, understand?"

"Yeah, sure, yeah. Whattaya want me to do?"

"I mean it, Mickey, you can't tell anyone. Not even Dale. In fact, *especially* not Dale."

"Okay, yeah, I know, so whattaya—"

"Let's go get a burger and talk about it."

In the car, Mickey was unable to hold still. He fidgeted with his seatbelt, rocked slightly back and forth.

Kit said, "I've got a lot of confidence in you, Mickey, so don't disappoint me."

"Okay, Kit, yeah, I won't, but you're gonna have to tell me what to do."

"You've got to listen to me very carefully, for one thing. We'll take plenty of time to go over it, but you've got to listen very carefully so you'll remember what to do when the time comes, and to do it *exactly* as I say."

"And I'm not s'posed to tell nobody, right?"

Kit grinned. "Right."

They ate lunch on the patio of a small café in town. Enormous hamburgers—Mickey's with a side of fries, Kit's with onion rings—and tall chocolate milkshakes. They ate very slowly because Kit talked a lot, and Mickey listened with more intensity in his eyes than Kit had ever seen there before. It was a long, slow lunch, but surprisingly pleasant. Kit was smiling when they left the restaurant.

He was still smiling when he stopped in front of the group home to drop Mickey off and gave him the .38 revolver in the bag.

«« — »»

When Kit got home, he found Emily sitting in front of the television watching a makeover on *Oprah*.

"My punishment doesn't include television privileges, too, does it?" she asked. Her tone was cold and she never took her eyes from the television.

"No. But if you're going to watch *Oprah*, it might not be a bad idea."

Emily's upper lip curled as she turned to him. "What's wrong with *Oprah*?"

"If I have to tell you, then there's no point in discussing it. Where's your mom?"

"She left with Geoff. Said she'd be back before dinner."

Kit went upstairs and changed into a pair of shorts, got the Michael Crichton novel he was reading. In the kitchen, he found Peter sitting at the table with a tall glass of milk, three cookies on a plate, and the San Francisco *Chronicle* open before him, deeply immersed in whatever he was reading.

"Hey, kid, what's up?" Kit said. He grabbed a soda from the refrigerator and the cordless phone from the wall.

Peter made a preoccupied, unintelligible sound of acknowledgement, but did not take his eyes from the paper.

Kit muttered, "Oh, that's good, Peter. I'm fine, thanks. You have fun, now." He walked out onto the redwood deck and reclined on the cushioned lounger. He called Gordo's cell phone—he had finished golfing and was having a cocktail at the Silverado Country Club—and told him to come to the back door of the store at nine that night.

Gordo laughed. "What'd you expect me to do, come in the front door at that hour? Crawl through a window, maybe?" He laughed again.

"I'll leave the back door unlocked. Just wanted you to know."

"You sure you don't want to come over to the country club and have a few drinks with me?"

"No, thanks, Gordo. I'll see you tonight."

Kit guessed it was not Gordo's first cocktail of the afternoon, and would not be his last. He smiled at the ironic possibility of Gordo killing himself at the wheel on his way to the store.

He popped open his soda, opened his book, and laid back to get a little afternoon sun while he waited for evening to come.

«« — »»

At night, the store seemed larger. Shadows lurked everywhere and sounds had a faint echo that could not be heard during business hours.

Kit arrived twenty minutes early, flipped on the light in the manager's office, then went upstairs to his own office. Seated himself at his desk and opened the bottom drawer. He checked the gun he kept there, made sure it was loaded. It was registered and licensed in Kit's name, completely legal. He had bought it after the store's first robbery, back when he was manager. Over the years, it had been robbed three times. Kit often wondered what kind of robber decided to break into a furniture store. Perhaps it was an effort to be original. He pushed the drawer closed.

He turned on the radio on the credenza behind him, listened to music as he went through the day's stack of mail. Four songs later, he was done, and turned off the radio as the news began.

Gordo was just coming through the door as Kit went down the stairs. He smelled of liquor and looked tired.

"What have you been doing all day?" Gordo asked. "I really wanted us to get in a game of golf this trip."

Kit shook his head, sighed. "I'm having problems at home. With Geoff."

"Again?"

"Had to go get him out of jail last night."

"Oh, no. What for?"

As he told Gordo what had happened the night before, Kit wandered into the manager's office, and Gordo followed. Kit perched on the front edge of the desk while Gordo dropped into a chair.

"I'm sorry to hear that," Gordo said, frowning.

"Marla took him to St. Helena today and put him into a rehab program at the hospital there. This is the second time he's gone into rehab, and she thinks it'll work, that he'll be fine afterward. I'm not as hopeful."

Gordo lit a cigarette. There was no smoking allowed anywhere in the store, so there were no ashtrays. After the first puff, he tapped the cigarette with an index finger over the concrete floor. "Makes me feel lucky. I've never had any problems like that with my kids."

"You never *see* your kids, Gordo," Kit said with a laugh.

"Yeah, that's probably got a lot to do with it."

"That's not all. Yesterday, Emily had her *tongue* pierced, for crying out loud."

Kit checked his watch, they chatted for a few more minutes, and he checked his watch again. He wondered why he felt no tension, no fear. He gently touched two fingers to the dressing on his neck as the subject changed to his tumor and the resident maggots. He explained the treatment to Gordo. Then checked his watch again.

Gordo stood and said, "Whattaya say we wrap things up here and go get a drink."

Kit looked at his watch again, this time for Gordo's benefit. "You know...that's not a bad idea. It's not too late. You stay right here, Gordo, I'll be back in a second." Kit slapped him on the shoulder as he left the office, then hurried up the stairs.

In his office, he went around the desk, eased into the chair. Opened the bottom drawer. Listened for almost a full minute.

Gordo's loud but winded voice from downstairs: "What in the hell do you think you're—"

Kit took the gun from the drawer when he heard the gunshot. He hurried out of the office and stopped at the top of the stairs.

Slivers of Bone

In a ragged, gurgling voice, Gordo screamed, "Oh God, oh God, oh—"

Two more gunshots.

Kit put a hand to the bandaged tumor on his neck. They were moving around in there. The sensation sent a shimmer of electricity over his shoulders and chest. Dr. Radnitch was wrong—he could feel them.

"Kit? Kuh-*Kiiiit!*"

"I'm coming," he said, rushing down the stairs. He held the gun behind his back in his right hand.

Gordo lay in the open doorway of the supervisor's office. Legs splayed, upper body inside the office, arms spread at his sides. One of the bullets had entered Gordo's throat and there was a great deal of blood on him. He did not move, and his open eyes were as glassy and soulless as a doll's.

Even with the mask on, Mickey looked as scared as he had sounded when he called for Kit. He wore a black hood over his head with a white, distorted, agonized face on the front. It was the same mask the killers had worn in the *Scream* movies. At his side, his quaking hand held the gun Kit had taken from Geoff's bedroom.

"Kuh-Kit, I'm scared," he whimpered. "I-I think I killed him."

"Yeah, he's dead, all right." Kit turned away from the body and smiled. "You did a good job, Mickey. I'm proud of you."

"Really?" He reached up and started to pull the mask off. "Y'mean I—"

"No, no, don't take the mask off! Leave it on for now."

His hand dropped. "Well, do I...do I get my job back?"

Kit's smile melted away. "I'm afraid not." He raised the gun and shot Mickey in the head.

The boy collapsed, and the gun chattered against the concrete floor, still clutched in his hand.

"Two down," Kit whispered to himself as he dropped his gun. He went upstairs to his office and called the police.

«««—»»»

"I was so sorry to hear about the shooting at your store," Dr. Radnitch said as he slowly removed the dressing on Kit's neck. He clicked his tongue. "So tragic. But thank God you weren't hurt. I'm sure it was painful enough without getting shot, too."

"Yeah," Kit said. His voice was low, a little hoarse. He sat still in the procedure chair. "It was pretty painful."

"How are you holding up? I hope you're seeing someone. Getting therapy, I mean. That sort of thing can leave some pretty deep scars."

Kit said nothing.

"How are the police handling it?"

"Self-defense. They said I don't have anything to worry about."

"Oh, this looks beautiful," Dr. Radnitch said with a grin in his voice. "It's coming along even better than I expected. Looks like your little friends will be done soon."

Creases cut across Kit's forehead as he slowly said, "Really? How soon?"

"Sooner than I thought. Now, hold still while I take them out."

Although it was obvious, it had not occurred to Kit that when the maggots were finished, Dr. Radnitch would stop sending him home with fresh ones every couple of days. The thought made him feel sad.

"How are the wife and kids?" Dr. Radnitch asked.

"They're fine," he lied. "Upset, naturally, because both of them were friends. Gordo and Mickey."

Dr. Radnitch clicked his tongue again. "So tragic."

"Yeah. It was."

After a moment, Dr. Radnitch said, "People just don't appreciate maggots enough. Everyone is too busy being disgusted by them to appreciate what they do. They eat up what we don't need. Look what they're doing for you, right?"

Kit smiled. "We could use something like that in life, don't you think?"

"What, you mean…giant maggots?" Dr. Radnitch laughed.

He kept smiling, but Kit did not laugh. He did not find it funny. Not at all.

With Gordo gone, Kit could begin to eat the necrotic tissue in the company. And the malignancies at home, in his family—he could eat those, too.

"Oh, I don't know how people would react to giant maggots, Kit," Dr. Radnitch said.

Still smiling. "Yeah. Stupid idea."